PROPHECY:
Elf Queen of Kiirajanna
(volume 1)

STEPHEN H. KING

(TOSK)

ISBN-13: 978-0-9989355-3-9

CONTENTS

Acknowledgments

As always with my novel-length efforts, the list of people I have to thank is longer than my ability to present them.

First, my beautiful wife Heide, for all the hours you managed without me as I banged on the keyboard, as well as all the hours you managed to listen to me read passage after passage, sounding out everything and getting it just right. Your advice was always valuable and your patience incredible.

To Jessa, my daughter, who not only provided the original cover art and the cool flipbook dragons, but also fielded the question, "How would a teenage girl say ____" more often than seemed possible, thank you as well. Your artistry is coming into its own in an impressive way.

To my initial readers, thank you. I owe each of you more than I can possibly pay, ever. Most of your advice I took, and some I didn't for artistic reasons, but your feedback was valuable beyond measure. So thank you, Jaime, Sue, MA, Lisa, Doug, Leslie (who's still the most awesome DM ever!), and Rebecca.

Finally, I send wonderful blessings and great thanks to the pro who made such a wonderful cover, Renee Barratt over at TheCoverCounts.com.

Opening

In hindsight, I'll admit that slugging the high priestess was probably a very bad idea.

As my feet pounded down the hall toward an escape I didn't figure I was gonna make, my new elf shoes makin' a ruckus on the stone floor, two thoughts came rushing at me. First, I really wished that I had my tennies on instead of the hard-soled shoes. Second, I should've thought about what a stupid thing it would be to hit a high priestess, and that well before I let go of my temper.

Oh, and third: Dad's gonna be ticked at me for it. That was a new one; I hadn't worried about my father's opinion before. Ever.

Sprinting, I cut toward the side exit of the cathedral, my slick soles making it tough, but not impossible, to turn. The acolytes standing guard would no doubt be waiting for me, alerted by some sort of elven voodoo that I couldn't possibly know about yet. They would be ready to catch me and send me back for whatever punishment punching their spiritual leader in the nose would bring. I didn't know.

At that moment I really didn't care. Yeah, I was *that* angry.

As I sprinted, it occurred to me to wonder how the high priestess had possibly seen it coming. My swing was epic, but she hadn't fallen. She hadn't even really winced. It wasn't from a lack of trying; I could throw a punch with the best of them. I'd only had one fight in school, and once word of it had spread most of my classmates got much nicer. Tommy had just caught me in a corner I couldn't get out of and for no apparent reason started mouthing off about stuff that shouldn't be mouthed off about—you know, Momma, single mother, and so on. I swung a closed fist, he hit the ground with a broken nose, and everybody left me—and Momma—alone from then on.

Until I met the elves, anyway.

Thinking about all that, I missed the turn.

It was easy enough to spin back using the next pillar for leverage. Without slowing down I cupped my right hand around the back of the smooth marble, put my weight into the spin, and I was able to whirl around the column quickly. I darted the few feet back down the empty hall toward the turn I should've made in the first place.

The hall was empty, amazingly. Empty, I wondered? Why weren't the acolytes chasing me? Had I somehow outdistanced them? There'd been several elves in the room when I'd snapped, lost my temper, and lashed out with a right hook, and I bet at least half of them could probably set new world records in track and field back on Earth, if they ever cared to go there and try. So why weren't they chasing me?

You know how people always yell at teenagers to look where we're going? They always seem to yell it at me, anyway. And I should've listened then, because while my head was turned back over my shoulder, I ran right smack-dab into somebody. Bam! The collision was actually hard enough that it and the grunt of whoever I'd run into echoed off of the exit door that stood, closed and probably locked, way down at the end of the hallway.

As we both tumbled to the hard stone floor, I took in some disturbing facts in the order that they came to me. First, the guy I'd collided with—and he was a guy, I knew because my head impacted right into the middle of his muscular chest—was easily a head taller than me, which was unusual because of my own height. Every time we'd had height and weight measurement days in P.E. they'd made a show of pointing out that the top of my head cleared over the six foot mark. I'd hated standing out so much, but it made the number of guys whose chest height matched my nose height really, really tiny, even among the elves of Kiirajanna.

The second, and more disturbing, fact was that he was wearing plush purple velvet robes adorned copiously with sparkling gold thread, and only one man I'd seen in the realm of the elves wore such finery.

Third, the bright golden medallion that my nose, and then my cheek, planted itself on bore an unmistakable seal with the stag and the raven. I'm surprised I don't have a stag's horns still imprinted on one side of my face.

Only one male elf in the realm had the authority to wear the stag and the raven: the Elf King, himself.

I tried to help him up, but he was having none of that as he rose on his own and fixed me with a powerful glare. His penetrating blue eyes asked so many wordless questions that I could only think of one thing to say.

I gave the elf king my sweetest smile, brightening my own blue eyes as much as humanly possible in the hopes of making an impact.

"Hi, Daddy. I can explain," I said in my sweetest voice.

ELLYLLON

elves, to an elf.

ELLYLL

both singular noun (male) and adjective (male)[1].

ELLYLLES

because females need more syllables than males, I guess.

[1] note the difference between this adjective and all others formed by adding 'aidd to the noun

A Long Overdue Meeting

I suppose I ought to start the story a little bit before the slugging.

I didn't grow up as the daughter of the elf king. That's probably pretty obvious by now, but I figured it needed saying.

No, instead, I grew up a middle-class, fairly normal daughter of a hard-working single mom. Unfortunately that was in the South, where such things aren't always all that accepted even nowadays.

I had other things keeping me from being Miss Popularity in school. I've always been a good bit taller and more athletic than most of the other kids, which makes a whole lot more sense to me now that I've seen my father, the insanely tall and athletic elf warrior who became the elf king. It made me a bit of a tomboy—a tall and fast tomboy, at that. I outran my friends on the track team a few times, which kept the coach asking when he'd see my sandy head out there. I never saw the point of running in circles, though.

What I never did get was that accent *thang*. If I got upset enough I'd drop a y'all or two, but that was about it. My mother, an English and music teacher in school, taught me to speak correct English—you know, stuff like "ain't isn't in the dictionary." I mean, now it is, but she didn't want to hear any of that. Back in second grade, when she moved us *north* to a small town not far from the Tennessee state line, the kids heard I'd moved from Philadelphia and started calling me a Yankee. I tried explaining that there's a town by that name in Mississippi too, but the smart kids that they were didn't want to hear it.

Then there's the breast thing. You know, those things that are supposed to grow at puberty? Mine didn't. Girls in gym class used to ask if I wore A cups for "Absent." Heh heh, yeah, that was funny, my butt.

So yeah, I had a hard time fitting in, and I dare say it was through no fault of my own. But I made it, and my, uh, top half eventually showed up to the party, and so everything seemed to be going all right by the time I graduated as the class valedictorian, with a letter of admission to freshman year of college at State in my hands. I was pretty happy, all things considered.

The next day, my life turned upside down.

I'd been out with Sarah, who was pretty much my only close friend, celebrating our new status as graduates. Now, Sarah's from the upper class, her daddy being the best-known pediatrician in town, but she's never been snooty about it. She's the brilliant one and I'm the hard worker, and together we placed first and second in nearly everything academic. She's been a good friend, and....

But no, that's not part of this story. Sorry.

Anyway, I came back from an afternoon of hanging out with Sarah to find a man sitting in the living room with Momma. I'd say strange man, but the strangest thing about him was that he seemed eerily familiar.

To make sure you understand how unusual that was, let me say that my mother never, ever dated. Not ever. She always wore her wedding ring and kept telling me stories, when I'd ask, about how great my father was and how he was sure to come back some day. When I was young, those stories were always amplified in my head by an active imagination; sometimes my daddy was a fairy prince, or a mysterious robber baron, or whatever my imagination could come up with on any given day. No matter the fantasy, someday soon Daddy was going to come back home and sweep us out of our normal, boring lives, and we'd all live—well, you know the line.

Happily. Ever. Fricking. After.

Right?

At some point—I can't really pinpoint when—I stopped having the stupid daydreams. My father obviously existed, or else I wouldn't be around to get angry at him, but his place in my world as some sort of super-exciting big-shot became more and more clearly just the product of a young girl's overactive imagination. Through high school, I just got increasingly cynical at my mother's insistence that he'd be back. Can you blame me? How many years do you have to go without someone to admit that he's gone, done, and left for good?

All that was why it was such a shock to see an eerily familiar guy sitting on the couch holding Momma's hand when I walked in.

I could tell he was tall and every bit as angular as me, even with him still sitting on the couch, and as I got closer I saw that he had the same strange shade of blue in his eyes that I did. Same nose. Same long ears. Same high forehead. A grin radiated all the way across his face, cheek muscles pulling lips into a long looping smile while the skin at his temples did the same for his eyes. Long, lean fingers curled around Momma's hands—hands that had been so rough at times, and so gentle at other times. He shared glances with my mother, his looks filled with an impossible amount of emotion and Momma's with doe-eyed affection.

The man finished muttering something he'd been sharing with my mother when I walked in, and she tittered in response. I don't think I've ever seen her laugh in a titter, but there it was. Obviously, she was completely smitten.

In a single smooth motion the man rose from the couch, Momma following his lead a little less gracefully.

"Alyssa," she said, excitement bubbling in her voice, "this is...."

Yeah, I already figured who he was, which was why I didn't let her finish her sentence before I closed the short distance between the front door and the couch. I just snapped. I punched him. Hard, with a punch to the solar plexus that should have dropped him like an overripe peach.

It didn't, so I hit him again.

That one didn't, either, so I hit him again.

And again.

I vaguely remember Momma's screaming as I looked this newcomer in the eyes, pushing all the years of frustrated dreams and hopes through my fists as I beat on his torso. I was hitting him harder than I'd hit anybody in my life. Not that I've hit that many people—you know, Tommy, and, well, that was about it up to that point. I think I was screaming something too, but I don't remember what it was for certain. It sure wasn't "bless your heart," I know that.

Through it all he just stood there smiling at me, one arm holding Momma protectively back away from the pummeling I was trying to deliver. I have to admit that he went up a notch or two in my estimation for that, but then again, there weren't any notches left for him to go down.

As all tantrums eventually do, my anger finally wore itself out and I let my hands drop to my sides.

Now, look, I know what you're thinking, me already having

slugged two people in the story, but no. I'm really not a violent person, normally. In high school I only used my fists in defense, and that only came up the one time. But there I was facing the guy who'd deserted us, him just showing up right after graduation with a big ole' smile on his face.

Tell me you wouldn't have hit him, too. I dare you.

'Course, the high priestess I slugged deserved it, too. She— no, wait, one part of the story at a time. I'll get there.

Anyway, as my anger wound down, I finally got to where I could hear what my mother was saying: "...not his fault he's had to be away!"

Oh, fine. I stopped. Nobody's ever called me unreasonable, after all. Besides, I was doing more damage to my fist than I was to his—my father's—solar plexus.

"Okay, Dad, so tell me. What's so important in *your* life that you had to miss all of mine?"

"I truly wish I could have been by your side throughout, my daughter, but my kingdom needed its king...."

"Oh, good *lord*. Genovia couldn't occasionally go without its king for a day or two?" I said, painting my angriest glare onto my face. *My kingdom needed its king*—does anybody on this side of reality talk like that? Hey, if he could make stuff up, so could I.

The man who was trying to worm his way in and become my father shook his head vacantly, missing the movie refer- ence. Momma caught it, though, and I saw anger burning in her eyes.

I should've taken her glare as a warning to stop, but I didn't. I was on a roll. "Will there be sparkly vampires or hob- bitses on a mission there waiting for us?"

"Alyssa Serena Miller," she said, drawing my name out in that white-hot voice only mothers know how to wield. I knew from experience that whatever words came next could be life or death for me. "You *will* take this seriously. You *will* listen to your father's story. *Do you hear me?*"

Yes, ma'am didn't seem meek enough, so I just nodded. It did the trick; Momma's eyes simmered down and she started giving the stranger those lovey-dovey looks again.

"Look, my beloved, Alyssa has every right to be angry. It's been a very long time for her to go without a father. Why don't we have a seat, and perhaps a cup of tea, and talk this through?" the man asked politely as he led my mother and me into the dining room.

Fine, I thought, sitting in my spot at the table. I sat quietly, eyes ransacking his appearance for clues as Momma got the hot water going.

For a so-called king, he was dressed fairly casually. At least, I guess it was casual attire; I've never seen what a king wears when he's not busy ruling. I'm not sure what I expected. Robes? A crown? A scepter? A fancy coat with frilly neck-line? Maybe all of those? This guy, though, looked more like a college professor in his normal-looking buttoned shirt under matching coat and slacks. He wasn't wearing a tie; I guessed that kings don't have to wear ties when they're not being royal.

He was still holding his gentle smile on his face, though I could tell that it took some effort. His eyes were doing the same to me that mine were to him.

Momma's return to the table with three cups of hot water and tea bags broke the ice that had frozen up between us.

"Do you see what you expected?" he asked.

"Mostly. Except for the king stuff, of course. I always imagined you were a prisoner somewhere, framed for a crime you didn't commit. Sometimes I saw you guilty of a crime of passion you did commit, though. Other times you were a secret agent, or a pirate."

"I am sorry to disappoint you, then."

"Well, if we must go with fantasy stuff, I guess king is a great big ole' step up from the other possibilities. Where is it that you're king of, anyway?"

"Kiirajanna."

"Oh." I'd never heard of it, despite actually paying attention through most of my geography course back in—what, tenth grade? Ninth? Whatever. "Never heard of it. Which continent is it on?"

The man looked at my mother, a surprised look on his face. "You never told her of the land of her heritage?" he asked.

Momma shrugged. "Some things are hard to explain, and— it always seemed to be the wrong time. Alyssa is such a pragmatic girl, and...."

The man silenced her with a gentle *shh* sound, bringing her hand up to his lips and kissing it gently. A smoothie, then.

He turned to me, a warm smile on his face, and opened his mouth and blew my mind.

"Alyssa, my daughter. You are my daughter, and it appears that you have inherited every bit of my blue eyes, my build, and my warrior tendencies." He looked down at my right fist meaningfully. "We have so much to talk of. It will take so long to teach you all that you have to learn. To start, though, Kiirajanna is the name for the otherlands. The realm of the elves, in other words. I am the king of the elves, and you were born to be their queen."

I looked at Momma in disbelief. "Is this some sort of weird Dungeons & Dragons thing?" She'd never been into the role playing before that I knew of, but we were already so far beyond strange that I couldn't imagine how it might get back to reality unless it was some sort of game. When she just smiled back at me and shook her head, I did the only thing I could think of. I panicked.

Wouldn't you?

My chair hit the floor as I put the table between the strange man and me. There was no telling, I reasoned, what he had done to my mother. My mind started racing over all the different drugs we'd learned about in school—not the ones kids do behind the band building, like pot and alcohol and stuff, but the other, stranger ones. The more powerful ones. The ones with strange names. The ones that make you see white bunnies and talking purple worms and—well, elf kings in your kitchen.

He sat there, though, still smiling and without a touch of concern showing. After several seconds of watching me inch toward the exit—he was sitting too close to the kitchen phone for me to just jump over there and call the cops—he opened his mouth and began to sing, quietly at first but beefing up the volume rapidly.

"Holl hamrantayrre sey theway thant, ahr heed eh noch"

It froze me in my tracks. No matter how much I didn't want to, and no matter how much I really didn't want to admit it, I recognized the words. 'All the stars' twinkles say, all through the night' the first line of the old lullaby went. The haunting melody flashed me back across the years to a very, very young age. Suddenly in my mind's eye I was young—very young; I don't know what age—and looking up into this man's face from the security of an old fashioned playpen as he crooned. I sat down heavily in a chair as I listened and allowed the memory to flood my mind once again.

"Therr morr orth ee vrro gorgonyant, ahr heed eh noch" - 'This is the way to the land of glory, all through the night'

"Golau ahrall hewe tehwehlhook" - 'Any other light is darkness'

"Ee ardanngos gweer broodverthook "- 'When true beauty shines down on us'

"Tehlyoor nevoid mehn tahwelook, ahr heed eh noch" - 'Heavenly family, peacefully over us, all through the night.'

"What—what was that?" I asked once the notes had faded, keeping my own voice soft in the hopes of not dispelling the moment that the man—my father—had created. Maybe, just maybe, with magic like that, the story might actually be true?

"It was a lullaby I used to sing to you."

"I—I know that. I actually understood what the words meant. I even remember hearing you sing it to me."

"I am not surprised, my daughter. You used to speak our tongue, back when you were a wee babe in swaddling blankets."

"It's beautiful," I said, my comment gushing with praise. I was still breathless. "Both the song and the language, I mean. Absolutely beautiful. And—and I used to talk like that?"

"You did. You were fluent in it once, as a child, when we all lived together in Wales. I am pleased that you remember that, from way back when you were the cutest little bundle of straw-haired cuteness."

I nodded, slowly, just about to the point of reaching my enough button. The thing was, I did remember it, sort of. It seemed a strange, magical time in my memories, a part that I'd just made up in a fit of overactive imagination. A mommy, and a daddy, I'd remembered in my dreams, but as he spun the song and the tale together, the images I'd put away sprang to life and the memories flooded back to me.

"You mean Wales, in England?" I asked.

"Wales, yes. It's the original point of connection between the realms of humans and elves. They still speak the old tongue there, in fact. But—England? Your mother brought you back to the United States for the high quality of education, and so now you say Wales is in England?" He grinned, the wide, face-consuming expression returning, and it eased the sting of his words a little.

"Hey, now," I said. My education had been just fine, and I

told him so. I'd just forgotten about the whole difference between England and Great Britain thing.

"I am certain it was. That said, you have apparently forgotten the language of your ancestors. Will you come with me to learn to speak it again? Without, hopefully, your new-found drawl?"

Even though I didn't think I had one, elves are apparently pretty sensitive to Mississippi accents, which is what started the punching thing later between me and the high priestess—but there I go again, mixing my stories. Anyway, I supposed that he'd proven that he was my father as much as was possible.

But there was one glaring problem still, and I saw it written all over Momma's face before she hid it behind one of her fake smiles.

"So you're taking Momma and me back to this elf kingdom with you this time?" I asked, hoping I'd misjudged.

He looked down at the table. Momma looked over at the blank wall. I saw right through both of them. I'd been right.

"She can't come, can she?"

"She is of human blood," my father said. "Unfortunately, that means that she cannot enter our world."

"And I can, because apparently I'm half-blood."

He nodded.

"So, if I get this right, you met Momma, got her pregnant, left her, and now you're coming back to take away the only family she has left."

"It was never quite as casual as you make it sound, but to answer your question directly: for the time being, yes."

"What's that supposed to mean? How long is a *time being* to an eternal elf?"

"Elves are not eternal, dear, no matter how much the storytellers entice you to believe so. In fact—no, that is not important now. What is important is for you to know that my intent is to take you back with me, assist you in taking your rightful place on the queen's throne in Kiirajanna, and then return here to my one true love."

"And abandon me in a strange land all by myself? Great plan."

"The queen is hardly all by herself. Besides, I believe you have been planning on doing much the same thing when you go away to college in the fall. Am I correct?"

He had me on that one. I tried another way. "And what if I don't wanna go?"

He looked surprised and thought for a minute. "I confess, I had not thought of that alternative. Other than carrying you back against your will, a prospect which I am firmly against, I suppose the answer is simple. You will stay here and never be the queen, I shall go back to Kiirajanna with no hope of ever returning, evil will triumph over good throughout the land, and—well, I guess that is that. Is that choice to be your path, my daughter?"

"*Hmmph.* Melodramatic much?" He sure had the guilt trip thing down pat.

"That was not melodrama, Alyssa. I was being honest."

Suddenly he spoke again in that strange lilting language, his voice this time picking up a scary intensity as he recited something that sounded like "Krayethenon, booth ee freneeness arr mangeni thrayig ashoob nee."

"So, what was *that*?" I asked.

"Words from the ancient prophecy. It means 'the queen with the dragon-shaped birth mark shall save us all.' Or, something like that, in any event. The exact translation is impossible to render into this Southern language you are so fond of using. Tell me, Alyssa, do you still have the dragon birth mark on your right shoulder?"

I did. It had always been a strange round-ish brown thing that Momma had just shrugged about when asked. Without speaking, I jumped up and ran to the bathroom to look at it in the mirror again.

Sure enough, now that he said dragon, I could see it. My birthmark was a curled-up dragon.

Dang it.

I walked back to the table, a defeated look on my face. When the chips have been down, I've always at least been compliant.

"Okay, fine. Dad. One last question, though. Why would these elves want a half-human to be their queen?"

"A good question with a very complicated answer, Alyssa. Part of it is simple genetics—many thousands of years ago elves and humans intermixed freely, and it is thought that those times were the best that Kiirajanna has ever seen."

"'It is thought'? You don't buy that, do you?" I had a hunch, and I went with it.

I was rewarded with a single nod. "You have always been a perceptive girl, a trait that will serve you well as the queen. And no, I do not. It is our nature—elf, and human too, I believe—to look more fondly upon the past than the past really deserves."

"Okay. So that's part of it, you said. Why else, then?"

"Tradition. My people—your people, soon, too—manage ourselves very closely to our traditions so that we maintain a very orderly society. Truth be told, nobody really questions why the king must find a human lady to bear the next queen by; we just accept it and do it. I must say, it worked out quite well for me."

"I'm sure," I said, looking across the table at Momma. She sure was a prize in my eyes. I'd wondered over the years why she didn't go find someone rich and—well, present—with as beautiful as she was. Now that I saw Tall, Handsome, and Royal, I kinda understood.

She smiled back at me, and then turned a goofy smile to her husband.

"Okay, makes sense, I suppose." It actually wasn't making much sense to me, but I was being compliant, remember? "When do we leave, then?"

He looked at my mother, a smile that bordered on lewd spreading across his face. "Our departure will wait till tomorrow, I believe."

My mother returned the same smile and then they got up and walked hand-in-hand out of the kitchen, leaving me alone with my tea, my knowledge of what they were fixing to do, and a great big-ole' helping of *'eww.'*

CYFEILLGARWCH

friendship. For some reason, a much harder word to say in the elf language than it is in English.

The King's Home

"Graceland?" I asked, my voice rising to a pitch I rarely hear myself using. It was unbelievable.

My newfound father looked back at me from the front seat of our old sedan where he rode beside Momma, a gleeful smile on his face as he nodded. "Indeed. It is the former home of Elvis Presley."

"I know what Graceland is. I just didn't expect us to find the entrance to Narnia here," I said, wiping the grogginess out of my eyes. I'd apparently slept for most of the drive, and I'd just come to as the car moved up to the parking attendant.

"Oh, you cannot find it here," he said, ignoring my sarcastic reference. "The ley-gate is close, but not at Graceland. Your mother and I were big fans of the King, though, and I have always wanted to see his home. We have plenty of time, after all."

I growled. They'd gotten me up before dawn, a feat that I rarely allowed to happen in the summer. I hadn't been allowed to pack much more than a few favorite outfits, either. Granted, I'm not one of those prissy types who takes three or four trunks of clothes to a week-long summer camp—yes, I've been to summer camp, and yes, I saw some of those—but I wanted to at least take a few normal sets of clothes.

No, he'd said, they could clothe me just fine once we got there. An elf princess, he'd said, doesn't wear jean shorts.

Blah. Elf princess, my butt. I was already not looking forward to the trip.

Sarah, my bestie and really the only significant tie I had to this place other than Momma, had of course quizzed me about where we were going when I'd called her over last night. I'd said, mostly honestly, that I had no idea. My long-lost dad was back from wherever he'd been hiding, and he was taking me back to his home to meet everybody.

"Hey, he's a hottie," she'd said after we walked back to my room to hang out for one last evening. That hadn't helped much; I wasn't sure whether to be grossed out or proud of it.

"You look a lot like him," she'd also said, and after the hottie comment I really wasn't sure what to do with that. My hair was sandy-brown and stiff like Momma's, while his was a flowing black mane, but my facial features could've been photocopied directly from his.

We'd spent the rest of the evening and much of the night giggling like we were little again, remembering strange stories of high school and making up stranger stories about what I would be facing in the great Somewhere. We exchanged mailing addresses after Dad gave me the one for the castle in Wales; apparently they even have an everyday inter-realm courier service going there. I played along with the jokes about being a newly-discovered princess, trying my best to discredit them without outright lying.

It wasn't hard. The honest truth was I had no idea what I was in store for, a nagging fact that kept me up well past Sarah's eventual departure.

Well, that, and a late-night visit from Momma. She padded into my room and presented me with a beautiful pendant. It was shiny silver spun into the form of a Celtic dragon. A bright blue gemstone eye sparkled in the moonlight when I turned it on the chain, and it mesmerized me so much that I probably could have spent an hour watching it glisten.

It was the most beautiful piece of jewelry I'd ever seen, and she refused to spill where it had come from beyond a couple of mouthed words: "family heirloom." I'd tried asking for more, but she just shushed me. Then, as I admired the amazing craftsmanship, she tousled my hair one last time and left as silently as she'd come in.

All that mystery combined with a really strange day to keep me up way into the morning hours. It couldn't have been more than a couple of hours from when I went to sleep till my new-found dad was shaking me out of bed to go.

Hence my growl.

"Oh, come, Alyssa. It's gonna be fun," Momma said.

"Or else, right?" She'd been dragging me into stuff I didn't wanna do for as long as I could remember, threatening me that I better have fun, or else. I almost always chose the former.

"Of course. Besides, now you get to see the King's House."

"That's what you said last night. I just didn't realize you meant this king."

It was fun, actually. Graceland was a destination everybody in my town talked about, but leaving the state—other than the short trips north to spend a day at the lake—wasn't done much, so I'd neither seen it for myself nor talked to anyone who had toured it in person. The mansion was pretty, and I swear the spot on the tour that they called the jungle room looked just like our living room did growing up. At least, it looked like our living room would've looked if the furniture in our house had matched. Then again, my mother liked decorating in the Early

Southern Garage Sale style, and to be honest, so did I.

Okay, I admit it, our living room didn't have a waterfall. But the shag carpet? That, in spades.

I gasped when we walked out behind the home; there were horses! I never knew that Elvis had huge pastures, but he did, and they still keep horses on them. One even trotted up to the fence opposite us, nickering at my father, who actually seemed to answer in the lilting language he'd used before.

"Beautiful," I said, not sure whether to apply the word more to his words or to the magnificent mare. "I've always had a thing for horses."

"Of course you have, dear," the elf king said quietly, turning and walking over to Momma, away from the other family that had walked up to pet the horse. "Our kind have a special connection to the animal kingdom."

"And all the fairies and pixies, too, right?" I said, following and giving him a wider than usual smirk to make my sarcasm obvious.

"Yes, of course. Those, too," he said, walking away with Momma in tow before I could gauge his expression for honesty. I stood there for a minute thinking about what he'd said, trying hard to keep my jaw from hitting the ground over the suggestion that fairies and pixies might actually exist.

They—they couldn't possibly, right? Finally I decided that he must've just been messing with me.

When we'd finally seen every inch of the mansion, the wall of gold and platinum records, the back gym, the jet, the other jet, the museums, the dining café, and everything else, we piled into the car and headed out, stopping near the river at what appeared to be a huge but deserted glass pyramid.

"Oh, a pyramid. How predictable," I said, my exhaustion from sleep deprivation and a long day of walking around Graceland bringing my sarcastic side back out.

Alright, so my sarcastic side is always out. At least I had tiredness to blame for it this time.

My new dad didn't seem to notice, though, wrapped as he was around my mother. I waited patiently for them to break the embrace.

...and waited....

...and waited....

When I couldn't bear sitting in the back seat any more, I grabbed my backpack and the walking stick he'd brought for me and walked a little way off into the evening light, reading the signs on the fence for lack of anything better to do. I ended up staring at a tall Egyptian-looking statue for quite some time.

"Ready, Alyssa?" a voice surprised me from behind, making me jump and spin around.

"Don't do that!"

Blue eyes fixed mine from under the cowl of a cloak that, in the dimming light, made my father's features nearly disappear. "You cannot tell me," he said, "that you failed to sense my approach."

I couldn't tell him that, at least not honestly. I'd always been able to sense people entering my space somehow. I shrugged.

"It's still rude."

"Alyssa, you are about to enter a realm where the definition of what is rude and what is not might not match your expectations."

"Yes, but we're not there yet. My realm, my rules," I said, a sudden extreme piquishness settling over me.

"Indeed," he said. "And on that note, it is time to enter your new realm for you to learn your new rules, as well as your new rule." I left him standing there, chuckling quietly over his play on words while I went back to say my own goodbye to Momma.

It was harder than I thought it would be. I realized, standing there holding back the tears, that I couldn't think of a single day in my life that I hadn't spent at least a few minutes of it with the woman who'd raised me up all on her own. I'd been ready—heck, I'd been looking forward to leaving home in the fall to go away to college, but that's just a dorm room kinda thing, with breaks over holidays. State is close enough to home that I could even spend most weekends there if I wanted. I'd been sure that I wouldn't want it, that getting away from home and out on my own would be a scary but wonderful adventure, but now that the moment of departure was right in my face, I questioned everything I'd been so sure about.

I kind of wanted to just stay home.

"Momma," I murmured into her soft, warm shoulder as we stood there beside the car, our arms grasping each other tight. "Can I just say no and go back home with you?"

"No, dear," she said. "You have to go."

"I don't want to. Really, I don't. They can choose somebody else for this princess stuff, can't they?" I don't whine often, but at least when I do it's sincere.

Pushing me away to arm's length, Momma said, "Alyssa, daughter, I love you more than I have loved anything on this world, ever before. Trust me, I'll miss you more than you can imagine. But this is the position you were born for. To be honest, I'm still overjoyed, amazed, and in a bit of disbelief that your father chose me to spend the rest of his life with once he comes back. That choice left me with a few challenging years to deal with, yes. But that choice also led to me having eighteen wonderful years with you, watching you grow up into the smart, strong young woman you are today. That was my time, and it has been wonderful beyond measure. And now we've come to *your* time, dear. You will be the elf queen, and trust me, you'll be the best queen the elves have ever had. Now, you just take the picture of me that you brought and set it out beside your bed when you get there. Talk to me through it every night. I'll hear, I promise. Come back to visit whenever you can, but Alyssa, darling, this is your moment to shine."

Emboldened and saddened both, I stood on the sidewalk and watched Momma get into the driver's seat of the old sedan, turn the key, put the engine into gear, and drive away.

"Ready to go, Alyssa?" my father's voice sounded from the darkness behind. I nodded, wiped a few leaky drips from my cheeks, and turned to follow him into my new life.

As we walked toward the massive pyramid, I took what might be my last opportunity to quiz him: "So, how will we know when we're at the ley-gate?" He'd told me over supper about the vortexes, where the link between the world I'd grown up in and the world of the elves coexisted. That was where creatures that were combinations of magic and matter, like the elves, could cross from one realm to the other, while creatures of pure matter, like humans, and creatures of pure magic, like faeries, could not. These places of power were spaced around the world, and of course they existed at the normal spots you'd expect—Stonehenge, the Bermuda Triangle, the Great Pyramid, and so on. But there were many more, he said, at less exotic locations.

Like, apparently, Memphis.

"The staff I brought for you will tell you when you're there. Just keep hold of it and you will know. With some training, you'll be able to pick out the closest ley-gate's location and distance from farther away."

"Um, yeah—this training stuff. Is that part negotiable, Dad? I'm not thinking that I'm really up for that, just out of school as I am. I was supposed to be having a summer off. Maybe I could still go take some time off from school, go to an elf beach, or something?"

My father chuckled and shook his head, and then said, "You will need the training as soon as you arrive, though, my daughter, and you really will enjoy it."

"We'll see." I wasn't convinced; I had really been looking forward to a long summer of leisure.

"What we have prepared for you is not just training. As part of the transition you will have the opportunity to learn all about your realm and its history, as well as the people who wrote their signatures upon the major events of the time spectrum. Most important, you will learn who your people really are."

"My people, hmm?"

"Yes, your people," my father said, turning a shadowy grin my way. "Have you ever felt completely at home in Mississippi?"

I ignored the question and changed the subject, "So, why did they put a ley-gate here by the river? Did there used to be something here that was iconic, or did the world know that someday Memphis would build a big glass pyramid over it?"

The *over* was because we'd taken a sudden turn; from inside the now-deserted athletic area the path I was following the Elf King on was definitely sloped downwards. Deeply downwards, in fact.

His voice came back to me from within the form-hiding cloak as he somehow opened yet another gate that I would've sworn should have been locked.

"Actually, the intersection was not in this location when I first came to this area. The energy was centered about—oh, what is the distance—thirty, forty leagues? About as far as we traveled to get here, but toward the northeast. There were ancient burial mounds placed there by the humans who used to walk the land. Once this pyramid was built, it focused and shifted the energies to this location instead."

"Wow, I didn't know humans have such power over energy flow."

"You—or, rather, they—do not. Structures do, though. At least, certain structures do. The pyramid is a particularly powerful one, and this one being used as a sports complex generated the tremendous energy required to shift a ley point."

"So, what happened to the spot it connects to on the other side when this side shifted?"

"Nothing, actually," he said, stopping briefly and looking back at me from under his cowl. "The locations at either end are not physical points but rather tendons of energy, and they do not have to correspond directly. That was an excellent query, though, my daughter."

I grinned despite myself.

"Ah," he said after walking in silence for a few more minutes, "here we are. Feel anything?"

I did, now that he mentioned it. My staff was starting to buzz in my hand, a slight vibration that was just a touch uncomfortable.

Around the next corner, we walked in to what appeared to be a central room in the depths underneath the complex. A small grate in the center of the floor probably served as a drain, though I couldn't see anything that might need to run off through it. As my father walked toward the grate, his staff began glowing with a slowly brightening blue light along the angular lines carved into it that I hadn't noticed before.

Oh great, I thought—*runes*. Really? As much as I really didn't want to, I was starting to believe that there might actually be something to the stories he'd been telling me. The birthmark, the Welsh lullaby—those were, well, cute. Runes that blinked to life, unbidden, though, were—well, serious. Seriously creepy, in a way, but serious, regardless. Still, it was his staff, and who knows what kind of buttons he'd had hidden on it for the runes, right?

I looked at my own staff: blank, no markings on it at all. If it wasn't still buzzing I'd've thought I got a dud, or at least one without a hidden "Magical Runes On" switch.

He stopped near the center of the room and looked expectantly back over his shoulder at me. "Coming, Alyssa?" he asked.

I took a deep breath for courage and marched in, watching my walking stick as I went. Sure enough, runes I'd swear weren't there when he'd handed me the staff flowed to life, runes that glowed brighter as I approached the middle of the room. My breath caught. I became a believer. Finally I stood next to him, both our staves giving the air around us a weird azure tint. I grinned ear to ear in anticipation despite myself and my former misgivings.

"Feel the energy of the vortex?" When I nodded, he continued, "Good. Now, rap your staff on the ground and will yourself into Kiirajanna by thinking the name," he said, and demonstrated, disappearing from sight as he did.

"At least I don't have to click my heels three times. Now that would be weird," I said, then realized there wasn't anybody around any longer to hear my sarcasm.

I really hate wasting good sarcasm!

I followed his instructions and suddenly found myself in a glade in the woods, my staff still glowing, facing my newfound father.

"Welcome to Kiirajanna," he said, a broad smile on his face as he gestured to a strange wheeled box at the edge of the clearing. Painted red with white trim, it looked like it might have been a carriage if it only came with horses to pull it. "Your transport to the castle awaits, my young princess."

That wouldn't be the last time I cringed at hearing that title.

First Day In A Foreign Land

Have I mentioned that I hate being woken up early in the summer? I think I have. If not, it's true. I hate being woken up early in the summer—hate, hate, hate it. And I should also explain that *early* means anytime before my eyes decide they're tired of being closed.

Momma does it, but only rarely and then only when there's something important going on, like a fire in the house or a trip to the lake. My new-found father had already done it once, too, because he wanted to see the King's mansion before taking me to Kiirajanna to see—well, the King's mansion. Go figure. Different king, and the royal castle in Kiirajanna didn't have anything resembling a jungle room or a wall of gold and platinum records, but it was still roughly the same idea without the shag carpet. I guess I didn't hold the early wake-up too heavily against him.

A little elf girl, though? She was toast, if it wasn't for the bear backing her up.

The somehow-self-powered carriage had dropped us off at the castle the night before. There hadn't been enough light out to see much of anything else, so I didn't bother looking. A servant—a servant? Really? Like I would ever have a servant?—whose name I was too tired to remember showed me to my room and helped tuck me into bed, an action I was too exhausted to think about, much less consider weird. I was asleep so fast I really don't remember closing my eyes.

"Princess Alyssa, it's time to wake up," a husky voice near my bed had the audacity to say. It even sounded eager, as though the girl actually liked the idea of rising early in the summer.

I opened one eye to see who the brave fool belonging to the voice was. She seemed young-ish, though I confess to having no idea how to judge the age of an elf. Medium-tall, with short reddish hair. Goofy smile, teeth showing under an upturned button nose. Same long ears people had made fun of me for back home. The brown tunic and light green trousers she had on were much simpler clothes than I'd have expected to see in the King's castle, but who was I to judge on my first morning there?

I could take her, I figured. Which, I hoped, meant I wouldn't have to; a simple growl would probably scare her away. Opening both eyes, I sat up halfway and sent my most menacing growl her direction.

That was when the bear popped its head up and over the side of the bed, growling right back at me. The fur on its wide neck stood straight up, giving the creature a demonic appearance to go with a menacing throaty growl.

Now, I have a pretty good growl, if I say so myself. It's not nearly that good, though. I ended it with a not-as-impressive squeak as I sprang to my feet on the other side of the bed in a move that must've looked pretty athletic.

"What.... What—why is there a *bear* in my room?" I stammered.

"Bear? What—no. Oh, no, Your Highness, Booboo is a wolverine."

Oh, a wolverine. Right. She said it like that was better, but it wasn't. Last I heard, bears eat salmon, wolverines eat people.

The elf girl must've seen the panic in my eyes—or perhaps in the fact that I had backed all the way to the corner of the room, cowering behind the sheet-shield I'd taken with me in my white-knuckled grip. Whichever it was, she started pulling backward on the waist-high shaggy brown beast's fur. "Down, Booboo. Down. This is the princess that you're scaring. Stop it!"

"Booboo?" I asked, finally ratcheting my fear down enough to make some sense out of what was happening. "You named that furry, mean little monster *Booboo*?"

"He only looks mean, Your Highness. Booboo wouldn't hurt you. Please believe me."

"Okay, fine. Look, I'll believe you if you can get him to put that growl away. It makes my skin crawl. And what is Booboo doing in my room?"

She looked confused and said, "Helping me wake you up, Your Highness. Booboo follows me everywhere."

Ignoring the strangeness of that, I went after the title. "Quit calling me Your Highness!" Once again I made a wrong move, apparently. As the little elf girl shrank back, the wolverine renewed the growl that would've sent Chuck Norris into a crouch, and then it strained forward, looking for all the world like it was just about to tear my throat apart.

I held my hands up, unfortunately letting the sheet-shield drop in the process, in the hopes of preventing the beast from attacking me. "Sorry, sorry. I'm a little grumpy when I wake up. But seriously, do you have to call me Your Highness with every breath?"

"What would you prefer I call you?"

I sighed. This had started out all wrong and was going

worse. "Um, Booboo's not gonna bite me if I walk over to you, is he?"

"Booboo, behave," she said to the beast before shaking her head. "No, Your—ma'am. He'll be good."

Unconvinced, I walked slowly around the foot of the bed till I was just inside handshaking distance of the elf. Extending my arm way out, I said, "Let's start over, then. My name is Alyssa. What's yours?"

Okay, in hindsight I really should have expected her, I guess, to take my outstretched hand the wrong way. I mean, I've seen enough movies, right? She did exactly what one of those movie characters would've done when meeting royalty: curtsied, a little clumsily, and kissed the top of the hand I was stretching out toward her.

"No, no, I meant to shake your hand, not have you kiss mine," I said, more annoyed with myself than her. "Up, up, up. Here, grab my hand like so, and shake." We managed to shake hands, mostly through my own effort. The elf played along, a bewildered look on her face.

"Is that the customary method for greeting princesses where you come from, ma'am?"

"No, it's the customary method for greeting friends."

"But we're not friends, ma'am. No offense intended, please, but you're the princess."

I couldn't help it. I sat down at the foot of the bed and sighed a long and frustrated exhalation. The day before I hadn't even believed in elves beyond the Santa story and the Keebler commercials, and now here I was in their castle. My first meeting with my first non-parental elf was going horribly wrong.

"Look, can we just start over? What's your name?"

"Sephaline, ma'am."

"Well, now, that's a very pretty name. But look, Sephaline, I think I'm going to have a lot of people bowing and scraping to me, right?" Sephaline hesitated but then nodded, and I continued, "So to get me through all of that, I'm going to need at least one friend I can count on. Now, I'm as good a judge of character as anyone, and I'd like to be friends with you. Can we do that, or is it completely forbidden?"

"It's not forbidden, exactly; it's just not normally done, ma'am," Sephaline said, a thoughtful expression on her face.

"Normally? How many princesses are there?"

"Just you. Well, and the queen's two daughters, but they'd never ask me to be friends. They're not in the same category as you, anyway. You're going to be the crown princess."

"Okay. I guess that makes sense. So how many princesses have you known, personally?"

"Just you."

"How can you say what's normally done, then?"

Her mind tussled with that for several moments before her face lit in a smile. "Friends, then, ma'am," she said, reaching out and shaking my hand a little harder than would've seemed normal back home. Still, I figured it was a good start.

"Alyssa," I corrected.

"Yes, Princess Alyssa," she agreed.

"Just Alyssa."

"Just Alyssa," she replied

Good lord, I thought. "So now that we have that straight, where's breakfast? I'm starving."

"You're not.... You're not going downstairs dressed like that, are you?"

"Why not? I'm the princess, right?" I asked, a wicked smile on my face.

"Well, yes, but the prince or other princesses or even the king might be there."

"So?"

"So you're dressed like a commoner."

"Yesterday I *was* a commoner."

"And today you're the princess of the realm, our future queen," Sephaline said as she crossed her arms stubbornly. "It would be an insult for you to not dress the part today."

As much as I wanted to ask who might be insulted, I held my tongue. She was right, I guessed.

"Okay, fine. What does a princess of the realm wear?"

"You could try looking in the princess of the realm's wardrobe."

So maybe, just maybe, this much familiarity could be a bad idea, I thought as I opened the wardrobe. I was relieved when I looked in, though, since most of the clothes were fairly simple sets of pants and shirts. I pulled out a pair of light linen bottoms and a matching shirt and held them out. When my new friend nodded, I stepped behind the divider and changed out of my crumpled clothes from yesterday. The jeans and t-shirt I'd apparently slept all night in went into a hamper in the corner.

Before I left the room I took a moment to take the small picture of Momma out of my bag and set it out on a nightstand by the bed. It was one of the few personal items I'd snagged on my sleepy way out the previous day, but I'd been too tired when I collapsed on the bed to dig it out. "Mornin', Momma!" I said and planted a kiss right on the glass, getting a little giggle out of Sephaline as a result. Hey, Sephaline could giggle all she wanted; the picture was a cute pose with Momma's poofy hair all done up, and I was already missing her.

On the way down I had a couple of minutes to quiz Sephaline about the going fashion trends, and was happy to find out that elves didn't wear dresses much in the castle, and almost never outside of it. In fact, she didn't know what one was till I described it for her, and then she acted scandalized at the description.

"No—pants?" she asked.

"None. Just a very long top."

"How do you...."

Being a tomboy who'd always loved the outdoors and hated dresses, myself, I knew what she was asking. "You don't." As I shrugged off her horrified expression, I continued, "it's not such a big loss to some girls."

Most of what I'd mistaken for dresses in my new wardrobe were, in fact, formal tops, it turned out. In most elf activities, Sephaline explained, the length of the top indicated the formality of the occasion. Regular shirts as I had picked out were perfect for a working breakfast, but later in the day it was common for elf ladies to change tops two or three times, each one longer than the one before until the evening dining blouse fell past the woman's knees.

And speaking of breakfast, it was good and plentiful. I breathed a sigh of relief when I saw a thick hunk of ham; somewhere in the back of my mind I'd been wondering if my new "people" were vegetarians. But no, it was eggs, ham, and biscuits—the only thing missing was Momma's white gravy.

Well, that, and the remainder of the castle inhabitants. Sephaline assured me that nearly a hundred people lived within the walls of the main building, yet breakfast was served to just her and me because by that time everybody else was out working. Apparently most elves rise with the crack of dawn, and I would be expected to join them soon enough.

She'd waited as long as she could handle it, and well after the normal breakfast time, then, before waking me up. Great. A society full of early birds.

"So, Booboo follows you everywhere?" I asked, trying to make conversation between bites.

"Of course. He's my—I believe the word in your language is 'familiar.'"

I was familiar with familiars—hah!—thanks to a couple of times being drawn into D&D. Sarah had liked a guy who played it, see, and she'd needed backup when he invited her over. It was a tolerable enough game once I got past the mountains of rules, like the whole crazy thing about which animals give what special abilities to the mage when chosen as a familiar, but the part I found really strange was watching the other players' antics. The whole *ooh, here I go rolling a die at you* act weirded me out in a creepy sort of way.

Anyway, I nodded. "I know what a familiar is, I think. So you're a magic user, then?"

I saw her freeze out of the corner of my eye and turned. She sat there, fork full of ham halfway to her mouth, glaring at me. Booboo apparently picked up on her mood, because he treated me to another ferocious growl.

"Okay, so what did I say?"

"You don't know?"

"Apparently not. Remember, if you would please, that I haven't exactly lived here my whole life like you have."

She breathed, finally, and Booboo's hair fell back onto his haunches. "Just don't ever call someone a magic user. It's one of the worst insults you can give."

"Worse than 'your mama wears army boots'?"

"Are army boots an insulting choice of footwear where you come from, Alyssa?"

"No, it's just that—oh, never mind. So calling somebody a magic user is a serious insult here. But why?"

"Honest elves don't do magic. That's for the criminals and the churls, and they're few and far between."

"You don't do magic?"

"You heard me, Alyssa."

"I did, but I'm confused, then. When my father brought me through the ley-gate last night, I could'a sworn that was magic.

Then we jumped into a carriage that moved without horses, and I sure didn't see any electric rails or engines—and that wasn't magic? How, then, did it move itself?"

"You do have a lot to learn, don't you?"

I could tell it was going to be a long day. Still, I just sat and stared at her, eyebrow raised, waiting for her to answer the question.

"What powers the carriages is earth energy," she finally explained. "It's the same thing that allows us to travel from realm to realm, and also to sing plants into growth. It helps some of us hunt more cleanly. That's just shaping natural forces, not playing with dark magic. Do you see the difference?"

I thought for a minute and assumed I had it. "So, teleporting between realms is good. Shooting magic missiles into the darkness is not. Is that about right?"

She nodded with an expression that was still curious. "Sort of, I guess, if these magic missiles are what I assume they must be. You'll learn more, I'm sure, when you start your lessons with the priests. Which, it appears, will be very soon," she said, pointing to two tan-robed figures who strode into the dining hall.

LL

a voiceless alveolar lateral fricative, the teacher said, like I should know what that means. Then she made the LL sound at me for nearly ten mi-nutes straight. Fricative, indeed.

Learning To Be The Queen

The priests led me away from the dining area; Sephaline and her little wolverine bear-thing went the other direction claiming to have their own training to attend to. *Oh, joy,* I thought, *my first day in my new digs and my only friend so far has already deserted me.*

The priests leading me were polite, yet firm. They showed no hint of the whole bowing *Your Highness* stuff that Sephaline had gushed at first. Ah, well; I'm really not a big fan of being bowed and scraped to. Really, I'm not.

There was a maze of corridors to go through, and at some point the walls stopped looking castle-like and started looking cathedral-like, if that makes sense. Think "hunting and battle art" morphing into "nature and religious art."

Apparently the castle and the cathedral were directly connected, anyway. If, that is, you consider a few miles of hallways directly connected. Then again, with all the turns, I'm not sure whether the priests took me the direct way or the *let's screw with the newbie* way. I was pretty certain, regardless, that I wouldn't be able to find my way back on my own.

Somewhere along the way I remembered that I had never seen the building from the outside in daylight. I'd have to do that sometime, I figured, now that the inside seemed so huge.

We reached some sort of main office after a while; it was simple and bare yet held an air of importance in kind of the same way an old book store holds an air of moldy books. The priests led me to a simple wooden chair that faced a desk, behind which a woman—well, an ancient female elf, anyway—sat. At least, I guessed she was ancient because the wrinkles on her face had wrinkles, and because the hand holding a quill pen looked shriveled and gray. Across her shoulder ran a much-wider sash than the ones worn by two priests I'd come in with, so I assumed she was someone important. Otherwise she wore the same nondescript brown robes as they did, under which I had to assume, based on my recent conversation, was a pair of pants.

Yes, I thought about checking, but I'm an imaginative troublemaker, not a stupid one.

After a few minutes she finished whatever she was writing on, pushed it to the side, and looked up at me. Nodding with all the warmth of a frozen polar bear, she said, "Greetings, Princess. It is good to finally meet you in person. I am High Priestess Naissa."

I think Booboo came across as more approachable than the high priestess did. But maybe that's just my preference for furry creatures over wizened, dour matrons coming out.

I wasn't sure what the protocol was to respond to someone who introduced herself as a high priestess, and I told her so. She smiled and said, "It is always best if we admit our areas of ignorance, young one. When one of the priesthood greets you, it is appropriate for one of your elevated standing to simply nod in return and say 'Greetings, Brother' or 'Greetings, Sister.' That said, please keep in mind that although on a social level you are my peer, and a superior to those who serve in the priesthood, while you are our student you should always maintain an appropriate degree of humility."

Appropriate degree of humility. Right-y-o. After that, I really wanted to check for pants. Instead, I kept my voice dreadfully level as I said, "No problem, High Priestess. How long am I to be a student?"

"Until you have learned what needs to be learned."

Gosh, I should have seen that coming.

"What will the scope of my lessons entail?" Obviously I needed to be more specific with her.

"History. Protocol. Etiquette. And other matters that the queen of the realm needs to know."

"I see. Will I learn magic?" I was just testing her, of course. Her reaction was nowhere near what I'd expected. Instead of looking like I'd just asked her if she would eat a live mudbug as Sephaline had, the High Priestess's face actually seized up, the wrinkles' wrinkles changing directions.

She replied slowly and in a voice reinforced with steel, "No. Magic is not taught here, child."

Well, then.

"My father used some sort of energy to pass through the ley-gate to get here, though. Will I learn that?"

"Of course," she said, her face relaxing and brightening. "All elves know how to shape and call the energies of nature to them. You shall, too."

"Shaping and calling the energies of nature to them sounds an awful lot like magic, High Priestess," I said, and was rewarded by her face puckering up even tighter than before.

"And you say this because you have expertise in magic, or in shaping and calling the energies of nature, child?"

"No, neither one. But when I've played magic games—" I started, and this time she cut me directly off, her voice slicing like a Ginsu.

"This is *not* a magic game. I would suggest that, *if* you wish to continue along the path toward becoming our queen, you stop even thinking in terms of either magic or games. You are not here to think on those things. You *are* here to learn the arts that come naturally to most elves as *young* children."

"Okay," I gave in. It was pretty obvious that I wasn't going to win. "That sounds like a plan, High Priestess. So when do I start?"

"Now, if you are ready. I'll have the brethren behind you lead you to your first lesson."

I admit, I was a little disappointed that my lessons wouldn't be handled personally by the high priestess, herself. I was, after all, a princess. *The* princess, or at least *the* crown princess, in fact, of, like, the whole realm, though I still didn't know what that meant. It—and I, for that matter—had to be important, though, right?

I saw just how important I was when the priests dumped me off into a classroom full of five-year-olds. The Monks, as I'd started calling them while I followed them silently through the halls, introduced me to the teacher in a low voice. She, in turn, introduced me to the kids in the class, and they all bowed.

You know, "they all bowed" should look far more impressive than it did in real life. You'd think, anyway, right? A bunch of adults bowing would've probably been impressive, though of course I would have had to object and pretend like I wasn't even a little bit thrilled. *No, no, no need to bow to me, please, my noble fellow elves*, and so on. But have you ever been bowed to by a bunch of five-year-olds? It's—well, it's just kinda silly, honestly.

Regardless, the bow-fest was over quickly enough, and then we began what turned into a series of morning and afternoon lessons with the kids. The Monks would pick me up at breakfast and lead me to the classroom, where I'd learn stuff that admittedly I should have learned back when I was five: language, etiquette, et cetera and et cetera ad infinitum ad nauseum, and so on. All that, just when I thought I would be headed off to college to study adult stuff with the rest of the newly-graduated adults after a wonderfully lazy, adult summer.

What a treat, right?

It really wasn't that hard to pick the mechanics of the language back up. I apparently remembered more than I realized from my early childhood. The language of the elves used the same alphabet as English did, which was nice, but they went by some really strange rules to pronounce things. For example, the great big wolverine that Seph had running around behind her was actually named *Bwbw*, since the b is the same but the w is used for the *oo* sound. The problem for me was that *Bwbw* consists of four consonants where I come from, and four consonants together can't make a word. Ah, well, I decided to keep thinking Booboo instead. I'd gotten Seph's name all wrong, too; the ph doesn't exist for elves, and the e I'd been putting at the end of Sephaline's name shouldn't be there, either, but to me *Sefalin* looks wrong when the word should rhyme with magazine. Again, I decided to just keep it wrong in my head.

So, yeah, I started my new life and learning experience with my best—and only—friend's name spelled incorrectly. Way to launch, right?

That first evening the Monks dumped me back off at the dining hall pretty early—way before I was ready to eat supper, anyway. Sephaline and her little pet, too, were there waiting on me.

"Been waiting long?" I asked.

"Not really. I just got here."

"Just out of curiosity, who planned this training schedule for me? And, no offense, but why are you in it?"

"Your father, of course. His Majesty thought you would be a little overwhelmed with everything new you have to learn, and so he asked me to help you settle in."

"So why didn't His Majesty step in to help me himself?"

She winked conspiratorially as we sat at the table. "He's a little busy. That, and he has no idea, he says—and it's true!—about what a girl would want to learn."

"Okay, so why you?"

"Why pick me to help you? Several reasons, I guess, but mostly because most of the other rangers my age are out in the woods practicing their crafts already. He said it was because of my wit and my charm and my intelligence and all the other stuff people say when they want to fluff you up, but the reality is that I stink at hunting, and so he must have figured that I was the best girl to have in here teaching you the basics of life."

"Huh. So I've got you, the mighty huntress, and BoBo the bear over there as my teachers, and a bunch of five-year-olds as my classmates. What a great way to start my summer."

"It's—Booboo, and he's a wolverine," Sephaline murmured, eyes cast down at the table. As the awkward silence spread across the room, I bit down on my lower lip. I knew from experience that Southern girls could be awfully cruel, hurling words that hit like daggers. I'd always despised my classmates who'd displayed a heap of ability with their razor-sharp tongues. Here I was proving myself to be one of them. I put my hand on her shoulder, and she lifted her hurt face toward me.

"I'm sorry, Sephaline. Where I'm from, sarcasm is used for humor sometimes, and I used it without thinking it might not be taken humorously," I said. I figured it's better to admit to being an incompetent humorist than a tired and cranky girl who just wanted to eat and go to bed. One could be looked at as a mistake, after all, while the other was a character flaw.

It worked. She smiled. And when I say smiled, I mean

beamed. One thing I've learned about elves is that if they're just grinning, they're not smiling. An elf shows happiness with her entire face, and I'm not exaggerating. Her chin lifts, her lips curl, her cheeks brighten, her forehead actually crinkles up, and her eyes practically become spotlights. It's incredible, really. That true elf smile nearly knocked me off the seat. No, I mean it. It was that powerful.

"Wow."

She released the fog lighting and tilted her head to one side. "Wow what?"

"I've never seen a human smile like that."

"No? How do your people smile, then?"

"Well, I like to think that you're my people now, but to answer your question, the humans where I come from have different levels of smile, depending." I showed her the I-like-you smile, the I'd-rather-be-ripping-your-throat-out smile, the I-think-you're-pathetic smile, and the real smile. Just the four; there was no point going into the many others.

"Why don't humans just say what they mean?"

"Um...." Okay, she'd stumped me. "I don't know. It's just the way we—they—are, I guess."

"Well, it's silly."

"I guess," I said, a little hurt myself this time. Silence descended on the table once again as servants brought an interesting spiced soup to start our meal.

I felt a hand on my shoulder and looked over. "I'm sorry, Alyssa. I didn't mean to insult you. It must be difficult, leaving the people you have known for years and trying overnight to become one of another, entirely different, group." She pulled it off far better than I did, dangit.

I smiled, careful to give her the real one I'd shown her earlier. She laughed, and I couldn't help joining her. Before long we were both gasping for air.

Supper was a fairly quiet thing. It was really good; some sort of roasted meat with root veggies. Sephaline identified everything as we ate. It wasn't very different from what I was used to. The turnips were green and yellow instead of purple and white, and they didn't call them by that name either, but turnips are turnips regardless.

After a while, I looked around. The quiet of the huge dining hall was unnerving.

"Where does everybody else eat?"

"In their homes."

"What about the people who call the palace their home?"

"Those who live in the palace eat here in the dining room."

"Didn't you tell me that there are a lot of elves who live in the palace?"

"I did. All the members of the royal court, several dozens of elves, including royalty, advisors, servants, and others, live in the palace. Why do you ask?"

"Because so far I haven't seen a single person look tempted to sit down here to eat with us."

"With me."

"What?"

Sephaline shrugged. "I'm a common ranger. None of the royalty would share a table with me."

"Elves are like that, too?" My heart sank a little; somehow I'd been thinking the old status games weren't played here.

"I thought it was pretty much universal," she said and shrugged. "Doesn't bother me. It means I get you to myself, really, up until you're ready to sit at the queen's table."

"Can I sit at the king's table instead?"

"Where does a minotaur sit down to eat?"

"A what?" She stumped me on that one.

"You know, the old joke. 'Where does a minotaur sit down to eat?' 'Anywhere he wants to.'"

"Oh. On Earth they tell that joke about a gorilla."

"Why would you joke about a gorilla? They are just a myth," she said, a look of confusion on her face. I just blinked my eyes, myself; the conversation was getting way too weird. She redirected it, though, continuing with, "Anyway, the point of the joke is that I am certain that the crown princess of the realm can probably sit anywhere she wants. Why, though, would you want to sit with a bunch of men to eat?"

I didn't have a good answer for that, so I made a point of handing the servant the plate on which I'd been served a really tasty dessert made from some sorts of fruit—a combination of berries and melon—with a whipped cream sort of topping.

CWTSH

a warm, friendly, safe hug[1]

[1]I'm too stuck in English to ask anybody for a cwtsh, though

A Father's Apology

Dinner done, I changed the subject.

"You'd think that my father, having not seen me for so many years, would at least want to stop by and say hi to his daughter. You know, maybe tell her how good it is for her to be here and see how she's taking to the new digs and all." I turned my gaze up from the now-empty table and looked at Sephaline, who was suddenly staring over my shoulder with a panicked expression on her face.

"He's standing right behind me, isn't he?"

She nodded timidly. A long, masculine hand clasped me over the shoulder and a cheerful laugh filled my ear. It was followed by my father's voice as he said, "Hello, Alyssa! It is good for you to be here. How are you taking to the new digs and all?"

Dang. As busy as my mind was being embarrassed, part of it also spun around wondering how he'd slipped up on me like that. I used to always be able to sense people behind me. I wasn't sure if it was the not-magic of the realm messing with me, or some super-sneaking power my father had, that caused me to miss his presence.

Sephaline quickly begged her way out of the hall; my father dismissed her with a wave and turned his attention immediately back to me. I tilted my head and chewed my lower lip in the way I've always faced down weird situations. With a shock, I realized he was doing the same thing.

Like father, like daughter, I guess.

"I really was asking, Alyssa. How are you taking to your new digs?"

"It's—a little strange."

"A whole new world, a whole new life, even a new language and culture, and all you can muster is 'a little strange'?"

"Okay, it's *very* strange. Better?"

"Much. Walk with me, please."

I still wasn't entirely sure whether to respond to him as my father or as the elf king, here in the castle with him all regal in his purple velvet robes—over pants, I noticed the hem!—and the medallion of office around his neck. That had to be okay, I reasoned, since I also wasn't quite sure how to respond to my father after all his years of absence, nor was I sure how to respond to the elf king in his royal finery. No matter which I chose, then, I was as likely to be wrong as to be right. Or, I figured, as likely to be right as to be wrong, depending how you look at it.

Eh, whatever. I decided to go with what felt right.

I walked with him in silence through the rest of the very long dining hall, through a small antechamber, and into the throne room, where two really spectacular thrones stood. He walked right past the two spectacular thrones, but I stopped to ogle them. Each one looked like it had been grown out of a massive golden vine. All except the cushions, of course, which were soft purple velvet and looked awfully comfortable.

I started to sit in one.

"Stop," my father said, a note of urgency in his voice. I did stop and looked at him, a question on my face as my butt pointed toward the velvet.

"The seat will be yours to occupy soon enough, but it is not yet, Alyssa. Sitting in the throne without a crown on your head is cause for punishment for all, future queen or no."

"It's an awfully nice throne," I said. I admit, it sounded pretty lame when I said it that way.

"It is indeed, but the crown that is requisite to sit in that throne has some weight that you are not yet prepared to bear."

"Right. So when will I be?" I walked toward him, detouring between the thrones, running my hand over the smooth golden surface as I wondered whether it was a tree painted gold or a piece of gold forged to look tree-like.

"That depends. This is not the place to discuss that, though. Please, follow me just a little bit farther."

He wasn't kidding about the distance; he walked directly to the curtain behind the thrones, pushed one aside, pressed open the panel behind it, and held it while I walked in. When I followed, he closed the wooden panel and gestured for me to have a seat in what was, basically, a man cave. Leather furniture and animal heads dominated most of the room, with a bar on one side.

He walked over to the bar. "Brandy? Or whiskey?" he asked over his shoulder, surprising me.

"I'm—I'm only eighteen, Dad, but I'm sure you know that. What's the drinking age here?"

"Drinking age?" he asked, turning to me looking confused.

"Yeah, you know. The age you have to be to consume alcohol. It's twenty-one back home."

My father shrugged and poured a deep hazel colored liquid into two small rounded glasses. He handed me one and held the other up in an obvious toast.

"Welcome to your new home, then, daughter. We lack anything resembling a 'drinking age' here. I will merely ask you to be careful in your consumption, because too much is bad for you, but surely you know that?"

I nodded, raised the glass to join the toast, and then sipped.

I should point out, by the way, that my mother was never a drinker, and I was always too scared of getting in trouble to do anything worth bragging about. My entire alcoholic experience up to that point consisted of one or two glasses of wine at really special occasions, a disgusting swig of beer once at a high school football game, and a tippling of my mother's "wassail" every Christmas.

The wassail had seemed like an alcoholic treat-fest, but apparently that drink was pretty weak, compared to what I sipped from the glass my father handed me. Wow, it was strong. I held back a cough, barely, and asked, "What is this?"

"Brandy. It is mellower than the whiskey, so I figured it would be a good one to start with. Perhaps I should have offered you weak mead instead?"

I glared at him for the implied insult. Was he serious? His half-smile made it impossible to tell. Apparently he'd learned the human method of tiered smiling during his time with Momma in Wales.

I tried a different tack. "I'll just tell the High Priestess Sternyface that your idea of teaching your daughter the important lessons of life is to get her drunk on brandy in your private room behind the thrones."

Okay, so he *hadn't* really been serious, because suddenly he was. Very serious, that is. The change was dramatic.

"It would be a tremendous favor to us both if you would refrain from telling anyone in the realm that you entered this room, Alyssa."

All I could really do was gulp at the intensity of the strange request and ask why.

"You currently stand in the king's private antechamber. None but I, my butler, and one or two high-ranking—male— elves have seen its contents. No female may enter, ever, by a custom that is older by far than the oldest living elf. Not even the queen. What I did in bringing you in here was wrong—*very* wrong—but I wanted a place where we could talk without being listened in upon. This is that place."

The going pattern, I noticed, was for my father's explanations to create more questions than they put away. This was no exception; I had so many questions swimming around in brandy vapor that I just picked the first one I thought of.

"So why did you need a private spot to talk to me? Am I about to find out that my real mission is to assassinate someone, or did you bring me here to describe a secret and horrible family curse I have to deal with?"

I hadn't expected the snort I got in reply, but I guess it didn't surprise me much. After the day I'd had, *nothing* was likely to surprise me much.

"So tell me, Alyssa, what did you really think of High Priestess Sternyface?" he asked, his expression calming back into the half-smile.

"Not much. I didn't spend much time with her, though. She sent me away to learn with the kids."

"The kids?" my father asked, perplexed.

"Yeah, this group that looked like five- and six-year olds, learning the basics of the language. She said I had to learn the simple things first. And—you didn't know that, did you?"

"I am but a king, not a god, Alyssa. I have never been, nor will I ever be, omniscient. I am also not in a position to command the High Priestess—um, Sternyface." My father grinned when he used the name I'd made up for her, and then he continued, "She occasionally listens to the queen, but that always seems to be by her own choice. Trust me, she rarely, if ever, listens to a single word I say. That said, she is, however, charged with your integration into elf society, as has been the case with all elf queens before you. Please keep that in mind as you criticize, rightfully or no, her training methods."

I nodded, and his expression softened as he continued, "Still, I have missed so much of your life thus far, and now I am overburdened in curiosity with what you are learning of the culture to which I am native. That is why I desire our private time together enough to buck millennia of tradition. Well, that is one reason. I trust the high priestess, certainly, but sometimes her teaching can be a little bit—biased. I plan to provide the balance to that. The other reason is simple yet far more important. Simply put, I have missed so much of your life that I cherish the opportunity to spend this time with you, my daughter. You have grown so much, so fast, so wonderfully, and so beautifully, and I am as proud of you as a father could ever be."

"Thank you, Dad. But I have to ask—if Momma's the love of your life, and I'm your only daughter, how'd you manage to spend so many years away from the two of us?" I admit, I was intrigued by the apparent king versus high priestess conflict, but the emotional question rang deeper. It must've been the brandy.

"I did not manage that."

"What do you mean?"

"I visited every year, Alyssa. Your mother and I would sneak off and—among other things, discuss whether it was appropriate for me to meet you then. We always decided no, for purely practical reasons, but it was never an easy decision."

"Oh." I gazed into the swirls of the brandy while strolling back through my memories. It clicked. Momma had disappeared nearly every year toward the end of summer. It was never for long, and never for anything major enough to raise my interest, but she'd always been a little punchy about it.

I felt his eyes on me and turned that way. "So, really, Dad, what's next? What's in store? How long do I have?"

He shrugged. "What is next is that you continue learning what it means to be an elf queen, Alyssa. Nobody really knows what that means in terms of time. Once you are ready, Naissa will let us know and we shall hold a grand coronation."

It all sounded too simple, and I said so.

"Well, Alyssa, it is not really that simple," he explained. "There is quite a lot to be learned, and there are several milestones along the way. You have quite a while before you are likely to be seated in the golden throne."

"So what happens then?"

He shrugged. "Then you step into your prophesied role, ruling the realm as its queen."

"So what does the current queen do? And why haven't I met her yet?"

"Last question first. You still have many things to learn before you are ready to meet the current queen. Things like basic elf courtesy—no, do not snarl at that. You are a wonderful young lady by all human standards, but you know nothing about how to properly function in elf society. As it stands now, were you not my daughter, I would dismiss you from my presence because of how little you know about being around royalty. Seriously, Alyssa, you will meet the queen, formally, once you are ready, and after that she will even take some part in your training. For now, though, enjoy your lessons as they are. Besides," he said with a chuckle, "if you call Naissa Sternyface, then I shudder to consider what you will think of the queen. Here, allow me."

I handed my father my now-empty glass. It was amazing how easily and well the subsequent sips had gone down after the first shock had passed. I hadn't noticed the glass going empty.

"So—why?"

"Because, my beloved daughter, your glass is quite empty."

"No, not that why."

My father sat down facing me, a warm smile on his face. "Which why are you asking, then, Alyssa?"

"All of them, I guess. I'm just not sure which one to ask first."

He shrugged. "I cannot answer all at once. Pick one, please."

"Alright. Here's a big one. Why does a girl who's never set foot in the kingdom before her eighteenth birthday get to be queen, no matter how much her father is the king? Did you and the current queen not work out or something? Can she not have children?"

"Now, that is a hard one. Can we go back to something like 'why did you pick the bedroom you did for me to sleep in?'"

"No, but now that you brought it up, I'm going to ask that one later. But I don't get the whole succession thing. It doesn't make any sense."

"We are a proud people, Alyssa. Our traditions mean a great deal to us, whether they necessarily make sense at the time or not."

"So you're saying the queen is traditionally a half-human?"

"I am saying that, yes."

"Born to the king and his chosen human bride."

"Yes, I have already said that."

"So what would you have done if I'd been a boy?"

"Kept trying."

I barely kept a great big *eww* from escaping my lips as I watched his eyebrows waggle up and down.

"But what if you'd never had a girl?"

"The high priestess would have intervened. I do not know

how, precisely, nor do I really wish to know, and it has only happened once before in a long line of succession. Do not get that look on your face, Alyssa. Your Earth-bound doctors have incredible powers for a group of practitioners of the healing arts on a non-energy-based realm. If they can do all they can do, why would the high priestess not be able to influence the gender of the royal baby?"

"I don't know; it just sounds icky to think about." It was past time to change the subject. "So who gets to be the king?"

"That depends on who you ask."

"Why does it depend on that?" I asked.

"Most people believe that the king is chosen by the outgoing queen, according to the wisdom accumulated through years of doing the job herself. As long as the outgoing rulers are popular, which we've always been, it's an easy solution that makes the people happy."

"Okay, that makes sense. So who is it, really?"

"Someone chosen by the committee when I am ready to step down."

"A committee? Elves have committees?"

"Well, yes. I know, committees have earned a bad reputation on Earth, but this is a small and rather effective one. They chose me, after all."

"Sure, Dad." I didn't feel like playing into anybody's ego, my father or not. "Who's on it?"

"It is a secret," he said, his grin quirked up enough that he looked like he was trying to avoid telling me who killed JFK.

Somehow I knew he was bluffing. "No, really, Dad. Who's on the committee?"

"No, really, Alyssa," he said. It was cute when he mimicked me the first time. Now it was getting irritating. "It really is a secret. Most elves believe that the outgoing queen gets to select the new king herself, which is considered quite fair indeed because the king's daughter becomes the new queen. But while the queen is the face of the decision, the king also has a say in it, as does the high priestess. Even more, each member of the committee has a specific role to play. The queen represents the interests of the crown in the decision. In short, her mission is to put forth the candidate who would become the most effective royal leader. The high priestess represents the interests of the realm, and all of its extended clans as well. The outgoing king, meanwhile, surveys the population, and in presenting the results he represents the voice of the people in the decision. It is, simply, not a simple matter."

"But—it's always an elf, right?"

"Indeed," he said, nodding.

"And the king and the queen aren't a couple. Not this time, or not never?" I could almost hear Momma cry out over the double-negative, but—well, I blame it on the brandy.

"Never. That would be a connection forbidden by custom."

"So whom do I get to choose from to fall in love and marry, if and when I decide to do so?"

Chortling, my father replied, "Spoken like a true elf queen. You get to choose from whomever you wish in the entire kingdom. Except, that is, for the king."

"The king, who is the most popular male elf in the kingdom."

"If the committee determines it should be so, yes. He might also be the best innate ruler, or the elf who will most effectively champion the causes that are important to the entire realm. If the committee is very lucky, those characteristics might all be found in the same elf, who is, to loop back to the original point, nevertheless forbidden to the queen—to you—as a romantic interest."

"Strange custom, that is."

"Perhaps. Do you know why first cousins cannot marry back

in your original world?"

"Actually, I think they can in Mississippi."

"What?" Maybe it was the alcohol, but somehow I'd actually brought him up short.

"Different states have different laws. Most of the laws forbid marrying a cousin, but not all states do. I think Mississippi—or wait, maybe it was Mississippi forbids it, but Alabama allows it. I don't know; I was never interested enough to research it further than the silly discussion we had in government class."

"Oh. Well, legal or no, I presume that you would not have done so regardless of what the law of the particular state said, yes? That is because of—what?"

I shrugged. "It's just—icky. People don't do it. Besides, as near as I can tell, I have no cousins to marry."

"Well, fine. What you are talking about, though, is mores. Cultural traditions, if you will. Here on Kiirajanna, you will find that the reason we have very few laws is that our traditions are held to and trusted so strongly."

"So what happens when somebody violates a tradition?"

"I get to cut off his head," he said with a perfectly straight face.

"You're joking, right?" He'd said it seriously enough that I wasn't sure, but I couldn't imagine decapitation being the punishment for a little mores-breaking.

"It's good to be the king," was all he said in return, and I couldn't tell how I should interpret his shrug. I sat and watched him intently, willing him to spill the real truth.

Finally, I won the staring contest. The elf king took a solemn swig of brandy, and then looked over at my glaring face, and then broke out into a chortle. He reached out and tousled my hair gently, saying, "Okay, okay. Has anyone ever told you that you inherited your mother's glare? I never could resist that look, but don't you dare try to take advantage of that fact. At least, not in public. No, Alyssa, I do not cut off anyone's head. I have never decapitated anyone, in fact, despite the fact that before I stepped up to take the crown I was one of the finest warriors in the land. Nor is it in elf custom to practice capital punishment."

"So what do you do when someone violates tradition, really?"

"As I said before, nearly everyone recognizes that our traditions are what define our society and make us who we are. We all hold the traditions to be vital, and they truly are so. There are no traditions that do not have a purpose in the betterment of society, and nothing needed for the betterment of society is not already woven into a tradition."

"So it never happens?"

"Well, now, you should never say never, Alyssa. I have had to banish elves from society for a period of time. Twice, it has occurred. The more grave the violation, the longer the period. The worst violations would result in banishment to Earth."

"That doesn't sound like a horrible punishment."

"Of course it does not, to you. You are from there, and have not seen much of Kiirajanna. Soon you will come to love this land as much as I do, and then it will seem a perfectly wretched imposition of justice."

"Is that how you're going to feel when it comes time to move back to be with Momma?"

"No. I do love this realm, but I love your mother more, Alyssa."

Well, that was awfully comforting to hear.

"So, back to the whole king and queen choice thing—you're telling me that it's basically a grand genetics experiment."

"It would be wrong to characterize it as an experiment, or for that matter anything grand, but yes, there is a genetic root to the tradition. There's an ancient story you'll likely hear sometime about two lovers and a library that point to a more emotional reason, but there are not many elves—only a few hundred thousand in total—and so there will always be a need to mix the gene pool up. Of course, there is a certain rationality of decision-making built into a system where the two rulers are in no danger of having lovers' spats, though as far as I know the real truth of it is buried several millennia ago."

"I guess I'll have to research it, then."

"Perhaps. You have far more important things to learn first, though, such as how to read the texts that you will be sourcing for your research once you actually reach that point. Right now, though, it is time to wind down for the night. Tomorrow will be a full day."

"When will I get to see the outside of this glorious castle?" One thing I was learning about brandy: it sure does lubricate the voice.

"Tomorrow. It is the week end, and so I have taken the liberty to plan a tour and a bit of merriment."

"That sounds like fun. Will Sephaline be invited?"

"I asked her to keep her calendar clear in order to accept your invitation if proffered."

"Good. I like her."

"I thought you would."

We passed in silence back through the hall on the first floor and up the grand staircase to the second, where I was pretty sure I remembered my room being. The good news, I found, was that two glasses of brandy didn't make it too hard to walk.

As we turned left on the second floor and started down the hall, I noticed something that I'd missed the first couple of times up and down.

"Wait," I said, turning around to look back down the way we'd come. Sure enough, the hall was obviously done up in his and hers ends in a way that went right past the point of being cute and up the path of bad cliché. The walls of the half that we were walking down were painted sky blue, and all the paintings on our side depicted hunting or battle scenes. The other side? Baby pink, with flowery artwork. Even the small tables played into the décor; the one on this side was made from stained wood and supported a masculine-looking blue vase, while the other side was painted white, had a vase with flowers, and was even topped off with a lace doily, of all things.

"Is that...?" I asked, not certain how to ask the question. It didn't matter; Dad figured it out and answered.

"The queen's wing. Guess what the hall you are in now is called."

"You split the second floor?"

"You do not expect us to sleep in the same room, do you?"

"Well—no, but...."

"The lord and lady of an estate should never sleep in the same room even when they are a couple, Alyssa. To do so would risk maidservants walking in on the master, or menservants walking in on the mistress. That would be—icky, I believe is the word you use to describe such things."

"Makes sense, I guess. Wouldn't want anything icky to make Momma jealous, after all. Hey, does the queen have any children?" It occurred to me right after asking that I thought I already knew the answer, but what the heck. I liked having my father explain things to me, for some weird daughtery reason I couldn't put my finger on. Maybe it was just the brandy.

"Three. The prince is about your age; the princesses a few years older and younger than you, respectively."

"How do they feel about my place, my arrival?"

"I do not believe their opinion has been entertained in the matter."

"Oh," I said, turning back down the blue hall. We walked in

silence to the next-to-last door on the left. I couldn't help noticing the huge crest painted on the door at the end; the stag and
the raven both peered at me from opposite sides of the slash.

My father saw me looking at it. "The royal crest, Alyssa. It
marks my door, as well as the door at the opposite end of the
hall. When you are queen, one of the first official acts you and
your chosen king take upon yourselves will be the design of
your own reign's crest."

"So who's the raven, and who's the stag?"

"It is—not that simple. Both icons represent both of us in
the symbology of our people. Ask me again when I am less
tired, though. Good night, my daughter." He kissed me on the
forehead and walked into his room, closing the crest-covered
door behind.

My own room felt a little bit alien. The night before, I'd
slipped into exhausted sleep too quickly, I guess, to have noticed how big and—well, and polished—it was. My bedroom
back at home was the standard kid's room, just large enough
for a bed, a dresser, and a nightstand. My new room in the castle could've fit a few of those bedrooms in with room to spare.
The walls were done up in decorative panels set off by white
molding, and real artwork was hung instead of the poster-sized
eye candy—you know, cowboys in jeans and, um, stuff—that I
kept pinned on the sheetrock in my room at home.

As I sat and—I'll just say 'adjusted' (no, I wasn't pouting!), I
noticed one panel in the wall that was different. It was funny,
in fact; that panel really should have had a neon sign on it that
said "Secret Door." There was spacing around it that didn't exist in other panels, and light glowed along one edge.

It was secret!

Looking closer, I couldn't see any way of closing it or locking
it from my side of the wall, and that bothered me. How would I
manage to hold off the trolls or whatever else might come

through it at night if I couldn't lock it?

Chuckling over my own overactive imagination, I pushed the panel inward, following its swing into another chamber.

As luck would have it, I ran right into a troll.

I guess I should say I ran into a very large elf who looked and smelled like a troll. The overall effect was the same, though. I bravely said "eek" and tried to jump back into my own room, staggering and losing my balance instead.

He caught me.

"Princess," he said, nodding as he set my feet securely down on the floor.

"Hi," I said as bravely as I could manage with a troll in my face.

"You should be in bed."

"Don't I get to decide that?"

He seemed to think about it for far longer than I thought the question required. While he was thinking, I took advantage of his diverted concentration to examine him closer. He was clad in thick black leather armor. The royal crest I'd seen outside was on his breastplate, which I had to suppose was a good thing. It was also, I noticed when I looked past him, exhibited distinctly on the breastplate of each of the other three elves looking my way from the small guard room I'd bravely stepped into.

I continued to suppose that the presence of my father's crest was a good thing, for lack of a better plan.

"So, who are you guys?" I asked.

"We're—um, we're your guards, Your Highness," the large and smelly elf I'd run into said.

"I have a hard time believing that. Guards are usually introduced in the light of day, right?"

"You weren't supposed to know about us."

Something about the way he said it—I'm not sure whether

it was the crestfallen expression or the sad tone—made it impossible for me not to laugh.

"Well, now I do," I said once I was done laughing. I thrust my hand out in a handshake pose. "So, my faithful guards, I'm Alyssa. What's your name?"

"Stith." He didn't take my hand.

"What dangers are you guarding me from, Stith?"

I stood for several long seconds waiting for a reply, and then I decided to bluff. "Tell me, or I'll let the king know you have failed in your duty."

Wrong bluff, I could tell as a grin spread across the lead elf's face.

"Princess," he said, "your ability to talk to the king serves as notice to him that we have succeeded in our duty."

Ah, well. I was tired. Really, really tired, and a little bit inebriated, too.

"Clearly, then," I said, drawing myself up as regally as I knew how after one day's training with five-year-olds, "you've been instructed to keep me safe, and for that I am exquisitely and royally grateful. I am so grateful, in fact, that I shall return to my own bedroom to get some rest now. If you have no objections."

They didn't object. Feeling silly as well as tired, I marched back through the not-so-secret doorway and shut it behind me. I remembered seeing some lightweight clothes that probably were meant as pajamas in what Seph had pointed out as 'the princess's wardrobe.' Suddenly feeling a lot more exposed than I did before I'd found the hidden guardroom, I slipped behind the partition and changed into them, and then, finally, I climbed into bed.

SEGURDOD YW CLOD Y CLEDD

a sword's credit is its lack of use. One of Dad's favorite sayings, telling me that it's best to rule without resorting to physical power.

Meeting The People

The next morning I was pleased to awaken in my room without a small bear in it. Or wolverine. Or, you know, the large furry thing that had wanted to eat my face, whatever it's called.

I mean, I was starting to like Sephaline, but.... *Booboo*? Really? That thing could rip somebody in half. And they called it Booboo?

And who let it into the castle?

I dressed quickly and started down, but Sephaline met me on the stairs, Booboo trailing right behind. She eyed the simple garb I'd chosen and nodded once.

"Good choice for the weekend. Your father has some traveling planned for you today."

"I know. He told me last night. I asked, and he agreed, that you could come along. Would you like to?"

Her face lit up again in one of those elf-grins. Gosh, they were an intoxicating thing to see. "Yes, I'd love to," she said.

Her approval of my clothing secured, I followed her into the dining hall. It was a completely different setup from the day before. My first morning, each place had been carefully set with plate, silverware, napkin, and glass, and the food had been brought out to me as I'd settled in. This morning, there were no place settings. Instead, baskets were lined up along the central table. In each basket was a different type of fruit or bread. Several people sat at the tables in what looked to be random order, eating and chatting. My father sat by himself at a long table at the end. As we entered, he waved us over.

"Alyssa! Sephaline. Please, grab some food and eat so that we may proceed with the day."

I did, mostly following Sephaline's lead. The things that looked like apples actually were apples, I was happy to find out. As I munched, I observed, "Sure is a different room from yesterday."

"It is the weekend, Alyssa," my father answered. "You are used to five days of work followed by two days of—well, more work for some people. Here, we all work for five days and take one day off. That is everyone, from the lowest rank of servants to the royalty. The kitchen staff sets the baskets out last night, and they will collect them early tomorrow morning to begin another week of work. At the same time, I cannot, by tradition, do anything deemed royal today. Every elf gets the day off to rest and relax. It is a nice system, wouldn't you say?"

"Well, sure, but what if there's an emergency of some sort?"

"An emergency? Like what?"

"Um, well, what if somebody attacks the realm? Don't your bodyguards have to work?"

"Who would attack on the weekend?"

I didn't have any answer to that so I let it go.

"I met Stith last night."

"I know."

More surprising than my father's lack of reaction was the complete lack of interest in the conversation from Sephaline.

She just sat there, eating a fruit that looked like a mango.

"So what I don't get," I continued, shifting back to the first topic. I didn't know enough to be able to mold either of the other subjects into questions that made sense. "I don't get why it's the weekend here. I graduated Friday night. Saturday I met you. Sunday we traveled here. Yesterday, then, was Monday. And now it's Saturday again?"

"Dydd Sadwrn, actually."

"Sure, Dydd Sadwrn. Just like Saturday, only backwards and with one of those *w* sounds that the elf language is so fond of. Why are our languages so similar sometimes and so different others?"

"You grew up speaking English, a language composited from a great many ancient tongues, including that of our original base on the human world. It is no surprise that there is overlap. But back to your original question, the day of the week in both worlds is largely arbitrary. The human world and ours share a rotation schedule and a pattern of light and dark, but there is really no reason for the days to align. When one calendar is based on seven days and the other six, the lack of alignment is practically guaranteed. The misalignment does, granted, cause everyone who travels between the worlds some confusion. Luckily for all of us, the humans are not particularly keen on maintaining anything resembling an actual weekend, and so it usually does not matter."

"I can see the confusion. I guess. But why six days instead of seven?"

"Why not six days? And why seven?" my father countered, and I had no idea how to answer. I made a mental note to ask Sternyface about it later.

"Right. Anyway, you're saying that I need to get used to a six day week in which the sixth is an absolute day of rest, right?"

"You are close. Sadwrn is an absolute day of not working, which is not quite the same as a day of rest. If we had to rest all day, it would be very boring."

"How so?"

"Well, the trip we are about to take is not going to be restful. It will, however, be enjoyable and most definitely not working. Speaking of the trip, are you ready to go?"

I was. As I started to rise, though, I noticed that Sephaline hadn't stirred. I figured she'd been focusing on eating quietly, though I hadn't paid any attention to her while my dad was telling me about the calendars. She wasn't, though. Instead, she was making doe-eyes at a boy over her half-eaten mango.

Boy isn't the right word. He looked about our age, but there was nothing in him other than gender that suggested the word boy. I could see why Sephaline had more interest in him than the fruit. He was, for lack of a better word, beautiful. Long curly black locks spilled around a strong, sharp-featured face. Sloping neck muscles led down to broad shoulders and a well-defined muscular torso wrapped in something yummy made of vibrant green silk and brown leather—traveling clothes, apparently. Well-made ones, at that.

To me, attitude is more important than looks, and he had that, too. He sat his bench seat as though it were a throne, eating quietly and mostly ignoring the three other young men sitting beside him, each of whom cast glances his way occasionally. He had his own merry band of groupies, it seemed.

In one dreadful moment, he looked up from his food, and I felt his eyes lock onto mine like an electrical shock. They were intense, black orbs that smoldered beneath Machiavellian eyebrows. Wrapped up in the intensity of that smoldering gaze was a clear message. It was kind of a combination of *I don't like you* mixed with a taste of *You don't belong here.*

Well. I guess I'd found at least one of the reasons Stith and crew were on guard.

I nudged Sephaline, rousing her from her adoring stupor and earning a surprised little *meep* sound. She self-consciously wrapped the remainder of her mango in a napkin, stuffed it into a pouch she was carrying, and joined us on our way out.

"What's with Prince Charming over there?" I asked.

"How'd you know who he was?" Sephaline looked startled.

Look, I know you're sitting there thinking the same thing I was: *No, really? Prince Charming? C'mon....* Hey, I was joking when I said it, but the elves were really good at surprising the heck out of me.

"Young ladies," my father's voice carried his disapproval back from where he continued to stride toward the front doors, causing us both to hurry up. When he got outside, he continued, "The prince has a name. A real one, even. Alyssa, that was Prince Keion. Keion is the middle child of the queen's, and is quite accomplished at nearly everything a young elf should be. When the time comes to select your team of advisors you would be well-advised to consider him for membership." He stopped continued in a quieter voice as we caught up to him. "As for what's with him, his voice has been the rather outspoken source of an opinion that traditions of old need to be changed sometimes, particularly in regard to succession. I believe he feels rather strongly that his older sister would make a better queen than you."

"He doesn't even know me."

"Nobody knows you, dear. You have lived away from your kind for all but two days of your life so far, and there are those who believe that you have done nothing but sit and eat earthly bonbons while Queen Talaith's children have labored to learn the details of governance here."

"Yeah, well, they're probably right."

"Nonsense. Talaith herself has come out in your defense,

reminding us that you know just as much as she did when she came to our land."

"But if there's gonna be friction...."

"Friction is part of life, whether you practice governance or not. How you handle the friction in your early time here will not only shape much of your time as a ruler, but will also teach you some valuable lessons. But we should probably hold the remainder of this conversation for more private times, and instead enjoy today's travels together."

It wasn't subtle but I got it. I looked at him and Sephaline and tried one of those elf-smiles on for size.

"That looks...." Sephaline said, her expression showing that she was having a difficult time finding the words to express her disapproval.

"Don't. Just don't," my father added, chuckling. "Smile as you would normally. Over time your actions and expressions will adapt naturally, but forcing them will only result in the macabre."

"That looked macabre?" I asked, a little stung.

"More like a parody of the macabre," my father said, still smiling. "Still pretty horrifying, though."

"It looked like a Morgen," Sephaline said, shivering a little as she said the word.

"What's a Morgen?"

"A mythical beast from fairy tales," my father cut in. "Earth's lore called them sirens, I believe. Creatures whose beautiful songs would lure men under water and then drown them. Now, just drop it. Get in to the carriage, please, so that we can be off."

I stepped up into the same horseless carriage we'd ridden from the portal to the castle. As it launched under its own power down the long wooded drive, I looked back over my shoulder to see the castle displayed in the sun. I whistled in appreciation.

"It's immense," I said.

"You were expecting small?"

"No, of course not. I just—well, it's really big." I counted four floors, if the windows were a good indication. Both ends of the main building disappeared into the distant trees. Parapets and towers with pennants waving soared high above the ground. The squat light grey of the stone walls contrasted with the green of the roof, which in turn set off the light blue of the pennants, and it all gleamed in the morning sun.

"Sure is different from what I grew up in."

"That was kind of the point of how you were reared, Alyssa. The elf queen—any good queen, really—needs to understand, respect, and empathize with what it means to come from humble roots. The money from the crown treasury could have set you and your mother up in the finest palaces back on Earth, but you needed to grow up the way you did. When I return to her side, of course, your mother will be in for a far different life than the one she has experienced thus far."

"She deserves it," I murmured, thinking back on all the times she'd gone without anything fancy as she provided for me. We'd never been poor, really, but we'd never been rich, either. While that had seemed like just a regular life just a few days ago, when I compared it to my father's life in the great big castle with tons of servants, the difference was pretty severe. It all made sense, what they'd done, but it still made me a little irritated considering what she'd been put through.

"She does, indeed," he agreed quietly, and then we both let the topic lapse into silence. I watched over my shoulder until the carriage went around the gentle bend in the road and the castle disappeared, then turned my attention to the passing forest.

I've always loved forests. Growing up at the edge of a small town made access to the wooded areas pretty easy. We had plenty of neighbors with lots of treed property, of course, but there were also some pretty nice public forests both north and south of the town, and I'd sometimes spent entire days out there, wandering and examining.

A lot of people, I think, don't realize how wild and varied a southern forest can be. Some can be as open as you please, with old trees overlooking a floor of grasses, rocks, and mosses. Sometimes it's shut off by either brambles or the great strangling vine known as kudzu. But I'd always felt at home in either type of woods; I could immerse myself in exploring all of it for hours.

This elf forest, though, was completely different. I know, I keep saying that about this place. At some point along my training I stopped being surprised at being surprised, but this wasn't that point.

This forest seemed alien to me, and that was a surprise.

Alien isn't exactly the right word, I guess. It seemed more manicured than alien. It was like somebody came out and told the trees how and where to grow so that each had the same amount of space, and then somebody managed the grass so that even without lawnmower marks it was more of a treed lawn than a forest. It was more than just a lack of lawnmower marks, though. The grass in the distance had subtle height differences I could see, height differences that made little swirls and patterns on the forest floor. It was like miniature crop circles had been planted in nearly every space between every tree, and the result was beautiful.

It wasn't just the trees and grass that looked hand-crafted. Oaks—I could tell them by the lobed shape of their leaves— each had leafy ivy vines spiraling perfectly up the trunk. The sight was both majestic and beautiful, thanks to the way the deep, lush green of the ivy leaves set off the depth of the ridges in the bark. Another tree I didn't recognize hosted at each of its bases a patch of tall purple flowers, similar to irises. Little purple, blue, and fuchsia pansies bloomed around a smaller variety of tree, while spread out through the forest little yellow and blue wildflowers were peeking their way up between the blades of grass.

Even the smells seemed too perfectly placed to be true. A heady scent of spring flower hung in the air, the bouquet light and crisp. The gentle breeze that poofed its rhythmic way through the trees occasionally replaced the flower aroma with its own, one that smelled more like fragrant pine.

With every poof, the tree leaves all around rattled a quiet rhythm to the same light tempo.

To complete the nauseatingly perfect scene, a squadron of butterflies flitted about in the sunlight just over my left shoulder. They were incredibly pretty, of course, but who would expect otherwise in an elf Utopia? Their wings were a spectacular emerald green and light crystal blue with bands of pearly iridescence worked in. I had a hard time catching a direct look at them, though I tried several times; somehow they knew every time I turned my head and scattered at those exact moments. When they separated, their colors blended right in with the leaves and the sky so I could only tell they were still there by the little flickers of motion their wing tips created.

After several attempts I got tired of trying, so I sighed and pitched my head directly forward. Of course, that was when one of the little buggers landed right on my shoulder. I noticed Dad's and Seph's glances and grins at my expense, and that just made me more irritated.

"Yeah, so a butterfly just landed on my shoulder. How Wonderland is that?" I asked, pouring as much sarcasm as I could into my voice.

"Alyssa, that is—not a butterfly," my father said, his eyebrows arched in amusement. He had the same good looks as Prince Charming, I couldn't help but notice as the streaming rays of sunlight lit up his features. No wonder Momma fell as hard as she did for him.

Wait. Not a butterfly? What?

I glanced over to my left shoulder, swiveling my neck as quickly as I could to make sure I got a good look. I didn't need to wrench my neck, it turned out, because the little beast just sat there and smiled at me.

Yes, I said it smiled. It did!

It didn't stay long. The creature leaped away from my shoulder with a shove of its tiny human-shaped limbs, squeaking in child-like laughter all the way back to its little flock that somehow, suddenly, I could see clearly. I watched it go, struck dumb in shock over having just seen the weirdest creature ever.

They didn't really fly away, just vanished. Slowly, too. It was like at the eye doctor when the letters go from clear to fuzzy, only there you know it's happening because she's fiddling with something in the optics. There were no optics—that I could see, anyway—to blame for the butter—um, people's—fading from where I could see them clearly to where I couldn't.

"Right. Not a butterfly," I muttered, mesmerized by the transparent flutters I still saw in the air and the tree leaves.

"The—*tylwyth teg*?" Seph started, her eyes shooting a question over to my father.

"Fairy folk," he answered.

"The fairy folk seem to have taken a liking to you," Seph said.

"They—I—" I stuttered, still lost in amazement, and then finally I came around to what Seph had said. I murmured, "Fairy folk? Fairies—they don't—but I guess they do exist."

"You thought I was kidding?" my father asked.

"Well, no! Yes. Maybe." Seph snickered, but I plowed on. "I mean, there's a difference between believing you when you say that a creature from the myths and legends of my childhood exists here, and having one set down on my shoulder."

"Indeed."

"How do you know?" I asked Seph.

"How do I know what?"

"That they like me. That's what you said, right?"

"Right. They're always around, but the elves who manage the forests report seeing them very rarely if at all, and usually then it's a report of an annoyance. The little scoundrels can cause an awful lot of trouble, and they seem to do it just for fun."

"Who manages the forests?" Fairies, manicured grass, perfectly placed flowers, and stately trees were all coming together to form a too-perfect picture. It couldn't be natural.

"We do," Sephaline said.

"We?"

"I told you I'm a ranger, right?"

"Right, which is.... Hey, speaking of that, where's Booboo?"

"Back there," Sephaline said, pointing to the tree line a few dozen feet behind us. "He didn't feel comfortable in the dining hall with the royalty there, so he waited for us outside. Right now, he is trying to stalk the fairies."

"He wouldn't eat them, would he?"

"He probably would, but right now he's more interested in playing with them, I sense."

"Fierce pet, there."

"Booboo is not a pet."

My father chuckled again, softly and to himself. His face was unreadable, but I figured he was enjoying watching us talk.

"So, anyway, I somehow figured that you rangers were

hunters, not forest wardens."

"We're both, actually, and scouts also. The primary defense of the kingdom is entrusted to us through our range of traveling and our ability to sense oncoming danger."

"Oh. Well, that does sound exciting. When was the last time the kingdom was attacked?"

"Um...." Oops, I stumped her again.

My father came to her rescue. "Approximately four hundred fifty-three years ago."

"Approximately that, huh?"

He responded with yet another wry smile. Apparently he was finding us far more entertaining than the tour.

"So who was it who did the attacking?"

"A group of trolls from the south. Their food supplies ran low and they decided ours might be easier to take than to ask for. We proved them wrong."

"Trolls? Oh, why not. Are there orcs and ogres, too?"

"I was fairly clear when I explained that this realm is similar to the one you grew up in, except that it's populated largely with magical creatures, yes?"

"You were, Father. I just—trolls seemed to be pushing it a bit."

He shrugged and then said, "So back to your original question, the rangers are charged with maintaining the sanctity and order of our forests. You've probably noticed that the forest around us looks different from the ones close by your former home, yes?"

I nodded. "It's why I asked."

"Good. Rangers are chosen for their ability to join their wills with the natural world around them. Some are hunters, indeed, but most work in the forests. You have probably wondered how the grass is so uniform throughout—it is not because of lawn maintenance, but rather because a ranger asked the grass to grow that way."

"They asked the grass? That's impressive, but I'm still kinda confused. Elves use their earth energy powers to convince acres and acres of grass to grow the way they want it to, yet when I ask about magic I get a verbal karate chop to the gut."

"The basic difference is easy, but a full explanation will have to wait till later," he said, gesturing to the road ahead that was obviously leading to a clearing. "All elves, you included, have an innate ability to connect with the world around us. I know that in your world you call that magic also, but it is really nothing more than an extension of Self out into the greater existence. Through this extension we do the things we have to do as stewards of this world. Magic, though, is an aggressive mutilation of that same process in which the practitioner rips the world around himself apart and puts it back together in an altered state. Many elves will tell you that magic does not exist, but that is just a ruse to prevent young ones falling to the sweet temptation of power. Magic is dangerous, and thus it is forbidden."

I nodded my understanding and said no more as the carriage rolled into what looked like a pretty big village. Children dashed around the street, many of them holding various sticks and hoops while some older kids ran after a soccer ball. With a shock, I realized that I recognized some of them from the *they all bowed* classroom experience that, though it was just yesterday, seemed like so long ago. A couple of the younger boys even stopped what they were doing to wave at me with great big grins on their faces.

They were dressed differently, of course. Very differently. The kids who'd worn stern gray and white in the classroom were now decked out in every color of the rainbow. It was a complete color-splosion, with every kid wearing a bright shirt over medium length shorts. The girls had colored ribbons worked through their elaborate and complex braids. As the carriage came to a stop, several of the children broke away from their skipping and running games and came up to touch my father's hand in what looked like a gesture of friendly respect.

Here and there, a few animals—a bird, a dog, and a couple of what looked like ground squirrels—stopped what they were doing to watch intently. Days before, I wouldn't have noticed, but after a few hours with Seph and Booboo I was proud to have recognized the diligence of familiars assigned to watch over the kids at play.

"You're a popular monarch," I said over the noise of the kids running up and back to exuberantly greet my father.

"That is kind of the point, dear."

"They taught me in government class that the point of being a monarch is to run your country well, not necessarily to be popular."

"And so this government class was taught by which experienced monarch, daughter?"

"None." He had a point.

"Was it based on surveys of effective monarchs?"

"No, I don't think so."

"Oh. Well, then, perhaps you should take my word for it," he replied with a gentle grin. Sephaline chortled; I shot her a glare in return.

I dropped the subject and watched as adults joined the children in pressing around to greet my father. I was amazed that everybody seemed equally pleased to meet him; back home, there'd always seemed to be somebody who couldn't be happy unless he was hating on whoever was in charge, no matter who it was.

Dad started introducing me as his daughter, a prospect that scared me as I recalled Prince Charming's reaction. The people in the village, though, seemed overjoyed to meet me as their future queen. Huge grins broke out as they said my name out loud. Some even curtsied or bowed, making me giggle in delight.

"Alyssa, stop giggling," my father stage-whispered over to me. "Nod your head in response, and smile, but do not giggle."

We made our way slowly up the street. The simple houses on each side were gaily decorated with paint and ribbons that were strung and tied haphazardly around most of the irregularly-shaped arches of the door and window frames. Some had gable roofs, but others were more simple lean-tos or A-frames, while some of the prettiest ones looked like they had been grown straight out of the ground. All were pretty small, compared to the normal home I'd grown up in.

"Do they decorate like this every weekend?"

"No, the houses look like this all the time," my father said. "It is our way."

"It sure is pretty."

As the road continued the houses grew larger and grander. At the end of the street loomed the front doors of a massive cathedral that both hunched over what remained of the road and slagged back into the hillside that I'd just noticed. On the right side of the street the houses continued back for some distance, but the left had one layer of solid, fairly large homes and then a massive grass-covered hill behind.

We stopped at the fountain in the circle in front of the cathedral entrance. "You have been in that building already," my father said out of the side of his mouth as we continued greeting elves.

"That's the church where I'm being trained? Oh, I didn't realize we'd come in a semi-circle. That, or it's a lot bigger tunnel from the castle to the cathedral than I'd realized."

"Semi-circle is correct. The castle is so large you cannot see the sacred hill behind it, but the road we followed leads completely around."

We finished greeting everyone who came out and accepted a snack of a few apples and other fruits from the townsfolk before we headed out of town on a road I hadn't noticed. We visited several other towns along the road, each one very similar to the first but without the cathedral. In every one, my father was hailed as a people's hero, and I got the sense that those same people were also happy to meet me. As hard as I tried to stay good and cynical, it really touched me. Remember what I said earlier about an elf's smile? Imagine a few dozen of those lighting up a village green. There's no way to keep your lip turned down at that.

After a couple of towns' worth of happy-happy stuff, my father pulled the coach over to the side of the green and stopped it with a gesture.

"What's up?" I asked Sephaline in my best stage whisper.

"Lunch," Sephaline answered simply, jumping off the coach to follow my father, who was already walking over to a group of elves seated underneath a large tree.

I walked over, not sure what to do, but Sephaline and my father made sure I figured it out. She waved me over grandly, her arm windmilling toward a spot in the group. He pressed a plate of fruit and other foods into my hands as I sat.

"These are the village elders, Alyssa," he said aloud to me and to the rest of the group at the same time. "I'd do the introductions, but it is against Sadwrn tradition to do anything that formal. Let's just sit, eat, and enjoy each others' company, and please, all, speak English and say your name before you speak the first time so that my newly arrived daughter may know you."

Lunch was an amazing thing. Not the food; that was all raw fruit and nuts helped out by a little meat jerky and some boiled eggs. These elves took their day of rest thing far more seriously than anybody I'd seen on Earth. What was amazing, though, was the seemingly heart-felt companionship. A couple of the village elders had been around a long, long time. Some of the group, meanwhile, were as young as my father apparently was, which near as I could tell from the ribbing was only a few dozen years—a young buck, in the elders' eyes. There was a camaraderie among them all, though, that defied description. They all spoke English, at my father's request, and there was constantly a story or two going on and a laugh being shared.

We ate, and bellies full, we rested for a while in the warmth of the sun. Then the three of us continued down the road to find more villages, more crowds of elves who adored my father. As we rode down tree-lined roads, the conversation—well, it flitted, for lack of a better word. Sephaline and I compared the forests we'd grown up in. My father and I bantered about little details of elf society, stuff like how many elves lived in a typical village like we'd been going through (several hundred to a few thousand, if you care) and how many villages there were (many hundreds, spread around the land and connected by well-maintained paths through manicured forests—again, if you care). The summer sun draped across us the whole way, and by the time we got back up to the castle I'd warmed up both outside and in. I know it sounds weird, but—have you ever felt like everything in the world was good? Like no matter what, it would all be okay—no, better than okay? As silly as all that sounds, I really felt that way.

I had three main thoughts running through my head as we returned to the castle.

First: I wouldn't mind at all being the elf queen if the elves were half as pleasant when they greeted me as they were when my father came around.

Second, this world was a lot more peaceful and joyful to live in than the one I'd just left.

Third, it seemed like I had a pretty easy path ahead of me to get to the queen's throne.

Turns out, I had most of that wrong.

An Arrow Misses

It didn't take long to find out how wrong I was about the peaceful and joyful bit.

After the ride, Sephaline and I went out for a walk through the forest. It was her element, after all, and I wanted to spend some time with her. As we strolled along I asked her all sorts of questions about how it had been growing up in Kiirajanna, and about her use of what wasn't to ever be called magic even though it looked an awful danged lot like it, and, well, all sorts of stuff. We'd walked probably half a mile, talking back and forth, when I saw a shiny piece of metal lying on the ground.

I stopped for a second and looked down at it, wondering why a piece of metal would be lying there in such a well-tended forest. Curious, I bent over to pick it up.

I never did figure out what it was, though, because as I bent over three things happened pretty much at the same time. The most significant thing involved an object passing by my head at high speed. It went zzzzzziiiiiiip as it flashed by, and it grabbed hold of a strand of my hair on its way. Then I heard a thwack sound as it buried itself in the tree behind me.

I'd heard an arrow hit a target enough times in summer camp to recognize the thwack, if not the zzzzzzziiiiiip. I immediately hit the dirt, dust and little organic bits making a cloud around me, covering me in grime and filling my nose and mouth. Not, I guess, that it would have done me any good to be lying there in the open if there had been another arrow flying at me, but at least it felt like the right thing to do.

At about the same time, a loud growl sounded from behind me. Out of the corner of my eye I saw a Booboo-colored streak flash out toward where I guessed the arrow must have come from. My gosh, that wolverine was fast.

The third thing that happened—and yes, I'm pretty sure this one happened after the other two—was Sephaline sounding off with a high-pitched *eep* from behind me. Right after that, she leaped ahead to stand in front of me, spread her arms out wide, and started chanting in a lilting language that I now recognized as the elf tongue. I could sort of see what she was doing, pushing a sphere of blue-ish energy out away from us, though I'd never seen energy before like that. I had to assume it was a shield.

After several long moments, my breath finally returned as I saw Booboo loping back toward us. The wolverine looked a lot more relaxed, I—I guess. I admit that *relaxed* is a useless description for a killing bundle of fur and claws, even compared to the bristly, toothy, growling beast that had left our side just moments before, but that was how it—he—appeared.

Sephaline relaxed a little too, I saw. Her chanting stopped, and she dropped her arms to her sides. When Booboo arrived, she dropped to one knee and scratched the evil-looking creature behind one ear while she cast a still-terrified glance back toward me.

Heck, I was lying in the dirt, I realized. Some princess I was turning out to be. Slowly I stood up and brushed myself off as much as I could, my eyes searching the woods for an arrow I had to assume was nocked and about to speed my way.

"He's gone," Seph said from her crouch beside Booboo.

"How do you know?"

"How many times do I need to remind you that I am a ranger?"

"Yeah, well, do I need to remind you that I'm the one who just had an arrow shot at her? You may need to remind me of that ranger stuff a lot more if this keeps up."

I walked over and stared at the arrow that was lodged deeply in the tree.

"What do you make of the markings on this arrow?" I asked, trying my best to sound like one of the detectives on the crime shows. I couldn't see any markings, truth be told, but I couldn't see the things they pointed out on the crime shows either.

"What markings? It's an arrow," Sephaline said. I glared at her, my crime scene moment botched forever. "What? It is. It's just an arrow. Some people in the realm do mark their arrows, but this one isn't, and I can't imagine anyone marking an arrow to be shot at you, because you're the future queen, and besides, who would believe the marking to be true and not a misdirection anyway because that's...."

"Okay, I get it," I said, interrupting her serious run-on. "What the heck was that *eep* business?"

"It's my battle cry."

"Your battle cry is *eep*?" I raised a suspicious eyebrow.

"You don't like it?"

"It's nothing to do with whether I like it or not. But to be honest, it sounded like a scared little girl."

"Well, I was scared. And I am a girl. A fairly little one, too, right?"

"Yeah, but...." Okay, she had me there. "I don't suppose when you Turn Undead, you say *shoo*, do you?"

"I'm not sure what you mean by turn undead, or by what it has to do with footwear."

"Footwear? It's shoo, not shoe—oh, never mind. No, I mean it. Never mind. It's a game I used to play with some friends. It's kind of a role-playing game, where we played the game while pretending to be el—er, dwarves and dragonkin and other stuff. We would say what we were going to do, and then roll dice to find out if—dammit, I'm so freaked out that I'm rambling, aren't I?"

"Probably, but I'm still wondering what's this *shoo* thing?"

"Someone I played D and D—well, this game—with played a character who turned, well, controlled, undead by saying *shoo*. It sounded ridiculous, but it worked."

"You're saying that *eep* sounds ridiculous."

"No, no, not ridiculous! Just, not very battle-cry-ish. Oh, never mind. Lookit, somebody just shot at me with an arrow. We should probably head back inside now."

I tried pulling the arrow out of the tree, but it was stuck too deep. Sephaline didn't seem to think it mattered much as evidence, anyway, so I went with her suggestion to just leave it and get back to the protection of the castle.

"What did Booboo find?" I asked as we walked.

"What do you mean?" I couldn't believe how resonant her voice was despite our pace. It was hard for me to say much at all, as fast as our steps were putting the shooting spot behind us.

"When he bounded off after the shooter. You said the shooter was gone. Did Booboo find any clues?"

"Alyssa, you seem to think that Booboo and I have long, drawn out conversations, but we do not. The extent of our communication is mental imagery that is passed back and forth. The fact that the shooter had obviously departed was about all I got from what Booboo sent."

"Oh. I hoped," I said, and then I let my voice dwindle down to the huffing and puffing of the exertion. No point expounding on what I'd hoped.

"You hoped it would be like this dee and dee thing you told me about?" she offered. I just shook my head, sure that I was unable to say anything that could be heard, anyway.

Along the way we decided to leave the story untold till I could get up to my room and clean up a little. I had no idea what Dad would do if he saw his only daughter covered in dust and dirt from having an arrow shot at her, and I didn't really want to find out. I left Sephaline and Booboo standing in the hall and climbed the stairs to the royal floor.

After resting and rinsing my skin off in the bath across the hall, I was able to much easier. In the warm comfort of my room—a princess's room, I couldn't help but think to myself as I spun around—I felt much better, much safer.

Thinking of how much I wanted sleep, as well as the comfort my bed would bring after I finally told my father about the walk and the arrow, I turned the covers down. It turned out to be a bad idea. Under the blanket, smeared across the soft satin sheets in something dark and goopy, were the words, "LEAVE OR DIE."

Now *that* was creepy.

Suddenly everybody was in my room, if by everybody you mean my father, Stith, and the guard detail from the not-so-hidden chamber. Dad gently helped me over and down into a seat, and along the way it occurred to me that I'd been screaming and should probably stop. Sephaline bounded in, followed closely by Booboo The Growling.

"Get Aerona," my father barked to one of the guards as he physically dragged Stith back into the guard room.

"Who's Aerona?" I asked Sephaline. For the second time in two days I felt mildly drunk, only this time I hadn't had any alcohol. Stress is weird that way.

"The biggest, baddest female guard in the kingdom. She'll keep anything else from happening," Sephaline said.

"Will she?" I asked. Sephaline nodded tentatively; she looked as troubled as I felt.

Since I wasn't yet fluent, or even conversant, in the elf language, I had no idea what my father yelled at Stith. I do know that he yelled at him, but pretty much the entire castle knew that much. Sephaline winced at some of the grander crescendos.

Maids arrived, fresh linens in hand. As they changed the bed out, I asked, "Hey Sephaline, what was that little love message written in?"

"Alyssa, you don't want to know."

"Yes I do."

"No, trust me, you do not. It's both disgusting and powerful."

"You're acting like it was unicorn blood," I said, my sarcasm gear set to full speed ahead.

Her eyes widened slightly, as though I'd landed on a truth she'd wanted to keep me away from. Unicorn blood, it was.

Unicorn blood? I felt myself going over the top, but I didn't care.

"Are you serious? I haven't been here a week yet and already somebody's leaving me messages in the blood of a creature I thought was just a myth not three days ago? Really? A unicorn?" She just kept staring, and I switched gears. "Hey, I thought the blood of a unicorn was only used as a drink by evil wizards to keep themselves alive."

Her puzzled look sent me into waves of laughter. You know, it's always struck me as weird how people in stories laugh at the most un-funny moments. I get it now, though. Once the initial rush of tension is done and over, you get a feeling I can only describe as euphoria. At least, I did. And I laughed. I laughed loud, and hard, and long, with everybody in the room just staring at me strangely, bless all the elves' blessed hearts.

I finally calmed myself down and wiped the tears from my eyes enough to notice that everybody in the room, including my father and a new arrival, had me fixed in a crossfire of concerned stares. I shrugged them all off and looked at the new elf. Tall and muscular, her frame, stance, and severe expression served as pretty solid clues that this was to be my new guard. The twin swords hanging from each hip, combined with scars across her forearms and one cheek, said she was pretty good at it.

"Well *helloooo*, Gorgeous," I said in my best Streisand impression. "You must be Aerona."

She nodded, once, and walked over to stand next to the wall by the door. So, friendly and charismatic weren't her thing. Not a big deal for a guard, right?

"Are you okay, Alyssa?" my father asked, concern written across his face.

"Oh, sure. Today's been peachy, what with a tour of the kingdom, an arrow shot at me, and a not-very-cryptic message written in blood across my bed."

"An arrow shot at you? Tell me about this." He swept a glare from Sephaline to me and back.

I told him the story, with Sephaline interjecting occasionally. As he listened, my father's face got red and his eyebrows came really close to meeting in the middle.

"Why did you not tell me immediately?"

I shrugged. "Figured I should change out of the dirty clothes first. You know, didn't want you too worried, Dad."

"If anyone in my kingdom attacks or threatens you, Daughter, I expect to be notified immediately."

"Yes, *Sir*." I couldn't help responding sarcastically to his martial tone. To the side, I saw Sephaline mouth the word *Majesty*. Oops.

He scowled and turned to Sephaline. "How far away was the shooter?"

"I think about a hundred feet, Your Majesty. At least, that's where I sensed the trace of energy that remained from where I assume he teleported away after the shot."

"Ah. And so I take it that you failed to sense his intent to fire at a mere hundred feet?"

She opened her mouth to answer, and then her eyes dropped to the floor. She shook her head.

Father's eyes flashed and he opened his mouth. With a sigh, he closed it again and spun his back to us. Several long breaths later he turned and said, in a now-calm voice that had just a hint of steel in its undergirders, "Tomorrow, Sephaline, we shall work on your tracking skills. For now, go to bed. Everyone, return to your places."

Everybody left the room but my father and the Amazonian standing by the door. He knelt down beside me and grasped my hand.

"Alyssa, I owe you an apology. I had heard grumblings from those who would see someone else be the queen, but I dismissed them as typical. Grumblings are a normal part of the succession process. No one, to my knowledge, has ever grumbled to this extent, though. That, plus the ability of our foe to sneak in and out of your room without triggering the protective wards, is the reason Aerona will stand physical guard while you sleep. You *will* be safe, one way or another, in my home."

"Thank you, Father," I said, looking up into his face. It seemed like there should be something more for me to say, but I'll be danged if I could think of it.

He left quickly, leaving me in my now-much-less-private room. I looked over at the woman standing impassively by the door. She was—still there. Forcing my legs to press my body out of the chair was difficult after the stresses of the day, but I managed to rise and stumble toward the bed anyway. Along the way, I decided to try and be nice to my new companion.

"So Aerona, thank you for being willing to take up guard duty on such short notice."

Her eyes met mine, absent even a touch of emotion. "You are welcome, Princess. It is my duty to the kingdom and to your father, its king."

"You're probably never going to be friendly to me, are you?"

"I am your protector, Princess, not your friend."

And, on that cheerful note, I climbed into bed. As I slipped under the covers, I pulled Momma's picture from the night-stand over to me, hugging her close to my chest. Lucky for her, my guard-not-friend didn't say a word about it.

I tried, unsuccessfully, to go to sleep.

CLATSIO

a fight. Not a real, formal fight, just somebody smacking somebody else in the face. There's apparently a difference to elves.

She Deserved It

The next several weeks went fairly smoothly, if by smoothly you mean no arrows shot at me or messages left in unicorn blood. Meanwhile, High Priestess Sternyface—Naissa—proved to be the bane of my existence.

And then I hit her.

Hopefully you know by now that I'm really not a violent person. In fact, I'm pretty much exactly the opposite. One thing Momma always taught me is *not* to fight. The next verse, though, was that if you have to, then fight like a boy, and fight to win. Because the consequences of *fight to win* scared me, I made a habit out of avoiding all fights, choosing instead to hide behind sarcasm and humor. Hey, it usually worked.

There was one I couldn't run from back in freshman year. Tommy, one of the bullies at school who thought he was pretty tough, kept following me around over lunch one day. He just kept picking and picking; for some reason he thought a fight with me would be good for him. I still don't get it. He was annoying but bearable up till he started in on my momma; next thing you know he went to the hospital with what I heard was a broken nose, and I went home for a few days of suspension. By the time I came back to school, everybody knew not to talk about my momma. I think that counts as one of those win-win things.

Naissa and I plodded along through our own little dysfunctional relationship. As the future elf queen, I figured she owed me a skosh of respect, while she apparently did not. Every time she spoke to me, the disdain in her voice was only barely hidden.

Luckily we didn't get much chance to speak at first. The lessons with the tykes lasted for a week, just long enough for me to get a handle on the language. That part was pretty easy; apparently I'd been fluent when I was younger, and I had a wonderful practice partner in Sephaline.

"Do all elves learn English?" I asked her, in English, one evening after a long session of reciting verb forms. Elvish—I guess that's what I should call it since they have no name for their own language—is pretty straightforward in its verb forms, with a simple addition of a word to identify the various tenses. Straightforward, but different from English.

"No. Your language is hard to learn, and only those of us who might have cause to speak it someday are taught."

"How do they know who might have cause to speak it someday?"

"Position, usually. Royalty obviously, and the priests and priestesses who use the portals to the human world for study and research are other clear choices. Some of the village elders also learn it as a secondary means of communication."

"But why you? I mean, no offense, but you're not royalty."

"Actually, I sort of am, or at least I will be. I'm the king's niece."

"You are? I thought you said you were a commoner."

"Yeah, that's the strange thing about being the king's niece.

Remember that he was a commoner before he was selected by the queen to be our king. The king lives in the castle, but his brother, my father, still lives in the old hut in the small village I came from. I was brought to the castle back when it was first decided—by your father, I guess—that I'd be the one to show you around, but there's never been any question in anybody's mind that I really don't belong here."

"That's silly. Of course you belong here, you and your Booboo too."

"Thank you."

Then it hit me. "Wait—that means we're...."

"Yes, it does. You didn't know that we're cousins?"

"We were destined to be together, apparently," I said, the statement coming out a little more sarcastically than I'd meant it to.

She shrugged; her sarcasm meter was still broken. "Pretty much. I was designated from early on to be your companion and tutor. They taught me English, and they tried to teach me customs and finery and all that other stuff, but then I became a ranger. I think I probably leaned toward becoming a ranger because of all the customs and finery and stuff, to be honest. Well, that, and meeting Booboo. Still, for every hour I got to train in ranger skills I had to endure several hours of etiquette lectures. That's why I'm not a very good ranger."

"You could'a been a contendah," I said, nodding.

"What?"

"Nothing," I said. I was going to have to work harder at remembering how useless it was to spout movie lines off to somebody who'd never seen a movie. I sat quietly and thought about what I'd just learned.

Cousins. I'd never had one before. To find one in elf land felt weird.

But I digress. Sorry.

Anyway, Naissa kept me in there with the kids just long enough for me to get the language down, and then transferred me into classes with the older youth, learning the basics of government and trade and stuff, and that sprinkled liberally through with private sessions with *her*.

Intolerable, I think, is a good way to describe our private sessions, except that every day I somehow found a way to tolerate them. The high priestess was just plain mean. I asked my father about it one night after supper, and he chuckled and said that that was just how she was. Her rough exterior, he explained, which I guess meant she was like a coconut. You know, rough on the outside, and soft and flaky on the inside.

Or something like that.

She attacked my accent, especially when I was practicing the silly elf incantations to do things like transfer energy from one plant to another or sing a tree into a shape. Problem is, I don't really have much of an accent normally, but when I get angry I start talking like a real Southern belle. The more she picked on it, the worse it got, and the madder I got, which in turn made my accent even worse. Y'all know what I mean?

At first the lessons on doing not-magic were pretty easy, stuff like "tell me what the tree is feeling." Trees only really have a few different feelings, it turns out, so if I guessed *serene* when the tree was standing still or *troubled* when it was being bent one way or another, I was pretty much guaranteed to be dead on. Later, though, I actually did have to connect to the tree's energy to sing it into growing faster or slower or sideways. It was hard at first, but it got a lot easier as long as Sternyface wasn't chiding me.

That's why I enjoyed my homework with Little Treebeard so much: it was away from Naissa.

Little Treebeard was a small elm sapling that was being grown in a floor pot. It was kinda cute, as little bitty elm trees go, and I could swear after all the tree singing that I could sense a sentience in it—hence, Treebeard. One of Sternyface's priests carried it for me back to my home away from home the second evening after I'd started my tree-singing lessons. My task, as she'd said and he reiterated before he bolted from Aerona's glare, was to sing the tree back to health first and then into a form that was both artistic and pleasing to look at.

Great. Sephaline got a wolverine familiar; I got a potted elm tree.

Singing Little Treebeard back to health wasn't too hard. The way Sternyface explained it, elves can't actually heal trees because that would mean using magic, which is forbidden. That's just fine, though, because trees have an incredible ability to heal themselves. All the elf does, she told me, is sing about love and joy and how good healing feels, and the tree will listen and work its own healthy—um, magic. She said *magic*; she really did that time, I swear.

I guess if a *tree* is working magic, it's hunky dory.

Like I said, though, it wasn't too hard to do. It felt silly, mumbling cute little phrases in the language of the elves while pretending to be following a lilting melody, all while Aerona the Battle Maiden glared around the room like she was waiting for the shadows to attack.

"Rwy'n dy garu di, gwellhad buan, coed yn gariad, gwella eich hun," I crooned softly, over and over. Aerona snickered. When I glared over my shoulder at her, she pointedly stared off into the dark corners of the room as though they were the enemies themselves.

"What?" I asked, my irritation slipping out into my voice.

"Nothing, Princess," she said, her face maintaining its epic solemnity.

"You didn't like my healing song?"

"It isn't mine to like or dislike, Princess. Your tree will heal or she will not. It's just...."

"Just what?"

"Just—an interesting selection of phrases you put together, is all, Princess."

"Interesting?" Last time I'd heard someone describe something as interesting, it wasn't a good thing. But I'd heard of errors in translations before, like the guy I knew who had tried to talk about 'the blind,' as in the group of people who can't see, in German, and it had come out as the blind you use to cover a window.

"You don't think my song will work?"

"If your tree appreciates short, disjointed platitudes, then it will work just fine, Princess."

"Disjointed platitudes?" I felt myself getting a little riled up, but shoved it back down. She was right, after all. I'd been singing, "I love you, get well soon, a tree is love, get better," over and over. It was disjointed as hell, truth be told, but that was about the extent of my poetic ability.

"So how do most elves sing trees to health?"

"I do not know, Princess. I haven't had the opportunity to observe most elves singing trees to health."

"Fine. How do *you* sing trees to health? And would you please quit calling me Princess with every sentence?" The two of us had hardly ever said two or three sentences in a row to each other, and so I hadn't realized how annoying the constant reminder was.

"Princess is the appropriate title for me to use when addressing you, but I will try to use it less frequently per your request. And I don't sing trees to health. It is not something those in my line of work do."

"How do you know that I'm doing it wrong, then?" I still couldn't help being a little defensive.

Aerona stopped glaring at the shadows to look at me directly and said, "I did not say that you were doing it wrong. I only said I found it interesting."

"Oh. Right," I said and turned back to my tree.

I'm still not sure what I was doing trying to pick a fight with the elf who was assigned the task of guarding my life. I'll just blame the frustration at sitting there learning silly stuff instead of—well, anything related to being a queen. With a couple of deep breaths I forced myself to settle back down, since I couldn't imagine an angry 'get well' song would do much for Little Treebeard.

The funny thing was that my short, disjointed platitudes worked. The next day I came up to my room after a long day of working on intonation and proper pronunciation with Sternyface, and the first thing my irritated, frustrated eyes lit on was a noticeably healthier Little Treebeard. I skipped over to her and, after a minute or two of examining the new shoots of life on the branches, turned to Aerona and said, "See? It worked!"

"Your song did indeed work, Princess. A very nice job."

"Now I just have to figure out how to turn her into a bonsai." My training hadn't touched on that at all, at least not yet. Healing was just a matter of asking the tree to heal itself, and even short, choppy, unmusical ways of doing that obviously worked. But to shape herself into an unnatural form? How was I supposed to ask that of L.T.?

"Into a what?"

"A bonsai. It's what the Japanese people back home call shaping a tree into a form it wouldn't naturally grow into."

"Shaping a tree into a form it wouldn't naturally grow into? That sounds like a tremendous waste of time."

"Yeah," I agreed absently, and then I realized a coolness: we had agreed on something! "Yeah! Exactly. A *tremendous* waste of time."

"Unless, of course," Aerona said, continuing to sweep the

darkened corners of the room with her eyes, "the objective is to teach the shaper something. Like patience, perhaps, or perseverance. Those are good lessons to teach anyone, but especially one who aspires to be a queen. Do you not agree, Princess?"

"Sure," I growled. I didn't, really. I mean, I knew deep down that she was right, but I'd just been argued into a corner by my bodyguard, of all people.

Over the next several days I learned how right Aerona had been about the true nature of tree shaping. Naissa wouldn't answer a direct question on how to get L.T. to shape herself other than to assure me that the correct answer didn't involve wrapping wire around any parts of her. Any parts of L.T., that is, not Sternyface, though there were many times when wrapping the high priestess up in wire would have appealed to me. She did give me hints, though, and those hints echoed Aerona's, believe it or not.

Patience and perseverance were the keys, she said.

The tree didn't care how I wanted it shaped, she said.

Singing the elf word for circle to her for hours and hours wouldn't make my tree want to become a circle, she said.

Keep trying; it'll come eventually, she said.

I was getting really tired of everything she said. It made me want to scream.

Once I gave up, though, it happened.

I'd spent an hour, easy, singing every word or phrase I could come up with to transmit the idea that I wanted my tree to form a circle. Little Treebeard, meanwhile, had spent that hour, easy, making it clear that she was ignoring me. Finally I ran out of phrases to use, and at the same time I gave up on the whole idea of L.T. ever forming a circular shape. Instead, I asked her, in Elvish of course, what shape she wanted to form. Almost instantly the image of a fully-grown, magnificent tree appeared in my mind. That wouldn't do at all, of course, but I held that knowledge back, hid it, because for better or for worse Little Treebeard was actually "talking" to me.

I shifted the magnificent tree shape into something closer to what I thought of when I heard the word bonsai, and though I felt an objection to it through the link we shared, she still started bending slightly into my mental image when I hummed a melody.

I sat back and reveled in the new understanding I'd come by. Singing a tree into a shape, it turned out, has nothing to do with the words you use, and even less to do with how well you carry a tune. Instead, it's all about the conversation, the relationship, you have with the tree.

Then I thought about Sarah, my old friend back home. If I ever shared my new wisdom with her, she'd think I was crazier than a dog in a hubcap factory. A sandwich or two short of a picnic, she'd call me.

Didn't matter, though. She was back on Earth, and I was in one of the fanciest rooms in Kiirajanna, my very own bodyguard watching over me while I hummed a tree into a pretty shape. A smile spread across my face and I got down to the task at hand. I thought of a shape, thought it as hard as I could, and started humming. The branches shifted. I kept humming, and before long Little Treebeard stood in a perfect spiral.

"That was a catchy tune, Princess. What was it?"

Unfortunately I had no idea, and Aerona nodded her understanding when I admitted it. I had been focusing so much on the tree and the mental image I wanted her to form that I'd never even heard what I was humming.

Aerona started humming Elvis's All Shook Up.

"Oh, um, that," I said. How was I going to explain the song choice? "One of my mother's favorite songs, from way before my time. Back when Elvis was the King."

"There are kings on Earth? I thought the humans were go-verned primarily by elected officials."

"No, no, Elvis wasn't that kind of king. He was a singer."

"What kind of king is a singer?"

"Not a king at all. It's just what we call them to make them sound cooler. Elvis was the king of rock and roll, Michael Jackson was the king of pop, and so on."

"So these people were not rulers—so who actually ruled this thing called pop?"

"No, nobody ruled anything, really. They just made a lot of gold and platinum records."

"Gold and platinum what?"

"Records. Round pieces of plastic—the ones that aren't gold or platinum, I guess. They have songs on them."

"That sounds like magic."

"It's not. It's—oh, never mind." I honestly had no idea how records worked, but that didn't matter right then. I'd finally sung a tree into shape. I'd passed the test and could move on.

Move on, we did. About two weeks into the not-magic les-sons, it happened. You know—*it*. The fight, short as it was.

Most of my lessons blurred together after a while, but this one still stands clear as a cold winter day in my memory. I was in the high priestess's chamber trying to sing a tree into remov-ing a knot. That's a tough spell to arrange, trust me. A knot is—well, you know what a knot is from. Getting a tree to re-move one is physically challenging because the tree has to re-route so many of its own fibers around whatever it was that caused the disturbance in the first place, but that's only half of the battle. It's also really dang tough to talk the tree into. Trees think knots look distinguished, believe it or not. The tree I was working on was really proud of its knot, so I had to focus hard. In so doing, I forgot to tame my accent, and since I was already irritated at Mr. Knotty Tree, it was apparently really noticeable.

Naissa started in on me. "What's wrong, human? Can't get past your inner hick today?"

I ignored her and kept singing. She'd taunted me before. It was clear that she didn't like me a lot, and she didn't respect me any at all. The taunts started as just muttering under her breath when I mispronounced a word, but they kept getting louder, stronger, more annoying.

"Y'all didn't ever do much tree singin' back down there in redneck land, did y'all?" Naissa asked, exaggerating the accent till it was almost comical. I wondered where she'd heard the word redneck, but I managed to keep singing. That tree was going to listen to me.

Naissa put her head right beside mine and started singing the same song I was, only her version was loud with a much-exaggerated accent that made it sound awful. I kept singing, not even giving her the satisfaction of a sideways glance.

"It's your horrible mush mouth, child. If you'd quit singing to the tree like a stupid southerner, he might listen to you," the high priestess sneered into my ear.

I kept telling myself that there was nothing to be gained by getting angry with either the tree or the high priestess, though I could tell Naissa was getting to me. My face heated up, and my eyes betrayed me by starting to leak.

Naissa could tell it, too. She sensed blood and pushed harder. I tried to shut her voice out and focus on the words of the incantation, but then she said the inexcusable: "That lousy human mother of y'all's should have taught y'all to speak in a civilized...."

That did it. I spun around to confront her over that insult, but somehow, all on its own, my fist flew up and hit her face. You. Don't. Talk. About. Momma. I think I even said that out loud, but all I really remember was watching what ended up being a pretty nicely-aimed right hook connect with Sterny-face's nose.

Pure, shocked silence rippled through the chamber.

It was strange, though. I'd thrown exactly the same punch in exactly the same way at Tommy, and he'd crumpled when it hit. I'd watched his face, in slow motion, slide to the right and then back to the center. I saw his eyes widen in shock and then dull again as he fell to the floor bleeding.

High Priestess Sternyface, on the other hand, didn't move, didn't flinch, didn't even widen her eyes. She just stood there with a creepy, evil grin on her face. It looked like my punch hadn't even really touched her, though my knuckles were pretty sure it had.

Suddenly it occurred to me what I'd done. I'd slugged the high priestess, the highest religious authority in the entire realm. It wasn't that I was scared of the consequences; it was that I didn't even know what the consequences of such a grave offense might be. That terrified me, and so I ran. I ran down the hall, toward the exit to the castle. I sprinted right into my father's arms. Well, sort of; first thing was my chin colliding with his chest. But you already know that part of the story. He chuckled and brushed himself off, and then escorted me back to the castle to relax for the rest of the day with him and one of his finest bottles of whiskey.

Eventually I calmed down enough to tell him the story.

The next day he accompanied me to the high priestess's chamber, assuring me the whole way that all would be fine.

It was all fine, apparently. Naissa and Father sat and joked about the incident, a fact that both relieved and infuriated me. It turns out I couldn't have hurt her no matter how hard I'd swung, since a high priestess always has energy-based wards shaped about her. Go figure.

She said, in much the same tone my junior English Comp

teacher had used explaining that I had a problem with run-on sentences, that she was pleased at having found my weak spot. Now we could work on making it less weak.

She was, however, disappointed that it was such a *weak* weak spot, bless her high priestess heart.

Then again, if she'd asked me, I could've just told her not to talk about Momma. It's not like I'm the only girl who reacts badly to somebody talking smack about her mother. Am I?

So, weakness discovered and all, I settled in to even more difficult lessons. Like how to hold my temper no matter what, which apparently was one of the most important things she had in mind to teach me.

You'd think that once she'd discovered my weakness, she would've gotten nicer to me.

She didn't.

DIM YN YR UN CAE

literally, not in the same field. Like the old "not in the same league," which is how the royal family looked at me.

The Royal Family

It wasn't long before the inevitable happened. One morning I was following Sephaline grumpily (me, not her) down to breakfast, and we met them—Prince Charming and his two sisters—at the head of the stairs. Sephaline gave one of her battle cries, squealing *eep* and leaping to defend a spot directly behind me.

I didn't have time to comment on her lack of bravery as I sized up the royal threesome.

The girl in front appeared to be the eldest, gussied up as she was in a formal light green gown and pearled headdress. I couldn't help wondering if she had pants on underneath as I looked at the other two. Keion walked just behind his sister and to the right, clad this time in a black velvet blouse embroidered in gold thread that clung tight to his rippling abs and really—well, never mind what it did to my knees. To the left walked another princess, this one wearing a much simpler combination of shorts and t-shirt.

They were obviously siblings. Each had perfectly-arched eyebrows over almond-shaped dark eyes and perfect, straight little noses, and their faces were all angled the same way, with high cheekbones streaking straight into long chins. Keion and the sister in front both had long, flowing, black hair that glistened with moisture when it moved. His was swept straight back into a mane, while hers was curled up into dainty ringlets that could only have been executed by an experienced, and expensive, hairdresser.

The sister in back was the odd one out. Her hair was a deep coppery red, worn with perfectly-feathered bangs that flew around and entered a waterfall that gushed straight downward and then stopped, resting gently over her shoulders, just kissing her collarbones in front. Between her hair and her outfit, it looked like she was trying extremely hard to make it look like she wasn't trying at all to be beautiful. Which she was, I have to add. Or, at least, she would have been if not for the ugly sneer that was plastered on her face.

Speaking of sneering, the expression each one wore provided the best differentiation. The princess in front had obviously never had a hard day in her life, and she'd apparently never met someone she couldn't rule, either. I was certain from her calm expression that she looked down her nose equally at everyone who wasn't lucky enough to be her. Keion's face could be read like a book; he was amused and arrogant at the same time. The third, meanwhile, was perfectly content wearing dill pickle face and apparently wanted to bite someone.

Quite the trio, they were.

I'd say they stopped and looked at me for the simplest way to tell it, but that wouldn't be quite right. I mean, they all three stopped. The princess in front didn't look at me, though. Instead, she regarded me. To get it exactly right, you have to not pronounce that second r. *Regahded.* Have you ever been regahded? She regahded me. I bet if I'd curtsied, she would have returned it. Only better. It was a meeting of two equals, where I wasn't quite as equal as she was. It was clear that she was a princess of the realm, and that she recognized me as one too, and that she was making an effort, difficult as it was, to not be disappointed in the poor little human girl who'd found her way into her presence, no matter how much the elf princess ought to be.

Well, at least she was the polite one. Keion met my eyes with the same frosty glare he'd owned the first time we saw each other. The jerk even seemed to know, and enjoy, what his physique was doing to me. I made up my mind right then and there to never, ever, let him know how good-looking I thought he was.

Younger sister in back, meanwhile, was much easier to read. She hated me. Her brother's glare was frosty, but hers was angrier than a Mississippi State fan after an Ole Miss win. It's a good thing looks can't really kill, or else I'd be dead now. Bless her heart, her vibes were hateful.

"Greetings," I offered, not sure what else to say. It was kinda obvious that they weren't going to just move out of the way and let me down the stairs to breakfast.

The older girl's eyes traveled from me to Sephaline and back, weighing the situation and our worthiness at the same time. Finally she nodded. "Greetings," she said in her native tongue, a lofty lilt to her voice. "You must be Princess Alyssa. I am Seren, eldest daughter of Queen Talaith and first princess of Kiirajanna. To my right is my brother, Keion, prince of the realm as well as its finest hunter and athlete." Her eyes flicked contemptuously to Sephaline as she said that, and then back to me as she continued, "And to my left, the golden swan of Kiirajanna, the Princess Meriel, my younger sister. I had hoped to make introductions before now, but you've been kept so busy under the burden of the training you've required in order to become familiar with our customs and language. I trust that the clerics are approaching your education with the requisite level of intensity?"

"Indeed, they have," I replied in the language of the elves. The insult she'd intended with her last bit was clear, but I figured it was best not to play into whatever game she was trying to run on me. I cut to the chase and said, "The customs and language of Kiirajanna are both beautiful and fascinating. I will be so very honored to become her queen."

Both Keion and Meriel sent even more dangerous glares my way, but Seren just smiled, nodded, and said, "I am glad to hear of your fascination. The tradition of crowning a half-human to be our queen has been one of our most time-honored, cherished practices." Both sister and brother broke off their stares of daggers at me and glared at the first princess at that. It looked like she'd just made a point to them instead of to me.

"I will enjoy getting to know all of you more, of course, but right now my training calls," I said, glancing meaningfully down toward the dining hall.

Seren nodded, the smile never leaving her face as she rotated her presence to the side, taking her siblings with her as she cleared the way for Sephaline and me to descend the stairs.

I'd tell you what I really thought of her, but Momma taught me not to talk like that. Just—bless her heart.

We got down to the dining hall before I dared risk a glance behind to see if they were following. I didn't want them to think I was worried about where they went, after all, even though I was. But when I looked back nobody was there.

Sephaline caught my movement and said, "Relax, Cousin. The members of the royal trio never come to breakfast here. Well, the princesses don't, anyway. You've already seen the prince stop by sometimes, but only when he has his merry band of followers with him."

"Why not? Where do they go to eat instead?"

"I don't know, and I don't know. Nobody ever sees fit to inform me of the royal trio's whereabouts."

I started to make a wisecrack about her position, but then remembered how seriously she took it and just smiled instead. I changed the subject. "So, it's Queen Talaith? The queen is named 'crown'? Isn't that fairly unimaginative?"

"I'm not sure how you define unimaginative, Alyssa, but all our queens are named Talaith. Until they retire, anyway."

"So I'm going to be Queen Talaith?"

"If you're going to be queen at all, yes."

"Oh. Thanks for the vote of confidence."

She shrugged. It really was quite a bit to take in, I guess, so I followed it with the smartest thing I could think of to ask. "Why?"

"Why what?"

"Why are all the queens named Talaith?"

"Why not?"

"Because...."

I suddenly realized that I didn't have a good answer. Why wouldn't all the queens be named the same thing? Weren't, um, the queens of, um, someplace back on Earth that I couldn't recall, named all the same?

We sat down to eat while I stewed over the treatment we'd—I'd—received from the royal trio. Finally I had to ask, "So, why do they hate me so much?"

"Hate is a very strong word, Alyssa."

"Oh, come on, Seph."

"Well, it is. You already know there is some guarded sentiment against a human becoming our queen. The three royal children, in particular, have probably the most reason of anyone to desire a change in the law of succession. Many say that Seren would make an excellent queen, and I have no doubt that she would. If she were *your* sister, wouldn't you be a little bit upset that she'll be cast off like that?"

"Oh, I'm not planning on just casting them off."

"Will you make them your personal servants, then?"

"Servants? Lord, no. I was thinking something more along the lines of asking them to be my advisors, Seph."

"Your advisors?"

"Look, I don't know. So far my training on elf court and customs has ranked somewhere between slim and none. There's nothing wrong with being advisors to the queen, right?"

"Perhaps."

"Perhaps what? You're talking in half-thoughts."

"Perhaps all sorts of things, Cousin. Perhaps they'll accept a position in your court. Perhaps they'll choose to be three of your top advisors, though if I were you I would always hold suspect the advice of Meriel. Perhaps you'll change the way you feel about them, or them about you, in the future. Perhaps a dragon will come down out of the sky and eat us all before we have to worry about it. Better?"

"No. It's not. Look, I'm somewhere I didn't grow up, and I don't know the rules or even who to trust. I don't even really know who to trust about who to trust. And still, you trust me to become queen?"

"We don't have a choice, Princess Alyssa, and neither do you."

"Sure I do. I can pop on back to Earth."

"Really? I mean, you can, but do you know where you would go to do that?"

"Um," I stalled, realizing she had me there. "I could ask the royal trio where to find the spot. They hate me enough to show me the way home, I bet."

"Nobody hates you, so cut it out with the pity party, Cousin."

"Pity party? Must I remind you that somebody shot an arrow at me the other night?"

"Um," Sephaline stalled. For once, I had her. "Well, okay,

there was that. But now it's time to stop dwelling on who hates you and who doesn't and get to your training for the day."

IGAM OGAM

literally, zigzag, but used to mean drunk.

Royal Training

My "training for the day," as luck would have it, was more hateful abuse by Seren, eldest daughter of Queen Talaith and first princess of Kiirajanna. When I walked in to the high priestess's office, Sternyface wasn't there. In her seat sat Seren, still gussied up and head held high. Seren's brother and sister stood behind, watching quietly as the first princess *regahded* me once again.

"Oh. Hi," I said, not sure what I was in for, but already figuring it was bad. I found myself wishing I could be back in Mississippi, happily swinging out on the front porch with Sarah as we prepared each other to go to college, just as I'd dreamed of not too long ago. Instead of the nice, normal, path to college, though, I was stuck in a strange place where everybody but my dad and my cousin seemed to hate me. But I thought again of Momma, and of her waiting for my father to return once I'd finished my elf queen training, and I decided yet again to grit my teeth and bear it. My time in Kiirajanna had, after all, been a little bit embarrassing, and a lot annoying, but it was nothing I couldn't handle.

"Greetings," Seren said, inclining her head slightly. "High Priestess Naissa has asked us to begin your training on the important matter of our people's royal court proceedings, Alyssa."

"Oh. Great," I said, still on edge from the morning's encounter.

"Sarcasm?" Seren drew the word out, looking down her nose at me.

"Ya think?"

"Would you prefer to not be trained on the intricacies of high court?"

"No. It's important to know that, I'm sure."

"So do you object to our qualifications as trainers?" Seren asked, managing to actually look confused.

"No. Not at all."

"What, then, is your concern?"

"What's my concern? I would have thought it clear. Why should I trust you to train me when you three hate me?"

Seren rose, her eyes meeting mine. She shook her head and said, "We do not hate you, Princess Alyssa. We are— disappointed that our future queen is currently so ill-equipped for the position, granted, but it is our duty and our pleasure to help make up the—the gaps—in your knowledge." Every pause was clearly meant to insult me. During the last one, I heard Meriel mutter "shortcomings" under her breath, a word neither her brother nor her sister acknowledged.

I shifted my glare from Seren to Meriel, and then back again. It didn't seem to be doing any good; in fact, Meriel seemed to actually enjoy receiving my glares, while Seren was completely indifferent.

"Look, since I've arrived I've been treated with hostility from more than one elf. One of your archers even tried to kill me the other evening. What was that snort for?" I asked Prince

Charming.

"Elf archers never *try* to kill," he said, black eyes boring through my own. "Elf archers always hit our target."

I thought about that for a moment. "So what are you saying? The arrow wasn't meant to hit me?"

"You were out in plain view. Had the arrow been intended to hit you, it would have, Princess."

"Oh." Well, heck, that threw the whole incident into a new light. "Well, I was moving. I had just stopped to look at something on the ground."

"Are you suggesting, Princess Alyssa, that an elf archer might not be able to hit a moving target?" Prince Charming asked. I thought of several possible answers, but it really wasn't worth the fight.

"I am not suggesting that, no. I am certain, given your warmest of assurances, that elf archers can hit whatever the heck they aim for, bless their hearts. Be that as it may, somebody clearly wants me to leave."

"Many people want you to leave," Seren said, taking charge of the conversation again. "I'm sorry, but that is apparently always the way it is when succession time draws near. I admit that I would be pleased to ascend the throne myself, despite my knowledge that it cannot ever be in accordance with our customs. The throne is yours, Alyssa, no matter who wants what, and I, for one, intend to see you prepared to bear the weight of the crown associated with it. To that end, are you ready for your lessons?"

I thought I was, so I nodded and they started. It turned out to be one exhausting, long day, though.

The topic was actually pretty interesting, all in all. Seren managed the teaching for nearly all of it, running late into the evening with barely a break for lunch. Elf society was complex, as I already knew, but I had no idea how much complexity went into the royal interactions. She started with the basics, including how elves were supposed to approach the royalty both in official status and unofficially in towns and fields. I asked about what I'd seen of my father's reception in the villages across Kiirajanna on Sadwrn, and she explained that elves with a history of approaching the sovereign in a certain way relaxed their approach over time. I should expect, she explained, a much more formal approach by everyone when I accepted the weight of the crown, but with the passage of time, and depending on my own personality and preferences, that formality would in all likelihood relax.

Good—I like relaxed.

We went over the subtleties of elf court politics, too, and both of Seren's siblings joined in an animated way. It seems there are as many opinions as there are rules about the politics of formal court. It's probably the same in human royal court too, but all I know about that is from books. On the other hand, I was getting ready to live real life out in elf royal court politics.

Or I was trying to, anyway.

Once we got down to learning, Seren kept her sister and brother pretty well in check, at least in their outward displays of hostility. The speech she'd given at the beginning seemed to help a lot. They weren't downright glowing in their hatred for my existence, at least. I still could tell I wasn't likely to be invited out to a movie with them. Not that there were movies to invite me to, but—well, you get the idea.

By the end of the day I was flat tuckered. Seren was a great teacher, alternating as she did between lecture, demonstration, and role-play. I mean, yeah, the subject was important to me; I knew that. But her methods drew me in, engaged me in the lessons as much as any classroom teacher I'd ever had. It was exhilarating, as well as exhausting.

I sort of stumbled back into the dining hall. Seph was there already, and she and Booboo looked at me with concerned expressions as I collapsed onto the bench beside them.

"Long day?" Seph asked.

"Quite. The royals took over to teach me the *niceties* of court, and they say they'll do it tomorrow too."

"Ugh. Must have been hell."

"It was, at first, but it got a lot better as the day went on and everybody got too tired to maintain their glares. I mean, they're never gonna be my friends, it looks like, but at least they didn't seem to hate me. And Seren taught me a lot."

"And the niceties of court sound like so much fun to learn," she said with a twinge of sarcasm that surprised me.

"Well, yeah. Haven't you ever wondered what was going on behind some of the subtle gestures in the throne room?"

"Alyssa, I've never been invited to the throne room to see the subtle gestures."

"Oh. I don't know why, but I figured the king's niece would be invited sometimes, ranger or no."

"You have that backward, actually."

"What do you mean?"

"A ranger is more likely to be invited to the court than the king's niece. You didn't pick up on that already? I'd've thought that trio of pretties would have made the point clearer. The king's daughter is the future queen, and so her blood is considered royal. The king, though, was selected by the queen, and so his blood kin aren't nearly as important."

I winced at my inability to correct her. I didn't know why my father had said the actual selection process for the king was supposed to be such a secret, but I held my tongue anyway.

"But the king's blood kin are—aren't they also the kin of the next queen?"

"The next queen, yes, and once she ascends to power, all of her kin are finally regarded as royal while the kin of the guy she picks are treated like dirt till his daughter ascends and then they're royal, too."

"That's strange. You know that's strange, right?"

"No, not really," Seph said. "It keeps there from being more than one important family around at once. Consider the example of the queen's kids. Imagine if there were two sets instead of one, how much turmoil that would cause, especially if one trio were in the process of falling out of power and the other were falling into it."

"Huh. Good point. So when I become queen, you'll be able to come to every court you wish."

"Gosh, I was so hoping you'd say that," Seph said, sarcasm rippling through her words, the vehemence in her tone surprising me again.

"Or, I suppose, you can just go play in the woods, Cousin. Whichever you desire most."

"Just one or the other? What if neither is my deepest desire?" Seph's eyes looked up at me playfully.

I curtsied gently and said, "Your wish is my desire, Cousin."

"Good. I shall remind you of that promise some day."

Uh, oh, I thought, wondering what I'd promised myself into. "So, um, what is your fondest wish, if I can ask, Seph?"

"Graceland."

"What?"

"Graceland. Where Elris lived. Your father has told me all about it, and so I want to switch over to your world long enough to see its wonders."

"Oh. Graceland. I see, I guess. It's Elvis, not Elris. So, um, well," I said, "I'll work on that, then, once I'm all trained up and on the throne. And on that note, I should probably head to bed so I'm ready for more of the training tomorrow." I really didn't have anything better to add. *Graceland....*

Sheesh.

Lessons in Frustration

I expected Prince Charming and his two sisters to join me at breakfast the next morning, but they didn't. At least, the two sisters didn't show up. Prince Charming was there, though, and he watched me eat breakfast with a leer on his face that I could see all the way across the dining hall. As soon as I finished, he rose and sauntered over to stand across the table from me.

"So, Princess, I see you are ready for more training," he said.

"I am. Will your sisters be joining us, or do you get to torture me solo today?"

The prince snorted and said, "I shall provide all the torture you need and desire today. If you will follow me?" He spun on his heel, launching his hair into a swirl that would've been good looking if it hadn't been so comically cliche. The prince didn't even stop to see if I was following him as he marched imperiously out of the dining hall and then right out of the castle.

I hurried to follow him out and completely around to the far side of the building. It was a long walk, but it didn't take much time to get there at the pace he was keeping. I hadn't ventured to that portion of the grounds yet, but then again having an arrow shot at me on my first walk had curtailed my desire for a lot of exploring. Still, it figures that the elven archers needed somewhere to practice, and so I wasn't surprised in the least to walk through a break in a thick hedge to find a target range set up.

"Have you ever shot an arrow from a bow, Princess?" Charming said, spinning suddenly to face me. Without taking his questioning look off of me, he reached over into a stand and removed a bow and three arrows. He spun around again, firing all three rapidly at one of the targets set up against the hedge on the other side. All three hit around the center of the bull-seye, a feat that didn't seem to surprise the prince. To be honest, it failed to surprise me too. The boy could shoot. Big deal.

"Nope," I said, trying to look as unimpressed as I could while I waited for him to continue the conversation. I didn't manage to keep my eyes away from the targets; they had aw-fully small bullseyes. In all the archery I'd ever watched—not that there'd been a lot, but I'd seen some—the centers of the targets always seemed to be a few inches in diameter. These little red dots were the size of a quarter, if they were that big. Around the red dot was a blue disk that wasn't any wider. Sub-sequent disks radiated outward, in alternating light and dark colors, for a total of ten colored bands in all. The rest of the tar-get, itself about three feet in diameter, was white. A wooden stake held the circle up at about chest-height. I counted eight targets spaced along the opposite end of the range, and won-dered how many archers would be trying to use them during whatever served as practice time.

"It is time you learned from a master, then," he said, smirk-ing as he stepped over to me and held the bow out.

I really wanted to laugh at the arrogant display, but I knew that wouldn't do much good. I took the bow instead, holding it to me and plucking the string like a guitar. I said, "Well, bless your heart, but you've given me a really tight bow. I just don't know how I could ever use it to hit those little circle thingies over there."

Yes, it's called a target. Yes, it's called a bullseye. I know all that. I wasn't going to play his game, though.

"You could at least try, Princess," Keion said without moving his teeth.

I shrugged and flounced as well as I could over to the tub with the arrows in it. Pulling one out I turned and nocked the arrow, pointing it at him as I drew it part-way. I asked, "Like this?"

I was impressed; he didn't even flinch. With one raised eyebrow, he said, "No, not at all like that, Princess. If you're quite done mocking the most revered of our pastimes and sports, perhaps I could help you fix your form?"

"I'm not mocking the most revered of our pastimes and sports. I'm mocking you. If you're quite done behaving like a preening peacock, perhaps I'll let you help me fix my form."

The prince's glare intensified, but he apparently got my point. He moved over to beside me, turning my body gently so that the arrow was pointed the correct direction. Gently he reached around me, showing me how to hold the bow. Now, I'd watched archery on TV and in the movies, and so I had an idea I was doing it wrong, but when he showed me how to hold my left arm out parallel to the ground and then pull the string back smoothly with my right hand, it felt—right. And strong. Stronger, I think, than I really had the strength to control.

"I wasn't kidding when I said this bow seems too heavy for me. You don't happen to have any beginner or girl bows, do you?"

Keion snorted in my ear. "That would be a baby's bow here, and no, there are none available. They're too small for you, anyway."

"So what do your sisters shoot when they come to the range?"

"Why would they come to the range?"

"Well, they're elves. I thought all elves shoot bows."

"Many do, but my sisters are princesses. Why would they need to learn to do something they'll never have to do?"

"Well, but—but I'm a princess. Why do I need to learn to do something that I'll never have to do?"

"You are not merely a princess. You will be our queen, Princess. You do have so much still to learn, don't you? The queen is expected to be an excellent archer, in part to defend herself and her people should the need ever arise, but also because she is the ceremonial leader for any contests or games for which she is in attendance. She shoots the first arrow in our midwinter games, for example. Our people rest a great deal of pride in how straight and quick my mother can fire a quiver of arrows. It's my job to bring you up to that level. If I can, that is."

The last bit made me angry enough that I shook him off. I snatched an arrow out of the bucket, drew the bow as he'd shown me, and launched toward the target.

It missed. It missed by a lot, in fact, thudding into the ground about three feet to the left of the base of the target.

Keion snorted again. I was so frustrated by then that it made me want to hit him, but I held back. My slugging of the priestess had shown me that hitting an elf in the face made as much sense as walking a cat, and besides, I was pretty sure the prince would be tougher than Sternyface.

"You put that blade of grass to rest quite well, Princess," he said. "Now, would you be interested in further instruction, or would Her Highness prefer to continue sending arrows down-range to strike in random places?"

"Fine. Instruct me. Don't insult me," I snapped at him, punctuating each syllable as I said it.

"As you wish," Keion said and then took up his position behind me again. He explained as he guided my hands that as a beginner I needed to look at aiming the arrow as two separate exercises. The first, easy, part was aiming the arrow horizontally. To do that I needed to sight down the length of the shaft, lining it up with the intended target. It got a bit more complicated, he told me, when considering the effect of any wind that might be blowing, but experience would tell me how to compensate for that. Also, he mentioned that side to side flexing in the arrow always resulted from releasing the string with fingers. It wouldn't normally change the flight of the arrow, Keion said, but it could if it were severe enough, which happened if the archer were sloppy enough with the release.

"Back home we have mechanical grippers that hold the string and release it the same way every time," I said.

"So you have practiced archery before?" he asked.

"Only a little. But it seems a lot easier to use the mechanical gripper thingies."

"Our people do not look to make archery easier, but to make it more accurate," Keion said with a sniff. I guess I should have expected that reaction.

The vertical aiming, he said, took much more experience to get right. As soon as the arrow left the bow it started dropping, which was something I could've told him. I did, after all, pay attention in science class. Every arrow, then, had to be aimed a little or a lot above the target depending on how far away the target was and how heavy the arrow was. Keion told me that it helped a lot to make sure that I gripped the bow and the string in the same place every time.

Fine. I let him guide me through aiming a few times and

SYNDOD

a surprise. I got lots of those my first summer in Kiirajanna.

Another Day With Dad

The next morning found me up and at 'em early on the archery range. Seph joined me to shoot a few arrows, and she proved that girls can, in fact, shoot. We swapped stories as I plinked arrows toward the targets, most missing widely but some actually hitting in the colored areas. To be honest, I had a hard time concentrating as the shrubs behind us continued their rattling announcement of Booboo's investigations.

"Archery practice? On Sadwrn?" a familiar voice asked from behind me. I whipped around and, holding the bow in one hand, wrapped both arms around my father.

"No, I mean it," my father said after our hug. "Why are you practicing on Sadwrn?"

"To get better at it," I said.

"Who says you need to get better at it so much that you should practice on the weekend?"

"Prince Keion said I need to practice every day."

"Of course he did. One would expect that sort of request for dedication from a perfectionistic jerk. You are not really going to shoot all those arrows, are you? That would cause so much extra work for the arrowsmiths if you do," he said.

"Oh. I hadn't thought about that."

"Well, you need to start thinking about that. And you also need to quit doing everything people tell you to. You are going to be our queen, my dear. People will tell you to do stuff just to see if you will do it if you keep this up."

I thought about what he said for several minutes, growing more and more disappointed in myself. Fact is, I had this secret crush on Prince Charming. Yeah, he was a jerk, but he was the best-looking jerk I'd ever been around. And soon enough I was going to outrank him. It—well, wrong as it might have been, I got some weird fantasies out of it.

"Sorry, Dad," I said.

"And quit apologizing," he said, glaring at me. "Alyssa, again I must point out that you will someday soon be our queen. Not a recent high school graduate, nor an eighteen year old Mississippi girl. The queen of all the elven people. Please, you must start thinking like a queen."

"I'm trying, Dad. I'm just still not certain how a queen thinks."

"Your teachers are not doing their jobs, then."

"No! No, they are. I'm just apparently not grasping their lessons. I wasn't raised to be the queen, after all."

"No queens are."

"It's kind of a silly way to go about choosing the next ruler, if you ask me," I said.

"I do not believe that anyone asked you. Some day you will understand."

Ugh. There was that phrase again. I'd been hearing it my entire life. *Some day you'll understand,* my mama had said, like some magical meteor of knowledge was going to wait till I hit a special age and plow down out of the sky to smack me upside the head.

No point objecting now, though.

"Dad, do you think I could shadow the current queen for a while, maybe?"

"Eventually, yes, but not now. You need to get the basics down before you can move on to the advanced lessons, my daughter."

"But Dad, the siblings hate me. Oh, Seren's fine, but she's obviously older and wiser than me. Prince Charming is in an entire other league of his own, just ask him. But Drizella just plain hates me, and doesn't bother to hide it.

"Drizella? You mean Meriel?" Dad tried to look cross, but the corner of his lip quirked up the same way mine always had when I'd been in the principal's office laying out the perfectly good reason why I'd stopped Mrs. Moody's boring history class with a joke again. I always sat there thinking *I will* not *crack a smile, I will* not *crack a smile*, over and over, when the reality was I thought it was dang funny.

So, yeah, I guess I was—well, never mind. One story at a time, right?

"Yes, Dad," I said, not bothering to hide my own grin. "Sorry, sometimes I make up little names that help me remember people better."

"That is fine, so long as you refrain from say them out loud. Besides, I thought that Drizella was the older sister. Was she not also the one with the darker hair?"

"I don't remember which was which, but I do remember she was the bossier, meaner—wait, how do *you* know that story?"

"Alyssa, I spent many years on Earth both before and after you were born. Though the prize was unquestionably worth it, wooing your mother was a long and challenging—"

"Dad, I really don't wanna hear any of your wooing stories," I cut in, shaking my head and looking away, doing everything I could not to imagine him and Momma doing—wooing stuff.

He chortled. I looked at him again, and he wasn't bothering to hide a smile at my expense. "Of course not, Alyssa," he said. "Suffice it to say that I have spent many years in the realm of your birth, and as a result I am quite familiar with many of your customs and stories."

"Makes sense," I said, nodding my head up and down. It did, at that. I mean, I hadn't really thought of it before, but my mother wasn't the type who would say, "Oh, you're the elf king? How 'bout you come back to my house tonight and let's make a princess together?" But that just brought up other things that bothered me.

"What was it about Momma that made the elf king choose her?"

"You really need to ask that, Alyssa?"

"Well, yeah. I mean, I think she walks on water, but that's because she's my momma. What is it about her, though, that attracted you?"

"Well, many things. Everything, to be honest. Your mother is the kindest, gentlest, sweetest woman I know. Plus she was open minded and very willing to learn, once I'd broken the story to her, all about the elves and our heritage. And, for a wonderfully unpretentious woman, she's got a kernel of command to her, as though she were one of a great ruling family at one time in her past. That we share an outlook on life and others who are in it was a true blessing."

"What outlook are you talking about?"

"Have you ever known your mother to hold a grudge for long? No. Have you seen her allow her spirits to slip in the face of a hardship? No. I tell you this, Alyssa: your mother would make a magnificent queen, herself, if she but had the blood."

"How'd you two meet?"

"I thought you wanted to avoid all of those wooing stories."

"Leave out the icky parts, please."

"The—*icky*—parts will indeed be left out, then, per your request, my daughter. I had only just embarked upon my quest when the elves I had selected to accompany me asked to go to the United States to experience this place that you call Disney World. It was neither truly magical nor truly a kingdom, as I am sure you know, but it did present us with quite an atmosphere for fun and frivolity. Your mother, by the purest of luck and coincidence, was also there with some of her friends from college, participating in a ritual I believe they call spring break or some such. One of the elves in my company decided to pick on one of the people running around in costume for how poorly he was pretending to be an elf, and I stood up for the poor chap. Your mother, who was sitting nearby, commented on how much she appreciated my doing so, and at that moment it was clear that we were soulmates."

"Aww, that's a nice story."

"Indeed. Our first kiss, in fact, was on the ride called Space Mountain."

"Now, see, that's the icky stuff I was talking about."

Dad chuckled again, and again at my uncomfortable expense. "Alyssa, surely you have shared a kiss with a boy you liked, too. How is that *icky*?"

"When it's my momma, Dad, it's icky."

"I suppose I shall leave the story off there, then."

"Probably a good idea," I said. Changing the topic quickly, I asked, "So how did you manage to run your kingdom while you were away finding a woman, doing icky stuff on roller coasters and such?"

"Well, I made perfectly certain to remain in contact with my regents back here in case of emergency, and besides, the queen is perfectly capable of making the kind of regular, sort of boring decisions that we make on a regular basis. All by herself, even. As will you, some day, when your king also goes off to find a human wife."

His comment reminded me of something else I'd been wondering. "Speaking of boring decisions and stuff, what, if anything, does the queen actually do here?"

"Quite a lot, Alyssa. Why do you ask the question in such a manner?"

"I never see her actually do anything, is all."

"You never see her, period, Alyssa, and that is by custom."

"So I'll never see the woman whose throne I'm somehow destined to take over?"

"You are far from destined to take it over, Alyssa. There is so much still you must learn and do and prove; the crown is hardly yours yet. But you will see her, as soon as you have learned and done and proven what you must in order to move to the next stage of your training."

"There are stages to the training?" Nobody had briefed me on how the training would happen, and to be honest I hadn't thought to ask.

"Certainly. Though you spoke our language fluently as a young child, you have of course forgotten most of it in the ages since, so before anyone would seriously consider your bid to be our monarch you had to learn to speak our native tongue again—a task, I must add, that you've accomplished nicely. There are also the matters of geography, history, customs, and so on that you must know regarding our lands and people before you consider ruling them. The first stage, really, is primarily a matter of proving that you are capable of adequately acculturating yourself."

"And the second stage?"

He grinned. "You shall find out soon enough. For now, though, concentrate on your lessons, and also on not calling anybody by your pet names to their faces. Okay?"

"Okay. So, Dad, do you have any other suggestions for a

more fun way to spend the day than at archery practice?"

"I was hoping you might ask," he said, grinning widely.

Before we left I asked him if there was truth to what Keion had told me about the arrowsmiths being the only ones able to retrieve the arrows. He nodded. "The prince tells you the truth. You have a good teacher, Alyssa. Keion is well-known through-out the realm for three things: his pride, his sportsmanship, and his skill with an arrow. And, I suppose, the young girls al-so know him for his good looks, right, Sephaline?" In reply she just *meeped* and spun—so that neither of us could see her blush, I guessed. Dad chuckled and said, "His looks do nothing for the remainder of the population, though. In any event, as much as I know his presence is distasteful to you, you must overlook that in order to glean all that you can from his know-ledge and skills."

Was the prince's presence distasteful? I thought about that for a few minutes as we walked back in silence around to the front doors of the castle. Yeah, the arrogance was annoying, but I kinda—no, no I didn't. As cute as he was, no. I refused to think of him in any way that might be looked at as positive, no matter what I'd been thinking while I'd been enthralled in his archery practice spell.

The three of us piled into one of the magic carriages and it lurched off. We didn't head toward the populated areas we'd seen on the previous tour, though. This time the carriage took us straight out into the forest. As we drove, I looked around and behind and had strange feelings that I'd seen the path be-fore.

"Are we headed back to where we, um, teleported, or what-ever it was, from Earth to here?" I asked.

"Going by the ley gate, yes. Teleport is not precisely what we did, though. Teleporting is forbidden. What we did was merely shift from one plane of existence to the other. You should ask the priestesses to teach you more once they get over the whole slugging incident."

Seph snickered at me; I gave her a rueful look in return. Okay, so I'd lost my temper. Once.

The cart slowed down a lot as we approached an open glade. Dad pointed; in the middle were a circle of standing stones, each a couple of feet wide and rising up to about my waist in height. It wasn't like Stonehenge or anything; the stones at the ley gate were all shaped differently. If they hadn't formed a perfect circle, in fact, I wouldn't have thought much of them.

"Here is where we made the transition," my father said as he jumped out of the stopped carriage. He walked into the circle and motioned me to follow. When I entered, he asked, "Can you feel the power, Alyssa?"

I could, and I told him so.

It felt weird. In my lessons with the priestesses I'd been able to grab hold of the magical life streaming around me, barely, and not for long. Still, I had. Here, though, the same power was rushing around. It was a difference as large as trying to catch raindrops in a sprinkling rain versus swimming in Pickwick Lake.

"Do not activate it," my father warned. "We would prefer to avoid going back to Earth today."

"Speak for yourself. I miss my momma."

"Yes, Alyssa, I do, too. However, we have business to attend to here first. There will be a time for reunion, but that time is not now. Patience, my future queen. You must have patience."

"That's what Sterny—Naissa keeps saying."

He turned his face away from mine, but not quickly enough to hide his grin. "I am sure she does, Alyssa."

"Alyssa said she'll take me to Graceland," Seph said as we stepped up into the carriage.

"Did she? She enjoyed our trip so much she wishes to make

it again with her cousin? What a surprise."

I shrugged. "Dad, I've been there before. It's just a big house to me."

"It was just a big house to you, yes. Now that you are better attuned to the powers that surround us, though, you will probably see it differently next time you go."

"I thought magic was only here, not on the Earth."

"Please quit using that word, Alyssa. You are technically correct, in that useful energy flows exist only here, but there do exist power grids on Earth. We went through one to get to here. I do not know if it is manipulable, since none of our kind has ever tried. Never tried, that I know of, anyway."

I shivered one last time and then left the circle, enjoying the sensation of power flow through me. I could even feel it outside the circle now that I knew what to look for.

Dad smiled as we continued deeper into the forest. "I can tell you enjoy the feeling of being swathed in the power. That is good."

"I do. But I'm still not sure I get the distinction between using the power, as we do, and whipping out magical spells, which is forbidden."

"One is passive, while the other is active. For better than that," he interrupted as I started to object, "ask the priestesses."

"They're all grumpy," I said.

"I wonder why."

"They were all grumpy even before I swung at Naissa."

"Of course they were. It is a monumental task to train the next queen, and your occasional sulking does not help."

I sighed. At first I wanted to be insulted that he said I was sulking, but he was right. Changing the subject to one where I wasn't in the wrong, I asked, "So has there been any luck in figuring out who shot the arrow at me?"

"No," Dad said, his face clouding over. "Unfortunately there is little to go on. We are being more careful to guard you against attacks like that in the future, but I am not certain we will ever determine who pulled that one off."

"We'll just have to go with our suspicions, eh, Dad?"

"If you have suspicions, Alyssa, I would love to hear them."

"Well, when I told the queen's kids about the event, Prince Charming snorted and told me that an elven archer wouldn't miss, but rather that the attacker could not have been aiming for me."

"He was correct in saying that. Go on."

"Well, his reaction was just so cold, so matter-of fact. And you know the queen's kids don't want me taking the throne."

"Alyssa, stop. I would prefer to believe that you would never accuse the prince of such a heinous deed."

"But...."

"Stop. Accusing the prince could lead to a schism in the palace that can never be repaired. Besides," he said with a sideways glance my way, "we know where he and all the other royals were that night. It was the first matter we investigated. Even practicing the forbidden spell craft could not have allowed him to be in two places at once."

Well, Dad had a point. I let the discussion fade off into silence as the carriage rolled smoothly through the woods.

Soon we approached another glade, one I could just make out by the open area in the treetops up ahead. Dad signaled the carriage to slow down, and we came to a complete stop just outside the ring of trees.

I gasped. I rubbed my eyes to make sure they were still working, and then blinked several times. No amount of rubbing and blinking changed the sight in front of me, though. It was a unicorn!

"Unicorns are—a myth," I said, the words tumbling out of

my mouth.

"On Earth, yes, they are. And so are elves. And trolls, and dragons, and fairies, and all manner of creature that can only exist in a magical realm," Dad said.

"Like Kiirajanna," I muttered, still not believing my eyes.

"Yes. Like Kiirajanna," he whispered.

"He's beautiful. Can I—can I go up to him?" I asked, looking at both Sephaline and my father. The one stood in the cart as captivated as I felt, a wide smile of radiant joy plastered across her face. My father, meanwhile, chuckled.

"She is a her, Alyssa," he said softly. "She may let you walk up to her, and she may not. There is probably no harm in trying, though."

"I don't have to be a virgin who's not on my period, do I?"

"No, of course not. Wait—you are not a virgin?" my father asked, his questioning eyes piercing me.

"No, I am, Dad. Yes, yes I am. I just remember hearing the part about virgins in the myths."

"In addition to the part about how drinking unicorn blood makes you live forever? That sort of thing?"

"Yeah," I said.

"Hogwash. Go on up and try to pet her. Do not make any sudden moves, though."

As I stepped out into the glade the unicorn's head swung to watch me. She nickered once, and then again. I took another couple of steps toward her, and she took one back away from me, swinging her head as if to say no. I was just about to give up on the possibility of petting a unicorn when a wordless melody drifted across the clearing. Both I and the unicorn spun our heads to look at the source: Sephaline. My cousin had climbed down from the carriage and was now standing just inside the ring of trees, crooning a soft, haunting, lyrical song. It was beautiful; as I listened to the notes running up and down I saw images of merry brooks playing their way through majestic forests.

It was incredible, and the unicorn seemed to be enjoying it as much as I was.

Seph winked at me and motioned me forward. She didn't have to tell me twice; I started walking in time to the music. Slowly I made my way to the center of the glade, the unicorn seemingly enthralled by Seph's song. Up close it—she—was even more beautiful than I'd imagined. Her brilliant white fur glistened and sparkled in the rays of the afternoon sun. Both her mane and her tail were made of longer hair so fine that it looked like strands of white silk. The only non-white spots on her body were her black eyes, which were now staring directly at me, and black hooves. Those eyes, ebony orbs that bore more intelligence and emotion than any horse's eyes I've ever seen, widened as I slowly reached my hand up. I found the soft spot at the base of the unicorn's neck where it meets the muscles of the forelegs, and ran my hand gently down several times.

I was petting a unicorn! How crazy is that? Of all the crazy thoughts, I suddenly really wanted my old cell phone. I'd left it behind on Earth for the obvious reason, but the camera might have worked still. What I wouldn't give for a selfie, I thought, and then I realized how silly the idea was.

Finally, not wanting to press my luck, I let my hand drop to my side and walked backward, away from the magnificent white beast. As I did, the melody ended, and the unicorn nickered at us again. Released from whatever spell had been holding her, she reared onto her hind legs, turned, and galloped off into the woods.

I sighed and then went back over to the carriage. I couldn't resist gathering Sephaline up into a great big hug.

"Thank you," I breathed into her ear.

"It's what I do, Cousin," she replied. "Well, one of the things that I do. All rangers are taught the calming songs. That was a special one meant for unicorns, and it was an important lesson to learn, of course, because although unicorns are rarely encountered, the last thing you want to face is an angry one."

"I suppose so, what with that horn and all."

"To kill a unicorn is considered one of our greatest sins," Dad broke in, "no matter whether you attacked it or it attacked you. So if you come out into these woods, make sure you bring a ranger with you in case you meet one. Sephaline is not kidding; they can be quite fearsome when provoked."

"Gotcha," I said, detaching myself from my cousin's hug and climbing up into the carriage seat.

"Seph, have you ever gotten to pet a unicorn like that?" I asked.

"Of course. It's part of ranger training. We come out as a group and the instructor leads each of us through singing a calming song while stroking the beautiful creature's mane as you did. We are introduced to many of the forest's creatures in that manner."

"Ah, kinda like Hagrid did at Hogwart's."

"This Hogwart's place has magical creatures?" Seph looked at me, curious.

"Yeah, but it's just a story." I sat down, but I found it impossible to sit still.

"What are you bouncing for, Alyssa?" Dad asked.

"I can't help it. I got to pet a unicorn!"

"Yes, you did. Now, let's head back to get some food," Dad said, his stern expression replaced with another smile as his face turned away from me.

"Thank you, Dad," I muttered as the carriage started back. There was no answer, but I'm sure he heard.

GWARCHEIDWAD

a guardian[1]

---

[1] It's a whole lot easier to say than it looks. Try it.

Attacked Again

When we pulled up to the castle, I sensed my father's tension suddenly shoot way up. He didn't even wait for the carriage to stop before he leaped out, landing at a run and calling out to us, "Follow me closely!" Booboo didn't need a second cue, as the wolverine darted from where it had been shadowing the cart and ran into the castle and up the stairs on my father's heels.

Sephaline and I followed, though our running speed was nothing compared to my father's. We caught up to him finally as he stood in my room, sharing his glare among Stith and the other black-clad members of my little guard detail.

"Where's Aerona?" Dad growled.

"Majesty, she's taken the day off. It is Sadw...."

"I know what day it is," the king snapped. "What happened?"

"We heard a rustling that shouldn't have been there, so we charged out to investigate. Someone in black robes was in the room, right over there across the bed. He didn't get to do whatever he was here for, though, because we charged him and he teleported out."

Booboo obviously didn't like what he was hearing, because the wolverine kept growling. It sounded eerie, more like a cat than a dog, sort of high-pitched and scarier than a raccoon caught in a trash can.

Dad pulled out his dagger and used the tip to pick at the sheets on my bed. I couldn't tell what he was looking for, just poking around kinda at random as he was. He turned his head to Sephaline and said, "Would you please tell that animal to shut up?"

As he finished his sentence, though, Dad spun around and whipped the dagger through the air toward the opposite wall. It didn't reach the wall; instead, it sank into something soft just a few inches short of where the wall was, making a *shlock* sound. An elf appeared, coming out of what must've been an invisibility spell, his throat gurgling as he dropped to the floor.

"Nice throw, Your Majesty," Stith said.

"Shut up," Dad barked. "Get that person out of this room and down to the guards. Get Aerona up here. You four are relieved of duty, as of now. Report to whomever is on currently as captain of the guard. Go!" The guards all appeared to be about to object, then thought better of it as two picked up the guy who had been hidden and all four left the room.

"Alfred!" Dad yelled.

"Yes, Sire?" Dad's butler's appearance in the doorway was immediate. Heckuva job, that, since it was the universal day off.

Dad looked at me. My own eyes had been riveted to the blood spot in my bedroom where the would-be assassin had fallen. "Please make my daughter up a bed in my sitting room. Just do it," he said when the butler started to object. "We can worry about improprieties later; for now we must worry more about her safety."

A shadow fell across the doorway as Aerona arrived. "Your Majesty, I—I am so sorry. That this attack happened is my fault. I shall—"

"You took a day off?" Dad asked, his eyebrows raising.

"I did, Sire."

"At Stith's insistence?"

"I take the responsibility for not being here, Sire."

"Just answer the question."

"Yes, he did suggest strongly that I needed and deserved a day off, and that today was a good candidate with the princess being away with you all day."

"Mm hmm. Hurry, get down to the captain's office. I want Stith locked up for questioning. I want the guy with the knife in his throat to survive till we can question him. And I want the four men he trusts the most up here to join your guard post in watching over my daughter."

"I—I'm not relieved, then, Sire?"

"Not at the moment. Now go."

As the woman thundered down the hall, Dad looked from me to Seph and back. "Well," he said. "Sephaline, would you have Booboo do a once-around just to make sure the room is empty?" Seph nodded and her wolverine started on its task. "So, that was an interesting development. Why are you laughing, Alyssa?"

I couldn't help snickering. "It's L.T., Dad," I said. When we'd entered the room Little Treebeard had actually connected with me, a warning flash of danger through the mental link we'd formed over the weeks of my singing. That wasn't the funny part, though. My little elm friend had taken exception to my 'Seph got a wolverine, and I got a tree' comment. She'd pouted for a while over it, too, and I'd found it funny then that somehow I seemed to have gotten the only tree in the realm with the ability to pout. When I'd entered the room tonight, though, Little Treebeard wanted to show me that she was every bit as ferocious as Booboo. I could almost hear the growls through the mental pressure she sent at me, and her branches were visibly shaking, spread out and angling toward the intruder.

A tree, growling. Growling because it's jealous of a wolverine, at that. Now that's funny.

I told Dad the story, and he actually spared us a grin and a snicker in spite of the worry lines on his face.

"Do you really think Stith is guilty?" I asked.

"Absolutely. There is no way he and his team should have missed that invisibility spell; palace guards are trained to sense that sort of nonsense. Either he is slipping, or he is guilty, and in either case I can't have him watching over you."

"What if they're under compulsion?" Seph asked.

"Then they must still be treated as guilty," Dad said, harshness in his voice. "I still cannot trust them. I am honestly not sure if I can trust anyone other than the two of you, so please, girls, keep your eyes peeled. Alyssa, you should know that it is scandalous for an adult female to sleep in the king's chambers. I would not make you do it, but it would make me feel much better to have my own guards in addition to Aerona watching over you tonight."

"Sure, Dad," I said. The whole propriety thing seemed kinda silly to me anyway. "I'm still trying to figure out what the first guy was trying to do. There's nothing over there."

"I suspect he was trying to do nothing. He was a diversion to draw attention away from the cloaked man."

"Diversion for whom? We weren't supposed to be here. If your suspicion is correct, Stith would've known about both, wouldn't he? So he wouldn't have needed a diversion, right?"

"Right, but what if he was involved but his men were not?"

I had to agree that Dad had a point. "This detectivy stuff

gets complicated."

"It does, indeed, especially if the goal is to keep you safe in so doing."

"Well, you did that. It was a nice throw, Dad."

"Thanks, Alyssa. Again, it should never have been needed."

"Hey, how did you know to sprint up here, Dad? You took off at a sprint from the cart before it stopped rolling outside in the driveway."

"Did you not sense the teleport, Alyssa?"

"Um, no. Did you, Seph?" She nodded bashfully. I snapped, "what, am I the only idiot here who can't do what an elf should be able to do?"

"You are the only one here who has not had the good fortune to have grown up in the realm, my dear," my father said soothingly. "Give it time, and work more closely with Sterny-face and her priests at your magic lessons," he said, his use of my term drawing a snicker from both Seph and me.

"So does this teleport bother you as much as the arrow-shooter's did?"

"Why would it not?"

"I'm still trying to figure out the whole deal with when it's good magic and when it's bad magic."

"If you—or I, anyway—can sense it, it is forbidden. If you have to work at it, it is forbidden. The only thing you may call a teleport we do are between the realms, and that only uses the ley power rather than an arcane incantation."

"So if it does anything useful, it's forbidden."

"You could say that, I suppose, but it is not the usefulness that defines the danger."

"I know that, Dad. I was kidding. Mostly, anyway. I'm still wondering why you went charging in, though. Aren't you, as the king, the last guy who should run right into a dangerous place?"

"Why should I be last? The king and queen are the leaders of the elven people, not the followers."

"Yeah, but...."

"But what?"

"I'm—not sure how to put it. Leaders—at least, leaders as I've seen them—always have body guards who take the bullets first so that the leaders can continue to lead. I can't imagine the President of the United States charging into a battle, except in that movie where he was a former fighter pilot and he led the flight against the aliens. It was—you've never seen it, have you?"

"This—movie? No, I have not. And I am not the President, an elected and mostly administrative leader. Nor will you be, Alyssa. Keion has not been teaching you archery for his health, after all. It is for your own health that you must learn to be not only the governess, but also the first defender of the realm. You and your chosen king, as much as I hate to speak of the matter, will nevertheless be joined together as fellow combatants in the last battle of the realm."

"Last battle? You're not being literal with that, are you?"

"Yes, unfortunately, I believe that I am."

"That sounds like that prophecy thing again, isn't it? The one that said I would be born with a dragon-shaped birthmark, right?"

"The prophecy—thing—is indeed the source of the belief that you will be the queen who leads the people of Kiirajanna through the final battle, yes."

"Gotcha. So, is this final battle the last battle before many years of peace, or is it more the final battle before doomsday?"

A soft muttering from behind told me of Aerona's return. I looked back to see her spinning her hand through what looked like a star shape in the air.

"What was that?" I asked her, curious, and earned only a

glare in return.

"You do not know?" Dad asked. I turned back to him, half-expecting a sarcastic look, but his face had a sincere question on it.

"No, I've never seen it before."

"I will have to talk to Sternyf—er, Naissa—then. I would prefer to believe that her lessons should have already covered both the wards and the curses as well as the old legends. None of us is getting any younger."

"Wards. Legends," the meaning behind my father's words hit me. "Are they part of this prophecy, too?"

"I do not believe so."

"So why don't you tell me about this prophecy, then?"

"It is a long story to tell."

"It's still early, Dad."

"Not early enough. It is a work that reportedly requires months, if not years, to read, an accomplishment that I cannot claim personally. To know what is contained therein, you will need to read it yourself."

"Okay, I will."

"How is your ancient written elvish?"

"All those squiggly marks, you mean?"

"Yes, Alyssa. Those squiggly marks are the root of all of our—your people's, now—language."

"I thought so. Not so good."

"Well, then you still have plenty to study."

"You're not going to just tell me the gist, are you?"

"And ruin your fun in reading them yourself? Of course not. Seriously, dear," Dad dropped his jovial tone when he saw my frustration rising, "you really do need to read the texts yourself. It is hard to get into, but a shorter translation from me would not do the matter justice."

"Fine. I'll ask about them tomorrow. After archery practice, that is. Speaking of which, when do I get to learn to toss a knife like you did?"

"Tomorrow."

"Tomorrow, really?"

"No, not really. And that was sarcasm, my daughter. You are our future queen. You have a lot to learn, certainly, but at some point you need to take over responsibility for your own training. You need to quit asking when you are to be learning a topic and begin informing your trainers what you need to learn."

"Oh. Okay. So, when will I learn when I need to learn what I need to learn?"

"Well, now that was an excellent question, convoluted though it may be, Alyssa. The fact is, the more that you learn about our culture and language, the more that what you do not know will become clearer to you. Keep applying yourself to your lessons, try not to punch anybody else in the face, and you will get there."

"Okay, Dad. I think." One little punch, and I'm fixing to hear about it for the rest of my life, aren't I?

An Ancient Relic

The next day I rose early, intent upon taking charge of my own training as my father had told me I should. To start, I figured I should signal my intention by dressing differently, putting on a dress instead of my normal shorts and shirt combo, and even accessorizing as my momma had taught me to.

It worked, sort of.

Now, I've worn dresses before, plenty of times. Back when, um—well, never mind that. I've worn them. But firing a hundred arrows with a bow in a flowing dress is far more difficult than they made out in all those cartoon movies. I mean, the action of shooting a bow isn't any different, but the concentration is tougher to maintain while your skirt is whipping about in the early morning breeze.

It's even more difficult to concentrate with Prince Charming whispering a compliment about your attire over your shoulder.

Luckily for my shooting he only whispered over my shoulder once. I can't remember exactly what he said, focused as I was on the bullseye, but it seemed sweet. At least, it had a sweet tone.

The rest of the time, Keion sat there and made it difficult to be me. I nocked an arrow, and just before it flew a loud, raspy cough shattered the silence of the glade. I jumped, and the bow jumped, and the arrow went sailing way over the target.

The prince snickered and said, "If you had any skill, Princess, you could manage the shot regardless of distractions."

I answered, without turning around, "We have already determined that I have no skill, Prince. Now I have to wonder why you are trying to convince me that in addition to my lack of skill, you have no couth."

"That was well returned, Princess. Smart answers will not help you, though, when you need to put the tip of an arrow into a very small spot."

I didn't grace him with a response.

I missed more shots than I hit that day, thanks to Charming's interference. He didn't just make sounds to distract me; he went out of his way to make shooting difficult. He sat on the observation bench and guffawed loudly. He snuck up behind me and pulled my hair. He puffed air into my ear as I aimed.

I could sort of see his point, but that seeing didn't make me want to kill him any less. He was annoying.

Regardless, I got my hundred shots in and headed to the trio's office for training. I didn't get any of the training I'd expected there, though.

The door, as usual, was closed, which was a good thing at that point. I needed a moment to stop, pull in a deep breath, and put on my best regal expression. Soon to be queen, I was. Ready to take control of my training, I would be. I would show them.

Finally, I figured I was ready. I drew myself up tall as I could, pulled my shoulders back and my chin high, threw the door open and marched in.

Seren gaped. That made me happy. But then she spoke, and I deflated a little when it came out why she was gaping.

"Is that—?" she muttered, her eyes frozen on my pendant. She came around the desk slowly, warily. She kept coming, stalking closer, till she was only a few feet from me, but she still leaned back, an almost-fearful expression on her face. She leaned in slowly, making a show of studying my pendant, and then when she was satisfied, her expression darkened even more. "It is," she confirmed to her siblings. "Where did—where did you get that? You—you should not wear that pendant—not at least until you are queen, Alyssa," she said.

"Why not?" I challenged. Since I'd entered the temple that morning, I'd already been getting a suspicion it was more than just a pendant, though. The normally cool silvery metal warmed up as soon as I walked into the hallway, and it had stayed warm ever since. It wasn't uncomfortable, just noticeable. And weird.

But Momma gave me that necklace, and I was danged if I was going to let them tell me not to wear it.

Meriel spoke up from the side, her face frozen in an angry glare for some reason. "Do you not feel the power coursing through that relic? Do you actually feel competent to command such power, fledgling as you are to the ancient mysticism of the people? Play dress up as you wish, little girl, but do not presume to don Draignerthol till you have earned the privilege."

"Sister," Seren said, "your purpose is noble, but your passion undercuts your message."

"Noble to insult the future queen every chance she gets? I'm learning that elves have a strange sense of nobility," I muttered, drawing an angry glare from both sisters. Keion, though, looked amused.

Draignerthol? I could speak enough of the language to recognize the translation as 'mighty dragon.' Ooh, that sounded cool. Still, they had to be wrong.

"This pendant can't possibly be this Draignerthol y'all are so afraid of. It was given to me by my mother," I said, mentally daring one of them to make a snide comment about Momma.

Seren quirked an eyebrow and got close enough to reach my chest. "May I?" she asked, more polite than I expected. When I nodded, she closed her eyes and touched the pendant. Immediately the blue gemstone eyes lit the room in a bright glow.

I couldn't help it. I gasped.

The elder elf princess opened her eyes and smiled at me. In a surprisingly kind voice she said, "Alyssa, how your mother came to be in possession of an ancient and powerful elven artifact is certainly an interesting question, one I suspect contains your father's actions in its answer, but there is absolutely no question that the pendant hanging on your chest is indeed Draignerthol. Few remnants of the magical era of Kiirajanna remain, and none are as storied—or so long missing—as this one. I'll ask you to pardon my sister's brash reaction, but Draignerthol has been presumed lost to our culture for thousands of years."

Drawing myself up from where I realized Meriel's blast had worn me down, I shrugged and lied as I thought a good monarch should. "Nothing to pardon, really." Meriel's sneer, together with another mostly-hidden smirk from Keion, told me I'd hit the mark with that one. Still, I had more important things to worry about than insulting Drizella, the evil stepsister, over there.

"So, since it's the topic of conversation anyway, what can you teach me about Draignerthol?" I asked.

Seren shared furtive glances with her siblings, and Meriel hurried past me and out the door. After the door closed, Seren said, "It's not our lesson to teach, Alyssa. My sister has gone to seek the presence and the lessons of Naissa. The High Priestess will hopefully educate us all a bit further."

"So we wait?" I asked, already knowing the answer.

"I don't see what the other option would be," Seren said. "Incidentally, Alyssa, my brother tells me your archery lessons are coming along nicely."

I have no idea why I blushed at that. It's not like I like the prince. He's an egotistic jerk. But he's also a good, and good looking, archery teacher, and so I guess I just couldn't help it.

She noticed, though, and shot him a glance. He noticed, too, and this time he didn't even try to hide his smirk.

Trying my best to cover all of that up, I said, "Your brother is a good teacher. Besides, you can't help but improve quickly at the rate of a hundred arrows a day."

"Though that is the typical practice regimen for our young archers, I always found the shooting to be tedious," Seren said.

"I don't. The discipline of the breath, combined with the repetitive motion of making every shot the same, make it better than Tai Chi," I said, hoping they didn't probe the comment. I was guessing, after all. I'd only ever seen Tai Chi done on TV.

"Ah. Well, I'm sure..." Seren started, but she was interrupted as the door whipped open and the High Priestess pretty much flew in, followed by a Meriel who I thought might actually be out of breath.

"Child—" Naissa breathed, looking at my pendant with an expression of wonder. "Where—where did you find that artifact?"

I shrugged, kind of pleased to have finally stumped Sternyface, but at the same time wishing I had a more exotic story to tell. "I'd love to say I discovered it on a long-lost beach in Tahiti, High Priestess, but the truth is less exciting. My mother gave it to me the night before I came here."

Naissa craned her neck to meet Seren's gaze, and the elder princess nodded. Finally catching her breath, the younger one said, "I bet the King had something to do with it." Naissa whipped her head around unbelievably fast to glare at Meriel, who actually shrank back with a cowed expression.

Amazed as I was at seeing the haughty Meriel driven down, I was glad to hear the High Priestess coming to my father's side as she said, "If the king played a part in Draignerthol coming into our future queen's possession, that is for His Majesty's consideration, not ours. Still, that would make for an interesting tale for him to tell us. You see, child," she said as she refocused her attention on me, "what you wear around your neck is...."

I finished the sentence for her. "...a great and powerful artifact from the earliest days of elven spell-weaving. I know, they've already told me that much. And Seren proved that it can bathe the room in a really cool blue light. But what is it used for?"

"Why, anything. It can be used for everything magical, truly, though of course nearly everything the pendant can be used for is now forbidden on Kiirajanna." Naissa lectured. If she was annoyed by my interruption she didn't show it. "It is to magical power what a lens is to light. Many magical lenses were created in the early days, but the one you wear is the most powerful of them all. With it, the sorceresses of old could focus destructive power that could be used to raze entire nations, fell entire forests, raise, or lower, or both, entire mountains. It was crafted early in the first epoch by the archmage Tyrion, who used its power to solidify his own land holdings and, over the course of many years, create the southern kingdom. His son inherited both the pendant and the throne, the latter of which he frittered away in rather meaningless wars against his neighbors. The pendant he lost upon his deathbed, having succumbed to a magical illness that is still suspected to have been assassination. It was ever-present in rumor and story, but no one confirmed a sighting for hundreds of years. Draignerthol reappeared just prior to the Sundering in the hands of the white sorceress Rhiannon, who wielded its power to knit closed the veil between the two worlds and thus end the battle. She, in a tremendous show of sacrifice, remained on the non-magical side, in the world you came from, Alyssa. The elder prophecies suggesting the return of Draignerthol to the lands at the same time as the return of the dragon queen have been considered mere wishful thinking, but—well, clearly, here it is."

"Wow," I said, wishing I could come up with something smarter to say but overwhelmed by the story as it was. I'd already been told the story of the epochs—four of them, in fact. The first was a time of widespread warfare that sounded an awful lot like what I'd read of the Middle Ages back on Earth. Hundreds of thousands, if not millions, of elves died through the ages back then as nations rose and fell, fueled in part by the armies of non-magical humans from the realm I'd come from. The end of that epoch we'd talked about; I already knew the heroic tale of Rhiannon singing the fabric between the magical and the non-magical shut and, in the process, sealing herself on Earth, forever bereft of the source of her own powers.

After the first epoch came, of course, the second. That epoch was famous mostly for what it didn't have: strife. After all of the battles of the first epoch, and then the loss of access to their non-magical pawns back on Earth, the elves settled down to fairly normal lives, if lives full of magic and mystery could be called normal. It was a golden time for the elves, a time when they all prospered.

It was the third epoch that was both the most interesting and the least documented. At least, it was the epoch from which the least documentation had survived. I actually listened with a great deal of interest as Naissa spun the tales of magical war followed by magical war. The realm was a lot larger than

I'd dreamed, it turned out. Those stories thoroughly enchanted me. Elven priests and priestesses and sorcerers and sorceresses went back and forth, developing new, stronger, better spells that could kill twice, three times the number of people that the previous spells could. Landscapes changed overnight, and an entire mountain was rumored to have disappeared once. The rifts between the magical and non-magical worlds had been re-opened, though this time they were left passable only to elves.

It was incredible.

It was the third epoch of Kiirajanna's history.

It was also the reason for the elves' current attitude toward magic. It wasn't that we couldn't wield it. It was that we shouldn't. Since the Treaty of 9962, when the Great Queen Somebody and the Wizard King Somebody Else signed the realms into what historians were calling the fourth epoch of peace, no one had considered even researching, much less casting, the powerful force-warping magic of the prior years.

Except, of course, for the elf who'd shot at me and then teleported. And the other attack, too. Naissa had already told me there was no way any but a very few elves would ever stoop so low, but I wasn't sure I believed her.

"So maybe Draignerthol stayed on the non-magical side of the rift and made its way into my mother's hands through completely non-magical means," I said.

"Maybe," Naissa said, her expression saying that she didn't think maybe. "Maybe your father, knowing the prophecies as he does, helped Draignerthol along in its journey."

I shrugged, not seeing any reason to care whether Dad had helped the pendant along. "Does it matter?"

"No, I suppose it does not," the High Priestess shocked me by agreeing with me, for once. "Although if we do have his efforts to thank, at least partly, for the return of such a significant relic of our past, we should bring that to his attention.

That is such an incredible find, after all. You must let us study it...."

"No," I said, my voice coming out more sharp than I'd thought it would. I softened my tone a little and said, "My momma gave me this, and I'm going to keep it close."

"I'm sure it maintains some sentimental value, Alyssa, and we can make certain to preserve that no matter what happens."

"But," I cut her off once again, "you won't need to. You can't use the pendant anyway, right? Nobody can, since the magic that it amplifies is forbidden. Right?"

"Right," the High Priestess said, her voice hesitant.

"So I will hold on to it to ensure its use does not happen. Anyway," I shifted the subject slightly, "you keep hinting about the prophecies. When are you going to teach them to me?"

"Whatever gave you the idea that I am going to teach you the prophecies?"

I shrugged and said, "It seems only fair. After all, there seems to be an awful lot in them about me." I heard three snorts from behind me and realized how that must've sounded, and quickly added, "No, that's not what I meant. But this ancient prophecy keeps getting thrust in my face, and so I'd sure like to find out what it says."

"I'm sure you would," the High Priestess said, the sarcasm in her voice causing three elf voices to chortle behind me.

"As the future queen, I need to know."

"Oh, well, then. Your future majesty, how's your ancient written elvish?" Naissa asked with an arched eyebrow.

"Funny, that's exactly what His Majesty said to me, without the double helping of sarcasm," I said.

"Well, then, I, too, shall say it without sarcasm. I am *not* going to teach you the prophecies. No elf is. It's too long a lesson to be passed along verbally. I will, however, be pleased to have you shown to where you can find the scrolls. I'm sure, given your silvery tongue, you can convince the archivist in the library to help you with any linguistic challenges you face."

"Fine," I said. "Lead the way, please."

She snorted at me once again. Apparently I was a good source of amusement. She said, "No. Not now, anyway. You have too much to learn to spend your training time traveling to a library that is days away solely in order to read ancient prophecy, no matter how much we may believe it applies to you personally. I will, however, instruct the temple guards to show you how to get there after your training, should you desire. Seren, please instruct our new scholar in the geography of this continent as it has changed through the four epochs, and if you have the opportunity, and she the ability, please also show her how to interpret the marks used by our ancestors to inscribe important works of literature."

The elder elf princess bowed her head and said, "Yes, High Priestess." I noticed the respect they paid her, really I did. I just didn't feel like copying it. It didn't matter, as Naissa nodded a goodbye to Seren and turned around to leave.

Halfway there, she stopped and looked back over her shoulder at me. She said, "Oh, and fair warning, our future queen. The library where the older scrolls are kept is not only a long and dangerous journey distant, but it is also dusty and might harbor a few vermin. You might be better served by less flowing attire if and when you go down to read the prophecies." I nodded, and she glided out of the door.

"I offended her, didn't I?" I asked as the door closed. I really didn't care what the answer was, but I was curious what the elf highborn would say.

"I think that a better word in your language would be exasperate, Alyssa," Seren said, and not unkindly. "The high priestess is used to receiving respect from all, even the king and the queen, and to be disrespected by her charge—yes, you have been assigned to her to teach, didn't you know?—even to the point of being physically assaulted is, well, repulsive to her. It goes against everything we've ever been taught as far as how any elf, much less a future elf queen, should behave."

"So you heard about the slugging, too," I said, feeling a little low about it. I'd felt a little low since it had happened, really, though I wouldn't bring myself to admit that to Sternyface.

"The whole castle has heard about the 'slugging,'" Seren said.

"Oh," was all I could muster.

"It will some day make its own epic tale," Meriel said with daggers in her grin, "how on feet aflame you sprinted away from the guards who were not following you, not to mention how low you managed to knock the king himself in bringing an end to your flight."

"I'm sure it will be," I replied, voice as cool as I could make it. "Though I'm also sure that history will show how disarmed the king was by the approach of his beautiful daughter."

"I'm sure," Seren agreed, apparently as a means of cutting us both off. "Now, can we begin the geography lesson with which we have been charged?"

LLANFAIRPWLLGWYNGYLLGOGERYCHWYRNDROBWLLLLANTYSILIOGOGOGOCH

The name of a town near where I was born in Wales. I spoke Welsh as a toddler, and now I speak Elf, which was the base language for Welsh, now, but no, I can't pronounce that town's name.

I Hate Geography

We did begin the geography lesson then, unfortunately, and no matter my desire to learn it, it was boring.

Oh, it had all the usual cast of characters. There was a mountain range over there, and a river beside it. There was a great lake somewhere, too, with a few towns around it that had been there since the first epoch. That last was important to the elves, too, though I didn't really get why.

The continent we were on was divided into four main regions. They were named Gogledd, Dwyrain, Gorllewyn, and—aw, heck, I'll just cut through the Elf for you. They were named North, South, East, and West, though I don't think I got the order right. Not very imaginative names, right? They did make sense as far as how the continent was divided, though. The North area was a land of snow and ice, where they had mild summers and winters that were cold as a banker's handshake. At some imaginary dividing line, apparently kept up by ranger weather magic—earth energy, that is—the East started, with its tall trees and massive mountains. The West, meanwhile, was a desert sheltered from the weather patterns of the remainder of the continent by a tall, jagged mountain range, while the South was, of all things, a tropical jungle.

The elves do love their cliches.

And in the middle was us, with our manicured forests and rolling mounds and great big castle and abbey, each setting back into a massive central hill. If only there'd been a Mount Doom somewhere nearby, I would've figured Tolkien had drawn the map.

I tried to pay attention, I really did. I'd hated geography back in junior high, and the royals' class reminded me vividly of why. At the time I'd thought I would never need to know the capitol of, say, France, or even Tennessee, and if I'd stayed there I would have probably been right. Here, though, I could see the importance. It wouldn't do, as they reminded me, for the elf queen to meet a subject from Somewheretown and have to ask "where is that?"

It didn't help that the names they threw at me were often just plain weird. I mean, who names a town Twffwllwch? It looked like a drunk monkey had sat down at a broken keyboard that didn't have any vowels on it and tried to type the sound of somebody gargling mouthwash. And yes, I'm smart enough to keep that comment to myself. I did stop Seren's lecture at that point long enough to ask a question, though.

"So, what is there in this Twffwllwch?" I stifled a grin; saying the name had actually felt like I was gargling mouthwash, and the mental image of the monkey trying to type the sounds I was making nearly made me lose it right there in front of the royal trio.

"Approximately five thousand elves."

"And?"

"And what, Alyssa?"

"And nothing, I guess. I just figured that at some point one of these towns would have something more interesting than 'approximately so many thousand elves.'"

"Something more interesting? Like what?"

I couldn't believe they didn't get it. "Like, oh, I don't know—a park, maybe. Botanical gardens. A library. A Piggly Wiggly or a Walmart, even. A thermonuclear weapons factory or a secret repository for alien technology, maybe. Something other than just houses, anyway."

"This Piggly Wiggly, it sounds like a children's center of some type?"

"Um, no. It's a grocery store," I said, already knowing they wouldn't understand that, either. Their mom, the queen, had probably never told them much about life on Earth. It was turning into a long talk over nothing, and with every breath I was getting more sorry I brought it up.

"A grocery store?" I was right—she didn't get it. At that point I found myself with a choice. Should I make up something way out there and have a little fun with the conversation, or just tell 'em the boring part and move on?

"It's where people go to buy their food." I chose Option B, hoping it would lead to an end to the geography lesson sooner.

"Why would they do that?"

"As opposed to having the palace cook staff bring their food to the table, you mean?"

"I'm aware that not everyone on Earth, just as not everyone on Kiirajanna, lives in palaces, Alyssa. But why would townsfolk buy their food instead of trading with their neighbors for it?"

That one I didn't have an answer for, so I just smiled and shrugged. I knew that at some point in the past on Earth we had been like that, but how we got from there to relying on su-permarkets for our food wasn't something I'd paid attention to in history class, I guess.

"If I had Wikipedia I could look it up for you, but I just don't know."

"Wikipedia?"

"It's a—oh, never mind." I was never going to win that one. "It's just a place to look stuff up. A library, sort of. Can we get back to the gripping list of towns on the eastern side of the continent, please?"

"Sarcasm?" Seren glared, one eyebrow raised.

"No, no. Not—well, okay, maybe a little. But it's what I need to know, so let's just get going so we can get done."

I would eventually have to learn the other continents too, and that excited me not at all. The one I was on, being the largest and most populous, was tough enough. Still, they had their own kingdoms, and their own royalty as a result, and the details were all important, they said. Everyone looked up to our continent, to our king and queen, for leadership, which meant that I would apparently some day be a sort of super-queen, but that supreme leadership role was, as the royal fam put it, tenuous at best.

I sighed.

"Bored, Princess?" Meriel asked.

"Yeah, a little. No, I'll be honest, I'm bored a lot. I never thought I'd be subjected to a lecture that was more dry than Mr. Dranson's history lessons, but you proved me wrong, bless your hearts. That, and going to intensive summer school in geography wasn't what I had in mind for doing right after I got my diploma."

Seren's expression was uncomfortable but not too bad. I was glad I hadn't taught them the real meaning of heart-blessing.

"If you have a way you'd prefer to learn, please let us know. We'll be overwhelmingly happy to hear of it," Meriel said, her tone making it clear that she was best buds with sarcasm.

"Ms. Danikowski. She taught history the old way, not by pointing to a map and telling us what happened there and on what date, but by telling us a story of the people involved, and working from that into the actual lesson. Surely the three of you know some stories. Let's try that."

"Converting a history lesson into story time? Humans have an—interesting—approach to learning," Seren mused. I could tell she didn't mean it unkindly, despite Meriel's snicker. "Okay, I think I can accommodate that. Let's try one and see how it works, okay?"

"You're not actually going to cater to *that*, are you, sister?"

"Dear Meriel, *that* is our future queen. Her education has been entrusted to us, no matter how much you would prefer to be enjoined in other pursuits. Do I need to ask Mother about granting you another lesson on duty to state?" Meriel shrank away from her sister, who turned back to me with a wry grin and said, "Besides, I must admit that giving lessons in the traditional way is every bit as boring as you say receiving them is, Alyssa. I—I think I'll enjoy trying it your way."

"It will be excellent practice for a vocation when you're old and grey, Sister, in a few years," Prince Charming said.

When Seren turned and stuck her tongue out at her brother, I figured there was some truth to it and asked, "Storyteller is a profession?"

He nodded. "Indeed. In the villages, it's one of the oldest and most honorable of professions. Second only, probably, to—um, never mind. Anyway, the competent storyteller need never worry about hunger, or more importantly, thirst, when traveling."

"Oh," I said. "A bard, then?"

"You call them bard, with a hard *deh* sound?" Seren asked. When I nodded, she smiled that crazy-wide elf smile of radiance. "Oh, Alyssa," she said, clapping her hands together at the apparent joy of it, "it is so pleasing to find so much of the old tongue in use in your world. Your—former world, that is.

Our term is bardd," she said, pronouncing it with the double d combination I'd come to know as a harder version of the *th*. "And yes, the bardd is revered throughout our lands. I do, of course, hope that I will never need to go into any type of profession, but if I do, that would be my choice."

"So just tell her a story already," Meriel snarled.

"Oh, I shall, but which one do I choose?"

"You're the bardd," Charming said. He plopped himself down into a chair and motioned for her to continue.

"Okay, fine. So, once, long ago, as you already know, the sorceress queen Rhiannon used the power of her pendant to seal the access between our worlds closed. She wasn't the only one involved, though. Many hundreds of elves—and humans, too—stood on this side and pressured the rifts closed. Included among them were a human mage named Alecsanddrha and a powerful elf sorceror...."

"Oh, not that story," her sister said. "It's so old."

"Shut up, Meriel," Keion shot, earning a glance of gratitude from Seren. "Proceed, Sis."

"Thank you, Keion. Meriel, it is old, but it's important. Besides, it can be used to explain geography, and not all tales are so convenient. So Alyssa, way back at the dawn of the second epoch, many thousands of years ago, many groups and clans came together out of a time of great strife. They knew that the only way to end the massive wars that threatened to tear our entire realm asunder was to shut off the flow of soldiers into it, and therefore they joined together in spite of their former status as enemies."

"To be honest, I did already know all that," I said. "Well, I did!" I defended myself as both Seren and Keion turned glares my way.

"Perhaps this would proceed more smoothly if we took up the traditional storytelling postures," Seren said, and her siblings pulled up three chairs in a semi-circle around her. I sat in the middle, as ordered by Charming's gesture, and the two each sat to one side and adopted eager expressions. Seren stood in the middle, shoulders back and nose in the air. She took a deep breath and began the story.

MAN A MAN A MWNCI

literally, spot and spot and monkey, which caught my ear because I vaguely remember having a monkey when I was young, for some reason. This, though, is how we say "might as well," which is probably how I ended up with a monkey when I was young.

A Love Story

Seren stood, head high, arms stretched out to each side, eyes nearly closed. She sucked in a deep breath, and then this is the enchanting story she told.

It is said that times of greatest turmoil create the greatest tales of love, and this is no exception. The wars had ravaged Kiirijanna for well over a century, with hundreds of thousands of men marching into battle on each side, all supported by elves wielding earth, wind, and fire shamelessly. Entire forests were burnt to the ground, mountains were turned asunder, and powerful rivers diverted from their former course or even made to disappear. In fact, by the time of the Miracle, the wars had gone on for so long that few remembered why they had begun in the first place. It was a time of great strife, of great loss, and of great sadness.

Finally did the elf queen Rhiannon come to her senses while

touring the desolation that had come to her lands. An ancient oak that had been badly burned in battle, yet was not quite dead, spoke to her in her mind of the pain and humiliation the wars were inflicting upon the forest and its creatures, and the shame and anguish the tree spirit's words put in her heart caused her to weep. It is said that she turned her magnificent gilt war chariot around that moment and returned to her castle, leaving both her troops and her fleeing foe to flounder in uncertainty. She returned to her tower, secure in all its protective spells, and she wept, and she wept, and she wept.

The cherished queen wept for one year and one day, and on the second day following the anniversary of the opening of her eyes she emerged from her tower. Her head was high, and her voice was shrill as she ordered emissaries sent to her enemies to request a council for peace. No matter how her advisors quailed and implored her to reconsider in light of their all but guaranteed eventual victory, she forced her will be done, and soon the fastest of her horses and her own cherished unicorns were dispatched far and wide.

Some of her messengers were met with taunts, or worse, but the queen had been absent from the war for so long that most were granted the ears of the rulers they sought. Their words, infused as they were with the magical energy of the tree spirits, moved elf queen, king, prince, and baroness, to in turn send their own detachment to listen further. Thus was secured a truce, the first peace the land had seen in dozens of years.

The detachments, followed by the actual patriarchs and matriarchs of each clan, met upon a hillock named Cysegredig. You already know this place, as it is the sacred hilltop into which both this cathedral and the current castle are built on opposite sides. There, above our heads, it was so many thousands of years ago, that the leaders of the elven race met to discuss our kind's future.

Now, remember, Alyssa, that the wars had by that time gone on for so long that none could recall why they had begun. Some were convinced that it was the warlike human spirit that had led us to such ends, and those voices wanted a purging of the elf bloodlines. Others proved more reasonable, holding that both human and elf were to blame.

Finally it was decided what must be done. The great queen, herself, agreed to sacrifice her magical inheritance as well as her standing by sealing herself on Earth for what she believed was all eternity. She alone lacked the power to perform such a tremendous feat, though, so she called all spell casters from all clans and all races together to help her weave the necessary energies.

The spell casters came, and they came in large numbers, and together they sealed the rift shut. That, then, would be an interesting enough story, if not for two of the spell casters. There was an elf prince from the east who proudly bore the name Afallon, from the sacred apple tree. He was young and both physically and magically strong, and many assumed he would take leadership of the elven hordes after the departure of Rhiannon.

Alas, that was not to be. At least, it was not to be for a long while, because of all the scandals he could have presented his race, it was a human lass who caught his heart. Alecsanddrha, of course, had been brought across the rift by the western clans, and so technically she was the enemy of Afallon. She, though, was taken by his regal figure, and he, in turn, was entranced by her long, flowing red hair as well as the knowledge she had gained of the arcane in the years since she had crossed over.

Keep in mind that by then humans and elves had been cross-breeding for some time, Alyssa. Thus, a human who could cast magical spells was not surprising. A human who could recall being raised on earth, though, and who had yet gained mastery of the arcane arts was something to be noted, and Alecsanddrha had that and beauty as well.

With those qualifications, then, she stole Afallon's heart. The two remained devoted to the magical challenge laid out before them, but in secret they made the vow of undying love. And that, to an elf, is a serious vow indeed, as it is made once, and only once.

The combined hosts camped upon Cysegredig for several weeks after the rift was closed, enjoying the peace that such mutual action had wrought. Alas, it was a peace that would not, or perhaps it could not, linger long. One chieftain or another infuriated his fellow in some way, or another, that is now lost to the pages of history, and soon enough old rivalries were remembered. Voices were raised, and steel was bared, but before a battle could break out the clerics stepped in. They declared this spot, this hill and its surroundings, sacred then and henceforth, and they sent the hosts back to their native lands.

This, of course, was a problem for Alecsanddrha and Afallon. They had come to the gathering in rival clans, and their chieftains were among those who had reinitiated the conflicts. That their clans' lands were very close together should have been good for the young lovers, but what it really meant was that war was enjoined almost immediately upon everyone's return, and as clashes became battles, the lines were staked out and fortified. They found it harder, and harder, and then impossible, to meet, to see their beloved's face, to clasp a loving hand to a tender heart, in the midst of such martial vigor.

They were wise, though, and they were both powerful in the art of nature-shifting that we still call upon to this day. From well inside the clan lines to the east, Afallon hid from his own while he sang into being a wondrous westward-pointing tunnel system. To protect it against military use in the event of discovery, he shaped a below-ground labyrinth, laying in false tunnels and elaborate traps. He was particularly proud, it is said, of his air inlet system that would snuff any torch brought into the tunnel.

You are, I am sure, wondering how he himself would navigate around such a dangerous place. The secret was in the glow crystals, magical lights he spirited away from his chieftain's cache. Afallon imbued them with his own magic, cued by a single word. And he had to choose that word well, because those who would do violence through his tunnel system could not be allowed to guess it even if they knew him or his beloved.

You know what he chose? Of course, you couldn't. That's the point, isn't it? Both he and his beloved, though, loved the fine exercise of reading. Alecsanddrha had even brought scrolls with her from Earth, and these were the most secretly treasured of her possessions. Thus, he instructed his magical lights to illuminate the path at the breathed word *darllen.* It is, as you know, our word for reading, and Afallon reasoned that no army would use that word on a march.

Birds were being watched as they traveled between the camps, so Afallon enlisted the aid of a young buck to carry word to Alecsanddrha of his plan. Soon she, too, was crafting tunnels with song, eastward bound in her case. She sang of her love, of their long and beautiful future together, and in so doing shaped long and beautiful paths underneath the countryside. While still a labyrinth, her effort was more of a maze, one designed to lead intruders astray for long, long periods of time. The false tunnels narrowed slowly, finally over the course of several miles coming to a point where a group of armed men would find it difficult to turn around. She carefully extracted glow crystals from the ground in her lands and used them in the same way Afallon had, lighting the way with the utterance of a single word.

Neither lover communicated the special word to the other for fear of interception of the message. Of course, they wouldn't. You already assumed that, didn't you?

The day finally came, many months after they had started their labor literally of love, when the tunnels met. By design, they had joined underneath a terrible no-man's-land, a rocky area between both clans that had been so tragically, magically blasted during the previous century of war that nothing could live within its smoky presence. Nothing, that is, except the love of two elf mages who climbed out of the tunnels and into each others' desolate arms.

It took enormous power to turn the center of the blight around to green again, but working together the couple did just that. First, they removed the poison from the ground in a small spot and planted a tree that Afallon had brought. Then they did the same thing to start a tree that Alecsanddrha had. Then the pair raised a magical melody such as had never been heard, and the tree spirits heard and were pleased, and they grew, and they grew.

As the trees took over the dank gray soil and twined together to form the beginnings of a home for them, the couple realized that the tunnels they had wisely crafted could not protect them against the eyes of sentries. Thus, they sang a different song, raising an illusory wall of blight to conceal their efforts. By then they were exhausted, and so they rested, together, finally two as one.

There, they remained for many months, singing together to bring their new abode into being. Every day their home grew as their love did the same.

With a safe and comfortable home, the couple began working on both his and her first love, books. Together they traveled, in disguise on this continent and openly on the others, collecting what works they could find. Their work was timely, too, as several of the elder libraries had been decimated in the wars and their books and scrolls were in dire need of care.

Care, they gave them, occasionally re-binding or even re-writing the ancient works to preserve the knowledge contained within. Soon, within the blighted ring of war's ultimate desolation, a small collection grew into the largest store of wisdom in all of Kiirajanna.

Then, one day a few years after the couple had first met in their tunnels under the damaged landscape, the brother of Afallon showed up. He was barely alive, his ability to avoid the deadliest of the tunnel system's traps his only savior. Once Alecsanddrha had used her powerful healing voice to sing him back to health, he explained the dire circumstances that had pressed him to track his brother. You see, the old chieftain had passed away. Some said his death was by accident, while others suggested a fouler reason. No matter the culprit, though, the people were clamoring for peace, and they were clamoring also for the return of the old bloodline, the first-born descendant in the line of the primal king of the elves.

They were clamoring for Afallon.

They were clamoring for Afallon, *not* Afallon and Alecsanddrha, the brother continued. She was, after all, not an elf, and for elves to follow a human, or even an elf king who was joined to a human, would be unthinkable to all.

"All, including you, Brother?" Afallon asked, and he was greatly saddened by the agreement in his brother's reluctant nod. He explained that, no matter her birthplace or birthright, he could never, ever leave his beloved. His brother would have to return to the people, he said, and tell them Afallon was no longer available to lead them. Afallon, he must claim, was dead.

It was not long after this that Alecsanddrha and Afallon were graced with the promise of another generation. Her belly swelled, and soon it was evident that not one, but two new heartbeats joined together with hers. The couple wept with joy every evening considering the future that twins would bring.

As the time for childbirth grew closer, Afallon sent word to his brother asking for a midwife's assistance. Alas, he was told, Afallon was dead and could need no assistance from his former tribe. Alecsanddrha, in a show of both trust and desperation, reached out to her former tribe asking the same, but the human girl was ignored. Alone, then, the couple set out to deliver the two babies into the world.

The first twin passed through the birth canal with no problem, entering the world with the smile and giggle that is customary with highborn elf babies. The second was much harder, though, attempting at first to pass into the world sideways and then backward. The long and painful birth process finally ended as Afallon pulled the screaming baby free of the mother's body, but Alecsanddrha was dying even as her second-born took its first life-giving breath. Her blood fell on the stone floor, draining along with it all of the happiness from Afallon's very existence.

With Alecsanddrha gone, Afallon knew he could not raise his two daughters on his own. He renamed his home Llyfrgell o Alecsanddrha, which translates to the library of his beloved. His daughters, both of whom had lived through the death of their mother as perfect little children, he named Gwenhwyvar and Gwenhwyvach, the root meaning fair and holy, and -var meaning greater while -vach means lesser, as you already know.

With great sadness in his heart, Afallon set wards on his former home, now his wife's tomb and the literary museum in her honor, and left with his twin babies to return to his clan. When he saw his brother he was enraged at the refusal to send midwifery help. Then, when his brother explained that all was better because of the outcome of that decision, Afallon's anger became darker. He slew his brother that moment with a dark, angry spell that reverberated from the mountainsides, shaking a great many elves out of their midnight slumber. When they emerged from their homes, they found Afallon returned, very much alive, and now very much their king.

In order to protect his beloved's final resting place, Afallon forged a peace with his neighboring clan that lasted many centuries. The Library continued to grow, gaining its own order of priests to oversee its collection as well as its enclosed tomb. It stands, in fact, to this day, though the blight that once surrounded it was eradicated with the passage of time.

You may be wondering what happened to Afallon's twin daughters, as well you should. They grew up sisters, though both of them despised that arrangement. In part, their animosity toward one another was fueled by the circumstances of their birth and their mother's death, and it was also spurred by the names their father had chosen for them. What happened to them both is another story, to be told at another time, but it is important to end this story with the news that one of the sisters became the most powerful queen Kiirajanna has ever seen, asserting her half-human birth as a sign of strength.

Thus was the dawning of a new age of Kiirajanna.

DW I'N DY GARU DI

"I love you," in the most beautiful language ever.
No, really -- try it, like this: doo-in dee garih dee.

A Story Partly Explained

Seren stood there for a minute as her last words echoed around the room. I couldn't tell whether she was more pleased with herself for telling a great story, or spent from the effort. She looked both.

"Wine. I think I would like some wine," the princess said. "Now I understand why the bardds prefer to drink so heavily, as stories like that transform the moisture in our throats to the feelings behind the words." She sat down as her brother brought her a glass of wine from the pitcher on the mantle.

"Very nice job, Sister," Keion said. "I have never heard that tale told so beautifully."

"I agree it was well done, but...." I said, not sure how to say what I was thinking.

"But what, Alyssa?" Seren asked, turning an open expression my way. She seemed to genuinely want to hear my opinion. Meanwhile, Meriel glared at me, apparently thinking I was about to make disparaging remarks about her sister's storytelling abilities. Nobody had permission, I guess, to disparage her sister quite like Meriel gave herself. It didn't matter; I wasn't about to do that.

"But— But, well, Gwenhwyvar? Afallon? Sounds like the story was taken right out of Arthurian legend."

"Hmm," Seren said, nodding. "That is an astute observation, but I must suggest that it is more likely to have been the other way around. After all, our legends are several millennia old, while yours are but one or two. Besides, you forget that since the first sundering, elves could go to the human world— and tell our stories—while humans could not return the favor."

"Yeah," I had to agree. "But where does Alecsanddrha fit into the old Earth stories? I mean, it must, because there actually was a fabled Library of Alexandria on Earth, somewhere— um, well, somewhere over in the Middle East. Morocco, or Turkey, I think. Wherever it was, its name doesn't sound at all like an elf name."

"She was not an elf, remember?" Seren said after taking a long pull from her wine glass.

"I do remember, but it seems such a coincidence with there being a Library of Alexandria in real life."

"Real life?" Keion interjected, sharply cutting me off with a glare that somehow also seemed amused. "You mean real life in your former realm on Earth, do you not, Alyssa? There was, in fact, a Library of Alecsanddrha in real life right here in Kiirajanna."

"Well, of course. But definitions aside, bless your heart, it's still quite a coincidence."

"Judging from when and how you say that phrase, I don't think you're actually wishing my heart to be blessed."

"Ya think?"

"No, I don't. But that is your point, is it not?" Keion shook his head and then said, "The English language seems to have suffered greatly in the years since our mother taught it to us."

"She wasn't from Mississippi, though, was she?"

"Well, considering the fact that I have absolutely no idea where this 'Mississippi' is, I would have to venture a guess that no, she was not from there. She was born in Oxford."

"Oh, I know where that is. It's not very far from my home, really."

"And yet, she sounds nothing like you," Keion said, his voice dripping with—something.

"Well, it is a college town. Maybe her mom was a teacher at Ole Miss or something."

"Old what?"

"Not old. *Ole* Miss. The University of Mississippi."

"We will have to ask her about that, I suppose. She told us about the University of Oxford, not the University of Mississippi."

"Hmm, I didn't know there was a University of Oxford there. The only University of Oxford I've heard about is—hey, you're British!" As soon as I'd said University of Oxford the memories had come unbidden of talks I'd had with my counselor about Rhodes Scholarships and which American colleges had earned the most—or, for that matter, any at all. He'd been convinced I was throwing my brain down the toilet by going to Mississippi State, apparently. I'd disagreed, but that was all water under the bridge now. Oxford, Mississippi, home of Ole Miss the University, is very different from Oxford, England, home of the University of Oxford and the Rhodes Scholarship. Coming back to the present, I felt my cheeks warm up in embarrassment over that mistake.

"No, dear. 'British' is such a llwdy distinction. We're elves, and so, now, are you," Seren said, her voice even and gentle. The word she used, though, was a new one. Llwdy— pronounced as she did with an uplifted nasally 'l' sound followed by 'you' and then 'dee'—wasn't a word I'd heard in Elf. I caught on to the intended slur against my human half from the context, though, and it stung a little.

"No, I meant—never mind," I said, realizing that arguing that their mother, the queen of the elves of Kiirajanna, had been born British—as well as human, too—would do more harm than good. "So, this library actually exists?" I changed the subject.

"It does," Seren said.

"I'd love to see it. How far from here is it?"

"Several days travel."

"And that's where the prophecy is housed, isn't it?"

"You catch on with the speed of a malwen."

"I do speak *some* Elf, you know," I said, ignoring the grins behind me and trying not to get angry over being compared to a snail.

"I did not know for certain, but I was hoping for it to be the case," Seren said.

"Have you been there? To the library?" I was really hoping to get back to where she'd almost been friendly to me.

"I have not. It is said to be both stately and enormous, though, and full of an incredible assortment of literature. In a way, I envy you your journey."

"If and when I have a chance to go," I said. "It's days away, as you said, and I'm not sure I can take the time away from my *lessons*."

"I would bet that you can find a way," Seren said. "That ranger cousin of yours, in spite of our gentle ridicule, has quite a lot to teach you as well. She could continue your lessons on the road, and then you would have all day to read the scrolls once you arrived."

"If this journey happens, I'd like to go too," Keion said. When his sisters looked surprised, he shrugged defensively and continued, "I've always wanted to read some of the works they are rumored to have there."

"You—read?" Meriel said, her voice scornfully disbelieving. Part of me felt bad for Keion, but at the same time it was a relief to see Drizella's venom directed somewhere else.

"Of course," he said, wiggling his eyebrows up and down. Apparently insults were nothing more than a family love greeting for the royal trio. Prince Charming continued with, "Well, that, and somebody will have to protect our future queen while at the same time continuing her self defense lessons. Would you prefer to traipse along and perform that duty, Sister Dear?"

"I'd rather eat dirt," Meriel said. "No offense intended, dear Alyssa."

"I'm sure," I replied, feeling the exact opposite. My 'bless your heart' had been exposed for the insult it was intended to be, so I left my best sarcastic tone alone in its place. The glare I got in return said *job well done.*

"Excellent," Seren said, her voice sounding like it really was a little bit less than excellent. "You are finally catching on to the fine art of sarcasm."

"Catching on? I've been using that art all my life."

"Using is such a general term. We elves wield sarcasm like a rapier, while llwdy bludgeon each other with it. You must develop a lighter touch."

"Hold on. You've used that word already: llwdy. It's a pretty word, but it's obviously a derogatory term. And I've not heard it before, either. What does it mean in the elven tongue?"

"Llwdy is not from our language, but has instead survived, as many of our greatest insults have, from a much more ancient tongue. Some scholars say it is the original tongue, both of elf and of human, that we now know of only through snippets and insults. You are correct, though, in your surmising that it is an insulting term for humans."

"My momma is a human, so be careful slinging that

around."

"Yes, so she is, and I have heard how vigorously you elect to defend her honor." Her smile curled itself up into a sarcastic leer before it dropped back into a sincere glimmer. "Fear not, Alyssa. I stand nothing to gain through inciting you to violence."

"You probably have wards built up around you, too."

"No. Only the most elevated among the priesthood use shielding energy, and then only when it is likely to be needed. I have naught but the best athlete and warrior in the realm as a brother, and I should remind you that that brother is standing just a single quick step to your side." I glanced sideways and saw his leer, and then I showed her my hands, open-palmed, as a gesture of peace.

She continued, "And now, I believe that our time is over."

I looked out the beautifully colored stained glass windows at the darkening sky and nodded. "I'll ask my father about the trip," I said, and then I skipped out the door to do exactly that. There was no point in wasting time.

To Plan A Trip

"Absolutely not," the Elf King said.

I should say: Daddy said. I'm not sure why I'd taken to calling and thinking of him as Daddy when I wanted something, I just rationalized it as all the years I never got to ask for anything when I was younger. It was an easy habit to fall into, anyway.

Only now, he wasn't looking like Daddy. I'd caught him at the tail end of a ruling session, or whatever you call those periods when the royal duo sat on their paired thrones and declared judgment upon all of the questions presented to them. The queen had left quickly when I entered, but he stayed, seated in his throne, his golden and bejeweled crown perched on his royal head, my father looking as regal as I can imagine anybody ever looking.

"Why not?" I asked, trying not to come off as intimidated.

"The Library of Alecsanddrha is several days of arduous and unprotected travel away. It was not that long ago that several attacks on your life occurred, remember? What makes you believe that I can ensure your safety as you journey that far away, daughter?"

"I bet Aerona can."

"I bet Aerona is not going to like you suggesting that she traipse across the continent so that you can read a scroll."

"Who cares? You're the king."

"And that line right there, my daughter dearest, is what leads a noble ruler into despot-ville nearly every time."

"So you just let your subjects decide what to do? What's the point of having a pretty crown, then?"

"Well, it *is* pretty. I like looking into the mirror and seeing it glitter and stuff. Do you not think it sets my eyes off just perfectly?" Dad turned his head toward the wall that actually was mirrored, of all things, and struck a beauty-queen-like pose, batting his eyelashes and smiling that dazzling elf smile I'd seen.

"Dad, that sounded—"

"Effeminate? Indeed. But I am the king, so who cares, right?" He turned back to me and relaxed into his chair, a pleasant smile replacing the too-giddy one.

"Okay, you got me. But still, I don't see the point of ruling if you're just going to leave everything up to the people."

"I am not leaving anything up to the people. I am saying no, both as your father and as your king."

"But you are saying no based on what Aerona might say."

"No, I am saying no based on what I believe. That said, what Aerona might say is important to me. Alyssa—and this is important, dear, because someday sooner than you realize you will be doing this same thing—ruling is not just about knowing what to do and telling everybody to do it. As a matter of fact, I have often found that others, no matter their station in society, can come up with much better ideas and solutions than mine. Being a ruler is about listening to the people, about understanding and caring and trying to help them solve their issues and continue their normal, happy lives. Yes, sometimes it does involve imposing your will upon others, but being a good ruler also requires knowing when to do that, and when not."

"How do you know?" I really was curious; what he was telling me had never occurred to me before. I'd always just thought—well, never mind. What I'd thought sounds dumb now.

He shrugged and said, "Sometimes, you don't know. Lots of times, at first. That is where experience comes in, honestly. At first you listen carefully, you think a lot about what people are capable of, and you admit it when you are wrong. Once you have built up some trust in your subjects, and you have learned who you can trust in turn, then it starts becoming easier, almost second nature. A good rule of thumb, though, is to gauge carefully the strength of someone's emotional ties to a situation. This rule of thumb applies to your own decisions, as well, by the way. The stronger someone is tied to a problem emotionally, the less chance they will come up with the best solution for themselves."

"So the more emotionally someone is tied to their problem, the more likely you're going to have to tick them off over it?"

"You can also put it that way, I suppose. It is not always a matter of angering your people, though. Often it is better to force them, in the manner of respect for the crown if nothing else, to calm down and explain the situation clearly. That, in itself, usually detaches them enough that they see what they can best do to resolve their issue."

"That's smooth," I said.

"*Smooth*? Okay, I suppose."

"So are there such things as dragons?"

"Where did that come from, Alyssa?"

I honestly wasn't sure, myself. Sometimes my brain just throws out random stuff, and when I'm around somebody I trust, my mouth just tosses it along, right out there. I wasn't going to tell Dad that, though.

"Sorry for the jump. It was something we talked about today. This pendant Mom gave me is the shape of a dragon, and my dragon birthmark was something you mentioned when you came to whisk me away to your strange world here. But that's the only place I've seen dragons, and nobody's talked about them, so I'm wondering if they really exist."

"You have petted a unicorn, and now you ask whether dragons exist?"

"Well, I wouldn't want to pet one of those. Would I?" I realized I wasn't really sure. Most of the stories I'd heard have dragons as mean creatures who exist to eat humans, and dwarves, and so on, but then again there was that old movie about the boy who had a nice dragon that nobody else could see. What did I know? Maybe dragons, in reality—if I could call the elf realm reality—were fluffy and cuddly like big sheep dogs?

Dad's expression confirmed that I had it right the first time, though. His eyes narrowed and he peered off into the distance with the same look Keion got when he'd showed off by shooting at a long target. "No," he finally said, his voice soft but hard. "You would definitely not want to pet one, if they still roamed the land. Luckily you will never have to worry about that, though, as the last dragon was killed—at great cost of elven life, mind you—several thousand years ago."

"What were they like?"

"Fearsome. According to legend, they stood our height when they hatched and continued growing their entire lives. Stories tell of adult dragons with dark leathery wings that spanned as wide as this castle. They had four legs, each tipped with several long, razor-sharp claws, and they were strong enough that they could rip an elf clean in half with them. The beasts were covered in scales, too—scales so hard that no archer could shoot through. It is that fact, I was told, that is the reason we developed such a devotion to accuracy. When your life depends upon your ability to hit an eye or a nostril, I suppose that you get pretty good at it."

"What color were they?"

"Depends on the story. They might have come in all colors, in fact, if all the old stories are correct. Most often, though, they were described as a deep, fiery red color, with orange vertical slits for eyes, and black glistening claws."

"Scary, but I bet the beasts wouldn't seem as scary if we still allowed elves the use of magic," I probed.

"Do not say that, Alyssa. Such a thought is evil. Besides, your assumption that the dragons were just beasts would have gotten you killed. Intelligent, they were, and quite strong in the use of magic, also."

"And they could breathe fire, I'd guess."

"Of course."

"Big, strong, sharp claws, fire breath, *and* powerful magic," I said, ticking off the dragon's weapons on my fingers. "That hardly sounds fair that they got that many strengths."

"Life is not fair, Alyssa. Just be thankful that they no longer exist."

"There's probably a bardd's tale about how the last one perished," I said, proud of myself for remembering the softer-sounding double d's at the end of the elf word.

"There is, indeed. Next time we see a bardd, I will make sure to request it." He gave me the *I know what you're going to ask, and the answer is already no* look.

"Seren told a bardd's tale today. It was really good." I hoped he'd catch what I wanted and do it anyway.

"That's nice."

His eyes said he'd caught what I wanted but the answer

was still no, so I went straight on in. "Some day, when we have time, would you tell me that story?" Not sure why that hit me like it did; once again, brain gushes stuff out, mouth gives it voice sometimes. It was just that I'd grown up dreaming for a dad to tell me stories. Silly thing to dream of, granted, but that was what seemed like a normal life to me. That was just how little girls who still had their daddies around grew up.

I gave him the eyes. You know, the sad little girl eyes that always melt a guy's heart? They even sometimes worked on Momma.

They worked on him. "Sure," he said around a capitulating sigh. "Just not tonight, because I have been talking all day and I am quite tired as a result. And do not tell anyone, please? It is one thing for a father to tell a story to his little girl, but we do not want people thinking that the king wants to be a bardd."

"Of course not, Daddy. Now, can we talk some more about that trip to Alecsanddrha?" I gave him the eyes again.

They didn't work.

"We can talk all night about it, but no, you are not going," he said as he hefted himself wearily from the throne. "On second thought, no, we cannot talk all night about it. I am tired, Alyssa, and it is time for dinner."

"Okay, Dad" was all I had time to say as he walked into his private study and closed the door behind him. I was going to have to work on that one.

Private Dinner with Seph

"No way, huh?" Seph asked around a mouthful of some sort of green vegetable.

I shook my head and then took a second to wash down the roast I'd been chewing on with a mouthful of cider. Mouth clear, I said, "No. He won't even consider letting me go to the library to read the prophecy that is supposedly written about me."

"Actually, Princess, he didn't say he won't let you go to the library. He just said he couldn't protect you there, and so at this time it is not advisable."

"Thanks for the clarification, Aerona," I glared over my shoulder at my linebacker of a bodyguard.

"You're welcome, Princess," she said. I've got to give it to her—the expression on her face put Sternyface to shame. Whether she caught my sarcasm or not was completely undetectable. It didn't matter, though; she kept on standing there, watching Seph and me eating our supper up in my room, her eyes sweeping from one wall to the next and back again, her stance invincible.

To be honest, it made me feel a lot more comfortable.

The other night, while I'd slept on a cot in the king's—Dad's—room with just my picture of Momma near, Aerona and some of the high priestess's most faithful followers, I'd been told, had scoured my room for traps. They'd gone wall to wall, floor to ceiling. They'd left nothing unturned, not even a pillow. I was glad I hadn't brought much of anything with me, or I'd have felt a lot more violated than I did when they told me about the search. As it was, I was mostly just happy that they'd gone to such effort.

The kitchen staff, most likely spurred on by my father, had insisted on serving us up in my room. It was to keep prying eyes away, they said, but I bet it was also to keep anyone from being able to target me in a room full of people. Oh, and to avoid the possibility of poisoning, too, I figured. That scared me, by the way. The fact that I might not be able to enjoy being in a gathering again for a long time really scared me, because I found myself liking the elves. I enjoyed sitting and talking with them, and over supper was the perfect time to do that.

Oh, well.

"So, what did they find out from Stith?" I asked Seph and ignored the hiss the question brought from Aerona. It brought a glare from Seph, too, though, and that wasn't a good sign.

"Stith didn't make it down to questioning," Seph said, glaring at a particularly challenging potato on her plate. The poor plant was taking all of Seph's ire that my friend was trying so hard not to direct my way.

"Did the potato kill him?" I asked, trying to inject some humor. "Bad potato! Bad!"

"Nobody killed Stith, Princess," Aerona said. "He was sent down under his own watch, and he apparently teleported out of the castle on the way."

"Another teleport I didn't sense," I said, really starting to feel picked on by the magic of the realm.

"No one did," Aerona said. "Stith just never reached the captain of the guard's room, though there wasn't any other path for him to take. The only possibility is that he teleported somewhere along the way without us feeling him go."

"But Dad—the King—sensed the teleport in this room from way out there," I said, pointing uselessly out of the room through the exterior wall. Yes, they knew where we'd been when Dad had leaped from the chariot to go charging up to my room. It was still pretty dang impressive to me, actually.

"Well, there are dampeners, at least according to legend, Princess."

"I'm still new to all this legend, Aerona, but if the enemy has dampeners, why didn't he use them the first time?"

For the first time, I saw an emotion wash across the elf brawler's face. I nearly gushed that it was a positive one, in fact. She actually looked impressed, and she said, "A sound observation, Princess. But the problem is that we do not know what the enemy has and what he has not. You must remember that we're still considering the possibility that the first attacker teleported specifically to steal our attention away from the second attacker's motion, as it was only your father's keen observation that ferreted out the second elf. It is entirely possible that he had a dampener but elected not to use it."

"So, basically, what we know is that we don't know much of anything specific."

"That is, basically, correct, Princess."

I sighed. It wasn't really going anywhere. "Aerona, could we by any chance have some girls time, some privacy? Just my cousin and me?"

She made a show of thinking about my request for several long moments. Finally she nodded and said, "I suppose that can be arranged, Princess. I would object, but that little monster keeps looking at my legs as though he's wondering if they'd be tasty with gwaed sauce. I'll be right outside the door should you need me."

She stepped out into the hall and closed the door behind her.

"Do I want to know what gwaed sauce is?" I asked Seph. She crinkled her nose and shook her head.

"That's what I thought. Now, about the library—"

"Your father said no," she said, surprising me with how quickly she figured out where I was going with it.

"So?"

"I should hardly need to remind you of this, as often as you remind me, but your father is His Royal Majesty, the Elf King. The ruler of all of Kiirajanna. It is a capital crime to disobey him. And capital means—"

"I know what a capital crime is. Surely he wouldn't put his beloved daughter, the bearer of the fabled birthmark, to death," I argued, really hoping she would agree.

"Surely you wouldn't put him in a position where he has to make that choice," she said.

"I'm thinking about it. And don't call me Shirley," I joked.

"I didn't call you Shirley," she said, her head tilting into her confused pose.

"I know, sorry. It's just a line from an old movie."

"What's a movie?"

How do you explain something like a movie to someone who's never even been to the human realm of Earth? She'd just think it was magic, and thus forbidden and evil and stuff. Heck, I thought it was magic most of the time, and I had a vague idea how it worked. "Never mind," I said. "It's just an old Earth storytelling method."

"Oh, a bardd!" Her face lit up, and I hated to unlight it for her.

"No, not a bardd. It's kind of an automated storyteller with pictures." I mentally kicked myself; I had, after all, decided not to explain because of the possible reference to magic, and there it was.

Luckily she didn't take the bait. Instead she focused on the outcome and said, "An automated storyteller? It sounds boring."

"It can be, especially the—oh, never mind," I said. Once again I'd been about to be sarcastic, and that would've just taken the talk back where I didn't want it to go.

See? I was trainable, no matter what the nasal trio said.

"So," I plunged ahead, "back to the topic at hand: our trip. You are coming with me, right? It'll be so exciting!"

"Alyssa, you're speaking pure madness."

"No, I'm not. He'll never expect just the two of us to set out across the land. And who better to protect me than my ranger cousin and her familiar Booboo?"

"I think that's the first time you've gotten his name right," Seph said, and she was right. I'd done it on purpose. No point telling her that, though. It would spoil the advantage.

"So you'll come?"

"No. His Majesty will expect precisely that trick from you. You're his daughter, after all. You should hear the tales of the exploits he got into when he was younger."

"I should," I agreed. Matter of fact, I really did want to hear those tales, but I had a more important job at the moment. "But later. Even if he expects it, what's he going to do? Bind me to the castle so I can't leave?"

"He might do exactly that, Alyssa. And he'd be right to. You only have one life. One. There are obviously a group of people who want to see you dead. You owe it to yourself, and to your father, and to the entire realm to stay safe from that group of people. I'm not sure where you got the idea that I could protect you, but I'm not that advanced in my training. Rangers my age are out there picking up pine cones, not guarding future queens on forbidden journeys. No. Just—no. Really, Alyssa. I mean no."

"You're going to make me travel to the library by myself?" Heck, I wasn't immune to guilt, so I figured she might not be either.

"Would you rather I just told your father and stopped you?"

"Well, no."

"Then drop it, please, Alyssa. I don't want to be a taleteller, but I will to save your life."

"Okay, fine," I said. I let it go, but I could tell from the glimmer in her expression that I had an opening with the argument.

We ate the rest of our food quietly, neither of us apparently wanting to re-hash the argument we'd just finished.

"Good night, Seph," I said as she left. She replied and walked out, Aerona marched in, and I settled down to dream of a trip to see the library.

Learning the Script

The next few evenings were the same. The kitchen staff insisted upon serving my and Seph's suppers in the privacy, comfort, and safety of my room, and Aerona stood guard over us till we told her to go into the hall, and then we bickered over my desire to go to the library. Seph didn't seem to get tired of saying no, a fact that I took to be a good omen.

My training, on the other hand, changed a lot. The next morning I sauntered into the siblings' office and told them I wanted to learn to read ancient written elvish, and that was that. They agreed way too cheerfully, and then I found out why. None of them was—I'm not sure if interested or qualified is the better word to use—in teaching that language. Each one said, a little too fast and loud, that of course he or she could read it him or herself, but that it wasn't a topic they should teach me. Uh, huh. I figure none of them really knew the language. At least, not very well.

Thus it was that a kind old priestess was assigned to teach me to read the little scribbles of the ancient writings. And, by the way, it was a good thing she was kind, because it was hard.

She didn't start off teaching me about letters and scribbles at all, actually. Instead, she started telling me about trees and bushes. When I interrupted that I was there to learn to read, not do forestry, she just smiled at me like I was a special sort of child, nodded, and continued her litany of trees. It was birch, and then alder, and then—oh, you probably don't care, do you? I don't want to bore you as much as I was.

I mean, she used the elf words for the trees instead of English, but it was still just a litany of trees.

Finally, after several mind-numbing hours of saying and repeating the trees and plants, in order from birch to gooseberry, the old priestess whose name I can't remember rose from her chair in silence. I was overjoyed, just by a single movement. Then she motioned me up to the chalkboard and pressed a piece of chalk into my hand. I was elated!

Then I started drawing trees with her, and my elation dimmed.

Well, they weren't real trees. It was really just lines that represented trees. Birch, for example, was a horizontal line on top of a vertical one—more of a "T" shape. Willow was like a T with four trunks, which I understood since we had a beautifully overhung weeping willow tree in our yard back home. Some trees had their horizontal bar at the bottom, and some in the middle. Some of the trees with bars in the middle had slanted trunks. It was all confusing, but her explanations of the nature of the trees and bushes helped the pictographs slowly make more sense.

She sent me to supper after we'd been through the drawings a couple of times, making me promise to come directly back to that room after archery practice in the morning. After a whole day of trees and bushes I wasn't sure that was a great use of my time, but I agreed anyway. After all, I'd asked for it, and from the look on the old elf's face the chance to teach me what she knew was the thrill of her life.

I told Seph about the trees over supper.

"That's how they teach the alphabet," she said, nodding like it was the most normal thing in the world.

"It's trees and bushes," I said, unable to believe it was normal.

"That's the alphabet, Alyssa. Our alphabet is based on the world in which we exist. Show me the symbol for birch."

I drew it out using my finger on the bed spread.

She nodded and said, "Yes, that's birch. That's our letter b. It's the first letter of the alphabet. See how easy it is?"

I sat back and thought for a second, not sure I saw the connection or the easiness. "B is the *first* letter of the alphabet?" I asked. When she nodded emphatically, I asked, "Why aren't the letters in order?"

"They are in order, Alyssa."

"No, they're not. A comes first."

"A, the vowel? When does a vowel come first?"

"It—oh, I get it. The elf alphabet strips the vowels out to the end. So it goes b, c, d...." As vigorously as she shook her head I was surprised she didn't hurt her eyes or her neck.

"No, silly. It goes b, l, f, and so on."

"Why are they so out of order?"

"Alyssa, they're *in order*. They're in order to us, anyway. Your alphabet may be all mixed up, but ours is just fine."

"Oh," was all I said, and then I went back to eating and thinking. Thinking, and eating. Thinking, eating, and asking about a trip to the library, only to get shot down again.

I was going to win her over, I was sure.

The next day the kind old priestess morphed into an evil little taskmistress. She started me out reciting the plants, and when I so much as paused she made me start on it again, from the top, and with feeling. "No! Again! No! Again!" was the mantra of the morning.

I started to think that I was going to spend life hating trees.

Finally I just stopped. "Can. I. Get. Some. Water?" I asked, my breaths making each word into its own sentence.

She just nodded and glared.

"Where did the nice teacher I knew yesterday go?" I asked after a gulp of cool refreshment.

She just glared at me without responding.

I finally got it. I don't know how many times in a row she made me get through the plants list without error, but it was a bunch. Eventually, though, practice makes perfect, and practice also makes me perfectly irritated. I *was* irritated, but she finally let me take to the board with chalk.

Once again, though, the nice priestess of the day before had been replaced by her evil doppelganger. Now, instead of repeating adages about trees and bushes and their resemblances to stick figures, she stood guard as I made neat lines of scrawls that passed for letters on the board, in order, one after another. Scritch scrawl scree scritch scratch, erase, scritch scrawl scree scritch scratch, erase, and so on it went. And went. And went. For hours, it went like that. Any error, whether it was a pause in the scritching or a line slightly out of place, caused another "No! Erase!" after which I started again.

It was a real drag.

That night, my stories about the trials and tribulations of learning to read were met with snickering. Apparently this same evil old lady teaches everybody to read the script. It's one of those hazing things that, once you get through, you think, "Hey, this is something everybody should have to do." I sighed at Seph's giggles and went on to pitch, and get shot down on, my latest ideas for the trip to the library.

The next day I walked in ready to punch her in the face if she said, "No! Again!" one more time, in spite of my father's request not to behave so un-ladylike again. As polite Southern ladies used to say back when they cared what others thought of what they said, "Kiss my grits."

She didn't, though. Luckily for me and my grits, the nice priestess was the one who showed up and started actually, finally, going through the alphabet. Yay!

It turned out to be just like Seph said. The trees and bushes *were* the alphabet. And no, they weren't in the same order as the English letters, but that was okay since I'd spent the entire day before going over and over the order of the trees and bushes.

I finally got it, in a great big ole' flash of the obvious.

Before long we ate a quick lunch and were into actually writing words out in the script I had learned. It was fun. I actually got giddy with the enjoyment of it all.

Just for fun, I started writing out the name of my pendant (which had stayed in my pouch since the episode over it). I got to the H in the last few letters before she stopped me.

"Do not write that name," she said, eyes wide in what I guessed was fear.

"Why not?"

"It is holy, and it is cursed," she said. "Now, let us continue with the names of the months."

And so it went, until it was time for supper. She excited me at first by telling me to ask the guards the following morning to escort me to the library for further education, but then she explained, "Here in the temple we do not have the widest collection of works, but we certainly have enough for our future queen to practice reading with."

Ah. Not that library.

Still, I tried to use it. That night, I waited till Aerona was out of the room to brag to Seph, "Tomorrow I get to go to the library!"

She'd been through it before, though. She nodded and said, "And maybe in our library here the princess will find a manuscript that will make her happy instead of drawing her to the forbidden journey to the forbidden areas."

"The library is a forbidden area?" I asked. This was the first I'd heard of that. The story had said that the blight of the wars that surrounded the Library of Alecsanddrha had gone away.

"Well, to you, at this point, yes," Seph said. "Your father has forbidden it. To most of us, there's just a caution attached to traveling there."

"What kind of caution?" I asked, feeling my curiosity grow.

"The *be careful or you may die here* kind of caution, what else? It's never been all that healthy of a trip, Alyssa, and it's still not. I know the stories you heard tell that the blight is cured, but the forest surrounding the Library of Alecsanddrha has never forgotten, or forgiven, elves for what we did to it. It's a dangerous place even now."

"How do you know this and the bardds do not?" I asked.

"Really? You have to ask that?" Seph actually seemed wounded by the question.

"I—I don't get how what I said was wrong," I explained, hands out in what I hoped would be a gesture of Sephaline-calming.

It worked, a little. "You're new here, Cousin, so I understand. But the bardds tell tales that will be interesting to listen to. You probably have never been around someone who would embellish tales at will in order to make more people interested in hearing them—"

"Yes, I have. It's called Fox News," I interrupted.

"Oh. Well, this Fox is like our bardds, then. Meanwhile, I'm a ranger. You know what rangers do, don't you, Alyssa?"

"Of course I do," I said. I really didn't, but I didn't want to belittle her occupation.

"No, you don't," she said, apparently correctly judging my facial expression. "You think we're just groundskeepers, but we tend to the planet in far deeper ways. Ways you can't possibly understand till you've experienced them. Alyssa, I can touch the ground here and tell how the former blight around the library, several hundred leagues away, is feeling. I know how the land thinks. My brethren communicate—really, totally, effectively communicate—with Kiirajanna and her agents, and we know what is going on.

"Alyssa," she said after drawing a deep, meaningful breath, "there is something going on at the Library of Alecsanddrha. Something so deep and sinister that, believe it or not, I'm scared to go. The blight is returning. I'm sorry I haven't been completely honest with you, but that's why I've been so against the trip. Well, that, and a certain bit of command from your father, the king."

"Okay, I understand," I said, though to be honest, I didn't really understand why the potential danger in such a beautifully perfect elf forest trumped the future queen's need to read the prophecy that was written mostly about her.

The next day was mostly spent in heaven. I mean the library, but I'm sure you figured that out. I've always loved libraries, and in the abbey library I was undeniably the future queen, or at least I was treated that way. The nice old elf who'd been teaching me started me out with some basic reading books, but she let me progress quickly at my own pace, and before lunch she left me there to my own interests.

"Do you have anything listing the collection at the Library of Alecsanddrha?" I asked the head librarian after lunch, which we ate outside the library, because food was forbidden inside. Of course, they did. I reviewed it for ranger-specific information and found several scrolls that were only located there.

That was gold for my argument in favor of the trip. I wrote

the titles all down. In ancient Elvish, of course. Seph would hear all about them over supper.

The Elves Can Party

As luck had it, she didn't hear all about the ranger scrolls over supper. She wasn't there.

The dining staff shrugged. Some mission she was on, they said. Would be back by morning, they said. Her Highness the Princess Alyssa would dine alone that evening in her room, they said. Aerona would take sup with the princess, they said.

Jerks.

I mean, I can eat all by myself. I did it often through high school, taking my supper to my room and eating over a book. But I'd grown kinda used to my cousin's presence, even when we were sitting there without words, and suddenly, for some reason, I missed that.

"Aerona, what do elves do at night?" I asked when the last bite was done. I'd drawn the silent meal out as long as I could, but eventually there was a vegetable of some sort—a pea, I think—that just couldn't be cut down into two bites any more, and so I had to put the whole thing in my mouth, chew, and swallow it. Yum.

"I don't understand the question, Princess," she said, her

eyes continuing their constant defensive sweep of the room.

"You know, at night. When they're bored. When there's nobody to talk to."

"You could talk to me, Princess."

"Not until you stop calling me Princess."

"Oh. Well, that is a problem, then, Princess."

"So when there's no TV, and no radio, and no CDs to play in a CD player that doesn't exist, what do elf girls do to entertain themselves?"

"I won't pretend to know of those things you speak, but elf girls do all sorts of things to entertain themselves."

"Like what? What did you do when you were a little girl alone in your room, Aerona?"

"I usually practiced throwing knives, Princess."

"Of course you did," I said. Why wasn't I surprised? "So riddle me this, Aerona. Is there anyplace close by to listen to singing, or watch dancing?"

"Yes, there is, Princess."

"Where?"

"I don't believe, Princess, that I was ordered by His Majesty to contribute to any of your quests to be delinquent."

"But you won't stand in the way of my quest to be delinquent, will you?"

"It depends upon the nature of the quest."

She shouldn't have said that. I rose from my seat and walked out the door. She followed, of course, but didn't stop me.

I walked down the stairs into the main foyer of the castle. She continued following, her eyes still darting from side to side, up and around me, alert for any possible threat. She moved so much like a cat that I imagined her with a twitching tail.

"Are you gonna follow me all the way to the singing?" I asked.

"She would unless I asked her to stop," a familiar voice

boomed from the bottom of the stairs, and my father's figure stepped out into the light.

"Oh, hi, Daddy," I said, grinning innocently.

"Don't *hi Daddy* me. You were about to defy orders to leave the castle grounds at night, when you are at your most vulnerable, were you not?"

"No, I don't think so. I mean, yes, I was about to leave the castle grounds at night, but I don't recall being given orders not to." I finished my descent of the stairs and turned to face him, my hands on my hips in my best show of actual defiance.

"Well," he said, his mouth twisting in confusion for a moment before he looked up to Aerona and said, "Did you not relay the orders forbidding her departure from the castle without permission?"

"Sire, I don't believe I've ever heard such orders to relay them," Aerona said, her tone the same level voice she'd been using with me.

"Oh. Well, that represents *such* a horrible lack of fatherly foresight. Consider such a ban enacted, unless I am invited to go with her. Would you please relay that to the subject, Aerona?"

Her voice didn't show a hint of humor at what I found very silly as she turned to me and said, "Princess, His Royal Majesty the King of all Kiirajanna has decreed that you shall not leave the castle premises unless you invite His Royal Highness to attend such departure."

"At night," the king added. "Otherwise, she can't go study during the day."

"At night, Princess," Aerona dutifully echoed.

"Hmm," I grunted, seeing the obvious hole but wondering if I should exploit it. "So, Dad, if I invite you to go with me, even if you don't go, I can go?"

"As long as you do not rescind the invitation."

"Well, then, would you like to go find some singing and dancing with me? Dad?"

"I would, indeed. Let's go."

"Do you know where we're going?" I asked as we stepped outside into the chilly night air.

"To find some singing and dancing, I believe your invitation said."

"Do you know where we can find some singing and dancing, then?"

"Yes, I do," he said, his shadowed face bearing a cryptic smile.

"Are you gonna lead us there?" I asked as he stopped at the foot of the stairs.

"Where would be the fun in that? You invited me to go with you to find some singing and dancing, not to direct you to the singing and dancing."

I sighed. He had a point, as annoying as it was. Part of me felt like turning around and just marching back up to bed. Luckily, that was a small part. "Okay," I said, "let's find some singing and dancing. Can you give me a hint which way to go first?"

"I can," Dad said, "But should I? Let me ask you this, Alyssa. Had I allowed you to continue your initial quest unimpeded, which direction would you have gone from here, on your own?"

Good question. "Um," I started, and then I stopped and thought for a moment. "That way," I said, pointing to the left.

"Why that way?"

"I don't really know. Gut feeling, I guess?" I was telling the truth; I didn't have any idea why I'd picked that direction, but it felt right.

"You are an elf, dear. A half elf, by blood, but now a full elf by living arrangement. Elves have gut feelings. Elves trust our gut feelings. You must work at letting your gut feeling become a stronger driving force."

"Okay, I'll do that. But is that way the right way?"

"Absolutely. If your gut tells you it is the right way to go, then it is the right way to go."

"So we'll find singing and dancing that way?" I asked, still not really believing the whole gut thing.

"Maybe. Maybe not. Probably. You were telling your gut that you wanted to find singing and dancing, and odds are good that the path you found will lead to singing and dancing. If it does not, then whatever it does lead to will be better than singing and dancing would be."

"I can't think of anything that would be better than singing and dancing would be, at least not right now," I said.

"Stop thinking so much, dear. You must learn to respect what you feel."

"Alright, can we call that enough esoteric stuff for one night? I just want to get to the fun stuff before it ends."

He tousled my hair and looked over at me, his wide grin making his eyes twinkle in the dim light. "Certainly we can, my daughter. Step into the coach and we will be away. Aerona, please watch her room to make certain that no traps can be laid for her in our absence." The female elf linebacker nodded and reentered the castle while Dad and I mounted another horseless coach that had appeared at our side.

We left the castle's lights behind as the carriage rumbled into the darkness of the forest. It felt like we were following the same path we'd taken during the tour Dad took us on my first weekend in Kiirajanna, but I couldn't tell in the night. Regardless, the coach ride was nice. I took a seat, and Dad sat right beside me and draped a protective and warm arm around my shoulders. We rode in silence for several minutes, my head leaned back so I could see the millions of stars whose light twinkled down between the tree branches.

It was beautiful, and peaceful as well.

Along the way, though, I couldn't help it. I had so many questions left unanswered, and so far I'd had so few chances with my dad. "Dad?" I asked, interrupting the peaceful silence.

"Yes, dear?"

"Who's the raven and who's the stag?"

"Huh? Oh, you mean on the royal crest?"

"Yes. You told me to ask you again when you were less tired, right?"

"I think I did, actually, now that you mention it. The fact is that neither of us is the raven, and neither is the stag. The two animals, together, represent the important aspects of our mutual reign. The raven represents continuing wisdom, and its symbology is simple. The stag, though, is far more complex. It represents strength, to be sure, but it also represents a link between the worlds of mundane and of energy, as do both I and Queen Talaith. In selecting those two animals for our crest, we managed to bridge the gap between simplicity and complexity as well as that of mundane and energy. Clever, no?"

"It is clever, yes," I agreed. It was awfully clever, at that. I realized that I and whoever was chosen for my king would need to work closely to present such a multifaceted pairing for our crest animals.

Then I dropped the conversation and just enjoyed the rest of the fairly short ride in silence.

I heard it before I saw it. A light trilling note made its way through the trees to us, and it disappeared to be replaced by a scale of deeper, and softer, notes. As the carriage rode on, the sound resolved itself into an old-fashioned-sounding jig, and then the lights of the village came into view.

"Well, Alyssa, it looks as though following your gut did find some singing and dancing," my father whispered into my ear. "Just so you know," he continued in a lower voice, "elves gather in the central square of most villages at night to join together in song and dance. It is one of our regular pastimes. If you wish to join in the dancing, you have but to stand up and approach the circle. No one will mind teaching you the song or the steps, as this is truly our way to celebrate life. The fact that I am king, and that you are my daughter, means nothing while the reel plays."

"I understand, and this is exactly what I was looking for," I said. Growing up, Momma sent me to church camp over the summers for reasons I never really knew. I didn't get into the religious stuff, but I did love the nighttime singing around the fires. I loved the dancing, too, when that happened, but it was really rare at church camps.

Not in an elf village, though.

As we approached, I watched the dancing elves. There didn't seem to be a specific pattern to it. They would swivel around a bit, and then skip and hop to one side or the other.

"Are there actual dances with patterns of steps to follow?" I asked.

"There are," Dad said, "but they're rarely danced at nighttime events. The point, really, is to just get out there and wiggle however feels right."

"Hmm, I'll try."

"You will succeed, I am sure. It is—well, it is quite easy, to tell the truth."

The carriage rolled slowly to a stop, but Dad didn't wait. He leaped out and strode over to the party, joining in on the shimmying in the middle without a hitch.

As it turned out, he was right. These same elves had welcomed Dad as their king—as their beloved king, for that matter—just days before, but at the party they welcomed one of their own.

Putting his hands over his head, he whirled a few times and

then clutched his dancing neighbor's hand and spun her around too. Both elves, king and commoner, threw up their heads to face the rising moon and laughed together.

It was hypnotic. The music sounded like what I've always imagined a Ren Fair would sound like, played on strange flute-like instruments and little round drums that the elves held to their chests or down between their knees. They weren't always playing the same notes, or even the same song, but nobody really seemed to care. The singers mostly just wailed out notes in voices that were beautifully happy. Some sang words in elvish, though; I caught a line about a boy and his hoop over there, and another line that sounded like it was talking about a maiden going for a walk from over on the other side.

All in all, it was such a joyous cacophony that I couldn't help myself. My foot started tapping, and my face broke out into what felt like one of those large elf smiles.

Soon after my foot got revved up, my father appeared at my side. He grabbed my hand and pulled me into the mad crush of people, his other arm waving sinuously overhead and his hips and knees making little circles. I laughed, mostly at him, and then I started doing the same thing. I couldn't help it, really.

They had the plague of joy going, and I caught it completely.

A long time later, I staggered to the side. I thought it was the side I'd started on, but I couldn't tell through the loops that my head was spinning. My butt plunked onto the ground all on its own, and my now-grounded equilibrium thanked it. I was breathing heavy, but not so much that my feet stopped tapping on the ground.

Before long, Legolas, of all people, plopped down beside me. "Alyssa, right?"

"Yes. You?" I struggled to ask between heaves of my chest. I looked over at his profile; he really was was a spitting image for Legolas, the elf from the Hobbit. All in all, a pretty good looking elf. He had nothing on Prince Charming, of course, but his exotic face had high cheekbones and eyebrows that arched way up into the night.

"Gwyn," he said, tossing a smile at me. I could see that his chiseled nose fit well with the angles of his face, and his bright blue eyes were dazzling. For the first time ever, I felt the tingly feeling I'd only heard about before.

I've always been different. Indifferent, in fact, to boys. I'd watched the girls in high school swooning over this or that football player or boy band member, but they never did anything for me.

Now, though, I felt it. I'm not sure if it was the music, or the atmosphere, or what, but I actually wanted to fall into this guy's arms.

"Ydych chi'n hoffi fy pentref?" he asked in the elvish tongue. *Do you like my village?*

"Ydw," I said, my head spinning. *Yes.*

"Would you like to see more of it?" he asked in English, as though my head wasn't spinning enough.

"Alyssa, there you are," my father said, striding up and breaking the mood.

"Hi, Dad. This is Gwyn," I said, hoping I managed to say it without slurring the words.

"Yes, I already know Gwyn," my father said with a strange, shadowed smile. I looked over at Gwyn, who seemed nervous. "Alyssa, it is getting late, and you need to be up for more lessons tomorrow. We should head back home now."

"Okay, Dad. Just let me say bye to my new friend here." Why was I still slurring my words?

Dad crossed his muscular arms and looked directly at Gwyn, who gulped. My new friend turned to me and muttered, "Bye, Alyssa, and good night to you," and then shot out of the circle like his feet were on fire.

"Let's go, Alyssa," Dad said, helping me up.

Carriage bumping under me on the way back, the cool night air cleared my head a little. "That was a heck of a party," I said.

"It was," my father agreed. I noticed that his arm was still draped protectively around my shoulder. "Alyssa, I should have warned you about the chifol weed. They burn it for the parties, and its smoke is a mild intoxicant. It helps us dance and party while dropping our inhibitions, but sometimes it drops our inhibitions too much."

"Oh? I couldn't tell," I said, still wondering what Gwyn was up to that night.

"I bet. Look, my beloved daughter, the boy you met tonight is nothing but trouble. You should avoid him."

"I will, Dad. I will," I said, visions of the handsome elf with the sky-high eyebrows still swimming in my head and making my stomach flutter. I mean, Legolas. Really, an elf Legolas. My next letter back to Sarah, I could tell her that I had danced with Legolas!

To Ride And Shoot

My conscience slowly surfaced the next morning from the weirdest dream. In it, I was staring into the hot air of a furnace with a smelly fish wiping my face with a wet rag. As I came to, I realized that the furnace was actually breathing hot air at me, and that it was the breathing that stank like smelly fish. The final strange realization was that what was wiping my face wasn't a wet rag, but instead it was a tongue.

A tongue!?

My eyes slammed open to see the tongue of a dog-like thing licking my face. I couldn't help it; I snarled and sat up. Booboo, sweet little thing that he is, slurped his tongue back into his mouth and snarled at me in return.

"Hey! Hey! Hey! Stop!" Seph said, the urgency in her voice kept just low enough to avoid Aerona charging in.

"Booboo was licking my face," I complained.

"He was just trying to wake you up gently."

"Well, he failed," I said, still irritated. "Is there really any way to be woken up by a wolverine that's *gentle*? And since when do I need waking up at all?"

"Since the sun rose an hour ago and you're still sleeping," Seph said, still pouting a little.

"Oh. I guess the party last night was a bit too much."

"You wanted to sing and dance, I heard."

"I did," I said with a sigh. "I didn't realize how late you—we—can go with that. Hey, where'd you go last night?"

"I had some stuff to go get," she said, her eyes shifting around the room. "Hey, I want to take you to archery practice."

"I always go to archery practice," I said, finally rising from bed and walking behind the screening dividers to change into my study clothes.

"No, not like that. I meant my archery practice. Have you ever ridden a horse?"

"No, but I've watched others do it on TV, and it didn't look that hard. Wait, are you talking about riding a horse and practicing archery at the same time, or are you talking about riding a horse to the archery range, getting off, and then shooting?"

"The first. Your aim has become good enough that you should be able to handle it on horseback."

"Wait, wait, wait." I stopped to grab what early-morning thoughts I could. The conversation was getting weird. "I have never ridden a horse before. You caught that, right? I can't imagine riding a horse while shooting arrows at something, let alone hitting anything in the process."

"You said you'd watched it on TB, whatever that is, though."

"Uh, TV. TB is—never mind. Look, I was joking. I mean, yes, I've watched it, and well, yeah, it didn't look that hard, but seriously? Riding and shooting arrows at the same time?"

"It's the next logical step in your progression, Alyssa, and you were right when you said riding a horse isn't all that hard. We'll go for a short ride first to ease your concerns, and then we'll run the archery course."

As much as I'd argued, I was actually excited. So excited, in fact, that I barely ate anything for breakfast. We skipped around the regular archery lanes I'd been using for practice and headed for the stables out past them. There, Seph introduced me to Awel, a mare she'd picked for me. Her name meant breeze.

Gentle breeze, I hoped.

Along the way she'd explained the basics—squeeze the horse's side firmly with your knees, use knees to steer, lean back going down and forward going up, and so on. I had to agree, it sounded easy enough.

It was easy enough, I suppose. At least, once I got past the embarrassing little incident of getting up onto Awel, it was easy. Even that part wasn't that hard; I just didn't expect the stirrup to slide down when I tried to use it to spring up, and then I was glad I had a good grip on the pommel or else I would've ended up on the ground on my back.

Awel still turned her head around to look and laugh at me, but we got past that.

She wasn't too far off of gentle, either. She didn't like walking much, it seemed, so she'd break out into a trot whenever she could. "Post! Don't forget to post!" Seph kept calling to me, and finally I understood why she'd taught me how to do that. The trot, you see, isn't fun to ride. The horse's hooves go clip-clop-clip-clop over and over, and at the same time the horse's back goes up and down and up and down. That'd be fine if I didn't have a backbone.

But I do.

And the trot, with its constant up and down—or, more accurately, up and slam and up and slam—movement, hurts it. In fact, it hurts the backbone and the entire portion of the body that usually rests against the horse's back.

The answer Seph taught me was something called the post,

in which I was supposed to imagine my upper body as a literal post, rigidly hovering above the horse, not meeting the up and down of the horse's back but instead staying at a constant height.

How's that done, you ask? No, really, you should ask. C'mon. Because the answer seems obvious, but it actually hurts only a little bit less than the up-slam stuff.

The answer is, to maintain a post, the horse's rider—me!—has to keep her legs flexed so that they act like springs. This is while, I have to remind you, I was trying to keep inward pressure with my knees to guide Awel. The constant pressure in two different directions hurts. It hurts a lot, in fact.

We loped a little, and we galloped a little, and they were fun—and a lot easier on my legs—but Seph had explained on the way over that we wouldn't train on those gaits often because the horses couldn't maintain them for very long. The trot was the gait that the horses preferred, and a good horse could trot for hours without tiring out, so that, then, was what we needed to work on.

I finally just about got the posting thing down when we came up to two trees that were painted red. At least, I assumed they were painted till I got closer and saw that the bark was actually a bright red color, though they looked like the same kind of trees as all the others. We stopped there to catch our breath and for Seph to clue me in.

First, though, I was curious about the strange red trunks. "Do you—rangers, that is—do this?"

"The red?"

"Yeah."

"Uh huh."

"How?"

Seph shrugged and said, "We ask them to, silly."

And that was that. She launched into a thorough description of the course as it was laid out, what I was expected to shoot at, what I was expected not to shoot at—and yes, they had non-targets scattered through the woods as well—and all the basic safety stuff.

"And don't forget to post," she reminded me.

"Right," I said. "So I'm supposed to think about steering the horse with my knees, and I'm supposed to think about posting, all the while I'm thinking about putting an arrow through the center of targets that pop up?"

"Nope. By this point in your archery training, you should not need to think about putting an arrow through the center of targets that pop up, Alyssa. That's why the hundred arrows every morning. It's supposed to be something that just happens."

"Yes, ma'am."

"Is ma'am an insult where you come from?"

"No, not unless you say it like one."

Seph sighed. "Your world is full of contradictions, Alyssa."

"Well, considering that this is my world now, I have to agree with you. Who makes w's into vowels, hmm?"

"I don't understand what you're talking about, but there are other riders approaching who will also wish to use the lane. You should go."

"Fine," I said and nudged Awel into a trot between the trees. My ploy to rest my burning thighs had only worked a little, and as soon as I clamped down into a controlled post they screamed at me once again.

The course was easy enough at a trot. I'd imagined screaming through at a gallop like I'd seen in the movies, but at a trot I had plenty of time to make each shot. I missed the first, wide by a lot, and then heard Seph's voice from pretty far behind as she reminded me not to think about the archery part.

It worked. I hit every target after that one. By the end of

the course, I was nailing the targets, smack dead center.

It was a good exercise, I decided at the end. Forcing me to concentrate on staying on the horse's back made the archery part more fluid, more natural.

"Great job, Cousin!" Seph called as she exited the course after me. We put our bows across our backs and bent forward to enjoy a gallop back to the stables. It was exhilarating.

Then came Embarrassing Moment Number Two. I used my hands to spring off of Awel's back, just like I'd seen done in the movies, and as soon as my feet hit the ground I went sprawling into the dust as my overused and abused thighs refused to hold me up.

"Oh. Ow. Whoa, that hurt," is what I think I said as I rolled up and onto my knees in as dignified a pose as I could manage. The dignified part didn't work; Seph cracked up loudly, and from within the barn I heard snickers.

"Need a hand up, Princess?" came from behind me. Dangit, I recognized that voice.

"No. I'm. Fine," I said through my teeth as I forced my legs under me and turned to face Prince Charming. His grin made my whole face feel like it was about to catch on fire, but at least he wasn't laughing.

He looked down at my legs. "I can suggest some exercises to help you with your riding muscles, if you'd like." He looked back up and into my eyes, his own eyes sparkling with laughter that he wasn't allowing out of his mouth, I was sure.

That just made it worse.

"No. Thank you, but I can manage," I growled and spun away, stalking back toward the castle. At least, I tried to stalk meaningfully back toward the castle. It actually was more of a wibbly-wobbly rolly kind of walking thing with a huff added to the top.

Men.

Seph caught up to me pretty quickly. I mean, it wasn't hard to do. "You okay, Alyssa?" she asked, her face serious but sporting eyes that also sparkled with held-back giggles.

"Fine. You?" I asked and continued, eyes locked toward the castle, not looking at anything else.

"You know, it's normal—" she said, but I cut her off.

"Normal to make a fool of myself in front of a guy? Yes, I know."

"Well, it *is* the Prince Keion. He's not just any guy."

That sure didn't help, either. "I know who it is," I growled, my jaws clenching in frustration. "I just—I need some time to myself today."

"Going to the abbey library to drink your troubles away in the words of a scroll?"

"That's the plan, unless you have a better one."

She didn't, and so I did. Spend the day in the library, that is.

AR Y GWEILL

literally, on knitting needles, but it's used to describe something in progress (like learning all this elf lore was to me).

Studying In The Library

I did manage to simmer down, surrounded for the rest of the day as I was by books and scrolls. The abbey's library was small, but there was plenty to read, and so I was happy. I was even happier that the priestess who served as librarian was willing to bring the books from their shelves to her "Princess" so I didn't have to work my still-screaming legs out any more.

It was too bad the abbey's library didn't have access to Wikipedia. Most of the scrolls it contained were on esoteric elements of priest m—well, I can't think of anything to call it other than the 'm' word—magic. I'd read a little in history class about Native American shamanism, and what was in the scrolls reminded me of what I remembered there. It was basically along the lines of using the forces of the world around us to shape that world in gentle ways.

The more I read about magic there in the small cloistered library on the magical elf realm of Kiirajanna, the more I would've given to spend a little while with the magic of the Internet as presented by Google, in order to look all that stuff up again.

In addition to shamanism, apparently the library held a fair amount of works on astronomy, too. Practical astronomy, at least. I remembered while browsing a scroll that happened to mention weeks that I hadn't managed to ask the high priestess about the difference between six-day weeks and seven-day weeks, so I asked the librarian. She grinned that scary-happy elf grin and bustled away, returning a few minutes later with a thick, bound book.

"Here, my dear, is a study of calendars and the measuring of the passage of time."

Oh, great. I wanted a simple explanation on why the elves had weeks that were six days long, and she brought me a tome-length study on the passage of time.

It did get interesting, though. It got interesting, I should say, once I flipped past the chapters on variations in the Indian calendars, and the Chinese calendars, and so on, all of which happened while the elves of Kiirajanna were merrily enjoying their six-day weeks. I mean, while the elves made it simple, the whole calendar-making thing on Earth got pretty confusing until the Romans came along and inserted ego into the process, thus making it even more confusing. Bless their hearts.

Basically, to make a long story short, humans (and elves, too) had two things, and only two things, on which to base their measurements of the passage of time: the moon and the sun. The problem facing both the early humans and the elves, though, was that the moon and the sun don't match. The sun is on a three hundred and sixty-five day cycle, while the moon takes twenty-eight, ish, days to get around the Earth, except that by the time the moon gets around, the Earth has also moved a little. Therefore, it actually takes the moon nearly thirty days to complete a full lunar spin cycle as viewed from the Earth's surface.

The elves just focused on that thirty. It's a nice, even number that's divisible by six and by five. Well, and three and ten also, but those don't make sense when we're talking about weeks. It was because of the number thirty, then, that early on the elves decided on weeks of six days, consisting of five days of work and one Sadwrn. That provided a total of five days of rest per lunar cycle, which in turn just happened to match the number of fingers on one hand. Brilliant! It was a beautiful system, and entirely based on the moon, with a few extra Sadwrns tossed in at the end of each year to keep New Year's celebration honest and accurate. Because, well, you know: elves like to party.

Back on Earth, along came the Romans. They got a little weird with the emperors naming months after themselves and so on. Plus, they focused on years more than months, since years were tied to growing seasons and, further, to something that was even more important: taxes. There were several different lengths of the years as time went on, each determined by whose mathematicians were being listened to. Finally Julius settled in on a seven-day Julian calendar, and then after several hundred years Gregory added a little correction to his Gregorian calendar that made it line up New Year's celebrations (and Easter, too) correctly each year.

And thus, the seven-day week with an accurate calendar settled in on Earth, while all along the six-day week had been clocking along just fine on Kiirajanna.

And that's the difference.

While I was on a roll, I also asked why Kiirajanna, the name of the world of the elves, was impossible to spell in the language of the elves. There's no k, no j, and no double letters like I'd actually seen in the scrolls. For that, unfortunately, the librarian just shrugged. "Original language," she said, though she wasn't sure what the language was, nor did she have any references for it. She confirmed that it was the same language llwdy had come from, at least, and she tossed out a few other ancient-language insults that I stored up to use later. Otherwise, she knew nothing about it. That was strange. But it was very interesting, anyway—I'd have to look up the original language some time when I was in a bigger library.

Learning all of that, and being immersed in a sea of books at the same time, made me happy, to be sure. But what made me happiest, honestly, was that Prince Charming was completely absent for the entire time I was at the library. It was, therefore, by definition, a wonderful experience.

Unfortunately, I bumped into him on the way back up to my room for my supper-in-exile. He was coming down the stairs, and he stopped in front of me and stared down at my legs. "Feeling better, Princess?" was all he asked, his sneer drawing a touch of ugly across his face, but that was enough to bring heat to my own face once again.

I did the most adult thing I could think of: I snarled and darted around him, ignoring as much as I could the soft chortles I heard from behind as I strode purposely up the stairs and toward the sanctuary of my own room.

Men.

Seph was in my room already when I got there. "Feeling better, Alyssa?" she asked, but it didn't sting nearly as badly as it had when Keion had said it.

"Yeah, I suppose."

"That falling down on the first time thing is completely normal, you know, and some day you'll get to laugh at someone else's expense when they do it."

"I kinda hope not." I sure didn't want to be guilty of adding to somebody else's embarrassment.

"Well, be that as it may, your shots were great. I hear the prince is quite proud of your progress."

"How does he know?"

"His men are the ones in charge of the riding courses. He knows everything that happens on them."

"I should've known. Why did you take me on the course, then, if it would just embarrass me?"

Seph stopped working on the piece of wood she was shaping and looked me straight in the eyes. "It didn't just embarrass you, Alyssa. It taught you. Looking at your shooting as you exited the course, I was amazed. You took to riding archery like a native-born elf, Cousin."

"I suppose," I said again.

"And one more thing. You need to get over your infatuation with Prince Keion. He's already promised to someone else."

"I'm not—wait, what? He's engaged?" I asked, confused. He didn't wear any sort of—well, anything—then again, I don't know what an engaged elf should wear.

"No, not engaged. He's never met her. But she's a princess from a minor region, and her parents and his mother decided it would be good for the two to wed."

"Oh, great. So arranged marriages are a thing here, too?"

"Not usually, Alyssa. Only in special cases of wealth or power. Both are applicable, in this situation."

"When will the wedding happen?" I asked, a strange let-down feeling creeping over me. I tried not to show it.

"Not for several years. She has to come of age first," Seph said, tossing it out there like it was completely normal.

"What's of age?"

"Fourteen."

"She's not even—he's—they're—she's—he'll be—like her father," I blurted out.

"Like her father, only more powerful. And with her father's lands and holdings. It's a good deal for everybody, I suppose," she said, still shaping her little wood piece like it was the only thing that mattered.

"I guess so," I said, and I tried to make myself believe it. Luckily the food arrived at that moment and gave us a reason to stop talking about Prince Charming, who I most certainly did *not* have a crush on.

Men.

When we finished our dinners, Aerona excused herself automatically to stand in the hall. We were training her well, I figured. When the door shut, I inhaled to start telling Seph about the ranger scrolls at the big library, but she cut me off.

"So, tomorrow is Sadwrn. Tomorrow morning, then, you need to rise before the sun, because we need to take off before dawn. You'll tell Aerona that you're going to my room for an early morning game of peroogle before breakfast, and that she can go take some time off because you'll be safe with me. I'll be downstairs in the third room on the left, very nearly underneath this room. Count three doors and then knock two times softly on the third. I've already gathered supplies and traveling clothes and a couple of cloaks, so don't bring anything."

My mind was racing; I couldn't believe what I was hearing. "What?" I asked. "You're actually going to go with me to the Library of Alecsanddrha?"

"Yes," she said. "Isn't that what you've been asking for?"

"It is. I just didn't expect you to say yes without more argument."

"But you expected me to say yes eventually, right?"

She had a point. I'd known from the first time I'd brought the subject up that she would eventually say yes. I nodded and grinned, holding my hands out to take the sting out of it for her.

She just shrugged it off and asked, "So why should I make any further argument out of it?"

I couldn't really answer the question, so I went into planning mode. "How long will it take us?"

"Nearly three full days at a walk-trot pace. I assume your legs can handle a seat on a horse for that long, though I can promise that by the time we get to the library they'll be stronger than you ever imagined. The stable handlers won't be working tomorrow, so it's a perfect day to sneak away. We'll be a full day's ride before anyone knows we're gone."

"Won't this get you in trouble with the king?"

"*Now* you're worried about that? What happened before when I argued about it?"

She was right, again. But the excitement of the journey had me thinking and saying dumb things. We made more plans, and she explained what we'd be eating and how she'd packed enough food for a few days' journey. I asked about the blight, and she shrugged it off, but I could tell by the tension in her face that she was at least a little bit worried about it.

She didn't stay long, claiming that I needed plenty of sleep to be fresh for the start of the trip the next morning.

Sleep? Ha. I had a hard time lying in my bed instead of dancing around the room in front of Aerona.

FEL HWCH AR Y RHEW

literally, like a pig on ice, and we all know how silly a pig on ice would look. At least we would, if we got much ice in Mississippi.

Followed

"Chhhh!" Seph hissed at Booboo to quieten down as she opened the door in the morning. I'd counted three doors and knocked twice on the third just as she said, and the wolverine's growl sounded like it was going to wake the entire castle. I slipped into the room and closed the door quickly and as quietly as I could manage.

Inside, Seph had two backpacks neatly laid side by side, each packed with a bedroll underneath and what looked like a poncho strapped on top. They were surprisingly heavy.

"By the way, what is peroogle?" I whispered as I shouldered the weight and worked the straps around so they were tight.

"It's a dice game, why?" she whispered back.

"Well, you and I are supposed to be playing peroogle. I could say I didn't know what it was when I was headed down here, but after the fact I probably ought to know a little bit about the game. Right?"

"Alyssa, by the time we return, she'll have figured out that we didn't play peroogle," Seph whispered as she reached for the door. "But I am bringing dice, so I'll teach you along the way.

It's a simple game, usually for betting. Now, let's go quietly," she said as she slipped the thick wool hood of her plain dark cloak over her head and darted out of the door on silent footsteps.

I followed as quietly as I could. I'm no ranger, but I can sneak when I want to. Before I left, though, I slipped a note onto Seph's bed, labeled "The King's Eyes Only." I'd stayed up a little late practicing my written script, according to what I told Aerona. What I'd written, in what I figured was the most perfect lettering possible, was all sorts of apologies for going against his will, explaining that I had to follow my destiny, and I had to know it to follow it. Oh, and I asked him to have someone take care of Little Treebeard while I was gone. I figured if I'd left it in my own room Aerona would've know what was up, but that Seph's room wouldn't be searched till after it was obvious that we were gone.

We managed to make it the whole way out of the castle, by the archery range to snag some bows and a whole bunch of arrows just in case, and then to our horses without meeting anybody. At the stables the horses nickered a little while we saddled them—a trick Seph had to teach me in the very dim light of early dawn—but otherwise all was still and silent as we made our way out of the castle grounds proper and south through the forest.

The elation and excitement wore off quickly. And by quickly, I mean nearly immediately. Once the horses had quietly walked out of the immediate grounds, Seph made a little clicking noise with her mouth and suddenly her mount and Awel set off at that most painful of gaits, the trot. I was quickly transported in my memory back to the day before: up, down, up, down, up, ow, up, ow, up, ow.... I tried posting like I had the day before and instantly my thighs started screaming. The weight of the backpack only made it worse. Finally I slumped forward in the saddle, letting my butt move up and down without the weight of my upper body and the backpack on it, and just relaxed my legs. It still jarred, but it didn't make me want to scream with every other step Awel took.

I let my mind wander, my face planted in Awel's mane and arms around her neck. As I bounced along, I wondered what we would find at the library. What was causing the blight to expand again? Why was it that everyone seemed so afraid of me going? More importantly, what would the prophecy say about my future? Would I even be able to read and understand it?

Suddenly Awel stopped. I whipped my eyes up and around, the seventh scenario of our arrival at Alecsanddrha blinking out as my brain was interrupted halfway through it. But there was no danger, at least none imminent. Seph had just called a halt, and it was actually, finally, daylight.

"You okay, Cousin?" she called to me as she leaped down and pulled her pack off. From the top of the pack she pulled a few hunks of sausage and cheese and started slicing some off.

"Yeah, sure. Don't mind me. I'm just as comfortable as I can be right on up here," I called from the back of Awel. I had absolutely no idea how I was going to get down. My legs were useless lumps of throbbing mass at the moment, and the pack on my back felt like it weighed a thousand pounds, pushing my chest down onto the pommel of the saddle.

She laughed. "Alyssa," she said, sauntering over toward me, "you're a terrible liar."

Once she'd helped me peel myself off of the horse and land softly enough on the ground that it didn't hurt much more than the riding had, I sighed and rolled over to sit up, leaning onto the still-attached backpack. I looked up at her smiling face and asked, "I don't suppose it's too late to turn back, is it?"

She nodded and held out a hunk of sausage for me to eat. She nibbled on the cheese, and then said, "Once we've had a good break I'll tie our packs to our horses, and we can use your cloak now as a cushion, so the ride going forward will be easy. We had to leave so silently this morning that I couldn't do all of that."

"I'll believe it once I've seen it," I said, grumbling about the characterization of the ride going forward as *easy*. The mere thought of climbing back up into the saddle seized my stomach in vise grips of dread.

"Oh, stop it. What doesn't kill us, makes us stronger, remember?" she said.

"What doesn't kill me better run for its own life," I responded. We laughed, and the action of that gave me enough energy to shrug myself out of the pack and spin around onto my hands and knees. With a heave, I rose to my feet. "Those muscles I abused yesterday are really screaming at me today," I said, trying to stretch but only managing to look like a flailing chicken.

"Here," she said, handing me a small brown leather pouch. I opened its narrow mouth and saw twigs inside. "I figured you might have some soreness today so I brought a stock of helygen sticks. Chew on it as we ride, but don't swallow it."

"Helygen—haven't heard of it. What is it?"

"It's a tree. That tree," she said, pointing to one of the droopy willows we'd been passing. "Didn't you learn the names of the trees when you learned the alphabet?"

"I did learn the trees, but—oh, right. Trees. Helyg is what I learned. That's one of those weird singular-plural things."

"Right. The number of syllables in the plural fits the chant better. Basic grammar lessons aside, though, chewing the branches of the *helygen* tree helps relieve pain. Now, are you ready to go?"

I nodded, reluctantly. I glanced down into the pouch, wondering how much of this helygen branch I was going to end up needing before the trip was over.

I've never been much of a medicine-taker, but what I wouldn't have done right then for a Tylenol!

I helped Seph tie our packs behind the saddles. She was surprisingly careful to balance them, explaining that just having a little more weight on one side of the horse could cause the mare to have problems with her gait. Then up I went, with her help this time, and slowly settled my sore butt into the now-cushioned saddle. It still hurt, just not quite as much.

The sticks tasted awful, but they did seem to help with my lower back pain as we trotted along. My leg muscles seemed to scream less, too, which probably means I just got good at ignoring them.

We kept going, taking short breaks every hour or so. We ate—more sausage and cheese and some fruit—when the sun was high in the sky. Seph rode first, seeming to know where she was going, trail or no, while Booboo raced from side to side, ahead of us and behind, scouting for danger. I didn't do much, honestly. Awel trotted on like a trooper, and I rode numbly on her back, eyes swiveling around to take in the never-changing scenery. Occasionally a hill would loom to one side or another, but none of the hills counted for more than mounds of earth. The trees didn't change; they were a constant mix of oak, willow, pine, and a few other varieties I didn't know. I saw a few birds, but—well, I'll shorten the boring part by saying that nothing major happened.

We settled in to cook dinner and spread out our bedrolls in a small deserted, but surprisingly well-kept, log cabin that had been erected just beside the first creek we'd come across on our journey. Seph seemed to have been looking for it, since she made a little happy sound when she saw the creek and set out to following it directly.

"Looks like somebody was expecting us," I said as I reclined my sore body in a form-fitting chair and watched Seph light a cooking fire with wood that had awaited our arrival.

"No more than anyone else," Seph said, shrugging, and then she stepped back with a smile as flames licked up from the kindling and started tickling the smaller firewood, sending tendrils of smoke upward. "This is a ranger cabin. There are many of these retreats scattered around, and we all make certain to keep them stocked with food and firewood for each other."

"Aren't you scared somebody who's not a ranger will stay in one?"

"Those who aren't rangers stay in them more often than those who are rangers do. Why would that scare us?"

Good question. I thought about it and couldn't find a reason I'd worry about it if I were a ranger. I'd worry back where I'd grown up that somebody would abuse the privilege, but elf society just didn't seem to do that.

Seph cheered when she found a teapot in one of the slapped-together cabinets. She walked outside and filled it in the creek, and once it was hot she used our little tin cups she'd packed to steep some herbs for tea. Without honey or sugar the tea was bitter, but she explained it had several herbs, including more of the bark from the willow branches, and it was good for curing whatever ailed us.

Which, at the moment, was a pretty big list.

Tea made, Seph put some dried meat and vegetables from our packs into a pot of water. She added some herbs and let it boil as we sat and enjoyed the silence of the evening together.

"What do you think?" she asked after she'd used our cups to scoop out some soup from the pot.

I tasted it carefully, since it was hot. "It, um, could probably use some broth," I said, unwilling to hurt her feelings by telling her how awful it really tasted. It was like eating hot dishwater with vegetables and mostly softened jerky mixed in.

"It tastes awful," she corrected me with a grimace, saying what I was actually thinking, "but it's what we eat on the road. It keeps you fueled and going, and doesn't require a lot of weight or room in the backpacks."

"Okay, so yes, it tastes awful," I agreed. It didn't matter; I was hungrier than a woodpecker with a headache. I was so hungry that I could eat a—well, a lot of soup. I did, and Booboo got a helping too, and then I helped her clean up.

"Too bad you can't sing the soup into tasting better."

"Uh huh," she said. She was catching on to my sarcastic dry wit, obviously.

"So, what is this peroogle?" I asked.

"I told you, it's a dice game, silly," Seph said, grinning at me from across the rickety table. I started to object, and she pulled two dice out of her pouch and tossed them across to me. "I know, I know, I promised to teach you, but now that dinner's eaten we have nothing to gamble with."

"As a kid, we used to play poker with pennies. Nobody got to keep the pennies; it was just a way of tracking who would win if we were playing for real."

"We don't have any of these pennies, either, do we?"

"No, but I saw some pebbles outside. Let's get some and pretend like they're gold pieces."

"Why would we do that?"

"Well, there are plenty of pebbles, so they're easy to use."

"No," Seph said, shaking her head, a confused look on her face. "Why would we pretend like they're gold pieces?"

That stopped me; I realized that I hadn't seen any money of any type being used. Granted, I lived in the castle and got everything for free, but surely they used something as cash.

"I'm sorry. I kind of assumed elves would use gold pieces as money like in D and—a board game we used to play back home. What do we use for cash, if not gold pieces?"

"What is cash?" she asked, still looking bewildered, so I explained what I knew of the structure and purpose of the monetary system.

"I'll show you a dollar bill when I get back to my room in the castle," I said. "I'm pretty sure I had one or two the night I crossed over."

"That would be interesting, but I still do not understand. You're telling me that humans use green ink to print paper that, because of the green ink, gains special value and can be used to trade for items?"

"Well, it's not just the green ink."

"Is it some sort of magic? But wait, there is no magic on that side of the portals."

"It is some sort of magic, I guess, if you consider the word of the government to be magic," I explained. I was really reaching with that, but without it I had absolutely no idea how to explain what green paper had to do with purchasing stuff.

"So it would be the same here if your father wrote special words on leaves and told the people to use them for trade," she said.

"Um, yeah, I think."

"But why would he do that?" she was still confused, and I could tell I wasn't going to be able to fix that.

I took one last stab, though, and said, "Cash produced by the government standardizes the amount each thing is worth, giving a basic unit of value that all can agree upon. That's what they taught us in the class on it, anyway."

"Okay, but why would I and another ranger, say, out here in the woods doing a trade, care what your father thinks of the value of our two items?"

"Well, you probably wouldn't, but others might. Besides, having currency also enables the accumulation of wealth." There, that one finally slipped out of the dark passages of my high school memories.

"But why would the government create a system that promotes evil?"

"Huh?"

"When we were discussing your religions the other night, you said the accumulation of wealth was evil, did you not?"

"No, I did not. I did say there's a proverb, one of the few I can recall, that says a wealthy man isn't likely to enter into the kingdom of heaven."

"Because it's evil, right?"

"Um, no, I don't think so."

"So this wealthy man is unable to obtain his eternal reward because he did something good?"

"Well, no, but—look, I don't suppose elves have any way of accumulating wealth?"

"Some have larger holdings than others, I suppose. But that's hardly a matter of gathering pieces of paper."

"Look, can we just play dice?" I felt like a hound dog that had just chased its own tail for an hour.

"Sure. Should we go get the pebbles together?"

We did, and several minutes later we were seated at the table with a pile of perfectly smooth pebbles in front of each of us. The game turned out to be a little complicated for just using two dice. She let me play first, and so I started my turn by rolling the two smooth wooden dice Seph had carved and painted herself onto the table to determine what she called the prif, the elf word for primary. It had to come up between a five and a nine to count, and on my first roll I got a four on one die and a three on the other—seven. She said it was the best possible prif, so since it was time to bet, I pushed out three stones instead of just one. Next roll: the siawns, the elf word for chance. That was the complicated part; if it equaled the prif then I won, which in this case meant Seph would give me three pebbles from her pile. If I got a two or a three or a twelve, I would lose and she could take my three pebbles. Also, because the prif was a seven, if the siawns was an eleven I would win. Had the prif been a five or a nine, both eleven and twelve would lose. Had the prif been a six or an eight, meanwhile, an eleven would lose while a twelve would win.

See what I mean about it being complicated?

I rolled a ten. "Start over?" I asked, hoping that it would be that simple. It wasn't. I had to roll again, only now the prif was bad and the siawns was good.

I rolled a six. Again, she said. A five. Again. The next time the dice came up a three and a four, and Seph gleefully reached out and hauled my three pebbles over to her stack.

"See how much fun it is?"

"Um, no, I don't. It's an awful lot of rules for just a few pebbles. Maybe if we were playing for real gold, but—"

"Why are you so hung up on gold, Cousin?"

"Because it's pretty, and it's valuable. The castle is bedazzled in it, haven't you noticed?"

"Pretty, yes, but valuable? It's only so, from what I've heard, in your world, where the humans cannot just sing it out of the ground."

"Oh." I hadn't thought of that possibility. "But this is my world now, remember?"

"Would you like me to walk out to the stream and sing some up right now?"

"That would mean we get to carry it the rest of the way, wouldn't it?"

"Only if you wanted to keep it. Honestly, a good sausage is worth more than the same weight in gold here."

"Nah. But if gold is worthless, what can we play for that's worth more than pebbles?"

"We don't have anything, really. What's mine is yours already, Alyssa."

"How about a foot rub?"

"Why would rubbing a foot have any value?"

"My momma and I used to play for a foot rub back when I was a little younger. I always tried to lose because she always seemed to need one after a long day on her feet. She said it was an occupational hazard of being a teacher."

"Oh. Well, a foot rub it is, then, though if you win you'll have to explain the trick of it."

She scooped up the dice and rolled two threes. "A prif of six," she said as she reached out and set the dice rolling again. Boxcars this time. "A twelve! I win. Now you can show me how a foot rub is done instead of just telling me."

There are several secrets I've learned to doing a good foot rub. One is to start on clean feet, and Seph's feet really needed cleaning after a day in the saddle. Once you get to rubbing, though, the trick is to follow the lines of pressure that go along and around the foot. Some people focus on the hard parts that usually are where it hurts: the ball of the foot and the heel. Instead, though, you should rub between the landmarks, gently kneading out the ache.

It worked. By the time I was done she had that ridiculously beatific elf-smile stretched from one ear to the other. "Wow, that was really worth winning," she said. "So a foot rub is actually a feet rub."

"I guess," I said, not interested in getting into any other weird discussions. In silence we laid out our bedrolls and went to sleep.

The next day Seph pushed me right out of my bedroll way before it was dawn. Muttering some sort of useless chatter about early birds and such, she bustled around and got everything together before I even really got my eyes open. "They know we're gone by now, so we have to get going get going get going!" she chirped way too loudly for my morning sensitivities, bless her heart.

It was the same routine as the day before: ride for a while, then stop for breakfast, then ride more. The good news is that I was a whole lot less sore; this riding thing seemed to be growing on me. We followed the creek for a long while, and then we crossed when it turned so that we kept our horses' noses pointed south.

I lost track of time as Awel's hooves patted out a clop-clop-clop-clop sound, paired with her back doing a down-up-down-up motion, with which my thighs naturally picked up a flex-give-flex-give pattern. Sometime around noon, then, I realized that Seph and Booboo were both tense and wary. More so than they normally were, I should add. I pushed Awel into a short lope to catch up, and then asked Seph what was wrong.

"We're being followed," she whispered.

"By who?" I asked, trying to match her tone.

"I don't know," she whispered back. I realized, and mentioned, how silly a question I'd asked her—how could she be expected to know who was following us?—and she shook her head. "No," she said, "I *should* be able to tell. It's something rangers learn to do. Whoever is following us is masking his identity."

"Is he a ranger too?" I asked, started to feel concerned.

"No. If he were a ranger too, I wouldn't know that we were being followed," she said.

"So he's good, but not that good, then? Okay, so what's the plan?" I asked. "Do we just keep going until he, whoever he is, catches up to us?"

"They'd take away my ranger pin if I were happy with that plan. No, we'll reach a hillock in a little while. Once we get over it, you spur Awel into a short gallop and I'll ask the trees to catch whoever is behind us when I circle around. You gallop to the count of two hundred then circle back, too. Then, Booboo can eat him."

That's how it happened, at least all but the part about Booboo eating somebody. We made a path right over the top of the hill, and between two willow trees Seph said, "Go." I squeezed my knees a couple of times and Awel, who I think had been chafing to go a little faster, leaped out into a gallop. I counted to two hundred and turned the reluctant mare around to lope back toward where I heard a man's voice cursing punctuated by Sephaline's crystal-clear laughter and an occasional long, drawn-out hiss that could only come from Booboo the Fierce.

BLEWYN O'I DRWYN

literally, a hair from his nose, in the sense that pulling one means doing something mean to him, bless his black little heart[1].

[1] Nope, not thinking of Prince Charming at all while I write this. Nope, not at all!

Fancy Meeting You Here

I couldn't help giggling over what I saw as Awel loped into the clearing. Suspended upside down in the air by willow branches was none other than Keion, first prince and finest hunter of all Kiirajanna and light of Queen Talaith's eyes. He thrashed, trying to get out of the living entanglement, as the horse he'd obviously been riding stood nervously watching to the side.

My giggles turned into a full-out guffaw when I heard tiny chirps of challenge surrounding the prince, and in my sideways glances caught tylwyth teg flying about, taunting him. With my eyes on his face, I saw a flicker of motion dart in as one of the fairy folk pinched his side and then darted back out of range of his enraged shaking.

He stopped mid-stream with his cursing at Seph to turn to me when I laughed.

"*Twp!*" he hurled the elvish insult, accusing me of severe lack of intelligence. Ooh, that would have hurt if he hadn't been the one dangling upside down in the willow branches. I just sat on Awel's back and laughed louder.

I couldn't help it. I called out, "Well, Prince, fancy meeting you here."

"*LET ME DOWN, RANGER!*" the upside-down elf bellowed.

"Answer me first, Prince," she said. "Why were you following us?"

"Because the King asked me to, you stupid little girl. He wanted to make certain his daughter made it to the library and back with both her information and her head."

"How did you catch up to us with a day's head start, then?" I asked.

"I've been following you since you left yesterday morning, Princess. Your cousin is nearly untrackable, but *you* are quite easy to follow."

"You lie. If you've been following us since we left, there's no way you were doing it at my father's request. He didn't even know we were...." My words trailed off as I noticed Sepheline shaking her head at me.

"Were you not a princess and future queen of the realm, I would cut out your tongue for that insult, Alyssa," Keion said with venom in his tone. "And it is you who are wrong. Your father is the one who planned this expedition."

I looked to Seph for support, but she just shook her head. "It was I who misled you, Alyssa, but only because your father asked me to. He wanted you to sneak out under cover of darkness, and he believed that if you did not fear his catching you and keeping you from going, you would not have kept the departure as quiet as you needed to."

"Who was in on it, then?" I asked.

"Your cousin, me, and the master of provisions were all," Keion said from the spot where he still hung. "Even Aerona was left in the dark, at least till well after your departure, according to the plan. Your father, despite his desire to let you see through with your quest, really does fear for your safety while the realm is under the degree of chaos that it is. You've been attacked thrice while on his castle grounds, and that makes him feel particularly impotent in protecting you when you are away. Regardless, he asked me to confess to you in his name, once the truth of this expedition finally came out, that the trip to sing and dance was a bit staged as well. He wanted to spend an evening with you enjoying life before he let you head off into the great danger of the blight and the library."

As low as I felt at being duped, I couldn't let Keion see it, so I turned to him and said, "Thank you for the truth. But you would have a difficult time cutting out anyone's tongue, Keion, suspended as you are between the willow trees. And I'll apologize for the accusation of lying when you apologize for calling me stupid."

"But the difference, dearest Princess, is that I hold myself to the highest standards of integrity, and so your accusation of lying was a severe insult. You, on the other hand, were actually acting fairly stupid at the time."

I shrugged, still unwilling to give ground. "And yet you're still the one imprisoned upside down in the trees, awaiting our mercy. How does that make us the stupid ones?"

Keion's face untwisted. "Well, yes," he said. "There is that. Let me down, Ranger Sepheline"

"Please?" Seph said, a wicked smile on her face.

"Oh, give it a rest, would you? Fine. Sure, *please*, Ranger Sepheline, let me down from your great and glorious willow tree trap."

Seph motioned and the trees let go of the prince. I expected him to hit the ground awkwardly, but he spun and landed with catlike grace instead and then pressed himself up to his full height.

"And now that my presence is revealed, ladies, I must ask you in your father, His Majesty the King's name, if I may accompany you to the Library of Alecsanddrha."

"We would enjoy your presence and welcome your assistance," I said, cutting Seph off. She glared at me, but I really didn't care what she was about to say. We were getting our own Prince Charming added to the party.

And that made me happy.

The Old Ranger

As the shadows lengthened, the prince and I rode up to where Sephaline waited for us. Booboo still apparently didn't quite trust Keion, judging from the quiet snarling sound the wolverine kept making as we closed the gap to speaking distance.

"What's ahead, ranger?" Keion asked. He'd been surly ever since we'd caught him sneaking behind us. I really couldn't blame him when I thought about it; we hadn't been all that nice with the hanging upside down and stuff, after all, and the giggling hadn't helped either. Then again, he hadn't been all that nice to us, and so I figured that we were right about even.

Seph had spent more time than ever riding up ahead of us. In my little part-time fantasy I imagined she was leaving us alone for some ogling time, but I knew the reality. She didn't want to spend much time around him on the best of days, and now with his massive hunter-prince ego bruised it was even more prickly, no matter how hard she crushed on him, too. He was grumpier than a dog with its bone taken away, and that's what I had to put up with for the rest of the ride.

Bless his heart. Bless both of their hearts for lying to me, for that matter.

I'd tried asking him about his name, since it was the first time we'd been alone without a bow and arrow in my hands and a never-ending string of suggestions on how to use them better in his mouth. It's an awesome name, manly and melodic at the same time. Problem is, the first letter as he spelled it was a k, and that letter doesn't exist in the alphabet of the elves.

"Keion is an Irish name," he said in a flat, droning voice when I finally got him to speak. "It means 'born to rule.' My mother heard it and liked it a lot when she was growing up in Britain, and she brought it here without really caring whether it worked or not in the alphabet. Sometimes people get by spelling it with a c in the beginning, but I much prefer the k instead. It's more distinctive."

If by distinctive he meant that none of his people really knew how to write it, he was correct, but I let that go unsaid and just nodded. No point poking the bear, I figured.

Seph glowered at Keion as we rode up, her expression matching Booboo's growl. She took her profession seriously, but she didn't like being called just "ranger." She, also, decided it was best to let the bear go unpoked, though, and so she leveled a look at me as she answered Keion's question.

"There's another ranger cabin just over the next hill, and it's just about a perfect spot on the journey to spend the evening. We'll have some company, though. It's important that everybody be nice and polite, because the ranger we'll be sharing the cabin with is revered in my circles. It's old Owain, and it's said that he was rangering before these trees were little sprouts. He knows that we're coming, of course—what ranger wouldn't, and he's not just any ranger—but we owe it to one of his stature to approach with a degree of solemnity and comity."

Keion snorted. "I am a Prince of the Realm, and this is a Princess of—"

Sephaline cut him off angrily. "I know full well who you are, and I'll bet Owain already does, too. This man's been a legend since before you were in diapers, *pen bach*. You will show him the respect he deserves, prince or no. You hear me?"

I stood in shock; it was the first time I'd seen Seph's ire flare up like that. I wanted to applaud. My cousin does indignant better'n nearly anybody.

Keion's face turned bright red at the Elvish term. Apparently saying that somebody has a small head is a pretty severe insult. There was so much more I needed to learn about the language, things I'd never learn in a class of five-year-olds. It would have to come later, though, because it looked like a battle was about to break out.

Keion started reaching for the sword at his side, but Seph was in her element and she knew it. Booboo paced out to the left, looking at each of Keion's charger's knees in turn like he was planning which to bring down first. Then the trees started shaking. I remembered Little Treebeard's pitiful little growls at the attackers in my room and wondered what the huge elms and willows around us were doing in Seph's head. Keion must have wondered, too, since he glanced nervously around at the trees that were starting to lean in his direction. That apparently gave him second thoughts about the insult.

Holding both hands up and away from anything else, the prince said, "Okay, okay. Of course I will show your ranger legend the respect he deserves. I would ask that you do the same for me, though, ranger."

Booboo and Seph seemed to reach the same conclusion at the same time. Seph nodded. The trees relaxed back to their normal shapes. Booboo bounded back over to stand beside Seph.

"Look, you two," I growled. I'd had enough. "You're supposed to be following the king's request in escorting me to the library. It's not about who can hurl the best insult, or shoot the best arrow, or make the trees the most angry. Right? So just stop it, okay? If I get my way in one thing on this journey, it'll be that you two *stop* behaving like children toward each other. And I mean stop it right now. Seph, guide us on to meet your colleague, and Keion, you *will* behave appropriately as a Prince of the Realm. Seph, you *will* give Keion the respect he deserves, and Keion, you *will* do the same for Seph. *Do you understand me?*"

I don't just let go very often, but when I do, I guess I'm pretty good at it. Both of my companions nodded and pushed their horses silently up the trail.

It looked like we might have a nice, polite ride after all.

We rode up to the cabin, a log creation just like the one the previous night. It was getting pretty gloomy, but since the cabin was in a clearing I could see the man sitting out in front of it. He sat and watched as we rode up, his only movement the occasional raising of his arm to bring a long pipe stem up to his lips. His droopy leather hat matched his well-worn leather tunic and trousers, and as we got closer I could see that the all-brown outfit matched the wrinkled leathery skin on his face pretty well, too. We rode straight over to the post where his dappled horse stood quietly, getting down off of and then removing the weight of saddles and saddle bags from our own mounts, all in total silence. The old man's eyes followed every move we made.

Putting our bags and backpacks down beside the entry, we walked over to greet the ancient ranger. I kept glancing around, looking to see where and what his familiar was. After all, I figured, if Seph got a wolverine, no telling what a legendary ranger would have. A unicorn, perhaps? A saber-toothed cat? A mammoth? If not those, another fierce beast from our old earth myths? I couldn't wait to see, but the mystery of it also kinda scared me a little.

No matter how deeply I peered into the surrounding woods, I couldn't see any animals watching us, though.

Seph started the greeting process for us, bowing to him and saying a few words in the language of the elves. I remembered my lessons from the royal trio in which they instructed that it was best to speak in that language to all commoners, since many of them have never learned English. It's rude, they said, to assume someone in a village out away from the castle complex would speak anything but the native tongue. I hoped my inner elf was up to the task.

I didn't need to worry. The ancient man with a face that looked like the rough bark of a tree nodded briefly to Sephaline and then turned to look directly into my eyes. "Princess Alyssa," he said in English, "I have heard much of your coming. It is fortunate that I am granted this opportunity to meet you."

"And this is..." Seph started, switching to English herself and trying to finish the introductory ritual before Owain cut her off.

"Prince Keion, hunter-champion of the realm and steadiest aim in all Kiirajanna. Yes, I know of you, too, young man, and am honored to make your acquaintance. As I am yours, Ranger Sephaline. You have learned and accomplished much for one so young."

"Thank you, R..." Seph said before Owain cut her off again. Apparently being that age meant everything was a hurry to get out.

"Those were some mighty fireworks indeed that you three unleashed over the hill. You almost had me come running to save you from a dragon, as much of a commotion as you made."

"We had a disagreement, Ranger Owain," Seph said. She

actually looked chastised.

"A disagreement? Just a disagreement, eh? I'd hate to see what you would do if you had a fight!" Owain said, his voice coming out in a bark of a laugh. "What do you keep looking around for, Princess?"

"I'm looking for your familiar," I said. Seph turned a horrified look my direction; I guessed a moment too late that it's rude to ask a ranger such things.

"Oh, relax, Sephaline. One of the advantages of being a ranger is that you get to spend so much time away from court and the rest of elf civilization that you can forget all about the nonsense rules if you want to. Alyssa, my familiar is right in front of you. Come, Eryr, say hello!"

I tensed, wondering what mighty beast would respond to Owain's call. After several seconds of nothing approaching, though, I was just about ready to relax again when a *chirp* right by my ear made me jump like a scared deer. A little red cardinal landed lightly on my right shoulder, and my heartbeat returned to normal as Owain exploded in laughter.

"You were expecting a dragon, perhaps, Princess? Or an eagle?" he asked between laughs.

"Well—no. Yes," I corrected myself, trying to get a grasp on my confusion. "That is what you named her, right? Eagle?"

"Eryr is a him, Alyssa. Females of his species are brown. And why would I name him cardinal, since everyone can already see that about him? Familiars should be named first according to their wishes, and second according to their inner rather than their outer natures. It is too bad, I must say, that we elves are not named similarly."

"What would you be named if we were?" I asked, curious.

"A very good question, my young princess. In fact, I am a perfect example of the problem with my theory. You see, I would have had many different names over the years if we were named such. Now? Rhyddid, I think—liberty—as that is the quality of life that is closest to my heart. I can remember feeling strongly about the names Amddiffynnydd—protector—and Gwarchodwyr—babysitter—at different times in my past. The current title, by the way, is primarily the result of your father's ruling style. Not all kings have allowed us to roam and manage the forest as we see fit."

"I'll make sure to tell him that when we get back."

"Thank you, but there's no need. I am certain that he knows. Now, you must forgive an old man his curiosity. Where are three such good-looking and important youths going to in the forest without the benefit of the king's guard?"

We'd talked about what to tell him if he asked. The consensus we'd reached was that there wasn't any reason to lie to him, and besides, he could probably tell if it was a lie anyway. Not, Seph told us, because of any special ranger mind-reading power, but rather because he'd been around for so long he was a grand master at sensing things like that.

So I told him.

He nodded, his old eyes looking off into the distance as he scratched his chin thoughtfully. We sat quietly, waiting for his inevitable wise commentary about the path that stretched out ahead of us.

We waited a while. I was just about to shake his shoulder to make sure he was still awake when he swung his gaze back from outer space and looked at me from under raised eyebrows. "An ambitious plan, that is."

"Yes, it is, which is why I was hoping to trouble you for your wisdom regarding what is in front of us and how to face it." I seethed inside. *An ambitious plan*? That was all he had to offer?

"Do you want travel advice, or do you really want to know what I believe you should do?"

"I want the aid of your wisdom, Ranger Owain."

"Then go home."

"I—uh, I want the aid of your *other* wisdom, Ranger Owain," I said, trying to make light of the fact that I wanted to throttle the old geezer. Go home? After coming as far as we had? Right. I could just see myself explaining our trip to Aerona: *well, we slipped out after lying to you, then we got almost there, and some old guy told us to come back so we did.* Ha! Nope.

Not gonna happen, I told myself.

He snorted. "I might as well tell the trees not to shed their leaves in the fall, right? I tell you to turn around based on many reasons, none of which you're likely to take seriously. Something evil, something serious, stirs in the middle of the blight that surrounds the great Library of Alecsanddrha. The blight itself has grown bigger, and worse, it's taken on what can only be described as denizens. Now, don't look so gleeful, prince. I do not doubt your battle prowess, either of you, Ranger Sephaline or Prince Keion, but I have to tell you that I doubt whether the two of you working together could make it safely across the blight as it is now. And then there's—well, something. I'm not sure what it is, but I hear, and I sense, a growing power, a growing evil, in the middle. Once you get across it safely, dealing with whatever has taken up residence there is—should be, anyway—the work of the entire council of rangers, not two kids and a princess. Go home, bring the King's army back with you, and attack the problem that way."

"Why not bring the entire council of rangers instead of the army? Wouldn't that be a better way to attack it?" I asked, hoping I wasn't showing too much naivety.

The old ranger looked at me, his eyes softening, and he puffed on his pipe before answering. "Better, yes. But it's not likely to happen. Different monarchs have demanded different things of the council, you see. It is said that back when war gripped the land the rangers were a tight-knit cohort who could be called upon at a moment's notice. But those times are far in the past, and every monarch in the ages since has offered us more and more freedom."

"Freedom is a good thing, though, right?" I asked, thinking of both my father's discussion of the popularity of a king and the tone in Ranger Owain's voice when he spit out the word "freedom."

"Yes, and no. It's a very popular thing, to be sure. Everybody wants freedom, right? The problem, though, is that when most people get it, they don't do what needs to be done with it. Case in point, you give the ranger council freedom to operate according to what they believe are their most important priorities, as the monarchs have done more and more in our peaceful years, and you get in return a lackluster, half-assed approach to what should be a very disciplined regimen of monitoring the land for threats. At this point, in fact, I'm probably the only ranger around who knows there's anything going on at the library, and if I, or you, or anyone else were to ask the council to intervene, it would take them several passings of the moon just to determine a course of action."

We sat in silence for several long minutes, brooding in response to what he'd said. "What do you think is the nature of this growing evil?" Seph finally asked, drawing the conversation back to the matter in front of us.

"It is shielded from my senses, young ranger. All, that is, but my hearing, and it's difficult with an old man's ears to discern the source and nature of the screeches I hear at night."

"Well, we will find out what it is that is shielded, and also what it is that is doing the shielding," Keion said, his chest puffed out just a little too far for my comfort. At that moment he looked like a peacock in full plumage.

Owain just harumphed.

We moved inside to get some food in. Everybody including the old ranger grand master joined in on preparing supper. In fact, he played a key role. After Seph and Keion had added their stuff to the pot to be boiled, he sniffed his disdain. Pulling a root-thing out of his bag, he cut off a piece, peeled it, and chopped it into little pieces.

"Ranger fare is vile," he said, and we all nodded. "Ranger Sephaline, you should not settle for a lifetime of eating vile food. This root can be dug up in the early fall, in several spots a few hours south of the main castle where you live." He described the stalk and the leaves and how to find it.

"What do you call it?" Keion asked, sniffing the new, bright smell coming from the cook pot.

"I call it Bron, but that's only because I'm old and partly senile and need the companionship at night." Seph snickered at the joke; Bron is a common female elf name.

"It's called ginger back on Earth," I said. I'd only seen it used a few times, but the smell was unforgettable. I was really looking forward to tasting it, and I said so.

That night we enjoyed a flavorful stew for once, and after that Owain pulled out a small zither-like stringed instrument, set it on his lap, and played some simple but cheerful songs that we all sang along to.

Later Seph and I talked about familiars, while she excused herself to go outside and relieve herself and I, of course, accompanied her for safety and security and—well, you know, girl unity. While we walked I asked the question I hadn't been willing to brave with the ancient and revered ranger—why did a young upstart like her get a wolverine, while he got a cardinal?

"Hey, the cardinal is a cool bird," she said. "He's loyal, and quite smart as birds go. Plus there are many times I wish I had a familiar who could fly overhead and give me a bird's eye view of the area around me."

"But a wolverine is so protective. So tough," I argued.

"He is, which is why he's perfect for me in my role as the guide and protector of the future queen."

"Is that why you chose him?"

"I didn't choose him, Alyssa. Familiars choose rangers, not the other way around."

"How does that happen? Does a new ranger pass through a zoo of some sort?"

"No, Alyssa, though that's funny. All elves go on a dream quest to enter adulthood, and the young ranger is approached by an animal at some point during that quest. The joining is made then. It's a pairing for life."

"Oh. Wow, I didn't know that. Hey, Owain was saying that rangers name familiars according to the animal's desires. Was Booboo your wolverine's desire?"

"Um, sort of. He's a very playful wolverine, though you probably haven't seen much of that."

"Playful. No, I admit, Cousin, that I haven't seen much that could be called playful. I'll take your word for it, though."

We arrived back at the cabin with me understanding so much more about my cousin and her familiar. It was, all things including the lack of indoor plumbing considered, a pretty good night.

MOR DDU A BOL BUWCH

as dark as a cow's stomach, which, I guess, is pretty dang dark.

Crossing The Blight

"What do you know of the prophecies, Keion? I asked the prince as he sat across from me in the small, dark clearing we'd stopped for lunch in. I was really curious, for one thing, but I also hadn't had much of a chance to just sit and talk to Prince Charming. He was always accompanied by his sisters, the evil ones, except for the times outdoors when he had taught me how to shoot, and then it was all business. Now, though, with Seph off scouting the nearby blight, it was just him and me. After our cooking and singing together the night before the ice had broken, finally, and we were actually chatting like people who—well, people who didn't hate each other, at least.

Hey, it was a start.

"They're written in ancient Elvish," he said, and then he ripped another hunk of sausage off of the roll.

"And?"

"And nothing. Alyssa, I haven't read the prophecies, nor did I ever pay much attention to them. I've heard that there have been several, and that some pertain to you, and that many have already come true. That's all that I know of them. I'm a fighter, not a scholar."

"Not even a little bit curious?"

"Oh, I'm curious about a great many things in this world, but that doesn't mean I need to go investigate any of them. My primary need is to protect those who are close to me, and also to follow the requests of my king and queen."

"And your—" I started to ask a question I probably shouldn't ask about his young love interest, but Seph interrupted as she guided her mount thundering into the meadow, Booboo ambling along behind hissing with every step.

"We must ride!" she called. "Ready your bows!"

Keion and I hopped onto our horses. It made me proud how much I'd improved my horsemanship skills, especially in the day since we'd met up with Keion. I'm sure, by the way, that it had nothing to do with any desire to show off.

"What did you see, ranger?" Keion asked as his charger stepped up to the edge of the clearing near Seph. Seph and I had come to realize that his use of the title, far from being an implied insult, was really his way of showing respect, since he had explained to Owain that he actually looked up to the rangers quite a lot.

"The blight has grown, for one thing," she said. "We would still be half an hour's travel from it were it still the same size, but now it begins just a few minutes' ride over that hill. Worse, though, as Owain warned, the blight has taken on a hostility it did not have before. It used to be merely a swath of dead land, Alyssa, but now there are—creatures—on it, creatures who sensed my presence and began moving my direction with less than happy intentions."

"What manner of creatures?" Keion asked. "Do I need my sword more than my bow?"

"I saw birds, and what looked like reptiles. Otherwise I could not say, as what my eyes took in was outside of my experience. You should keep your sword limber, but your sure aim with your bow will be of use soonest."

"Well, then, if the denizens of the blight are already gathering to cut you off, there's no time to be wasted, is there? Let's be off," he said, and readied his bow as he pushed his horse into a trot. I followed, my knuckles turning white as I tightened my grip on the bow's handle, and Seph and Booboo brought up the rear.

As we crested the hill, we stopped. Keion whistled in appreciation, while I just sat in shock. Stretched out in front of us, as far as my eye could see, was complete desolation. I had been ready for maybe some withered plants and some dead leaves, but this was grey soil and muck. I could feel the menace that Seph was talking about, too. The blight did not want us to pass through, clearly. Way off in the distance I saw rocks jutting upward, a huge, spindly building perched upon them.

"That's the library, Alyssa," Seph said, her eyes following mine. "We need to move, Keion. The creatures that sensed me before sense all of us now, and they're already moving to cut us off. It's too far for an all-out gallop, so we'll need every meter of advantage that we can gain. Let's go, let's go."

Keion nudged his horse out into a ground-eating lope, and I didn't have to knee Awel too hard for her to get to the same pace. Seph and Booboo launched in right behind us. I wondered briefly if Booboo could keep up, but then I remembered that the lightning-fast wolverine had kept up with us the first day of riding, back when we'd galloped for a mile or so.

We hadn't gone far into the forbidding terrain when the first of the creatures came at us. A pair of the largest ravens I've ever seen screamed from the sky above and launched themselves our direction. Keion and I raised our bows and loosed arrows at the same time. His arrow hit its mark precisely; mine was nearly perfect. Both ravens fell out of the sky, but

I could see others circling up ahead.

"Don't focus on aiming, Alyssa," Keion chided without looking back. He'd sensed my error, then. "Shoot like I taught you," he reminded me as he nocked another arrow.

The lopes our horses were maintaining were an entirely different gait than the trot we'd used on the range. Where the trot had forced me to focus on the up and down springiness of my thighs to maintain a stable upper body to shoot with, the lope was much smoother up and down but had more surging front to back. I focused on adapting my seat to the different feel of Awel's new gait, nocked my second arrow, and let fly at the next set of ravens that attacked.

Three arrows left our group this time. Keion's arrow once again plunged into its target. So did mine and Seph's, but we had chosen the same bird. Keion's hand flew as he raised and shot another arrow, and the third raven fell. He did turn his head then, looking back to glare at both of us.

"I'll call my targets," Seph said from just behind. Keion nodded silently and turned to front again.

We kept the pace.

Five ravens came at us next. Keion's aim I could see as he was making it. From behind me, Seph called out "right!" I shot at the middle one, and three of the vile birds fell. "Right again!" Seph called out, and I drew and shot an arrow at the left bird as fast as I could. Seph's arrow flew before mine could, but we still managed to send the other two birds to the ground.

"What are we going to do when they send a whole flock at us?" I asked out loud.

"Shut up, Princess," Keion yelled over his shoulder. "No need to give them ideas."

"I'm sure they already thought of that, pretty boy," Seph said as about twenty birds wheeled up in front of us and started their approach.

"That's Prince to you, Ranger," Keion growled and nocked an arrow. I did the same, and counted while I was doing it. I was glad we'd brought a couple hundred arrows each; we might need them all just to get to the library.

"I'll go from the right, you do the middle," Seph called.

All three of us loosed arrows as the ravens came into range. As I watched my arrow fly and reached for another, I realized that Keion had already released two more. Seph's third was also flying already. I had thought I was good, but I sure couldn't keep up with that! I did my best, though, pulling and shooting arrow after arrow. Another, slightly smaller, flock joined in right behind the first one we were just finishing decimating, and we did the same to it, Keion's arrows reminding me of a machine gun, his right arm blurring as it moved rapidly between quiver and string.

And yet, despite his intense speed, every arrow Keion shot hit its mark.

The last of the birds fell, its body pierced by an arrow from Seph's bow, and a new menace made itself known with a high-pitched howl to the right followed by several to the left.

"Oh, great," Seph muttered. Booboo hissed from the center of our pack.

"Wolves?" I asked. I'd never seen a wolf before, but the pictures made them out to be majestic animals.

"Dire wolves," Keion said. "Whatever happens, stay together. Shoot for the face first and the chest second. Sometimes it takes three or four arrows to bring one down."

"Of course it does," I said. "Why should this be easy, after all?" I glanced up at the library on the hill; we'd covered maybe a third of the distance to it.

Maybe. Then again, I suck at judging long distances.

Growls came from the left and the right at the same time as the dire wolves appeared. They weren't anything like what was in the pictures back at home. They were lacking the long, rangy legs of wolves I'd seen, for one thing. Gray ragged fur barely covered gaunt bodies, and deep red eyes glowed a hatred for us as they charged, five on each side. A dozen more ravens came at us from above, too.

"Alyssa, get the ravens," Keion said as his first arrow sizzled at the lead wolf on the left. I didn't look to see where it hit, though, because I really didn't want to find out what the ravens could do to us up close. I drew and aimed, and shot—and missed. Drawing another arrow, I silently cussed myself—I knew better than to aim like that. My next shot found its mark, and the next one did too, and so did the next, and the next.

It wasn't going to be enough, though. The birds were coming toward us faster than I was killing them. At least two, maybe three, were going to make it to attack us.

Suddenly Keion's bow swung upward, and he rapid-fired three arrows, ending the raven flock's attack. "Don't miss again, Alyssa," he growled as he spun on his seat to shoot to the right. I glanced over to the left and saw five lumps of charcoal-grey fur shivering on the ground, one to three arrows sticking out of each one.

"We need to pick up the pace," Keion called as the last dire wolf on the right went down. "Can your little pet keep up, ranger?"

"Yes," Seph said. "My little *pet* is capable of—"

Keion howled a warbling war cry that launched his stallion into a full gallop. Awel obviously didn't want to be left alone out there and so she needed no urging from me to join him, and soon it felt like the three of us were flying across the desolation. As we rode, I glanced over my shoulder and saw, through the dust cloud, several sets of dull red eyes following us. Apparently the dire wolves can't quite keep up with horses that are rocking along at a full gallop. Looking down, I saw that apparently a wolverine can, and given that I told myself never to tick Booboo off.

Shooting an arrow at a gallop is different from shooting at a lope, too. The gallop is a lot smoother even than the lope, because it feels like the back of the horse is just floating along above the ground. It should be easier, then, but it's not. Part, I think, is the psychological fear involved with flying along so fast on the back of a horse while letting go of any hold you have so you can manage a bow. The other, real, part, though, is that the speed of the wind whipping by deflects the arrows a little as they're leaving your hand.

My first shot at a gallop, in fact, went way wide. An exasperated sigh by the prince caught my ears as I nocked another. For the second, my adjustment was right on, and the dire wolf I'd shot at went down in a heap with my arrow through his eye.

More dire wolves, more ravens, then more dire wolves and more ravens attacked us. No matter how fast our horses' pace was eating the ground underneath us, the blight still seemed to have unlimited foes to throw at us. We raced on, three bows acting nearly in unison, all the blight's efforts shot down before it could get to us.

And then I heard it.

Over to the left, a shrill screech sounded from one of the taller rock outcroppings. Suddenly the ravens and the wolves that had been chasing us wheeled away from their attacks and pursuit. It was like the bad guys were scared of the other bad guy, whoever it was.

Another screech rocked the air around us, and then two red leathery wings unfolded from the top of the rock. A crimson serpent's head slowly snaked up to take its place between the upraised wings, and then it turned two angry black eyes toward us.

"A dragon! I thought there weren't any of those left," I said, running my hand on Awel's neck to calm her down.

"There aren't. That's a wyvern, not a dragon," Seph's voice called out. It was harder to hear each other at the gallop, but Seph was shouting. So, apparently, was I.

"What's the difference?" It was an innocent question; what was peeling itself out of the outcropping to our front sure looked like a dragon. Small, maybe, but I'd never seen a full-sized dragon to compare it to, and I doubted that my companions had either.

Keion's answer settled it easily enough, though. "A dragon would have killed us already and be busy eating our corpses. With a wyvern, we might have a tiny chance of living."

"Oh. Well, that's better," I said, unable to quite contain my sarcasm.

"Shut up, you two. I need to concentrate," Seph growled as the wyvern snapped its wings completely out and, with another terrifying screech, took to flight. It really was pretty big, I realized as I watched it fly above us. The shadow of just its body covered all three horses at the same time.

It screeched again.

"Why does it keep up with that screech?" I asked.

"Wyverns love their prey terrified when they swoop in for the kill," Keion answered.

"Shut *up*, please. Somebody's trying to do something back here," Seph said.

"You're not...." I started to say but I let my voice trail off into the wind. She wanted quiet, so I'd give her quiet, for one thing, but I also figure it's a bad thing to remind someone she's not supposed to cast magical spells when she's about to cast a magical spell that might save your life.

I rode along, arrow nocked against the chance I might actually get to make a shot before the wyvern killed us all. It circled around once again and screeched, louder this time, and then stopped and hovered above our path, head following our galloping horses. I imagined the creature calculating the best path to take to swoop us all up.

Suddenly it bobbled a tiny bit to the left. Just a little, but I could tell from the way the wyvern batted its wings to correct the motion that it wasn't intentional. Maybe, I thought, whatever Seph was doing was starting to work.

Then the beast bobbled the other direction. As the wyvern flapped unevenly to right itself, a huge gust of wind caught its outstretched wing and flipped it over and around.

The screeches became strange little squawks as the wyvern tried to fly through the hurricane-style buffeting. I wanted to laugh, to shout, to cheer, but I didn't dare interrupt Seph as she worked. Nor did I dare turn my attention away from guiding Awel. That Seph could guide her galloping horse toward the only opening I saw in the wall surrounding the library while shaping the wind into a furious storm was impressive, but I was pretty sure I could do no such thing. The gates looked tiny from a distance and didn't get much larger as the three of us closed in.

Then, finally, we were through the two narrow gates of the wall that stood around the library's grounds. The blighted grey ground disappeared right at the wall, and green grass lay under foot again. I looked around at the nondescript ten or twelve foot tall black wall as we rushed through—it sure didn't seem substantial enough to keep the wolves, the ravens, or the wyvern out.

As soon as we were through the gate, the wyvern that we'd all been running from righted itself and flew peacefully back to its rock. At the same time, the gates slammed shut entirely of their own will, it seemed, and three ancient-looking elves appeared at the foot of the main stairs leading into the building. The trio processed down and along the well-tended gravel path through the front grounds of the library toward where our horses now stood panting.

"Greetings, travelers," the one in the center said as he slipped his black cowl off of his head, putting the ancient ridged skin of his solemn face on display. "It brings my heart joy to see that you made it successfully past the newest challenge in the blight. The wards inscribed upon the gate and the walls protect us from such beasts, but there is little we can do out there to convince it to go elsewhere. Regardless, you have arrived, and you are safe here, and so I bid you welcome to the hallowed grounds of the Library of Alecsanddrha. I am Gethin, the head librarian."

The Library of Alecsanddrha

Keion was the first to react, swinging his long leg up and around and leaping off of his charger. "Greetings, Librarian Gethin," he said, making a show of athleticism that didn't really go with how out of breath he sounded. "I am Keion, a seeker of the ancient lore."

We'd rehearsed this bit. As little reason as we had to distrust the librarians, there were still ears in every wall, danger behind every corner. No point waltzing in to a parade of "I'm the Prince" and "I'm the Princess." Simple pilgrims, seekers of the ancient lore as they were called, would be our identities as we searched the library's holdings for clues. Besides, seekers of the ancient lore wasn't far off from the truth, as it was.

Seph and I both climbed down from our horses and nodded to the librarians as we introduced ourselves as seekers of the ancient lore. They just nodded, and smiled. It felt kind of good, for once not being the object of the genuflection that was normal for elves meeting their princess.

I looked past the librarians toward the library itself. It was truly beautiful, in a dark and forbidding sort of way. It looked like what you might get if the Addams Family could've sung their house out of nature and into existence. I mean, I hadn't been sure what to expect—what does anybody think an elf library might look like? A cathedral, sure, or a castle, I would've had a mental image going in. But a library? The ones back home are in normal buildings, so I just figured this would be, too.

The building wasn't really normal, but it was close enough for something big enough to house what I'd read was a huge trove of information. It was narrow in the front, and its black walls looked very long. A front porch was nonexistent, probably because they didn't expect many people to sit out on Old Gothic furniture and chat. The building was a few stories tall, and an irregular slate roof was stretched across its top. Afallon's ability to sing a building into anything resembling a sturdy, attractive shape became something I seriously questioned. Then again, it had been a long, long time since then, and who knew if the librarians responsible for the building had the same singing ability or if they just attacked it with standard hammers and stuff. Nobody back on Earth could properly replicate Elvis, after all.

"Three seekers at once! What a wonderful thing. As you can probably tell, we do not get many visitors, much less seekers, these days," Gethin said. The trio's faces were steady, unemotional, unreadable.

"Small wonder. Do seekers normally get ravaged by the blight's welcome as we did?" Keion asked. It probably wasn't really a question a seeker would ask, since we figured most of them were only interested in reading books, but I figured our cover was already pretty tenuous with the shooting our way through the monsters and then the whole wyvern thing and all. He probably figured the same.

"The wyvern that accompanied your entrance only recently

settled in," Gethin said. "As I said earlier, our offensive capabilities are extremely limited, and we have not yet had an opportunity to find a way to use the little bit we have available to convince it to find another home. You are the first seekers to be bothered by the beast."

"We do the seekers an injustice, Gethin, by making them stand here in the courtyard instead of taking refreshment inside," one of the librarians said.

"Aye, Lefan," Gethin said. "Iago, take the seekers' horses, please, while we see to their stomachs."

"No," Keion said, shaking his head and raising his hand to stop Iago. "Thank you, but no. These horses have been our faithful companions for many leagues, and we would like to see them to their stalls ourselves."

"As you wish," Gethin said. "Please join us inside when you are ready. And," he added, turning around and then twisting his face back over his shoulder, "your—pet—is welcome inside too, so long as it is—"

"He is," Seph interrupted. "I have trained him well."

"I see," Gethin said and led the other two librarians back inside the hall. I wondered what, exactly, he 'saw,' besides one agitated and fairly pissed off wolverine.

Once the front door closed behind the three robed men, Keion turned on Seph and said, "It didn't do our story much good that your *pet* was *hissing* at the librarians the entire time."

She shrugged and looked confused. "Booboo doesn't normally react like that. Sorry. I'm getting strange signals from him. He's reacting to the librarians as though they were wyverns."

"Wyverns? They're very clearly not beasts," Keion said.

"I know. He must just be stressed out over that run we did. Aren't you a little bit stressed?"

Keion took a deep breath and turned to me before answering. "I am, but I'll be okay. How are you doing, Alyssa?"

I was the same as he was, and I told him so. As we led the horses off to the stable, I asked, "So how many wyverns have you fought in your travels?"

"None," Keion said. "They're a very rare beast, preferring to remain as far away from elves as possible. You, ranger?"

"None," she said. "I haven't ever even sensed one. Unicorns will pack together if a wyvern comes around, it is said, and fight the evil beast off as one unit, and from what I've heard you haven't lived till you've witnessed a squad of unicorns in a fight."

"Well, I would just as soon not witness that at all," I said. "But now that it's over, I have to ask: how did you do that bit of magic there?"

"That *wasn't* magic, Alyssa," Seph said. "The wind was already there, I just asked it to bend a little faster than it normally does. It's no different from asking a tree to shape itself a certain way. Don't you see the difference between magic and ranger work yet?"

"Well, no, I'm not sure I do. What's the difference between the wind spell and a fireball?"

"Look, it's really quite simple. With a fireball, you're creating the fire," Keion said. "With the wind storm, you're just moving wind that already exists. Now, can we get to the horses? They're tired, and I'm tired, and I, for one, am looking forward to seeing the inside of the library."

We brushed the horses down in silence. Every so often a far-off howl of a dire wolf or the cry of a raven would make Awel tense up, but eventually she looked around at me with actual gratitude—I'd never thought a horse could express that—and I joined Keion and Seph with our backpacks, bows, and arrows. We slipped in to the library through the side door.

"Welcome," the librarian who'd been introduced as Iago said

to us as we gathered in the little chamber just inside the door. The mud room had a few small benches and some coat hooks, but otherwise was stark and darkly-paneled. It was actually pretty chilly inside the building, which smelled of old books and older furniture.

For the first time I got a close look at the gold-toned pin I'd seen on each of the librarian's black-robed breasts. It surprised me how much it resembled Draignerthol, but without the gemstone eyes. That, or my own pendant's power, at least as far as I could sense. I wondered why they'd picked that particular symbol to stand for the librarians, but I decided against asking. I was tired, and had already gotten enough exasperated replies for one day.

"I would be pleased to show you to the seekers' rooms. Is—your *pet*—going to be okay, Seeker Sephaline?"

Seph giggled, her way of defusing the situation, as Iago looked down his nose at Booboo, who was, in turn, snarling at the librarian. "Yes, yes, he's just had a long journey, and it was a hard last ride. Booboo, this is Iago, a librarian. Be nice to the librarians, or you won't get anything to eat tonight. Do you hear me?" Booboo apparently did. His fur settled back down onto his back, and he lowered his nose toward the floor and stopped making the noise that was causing my teeth to grind together.

"Thank you," Iago said and slowly led us down the dark paneled side hall to a series of closed doors. He opened the first and stepped in. "It is my hope that these accommodations will satisfy your needs. We have no serving staff, so we ask that all our guests join us in carrying our own water from the kitchen at the end of the hall. Our privy is an outdoor affair, on the other side of the stables, but chamber pots are available in each room. The tower bell is rung thrice each day to signify meal times, and upon its call we invite you to join us in the central dining hall, where I will lead you to next. Our head librarian has asked that you join him at the main table in hopes of recovery from your long journey and traumatic arrival, and to share some time for talking in comfort. Other times, should you be hungry or thirsty, you may avail yourself of our kitchen and pantry as you need. And now," Iago finished as he walked back out of the room and down the hall a little, "I will await your completion of your freshening observances, just down the hall. When all are done, it will be my pleasure to escort you to the main dining room's table." True to his word, he moved down the hall and stood.

"Well. rang—er, Sephaline, why don't you take the first room, then Alyssa, and then me? I would presume that our items are perfectly secure in our rooms here," Keion said, nearly blowing the cover—which was already pretty tenuous—by calling Seph 'ranger.' Still, I knew his placement of rooms was tactical; he wanted me between my two protectors, and I saw no reason to object.

The room was sparse, but I had kinda expected that, in the back of my mind anyway. These librarians were the same breed of folks as the old monks I'd heard about in my home world, and I didn't suppose they'd have much use for frilly sheets or indoor plumbing. The bed had a small pad and pillow and was made with a simple sheet and blanket. The sink was nothing more than a basin, beside which they'd already brought a pitcher of water—hot, I found out as I stuck a finger in it. Good. A washcloth and towel completed the sink area. The only other furniture was a simple bare wood chair and a matching wood table, bearing a candlestick with a few wax candles beside.

Homey. Not comfy, really, but it would do the job.

I set my backpack on the chair and laid my bow and arrows across the bed. I was still a little too jumpy to feel like unstringing the bow yet, and laying it flat was the best thing for it after the workout I'd given it. Longingly, I looked back over at the small wooden table and wished I could go back in time a few days and change my mind on not bringing the picture. What I wouldn't give for my little photo of Momma to prop up on the table and keep me company, to remind me that some-where out there was a perfectly sane little Southern home in a perfectly sane little Mississippi town. A place without wyverns looking to eat us, without ravens and dire wolves attacking, and without wolverines wanting to shred librarians.

A place, I thought with my first smile in what seemed like forever, where Momma could make it all right by tousling my hair and kissing my forehead.

I dipped the washcloth into the steaming pitcher and rubbed it over my face and along the back of my neck. That didn't replace the need for Momma's kiss, but it still felt so good that I did it again with a fresh sling of hot water. Then I noticed that the rivulets from the washcloth were washing away lines of proof that my arms were filthy, and so I settled in for a good scrub of all exposed skin, followed by a few luxurious moments of rubbing my now-clean areas with a towel. I still needed a good soak in a bath after a few days on the trail, but overall I felt pretty good.

I did, though, need to find a way to get a good bath some-time during my stay in the library.

DYNN

*tight, like a muscle is when you're drawn back
ready to fight or flee.*

Dinner and a Story

"So—Alyssa, Keion, and Sephaline. If I may cut through the veil of secrecy, I believe it's Princess Alyssa, Prince Keion, and Ranger Sephaline. Am I correct?" Gethin wasted no time in getting down to business once we were seated with a couple of trays of food in front of us.

I sat in shock, staring down at my food and feeling guilty for the story we'd told. I couldn't help but wonder how they had known, and whether the fact that they had known should bother me.

"You have seen through our ruse," Keion said, apparently thinking the same thing I was. "Should we be concerned?"

"Absolutely not. Your safety is assured here in the Library of Alecsanddrha. I am surprised that you even attempted the ruse, in fact."

"The king ordered us to travel under cover. I am sure you will understand His Highness's concern over his daughter's safety."

"Oh, of course, of course. So if I may ask, what is it that brings the half-elf princess to the Library of Alecsanddrha?"

I almost didn't hear that the question was directed at me, as absorbed as I was in the room. It was long and narrow, with a table big enough to seat forty or fifty people stretched out from one end to the other. Along the walls stood a series of evenly spaced, matching hutches, each containing simple porcelain dishes. The length of the wall was decorated with cloth tapestries designed with repeating simple shapes: flowers, stars, and so on. And yet, for all the repetition, it was obvious that one end of the room saw constant daily use while the other hadn't been used in a long, long time.

I did hear, though, and I turned to the head librarian, who sat at the end of the table. He already knew who we were, so there was no point in hiding any—or most, anyway—of the truth, I figured. "I am here to read the prophecies related to the Dragon Queen."

"You're going to be here a while, then," Gethin said, and Lefan snickered from behind a hunk of cheese.

"The prophecy is that long?" I asked, innocently.

"Long, yes, as well as convoluted and quite hard to read. The words of the prophecy itself are written in a single long scroll, in truth, but the scholarly commentary fills the entirety of one of our book chambers."

"Who wrote the prophecy?" I asked. As long as I was asking newbie questions, I might as well keep going.

"Unknown. Actually, a group of scholars meeting toward the beginning of the current epoch suggested that they were the work of multiple prophets. That theory is supported by the fact that there seem to be several voices in the writing, but that can also be effected when a single prophet ingests multiple different prophecy-inducing substances."

"Like LSD one day, and acid the next, and shrooms the following?" I asked, knowing they wouldn't catch the reference and not really caring.

"If by shrooms you refer to certain types of mushrooms, then yes, exactly like that. In fact, there are many who feel that the holding of the prophecy scroll is silly, that the work is simply the deranged rambling of a drug-addled lunatic."

"Most prophecies I've heard of have a set of critics who believe that about them," I said, nodding slowly like I knew what I was talking about. I didn't, but what would they know?

"Of course," Gethin said, smiling. "And we can certainly hope that the prophecy in question, if interpreted correctly as it stands now, is one that fits in that category, can we not?"

"We can, but why would we?" I asked. Personally, I thought it was cool having a prophecy written about me. Who wouldn't want to be the subject of an ancient seer's writings?

"Well, dear, how do you feel about the idea of burning down this library?"

"It's—it's horrible. It's a travesty," I said, using the biggest word I could come up with to impress the librarians.

"I agree wholeheartedly. And if you feel that way, then, you see, you cannot possibly be the Dragon Queen," Gethin said, his finger pointing at me, thrusting toward me with each syllable.

"Why not?"

"Because if you were, you'd be here to burn this library to the ground," he said.

"Tut, tut, Gethin. No point getting into such melodramatics. That part of the prophecy, after all, is not precisely clear on which library is to be burned to the ground, and analyses differ on what that part means, anyway" Iago interrupted.

"Well, yes, but it's fairly clear to me that the term 'original library' refers to this one. And she's definitely not here to burn this library down. You can see that in her eyes when she mentions books." Gethin had judged me right; I've been told by others that my eyes light up and sparkle when I talk about reading. I always just thought I was a nerd. He continued, "But that notwithstanding, the princess is also not here with all of her father's horses, nor, for that matter, all the king's men."

"No, but I kind of wish we were. Why are you staring at me like that?" I asked. As a group, the librarians had stopped eating and were eyeing me like I had just announced I was a librarian-eating vampire.

"Listen, the king's horses and the king's men are not here, and that is that," Gethin said to the other two librarians. "Now, go back to eating. Alyssa, you must be careful what you express a wish for, as that is one of the key signs of the prophesied burning of the library, and of the end times beyond as well."

"Okay, I will be more careful in the future, but I tell you that it doesn't matter. I would rather *die* than burn a single book, much less an entire library," I argued, shaking my head.

"Let us hope it does not come to that as a choice we must make," the head librarian said, and I felt a chill run down my spine at his words.

"Do you bear the mark of the dragon?" Lefan asked, his stare suddenly making me feel like an elementary kid being questioned by the principal. His question drew sharp looks from both of the other two librarians in addition to Keion, who looked furious.

"It is none of your business," my protective Prince Charming said through narrowed teeth.

"You are correct, Prince. My apologies," Lefan nodded his way out of the conversation, and then he rose and left the room.

"My colleague is a little bit abrupt sometimes with his questions," Gethin said. "Please forgive him for the lapse in judgment in directing such a rude query toward the princess."

I couldn't give much away; neither Seph nor Keion knew I had the birthmark, either. So I just nodded, and Iago rose. "If it would be your pleasure," the librarian said, "I would show you through the great halls of the library so that you may get a fresh start in the morning."

"Why in the morning?" I asked. "Is there a closing time I should be aware of?"

"The sun," Gethin said. "We are not equipped with glow lights or energy-powered sconces as is, I believe, your home castle. Thus it is that when the sun goes down, all we are left with is candles, and we have a dwindling supply of those. Should the need be pressing, of course, you are welcome to remain up and read by candle light, but we ask that normal research take place during the hours when the sun bathes the entirety of the internal chambers of the library with its glow thanks to the unique positioning of windows throughout."

"Oh, Can I see the windows?" I asked, thinking that such a system would be really cool.

"You cannot see most of them without climbing out onto the roof, and we do not recommend that activity for a princess of the realm, Alyssa. Iago will point out the internal interfaces as well as he can, but much of the working design is contained within the walls. I am sorry."

I tried not to let my disappointment show. Windows that aren't just windows, but instead form a channel for light to get into a room, is such a cool idea. "That's okay. Lead on, Iago. Keion, Seph, you two coming with?"

They did, after securing candles for each of us. The ground floor of the library, it turned out, contained the seekers' rooms, where we were staying, the kitchen, and the librarians' chambers, as well as the room we'd just eaten in. Overall, it was decorated in a style of early elf drab, with dark wood and dark furniture and only very occasional decoration to either. They let us glance into Iago's quarters, which for him was a more or less permanent home, and I was shocked to see that he didn't have much better, or more, furniture than was in the sparse guest rooms.

The kitchen was huge. That surprised me a little, considering how difficult it had been for us to get to the library and thus how rare visitors had to be, but I'd seen the size of the dining room, too. "Has the library entertained large parties?" I asked.

"Huge parties, Princess," Gethin said. "At times this facility has been used as a central meeting place for the realm, playing host to hundreds of members of the nobility. Those times, alas, are no longer, but I would welcome your consideration of our services once you rise to the throne."

The Tomb of Alecsanddrha was next on the agenda. Toward the rear of the building was a stairwell leading down, and it was creepy. Besides being dark, it was also irregularly curved, and the stone walls were darkened with dampness. It opened up, though, into a rectangular chamber, one that was about the same size as our living room back home, in which two stone caskets lay. One of the caskets was spectacular, still detailed after all the many years with the likeness of a woman and a book on the lid. I didn't need to read the text to know that I stood before the remains of Alecsanddrha herself.

The other casket was much less ornamented. The simple script along the top proclaimed that within the stone vessel lay Afallon, master of the castle and beloved of Alecsanddrha.

"I know who sang her sarcophagus into shape," I said, my voice echoing off the stone and making Seph jump and turn her head. "But who is responsible for laying Afallon to rest down here beside his beloved?"

Gethin nodded reverently and said, "Ah, that is a good question, Princess. It is not known who crafted the memorial to Afallon. It is suspected that it is the result of the efforts of one of their two daughters, though. I must presume you are already aware of the story of Gwenhwyvar and Gwenhwyvach, yes? Well, then, you must know that the two could never have worked together, even to bury their beloved father, and so it is said that one or the other, but not both, managed to lay him to rest beside the love of his life."

"Wouldn't it have been more likely to be Gwenhwyvar? She was, after all, the favored daughter," I said.

"That is, indeed, the argument made by many historians, Princess. And yet she was truly the most favored one, not only by him, but also seemingly by fate itself. Her life seemed blessed—oh, you do not know this story? We shall have to tell it sometime. To the point at hand, though, it was Gwenhwyvar's sister who remained closer to her father throughout the remainder of his life. Some say it was devotion to the old man, while others suggest it was her own need that kept them close. Regardless, that fact lends itself to the supposition that perhaps it was the lesser daughter who cared enough to bury her father down here."

"So, nobody has ever researched further?" I asked.

"Princess, you do my pride injury with your question. We who live and work here are historians at heart. We have researched the matter as far as is possible, only to find in the end that some truths are indeed lost to antiquity."

"I'm sorry, I didn't mean to do any injury."

Gethin nodded in reply and led us back up to the main floor, and then we set to climbing into the room I'd been dying to see: the one with the books.

Up a single central flight of stairs we found the wondrous area. Granted, I've only ever been in the public library in my little bitty town in Mississippi, and then in the very simple abbey library back at the castle. I thought both were grand, but neither of those compared to the cavernous ceilings—they must have been twenty feet high—supported by walls that were covered from bottom to top, and from side to side, with filled book shelves. In the area between the walls were other book cases that also stretched nearly to the ceiling. Several ladders stood in locations around the room for use, and one floor to ceiling ladder was available on rollers to reach books on the wall.

"How many books and scrolls are contained in the library?" I asked Iago.

He shrugged and looked confused. "I—I don't know. Why would one count them?"

"To judge and rank the size of the library, I suppose."

"But the size of the library isn't usefully to be gauged by a simple number of books contained within, but rather by the quality and relevance of information available therein. You could post ten thousand banns and decrees and have less useful information than is contained in but a few scrolls."

"I suppose so."

"Besides, who would have the time to count these books and scrolls even if it were important?"

"I never thought of that. What do the librarians here do all day, without patrons to guide? You don't, after all, have any computer databases to keep up to date." I'd really had to reach on the computers bit; the elf language didn't have a word for those. I ended up just kind of describing a talking box that knew lots of stuff, and that was strange enough to be ignored by the librarians.

"We spend nearly all our time preserving the works we have, Princess. We have librarians in other areas who send us newly discovered works, but we have not heard from them in a few years. But some of these manuscripts are thousands of years old, and as the paper they're written on wears out we rewrite it onto new material."

"Have the prophecies been rewritten, then?"

"Depending on which prophecies you are referring to, yes, from once or twice to several hundred times. But in answer to the question you didn't ask, each time the librarian takes special pains to ensure an exact copy is made. It would be unconscionable to change a work of such antiquity at the mere mark of a pen.”

My heart started beating faster when Iago announced that we had reached the room of prophecy, but I was disappointed when he opened the door to darkness. This room, he explained, had its light source pointed toward the rising sun, thus reinforcing from the earliest days that prophecy was a matter best studied by early risers.

“Am I permitted to remove works from here to the main library in order to study them?” I asked.

“Certainly. You may move the works here most anywhere on the grounds except the tunnels. As long as they do not leave the premises, we believe that study is best attempted wherever the seeker feels most comfortable. Except, of course, in your case, we ask that you not bring books and candles too close together. You know—prophecy, and all.”

“Sure thing,” I agreed. Prophecy be danged, no way I was going to burn the library down!

LLYFRGELL

a library. Near as I can tell there's no official heirarchy to libraries, but the one I found myself in was amazing!

Time To Read

I got up the next morning and tromped out to what served as an archery range as the sun rose. Keion and Seph were both already there, serving each other wisecracks and bets about their various accuracies.

When I walked up, Keion looked at me with a perturbed expression. "Alyssa, you should be in the library studying prophecy."

"You said I should start every morning, even Sadwrn, with a hundred arrows."

"Yes, of course I did. That was back in the safety of your father's castle. Now we're here in the Library of Alecsanddrha, surrounded by a blight that wants to kill us with a resident wyvern that wants to eat us, and populated by a group of librarians who apparently wonder if you're going to burn their home down, and who Booboo seems to think are as dangerous as they believe you are. I think it might be best for our chances of continued good health if you read as fast as you can."

"Well, now that you put it that way, I guess I'll head up to the library."

"Good idea. Hey, did you take a bath?"

"Not exactly. Why?"

"You smell better than you did yesterday."

"Thanks, Keion. I think. No, I just found some soap next to the wash basin and washed up with it before I went to bed last night. It made me feel like a girl again. You should try it"

"What makes you think I wish to feel like a girl?"

I snorted. "I don't. But you know what they say: 'cleanliness is next to godliness.'"

"Who says that?"

"I have no idea. I've just heard it a lot, back on my—my former—world." I'd been about to say my world, but I wanted everybody to know I'd accepted Kiirajanna as my home.

"They must not do many military campaigns on your—your former—world," Keion said, mimicking me.

"Oh, they do, they just believe in proper sanitation," I shot back and walked inside.

For breakfast I pulled some sausage and cheese from the kitchen pantry and headed right on up to the library with it. It was quiet there. Completely, dreadfully quiet. It felt like I'd gone out to a different planet, one where there wasn't another soul. I started reading the top of the first scroll labeled "Dragon Queen" but after several lines it started sounding like I really was reading the work of a deranged lunatic. The sentences, even the phrases, didn't make sense. The writer kept switching up present and future tense: "For unto us she will be born, she is healing and burning down at the same time!"

I wondered if my interpretation was wrong, so I picked up one of the scholarly books on the subject and started reading it. No, the scholar who wrote that also used the term deranged lunatic on more than one occasion.

I read the first chapter in the scholar's work and put my head in my hands, dejected. Why would Dad and so many others put so much faith in the work of a deranged lunatic like this? Why set me up to ride three days and nearly get killed in the blight just to find out for myself that the prophecy was gibberish?

The early bell rang, signaling a call to breakfast. I took a bite of the hunk of sausage instead; there was no way I was leaving. I went over to get another, more elementary-looking, scholarly work on the prophecy and started reading it.

Soon the door opened and Iago stepped in, carrying a small tray. He placed it down in front of me and said, "We thought you might like a little bit of sustenance to help you study."

I nodded, engrossed in the chapter. He left after uncovering the plate. It smelled good, but I had no interest in stopping to eat it. The book I'd picked up got into the language used in the prophecy in an unusual way. You should, the author suggested, read it in the sing-song way of the ancient storytellers, feeling free to leave some of the words out. While modern prophecy interpretation focused on the meaning of each individual word, the first epoch writer or writers who crafted the Dragon Queen prophecies did so for their own people in their own age, using their own lyrical storytelling technique, the work said.

It made a lot of sense.

I turned back to the scroll containing the prophecy and read more of it, letting my mind flit over the phrases and focus on the underlying current of meaning instead of the individual words. It really did make sense.

Finally.

The sound of the lunch bell made me jump. It seemed the portals that brought the daytime sun into the library also served as vibration chambers to focus the bell's clangs. Didn't matter; I wasn't really hungry. I looked at the cold breakfast still laying there, decided on a bite of sausage instead, and kept reading.

It didn't take long for Iago to return, once again carrying food. This time it was a bowl of stew with a hunk of bread. "Princess, you need to keep up your strength. It is said there was once a scholar named Heledd who perished inside this very library from too much reading and not enough sustenance. Tell me, are you finding anything interesting?"

I explained what I'd learned about the way to read the prophecy, and he nodded. "Indeed," he said, "that is one of the secrets we were prepared to divulge sometime today, assuming you didn't find it on your own and left frustrated. It is to your credit that you found that work."

"Thank you. By the way, where is the bit about 'all the king's horses, and all the king's men'? It sounds like a nursery rhyme I grew up hearing." I pushed the scroll toward Iago hoping for a turn and a point from him. Neither Dad nor Naissa ever mentioned that bit. Not that either of them had told me much of what I'd find in the prophecy, but somehow I would have thought that one of them should've told me about that bit.

"Actually, that part isn't in the prophecy, per se. It's a quote from a derivative work, a term we use for studies of the primary scroll, by Master Bryn in the third century of the current epoch. In the prophecy itself you'll find the part about the final days of the library describing a mighty host on horseback coming to fight alongside the Dragon Queen, and since the King of the Elves is the only one who could summon such a vast cavalry force, Master Bryn supposed it was his doing. I suspect he took the wording from the same nursery rhyme that you thought of—Humpty Dumpty, I presume?"

I nodded. "You know the nursery rhymes from my former realm?"

"Indeed I do. There's a work out there in the main collection that details a study Master Bryn undertook of Earth-based children's tales, one in which he described how the greater bulk of them came from our own fables. It's a fascinating work."

"I'm sure it is," I said. My words were just words, though; I had no desire to read a study on the sources of children's tales.

"Well, I'll let you get back to your efforts," Iago said. I nodded, and the room went silent once again, except for the sound of the scroll unrolling.

The bell echoed through the room again, and once again the sound made me jump. When I looked away from the scroll to get my bearings I noticed that the light in the room was quite a bit dimmer than it had been just a few—well, hours, it must have been—before. I knew it got too dark to read at dinner time, but the evidence of that surprised me. I looked one last time through the gloom at the works spread out across the table, decided I could assume nobody would mess with them in a deserted library, and went downstairs for dinner.

Iago cried out when I sat down the tray I'd carried down. "You haven't eaten lunch either, Princess! You must be starving. You must take care of yourself and eat while you are working; it wouldn't do for anything to happen to you while you are under our care. You wouldn't want your father upset at us, would you?"

"I'm not a little girl to be guilted into eating, Iago," I said. Not a little girl, but I was very, very tired after a long day of deciphering ancient elvish scribbles at a very slow rate. I poured myself a glass of cool water from the butler stand against the wall and slipped into a chair beside Seph. "Hey, guys. How was your day?" I asked.

"Boring," Seph and Keion both said at the same time.

"Aw, that's too bad. Maybe you could both come up to the library tomorrow and read books about—oh, about whatever you want to read about," I said, nibbling at the soup that had been put out for dinner. It was pretty good, but apparently Seph and Keion had failed to work up an appetite also.

"Maybe," Keion said, nodding and looking at his bowl as though he had zero energy left to eat or to nod, either one.

"How was your day?" Seph asked with the same amount of interest as Keion was displaying.

"Lovely," I said, and I launched into the tale of discovery I'd created. I stopped nearly halfway through, though, as only the librarians were really paying attention. "Hey," I said, "why don't you two go on to bed?"

"Okay," Seph said, and the pair of elves slipped out of their chairs and padded back toward our rooms. Moments later I heard their doors close. It was—weird. I would never have imagined either Seph or Keion—especially not Keion—to be so pliable. Ah, well, maybe boredom was something that elves really aren't good at dealing with, I figured.

Gethin shifted his plate of bread, cheese, and some type of fruit, down to sit across from me. He smiled one of those crazy elf smiles and said, "I would like to hear of the rest of your day's research, Alyssa. It is what I love about my job."

I managed to finish the story of the day's reading, though it wasn't nearly as fun telling the librarians about a book they must have already read as it would've been telling my friends. When I mentioned the part about derivative works he smiled and nodded, his head bobbing rapidly. "It is one of our proudest credits to be able to claim ownership of every known derivative work on the prophecy of the first epoch. They are all stored, as you know, in the same room as the prophecy itself. You were exactly right to seek their wisdom out. You haven't eaten but a few bites of your soup, though. Is it not to your liking?"

It was to my liking, actually; I just wasn't hungry. I explained that to him and he let me get away with just another few bites. I begged out and laid down on my bed. I hadn't realized how tired I was, and so I dozed off immediately.

A Sickness Overtakes

The next morning I sprang out of bed, tossed another couple of hunks of sausage and cheese in my pouch, and was up the stairs before the librarians could force the issue of me eating breakfast. My stomach objected to the thought of eating, for one thing, and the books weren't going to read themselves.

Well, maybe they would—elves, magical library and all—but that was beside the point.

First, before I started back in on the prophecy, I was interested in this Queen Rhiannon the White. She'd been the one to disappear, forever sequestered to the Earth, with Draignerthol around her neck. What was she like, I wondered?

I found a book on the ancient queen of the elves and read furiously. I mean, I wanted to know about Rhiannon, but I also wanted to get back to the prophecy. Besides, the book I'd found was more of a fable than a history—the queen did this, and she did that, and I was surprised that it didn't recall her walking across water.

Then I got to the section of the book that contained pictures, where I was struck dumb for several minutes. It seems elves back then took magical portraits, and since then, they've made an art out of reproducing the magical portraits exactly as they were shown. Somebody, in writing the book about Rhiannon, had worked at reproducing a perfect portrait of the great queen in order for those in the future to be able to enjoy her wise visage.

So I flipped the page to find a picture of Rhiannon the White.

I found myself staring at a perfect likeness of Momma.

It was too much to take in, to even imagine. I put the book down and returned to my task of reading the prophecy.

As I started reading, Iago pushed a tray of eggs and some sort of hash-like stuff at me anyway. I smiled and nodded and went back to reading without talking to him.

It wasn't that the prophecy had gotten any easier to read. In fact, if it had done anything, it had gotten harder. But I was into it now, and I had a rhythm going, and I really hated being disturbed. I jumped yet again when the lunch bell rang, and I shook my head soon after when Iago clucked his tongue over the still-full breakfast plate he swapped out with a bowl of stew for lunch. Without even looking at him, I waved him off.

I'm not hungry. I'm not a child. I'm reading. Go away. I wondered, if I just thought those phrases a little harder, whether he'd get them without me having to speak. Speaking, after all, was forbidden in a normal library, and this was so much more than a normal library.

It was, I remembered as I got to the passage they'd mentioned the other evening and it hit me between the eyes, the library that I was going to be responsible for burning down.

No. There was no way I would burn down a library. *No.* No way the prophecy was right. *NO!* I shouted at myself in the quiet safety of my own head as I sat back in the chair and stared at the ceiling.

Yet there it was, right there on the page in black inked squiggly lines.

Granted, what the librarian—I couldn't recall which—had said was correct. The prophecy didn't specify which library was to be burned. It didn't even really use the squiggle for library. Instead, the prophecy said that the Dragon Queen would burn down the 'structure that housed the prophecy' and other very important scrolls. That seemed like splitting hairs, though. I was going to be, if the overall tone of the prophecy were to be believed, the worst thing to happen to the recorded knowledge of the elves in *four epochs*.

I grabbed the closest reference and thumbed through it. Nope, it avoided the topic of library burning entirely. So I looked in another—nope. I pulled another general volume off the shelf, and didn't find reference to the situation in it, either. I went through book after book, stacking the ones I'd read through at the end of the table as I hunted for confirmation or denial of the fact that I, Alyssa, was to burn a library down.

The dinner bell rang. I ignored it, pulling another book down from the shelf and thumbing through it. It was surprisingly hard to read, but I managed. It had nothing, so I grabbed another.

The next book was even harder to read.

Suddenly a ferociously bright light blazed from the door, and I looked up from the darkened book to see a candelabra. "Oh," I said. "I guess it really has gotten dark in here."

Gethin's face smiled out at me from his cowl. It was really spooky, between that and the candle's flickering, wavering light and the shadows it tossed across the wrinkles on his face. "I am afraid, Alyssa, that the books have cast a rather powerful spell upon you. I am not certain we should allow you back up here."

I sure didn't want to hear that. "You wouldn't keep me from

reading the prophecy I came to read, would you?" I asked, my voice showing more stress than I wanted it to.

"Tonight, yes, I would. You're welcome to return to this chamber on the morrow, of course. I'm troubled, though, that you have been refusing to eat."

"I'm not refusing, Gethin. I just haven't been very hungry. You know how research can get. Here, lead me downstairs with your candle and I'll eat some right in front of you."

"As you wish," Gethin said, and he turned and started toward the stairs. I followed, glad that the light in the main hall of the library was a little less gone than that of the prophecy chamber.

I entered the dining room and stood for a moment in shock. Both Keion and Seph sat at the table draped in blankets, each looking miserable with his or her head hanging loose over their chest.

"Are y'all okay?" I asked.

Silence met my question.

"Hey! What's goin' on?" I asked a little more forcefully.

Keion shrugged and raised his head with an effort. With a weak grin he said, "Just a cold, Alyssa. We'll be fine soon. It's a good thing we're here in the warmth of the library with plenty of good food and water and the librarians to help us get over it. Just think what it would've been like had this illness overtaken us upon the road to here."

I didn't want to think of that, honestly. I sat and ate silently, and nobody else at the table seemed to mind the lack of conversation. Finally all three of us rose and shambled toward our bedrooms, Keion and Seph looking like my mom did when she got the flu, and me suddenly feeling very tired.

Hopefully I wasn't getting sick, myself. My chest felt warm as I thought about it, but by the time I laid down I'd convinced myself that it was just my fear talking. I wasn't going to get sick.

I couldn't get sick.

I didn't have time to get sick.

I had to figure out how I was going to burn the library down so I could keep from doing whatever it was.

I jumped out of bed even earlier the next day, intent on finding somewhere in the reference area that talked about a library burning down. Once again I tossed a hunk of sausage and one of cheese into my pouch and bounded up the stairs. Once again Iago pushed a plate of hot breakfast toward me inside the chamber of prophecy.

"Hey, Iago, since you're here, maybe you could fill me in on something," I said.

"It would be my pleasure, Princess," he said.

"Gethin said something about a derivative work that discussed the whole library burning thing further. I'd like to read that. Which one would it be?"

"I will bring it."

"Wait—what? I thought all the works related to the prophecy were in this room."

"All except that one, Princess. That one we keep in a— special place. The burning of libraries is a rather difficult topic to discuss, you understand."

"I do. Okay, thank you. Please bring it to me as soon as you can."

"I shall. And while I do, may I suggest you await its arrival while you eat your breakfast?"

"I'm not—oh, alright. I will eat my breakfast. Please, the book?"

He nodded and left, though he didn't go nearly fast enough for my impatience. I was stuck on that, and I wanted it. Because I'd told him I would, I sat down and took a few bites of breakfast. It didn't set well on my stomach, though; after the first bite my chest grew warm once again, and it stayed that way for as long as I kept eating. I started wondering if I had a stomach flu coming on, myself.

"Ah, excellent," Iago said, smiling and nodding as he laid another book down to the side. "I will leave this here for you to read once you are done." He watched me pick up another fork full of the vile stuff, and then he left.

I soothed my stomach by nibbling on the cheese I'd brought. Something was definitely wrong—was I coming down with the same bug that had Seph and Keion in its grip? That would be bad. Maybe I was set to burn the library down by accident in a flu-caused daze? Maybe I'd pass out and leave a candle burning?

I had to find out.

I opened the book Iago had brought and started reading. It turned out that the book wasn't about the prophecy; instead, it was about the library, its history and its future. It really was fascinating to my inner nerd how the elves over the centuries had sent librarians out to seek out and acquire works for their beloved home. There had always been three central librarians whose purpose was to live in and maintain the Library of Alecsanddrha proper, but there were hundreds of others who scouted. There were even librarians out there who fulfilled support roles; an entire chapter described how they managed to get the food to the library by crossing the blight. I wondered how they'd manage to do that now with the wolves and the ravens. And—no, I didn't want to think about that other thing that was flyign around just outside

The lunch bell rang, and Iago brought more stew. Once again the bowl had a delicious aroma that caught my nose as soon as he sat it down next to me. He smiled and nodded over my half-eaten breakfast, and then he left me to my reading.

My gosh, I thought, *will these people think of nothing but*

my need to eat?

I snacked on the stew while I read the second half of the book. It really was fascinating, even though it was basically a textbook on how the library was run.

Hey, I can't help it. Nerd or not, I've always wondered how a library is run.

Finally, I found in the last chapter what I was after. "The End Time According To Prophecy" it was called, and in it I read about how the prophecy said that the Dragon Queen, she who bore the birthmark of the dragon—me, in other words—would descend upon the library in a fit of rage and burn the whole thing down. It also used the "all the king's horses" line as it described the host I would lead across the blight, which the book suggested might be as narrow as a single horse's stride by the time this burning happened.

The last few pages told the librarians to stand ready in the final days. The words said that they shouldn't anger me, but that they should instead do all they could to prevent the prophecy from coming to fruition by appeasing my every wish. Perhaps, I thought, that meant to feed me every chance they got. I chuckled and took another bite of the stew, noticing once again how hot my chest felt. I took a bite of the sausage I'd brought up to the room: nothing. Obviously one of the spices in the soup made me break out into a sweat. Hot chili peppers had done that to me before, and though I didn't taste them specifically, there was definitely something spicy to it. I shoved the stew away and nibbled on the sausage hunk instead.

Thinking about what I'd just read, I pushed myself back a little from the table. Anger. Fear. An attacking horde of elven troops. A massive conflagration, started by my own hand, and on purpose. I laughed—there just wasn't any way I was that kind of queen, or that I would ever be that kind of queen, either.

I flipped slowly through the prophecy again till I found the part about the burning. I read it carefully. Nope. Didn't say anything about anger, or fear, or the attacking horde. Well, it did say there would be troops involved, but the prophet didn't say I led them. And the fire that destroyed the library? It just said there was one, not that I started it, and especially not that I did anything out of anger.

The bell rang again. I looked up and realized that somehow I'd run straight through my supply of daylight for the third day. I'd've called down for a candle, since I desperately wanted to stay up there and read, but I remembered that I hadn't seen Seph or Keion all day, and I was worried about them.

When I got to dinner, it ended up being just the three librarians and me. Seph and Keion hadn't felt up to dining at the table, they said. Gethin explained that he had called for a healer, who should be on site by tomorrow to see to my friends.

"How is a healer going to get through the blight that the three of us barely made it through with our bows singing and our arrows flying?"

Gethin smiled at my question and his voice bordered on condescension as he replied. "She will, I am sure, simply use the tunnels to get underneath the blight. We have been traveling to and from the library for centuries in that manner."

"But the blight is bigger than it has ever been," I said. I'd picked that up from reading the book about the library and then judging where the hill to the north had to have been in olden times. "Won't the tunnel entrances be within the borders of the blight?"

"No," Gethin said. "Don't worry, Princess. The healer will be here tomorrow to look after your friends. Meanwhile you should see to your own health and make sure you eat a full meal. You've hardly touched your food for three days."

"What is it with all the food? Are you just trying to stay on my good side?" I was tired enough after a day of reading that I was willing to just blurt it out.

"No, of course not, Princess," Gethin said. I didn't like the way he shared a smile with his fellow librarians; something about him was turning the trust I'd felt around. Was it the reading of the book that did that to me? Was it all in my mind, I wondered? He laid his hands out to the side and said in the slimiest, most salesman-like voice I'd heard yet, "We only care about your well-being, Alyssa."

"Well, I'm not hungry," I said, irritated by his goody-goody act, and irritated even more by the fact that it irritated me. "I'm going to check on my friends and then go to bed."

"Checking in on your friends would be inadvisable," Lefin cut in, a little too fast. Once again, I wondered if I was over-reacting and reading them wrong as a result. "Whatever they are coming down with may be highly contagious, and you would be safer not risking contamination yourself."

"I'm young and healthy enough," I said. It was true, though it was also true of both Seph and Keion. I was set on it, though, and I was darned if I'd let them win the argument. "A quick stop in isn't going to harm me." I rose from the chair and spun around, headed for the hall at a fast walk in case one of them tried to get around the table to stop me.

They didn't.

I entered Seph's room and gasped. It looked like she was already dead.

CER I GRAFU

literally, go and scratch; our way of saying "get lost."

The Power To Heal

I barely kept a whimper back as I ran to Seph's bedside and knelt down. Booboo was there, laying on the bed wedged in between Seph's body and the wall. The poor creature who was usually so feisty and ready for a fight turned a pitiful muzzle my way. I reached one hand over to rub Booboo's head while I ran my other hand over Seph's fevered forehead.

It was hot. She was running a really, really bad fever. I wasn't any sort of healer, much less for elves, so I had to just assume that it was a good thing that she was running a fever, because at least it meant she wasn't dead yet.

"Seph—Seph—can you hear me? Are you still in there? What can I do?" I heard my own voice tumble out. It's funny; when you're in that position, you really have no idea what to say. What I said struck me as completely ridiculous, but it was the best I could do.

Regardless, she was still in there, at least enough to mumble and moan a little. Booboo gave me a whimper, one that turned into a vicious snarl the next moment as he bared his teeth toward the door. I glanced up and saw Iago quickly closing it. Apparently they really were scared of contagion.

"What can I do?" I repeated. Booboo licked my hand and laid his head down on Seph's chest, giving me an impotent and unhappy whimper.

It sounded like a good idea to me, too, and in any event, it was the only thing I *could* do. I laid my head down beside Booboo's on Seph's chest.

My own chest got warm.

"Again?" I asked—out loud, I think. Booboo looked at me weird, anyway. I straightened my back and put my hand to my own chest, feeling for the source of the warmth.

The pendant!

I pulled Draignerthol out from inside my shirt. Its blue crystalline eyes were glowing like they had the day I'd shown it to Seren. The glow was fading, though, as was the warmth that radiated from it.

Strange.

It was a magical pendant, though. If the sisters and Sterny-face were to be believed, it was one of the most powerful magical pendants in the world, in fact.

Maybe?

Not daring to hope, I pulled the chain over my head and slipped Draignerthol inside Seph's shirt to lie against her chest. Instantly it warmed up and the eyes glowed brighter from within the blouse.

A few seconds later, Seph gasped. Her long, raspy breath sounded like someone who'd been drowning but was finally up and safe. Her eyes slammed open, much wider than I'd seen them before, and her back arched up off of the bed.

She breathed in normally, and her torso relaxed back down. She took another regular breath, and then her eyes relaxed to their normal openness and started searching around her. They finally settled on my face, and she quirked one side of her mouth up in a weak half-grin.

Booboo and I exchanged looks; he seemed as confused and happy and joyous and weirded out as I was. Granted, I don't know how I read all that in a wolverine's facial expression, but I did. I guess he and I had finally become friends.

"Well," I said, and then stopped when Seph looked panicked. She made a shh sound and glanced toward the door. I finished in a whisper, "welcome back to the land of the living, Cousin. If I can ask, what's got you so sick?"

"Poison," she murmured.

"Poison? There's no way," I said, shaking my head. "I ate the same thing—oh." I thought back to all the times my chest had felt warm. The pendant, the relic they apparently hadn't expected me to have, had been protecting me. I still had to ask, though. "How do you know?"

"A ranger knows poisons, Alyssa. I should have noticed its effects earlier, but they're using a rare distillation of the seed of the nernag bush, one that not only makes you ill but also addles your mind."

"Will it kill you?"

"Not anymore, thanks to you. That poison doesn't do anything by itself to kill, though, so no, it would not have killed me without other intervention."

"But why?"

"Why poison me, you mean?"

"Well, yeah," I said.

"I don't know, Cousin. They didn't confide in me before they poisoned me. If I had to assume, though, I'd say it's because you're going to burn their library down. They're going to stop you. You showed up with a couple of strong friends, and so they're doing what they can to neutralize us slowly."

"I'm not sure what to do now." I was terrified, honestly. Suddenly it all made sense; all of the librarians' overtures for my health had morphed into sinister attempts to do away with me, and I was stuck in a building with three of them and my disabled companions. Burning the place down didn't seem all that bad an idea any more, as much as it shocked me to think that.

"Is today Sadwrn?" Seph asked. I counted the days since we'd left, still not used to the strange six-day weeks. Yes, it was, I realized, and I told her that. "Ah, well, then, you need to go to sleep in your room. I'll be fine, since I suspect Booboo has convinced them not to come in while I'm under. I'll pretend to still be out. Keion should be fine for another day. Tomorrow, help will arrive."

"How do you know that?" Sometimes my cousin really surprised me.

"I called for help when I realized what was happening," Seph said. "I had lost my physical strength, but—"

"Princess," a voice called from the other side of the door, and a moment later it was joined by an urgent knock. "We must insist that you go to your own room now, as you've taken more than enough chances with contamination. Your friend will be okay until tomorrow when the healer arrives."

"They're right," Seph whispered. "Go, stay in your room. If you need me, bang on the wall. Oh, and put that pendant back under your shirt," she added quickly as I started up and toward the door with the chain grasped in my hand.

I stopped and slipped the chain back over my head, tucking both it and the pendant safely beneath my shirt and hoping that it couldn't be seen. I turned and shot Seph a wink, trying to look much more confident than I was. She hadn't told me who the help was; all I could assume was that I would soon see what "all the king's horses and all the king's men" looked like in action.

She closed her eyes and went back to looking rather dead.

Booboo, for his part, put on a good act for being dejected. I put my own sad face back on and opened the door, stepping out into the hall to face all three librarians.

PENDRAMWNWGL

a headlong way of running into something silly.
One of the coolest words ever: pen-dram-oo-noogl

Confrontation

"Well, hello," I said to the trio of librarians, my eyes flitting from Gethin to Lefan to Iago and back. The three were standing, arms crossed, in the hall, three pairs of eyes following my movements as I shut Seph's door close behind me. Their dark expressions scared me, while at the same time the knowledge of what they'd been doing infuriated me. I didn't want a confrontation, though, no matter how good my recent history said I was at getting into them. Not yet, anyway. If help was coming, there was no sense risking death before it got there. I needed to play it cool—we all needed to play it cool, for just a little while longer.

"I'm glad you wish to—" I started, but was interrupted.

"Princess," Gethin said as he stepped toward me, uncrossing his arms to hold his hands out in supplication, "we must ask you to not risk your health any more by visits to your sick friends. The healer will be here tomorrow, be assured, and—"

I lost my patience at that point. I didn't dare allow myself to go as far over the top as I'd gone when I'd punched Sister Sternyface in the lips, but I'd had enough of them for the night and I wanted to make sure they knew it. I didn't like anybody interrupting me, and it made me furious that they'd poisoned my friends and lied to me, telling me a healer was on his way when they were the ones who were responsible for the poison. I know, I know, I'd just thought about playing it cool, but I snapped. Again. Angrily, I stepped in toward Gethin and slammed my palm into his chest to knock him back. I kept my voice low and angry-sounding as I said, "I am not a child, Gethin, for you to worry ab—"

I stopped.

I didn't mean to hit him hard enough to do any major harm, I promise. I was just trying to make a point. Just one blam, my open palm right in to the middle of his chest where a man ought to be able to take a hit.

Ought to, anyway. You would think.

He apparently couldn't take the hit, but I'm not sure it was his fault. As my palm connected, a blue flash surrounded my hand and I heard a sizzling crackle. Draignerthol, from its position hidden under my dress, flared up so much that it became uncomfortably hot. Somehow the pendant had read my anger as intent to do real harm and pushed magic through my palm into Gethin's body. Some day I'll have to figure out what I did and how I did it, but I honestly have no idea what triggered the magical part of the attack. All I remember was my own shock at the reaction.

Gethin crumpled, his eyes rolling back in his head and what little color there had been suddenly washing out of his face. The other two librarians caught him and checked to make sure their head librarian was still breathing, and then they dragged him away while taking turns glaring back at me, their expressions a mix of terror and fury.

Once they turned the corner I was able to breathe again. Fighting down panic, I rushed over to Keion's room and entered, shutting the door quickly behind me. What I saw stopped me in my tracks. He looked even worse than Seph had; if I hadn't seen his chest flutter, I would've sworn he was already gone.

I didn't have time to be panicked or weak, though. I rushed to his bedside, ripped the chain holding Draignerthol up and over my head, and reached my hand inside his shirt to press the cold metal of the pendant onto his skin.

Just like with Seph earlier, first the pendant got warm, and then, after a few moments, Keion's eyes flew open and he gasped for air.

"Whrff—" he managed to say before I clamped my hand over his mouth for silence.

"Shh, Keion. They don't know you're okay, and that may be all that's keeping us alive." His eyebrows nearly met in the middle as confusion tightened the muscles in his face. I whispered the big parts, making sure he knew that the librarians were the ones poisoning us, and that they hopefully didn't know I had Draignerthol or that he and Seph were healed, and that reinforcements were on their way. I told him about knocking Gethin out with a shove, and his eyes grew wide.

"Mrgr," he mumbled through my hand. I moved it away, and he quietly repeated, "Magic. You said it was a blue flash, right?"

I nodded.

"That is magic, Alyssa. It is forbidden."

"Forbidden? That magic just saved our lives, Keion."

"The end does not justify the means, Alyssa. How—where— did you learn to do that?"

"I didn't. I don't even know what I did, much less how I did it. All I know is that I was angry, and I hit him, and blam, he went down. When we get back, assuming we make it back, I'll ask Naissa about it."

He shook his head and rose onto one elbow. "No, Alyssa. You must never tell the high priestess about your use of the forbidden powers. She's the chief in charge of all magic-hunting. Anyone else she would banish from the realm without question. I don't know what she'd do to the future queen if she found out, but it wouldn't be good."

I shuddered at the part about realm-banishment. As much as I'd questioned my place before, and as many times as I'd cringed at the title of princess, the place was starting to grow on me. Besides, my banishment would probably mean Dad could never go be with Momma. "So what should I do, then?"

"Aren't you the future queen?" he asked, using the same question my father would have posed if he'd been there, bless his heart. I nodded, but my terrified expression must have made him take pity on me for once. "Okay, here's what you're going to do. Go to your room. Try to relax enough to get some sleep; I'll be listening carefully for anything that might happen, and you will need your rest for tomorrow. In the morning, knock twice on the wall to let me know you are leaving and then go directly up to the library and look up what you can about magic until this help that Sephaline called for arrives."

I nodded, and he added, "Hopefully it's enough help to battle a wyvern, too."

I nodded again.

"Keion, I'm scared." I knew he already knew that, and I also figured he was likely to roast me over it, but I felt like it had to be blurted out to somebody. I wasn't just scared; I was terrified. He was the last elf I would've chosen to confide in if any other elves had been around, but he was all I had.

I was shocked, though, when instead of gloating he reached up and ran a hand through my hair once, and then again. "We all are, Alyssa," he murmured, his eyes locked on mine, his voice quiet but serious and strong. "There's nothing we can do but keep on pretending until tomorrow, if they let us go that long, and then—well, we'll see what happens. Whatever happens, though, know that I'm happy to be facing it at your side." As he talked, he stroked my hair in a gesture that was unbelievably comforting. For several minutes we sat in silence, our closeness creating an unspoken connection there that I'd never imagined possible with anyone, much less Prince Charming.

Without anything else really to say, I finally sighed, nodded, and rose from his bedside. I pulled Draignerthol back over my head and tucked it into the dress, and then padded back through the eerily silent hallway and into my own room.

DAWNSIO AR Y DIBYN

literally, dancing on the cliff; means something like "playing with fire."

The Battle For The Library

I didn't sleep that night, but that's no surprise. I tried, lay-ing there still and quiet in the dark, but all that did was make me replay my blue-tinged magical attack on Gethin over and over, and each time I watched him die by my own blue force-wielding hand instead of being hauled off to safety by the other two librarians.

Finally I couldn't stand the silence in my own head any more, so I got up. Figuring it had to be dawn, or nearly there, already, I grabbed my backpack to take upstairs with me. As I passed by Seph's door, though, the frantic scratching there stopped me.

I cracked the door and peered in. Seph was up; she grinned and invited me in with a move of her hand. I slipped in quietly and closed the door, and she came over and whispered, "Booboo wants to go with you to the library. That way I'll know if some-thing happens to you."

"You can..." I started to ask, and let the question fade. Of course she could communicate with Booboo; she was a ranger. I'd learned in one of the sessions on what magic is and what it isn't that a ranger's ability to communicate, even across long distances, with her familiar, as well as with other animals, was a power that counted as not magical, and so it was permitted. I still half-believed that Naissa made the distinction up as she went, but none of that mattered at the moment.

Seph nodded the answer to the question I hadn't finished asking, and then her face got serious. "Alyssa, what did you do last night?"

"What do you mean?"

"What do you mean, what do I mean? What was that brilliant explosion of force out in the hallway?"

"Oh, right, you can sense magic."

"I didn't *have* to be good at sensing magic to feel *that* happen. Alyssa, what did you do?"

"I have no idea, Seph. That's the thing. I don't know. I got angry, and I reached out to smack Gethin in the chest because he was coming at me. When my hand made contact, a blue light flashed and he collapsed."

"Well, be careful. Not only do they have whatever reason to poison you, but now you've attacked their leader. You might want to take your bow and arrows in addition to Booboo."

She had a point. I snuck back into my own room and grabbed everything I owned, and then I headed out into the library proper with Booboo on my heels, following me like a hungry cat follows a can opener.

The dining room was empty, and I breathed a silent word of thanks for that. Looking down it through the main doors, I saw that I'd been right about dawn. Either the librarians were rising late today, or they didn't want to see me. Hopefully, I thought, they were too busy tending to Gethin's needs to worry about somebody slipping up to the book area.

Carefully I took the stairs one at a time, avoiding everywhere I'd heard a squeak on previous trips. When I got up to where I could see in, I stopped on the stairs and looked around. Nothing. No movement, no sound. Booboo was calm, too. I breathed for what felt like the first time since I'd left my room and darted the rest of the way up the stairs. Moving at my fastest walk, I made it in to the room where the prophecy was kept and closed the door behind me.

I breathed again. I was safe.

At least, I was safe for the time being.

What to do, though? Suddenly the prophecy didn't seem so important. Instead, I went back out into the main library and grabbed a couple of books on magic. Back in the prophecy room, I sat down at the table with my back to the wall and settled in to start reading the one that looked the most like a primer on basic magical spell casting.

After a few hours the door creaked open, and Booboo snarled from his corner. I looked up to see Lefan standing in the open doorway, Iago right behind.

And Lefan had a bow drawn, arrow pointed at me.

Booboo snarled again and lunged. Giving them warning was apparently the wrong thing to do, though. Iago gestured with one hand and a magical blue glow flashed around Booboo. The wolverine stopped moving. Iago whipped his hand to the side and Booboo crashed into the book shelf, whimpering softly as he fell in a heap.

Magic. I blinked in surprise. I'd actually seen true magic being done, I realized. It wasn't just singing a tree into shape, or sensing what an animal was seeing. What Iago had done was real magic.

When I came back to reality from my astounded state of mind, I noticed that I'd stood up from behind the table when Lefan had entered the room. That was a mistake. Now, he had an easy shot.

Luckily, he didn't take his easy shot right away, and so I

asked, "Why?" It always worked for Scooby Doo's gang, after all, and I was grasping for any chance I could get to start him off monologuing.

"Why? It's quite simple, actually, Princess. We can't let the prophecy come to pass. The librarians assembled here will one day be known as the noble Cult of the Wyrm, whose duty it was to protect the assembled body of knowledge for the time when the dragons return and magic use is once again celebrated throughout the land."

Iago nodded and said, "We don't know how you managed the magic involved in poisoning Gethin, but that was a big mistake, *Princess*. He was the one who didn't want to kill you. He was sure that we could incapacitate you and drop you back off with our agents in your realm, and we'd never see or hear from you again. But no, you *want* to die, don't you?" Suddenly the guy who had been bringing me my food all this time seemed angry at me, taunting me. I couldn't see why.

Unless—unless they were scared.

That was it! They were *actually* scared of me. I'd evaded their trap, poisoned their leader, and they didn't know how.

They also didn't know that Seph was back in the land of the living, as well as the land of the shooting, I thought as I noticed a Seph-shaped shadow slip around behind the librarians and draw its bow.

I almost, but didn't, have time to rejoice before Seph's arrow buzzed in from behind. It caught Iago square in the back and dropped him to the floor with a thud. She drew another, but she wasn't fast enough. Lefan loosed his arrow my direction and teleported out of the doorway, disappearing a split second before Seph's second shot flew in and stuck in the edge of a book shelf.

Luckily for me, she'd distracted him enough that he missed, too. At least, he missed where I'd moved to, since when he glanced backward I dropped as fast as a sack of potatoes to the floor. The arrow made a thwack as it stuck, quivering, into the books behind where my head had been.

Suddenly the room came alive with magical energy. Pops sounded from all around the shelves as black-robed troops teleported in, each wearing a pin that I now knew identified them as Librarians of Alecsanddrha. That, or Cult of the Wyrm. Or maybe the two were the same, I thought.

Before long there were at least a dozen bad guys that I could see, and several other shadows moving around the stacks. Two had already grabbed a struggling Seph and held her, while three others had caught and dragged Keion out from where he had been trying to sneak up behind Lefan.

One of them was Stith. I suppose that shouldn't have surprised me. Near Stith I thought I recognized a couple other of the guards from the first detail that had been sent to stay in the room of trolls. All of them wore the same little dragon-shaped pin indicating cult membership.

"Come out where we can see your pretty little face, Princess," Lefan taunted. He didn't say or else what, but I had a pretty good idea what they had in mind to draw me out if I didn't come willingly. I wasn't willing to see my friends die on my account, so I mustered what little courage I had, rose to my feet, and stepped bravely out of the room.

"Alyssa! No!" Keion yelled, and Stith responded by turning around and punching him several times in the gut. Watching him hurt made me want to scream and lash out with— something. Anything. I glanced around and saw nothing useful.

"You weren't supposed to be here, Princess," Stith sneered. "You should have taken the hint the first time, when I shot the warning arrow. Or the second time with the fake unicorn blood, perhaps. At least you should have been bright enough to leave when our colleagues hid in your room. We wouldn't have to kill you now if you'd just paid attention to the messages earlier."

"Thanks, Stith," I said, not sure what else to do. Hey, it's not like twelfth grade civics class has a chapter on "what to do if you're ever stuck in a library with elf librarians who want to kill you because you might burn the library down." I was improvising, and not well. "I don't suppose you could've just told me one day, 'Hey, you need to give up the throne or else bad things will happen,' could you? I mean, I admit that the arrow's message was pretty loud, but it was also kinda ambiguous, right? I didn't get 'you should give up your throne' out of it, but rather 'somebody wants to kill....'"

"Shut up, both of you. You, just kill them all," Lefan growled to the elves holding Seph and Keion, and several things happened at once right after. A librarian standing behind Seph, and another standing behind the now-sagging Keion, each stepped forward and raised a dagger to kill my friends. Booboo, who had apparently come out of his stupor from being slammed against the books, shot out of the room headed straight for Lefan. Lefan, meanwhile, drew another arrow and let it fly, this one aimed straight at my heart.

At that same exact moment, I discovered how to manipulate magic.

All The King's Horses and All The King's Men

Suddenly I could see noises.

No, I'm not kidding. To find my way to being able to touch the magical energies I apparently had to get really, really angry, and having my friends about to be murdered while an arrow was shot to kill me pretty well did that. As I lost control of my anger, I gained control of the flows of magic. Vibrations in the air—noises, the flight of an arrow, and so on—were things I could reach out and pluck, playing with them to my heart's content. The very air around me jiggled with furious power.

I stopped the arrow. It really was just that simple; I reached out with my mind and grabbed hold of the air around it and tossed it to the side. I saw Booboo was nearly to Lefan, so I let him have the librarian and blasted the guys holding my friends with as much air-pressured force as I could manage.

They toppled. The daggers clattered to the ground. Seph and Keion both looked at me with wide eyes, bewildered expressions on both of their faces. I didn't care, though; I was in control.

I saw when the librarians raised the energy to teleport out, but there was no way I was going to let them get away with that. I surrounded the entire library chamber in a great big whirlwind. Books were flying, shelves crashing down, but again, I didn't care. The raw power I commanded was intense, amazing, thrilling—intoxicating, even. The librarians had hurt me, had hurt my friends, and finally, amazingly, sweetly, I had the ability to hurt them back.

I had power!

I stood, arms outstretched, my hair whipping back and forth around me in the vortex of the mighty wind tunnel I'd created. I couldn't help laughing as I watched the librarians tossed around the room like dolls, their bodies crumpling as they knocked over book shelves and slammed into heavy wooden tables. I took special pleasure in blasting a panicking Stith in the chest with the energy, and in watching him fall onto a table and then crash to the floor as it gave way. A few flying books passed close by; I redirected their path to bounce off of the head of my former guard shift leader.

He slumped, out cold.

The power felt alive. It felt good.

In a windstorm, by the way, you should bet on the wolverine, every time. Booboo's squat body pretty well ignored the typhoon I'd created, his muzzle darting back and forth, terrorizing the poor librarian. Lefan was screaming, most of the sound of it carried away by the tempest as blood flowed from several places on his body.

For the first time, thanks to the magic roaring through and about me, I was able to make a mental connection to Booboo. He was laughing, enjoying the pleasure of returning the terror the elf in black had inflicted upon Booboo's mistress. He wouldn't kill it—not yet, anyway—but would instead play with the elf a while more.

"ALYSSA!" invaded my indulgence. I stopped laughing and looked down to see Seph on her hands and knees on the floor, crawling toward me as fast as she could manage against the wind storm. *"Stop! Fire!"* she screamed again.

What? Fire?

I turned to look over my shoulder where she was pointing. Sure enough, the back corner, nearly a quarter of the main library space, was blazing.

"What happened?" I asked as I let the wind die down.

The librarians who could still move looked over at the fire and fled, either teleporting out or stumbling on unsteady legs down the stairs. I panicked, turning toward Seph to ask where the fire extinguisher would be, where there was a fire alarm, what we could do to put the fire out.

But the sickening truth was that this was Kiirajanna, not Earth. Fire extinguishers didn't exist, nor did fire alarms. There wasn't a fire department waiting to send a truck full of hot firemen out to help us. It was just me, and a great big blaze that I'd started myself, and a huge collection of scrolls and books that also served as fantastic fuel for the fire. The fire that I'd started—did I mention that already?

"Move, Princess!" Keion's voice intruded on my pity party as he grabbed my arm with his and yanked me toward the stairs. "I've got your stuff. *Come on!*"

It was a fast run, but it felt like it was slow motion. Librarians with broken bodies looked up at me from their heaps on the floor, their faces a mixture of shock, fear, and loathing. The crackling heat of the flames surrounded us all. Intensifying smoke made it hard to breathe as we fled from the inferno down the main stairs.

Downstairs the smoke was thinner. "Faster, Princess!" Keion said as he pulled me harder toward the big front doors. Suddenly he changed course and led us back toward the side entrance next to our rooms.

As I stumbled along to his dragging, I glanced back. Seph was right behind, and I was relieved to see Booboo running along right at her heels.

We were going to make it!

We tumbled out the side door and down the stone steps, and I realized the way wasn't totally clear yet. The library above us still burned, flames shooting out the windows as well as through the holes where the magnificent ducts had once channeled all-important light into the places used for reading. Meanwhile, the roof and tower of the library started falling apart. Huge hunks of slate and stone toppled from high up, falling silently before crashing and rolling to the ground, felling the scattering librarians as they tumbled.

One big chunk of the tower almost took us with it, crushing part of the roof right above and hitting the ground just a couple of feet from where we stood.

"Horses!" Keion yelled, breaking me out of my stunned stare once again to push me toward the stables.

I untied and pulled Awel out of her stall as quickly as I could, grabbing her saddle as I walked her directly out into the courtyard and through a gap in the wall that part of the roof had broken out. Seph came right behind, followed by Keion. Once we were on the other side of the block wall we stood, looking up at the flame-shrouded building that had mere minutes earlier been one of the largest repositories of information in the world.

Then I heard the screech.

I spun around, grabbing at my bow, but Keion slowed me down with an "Easy, there, Princess." He nodded toward the battle to our front, in which a couple of dozen of the librarians were holding the wyvern back with their magical spells. The librarians seemed to be winning, but I wasn't sure which team

I wanted to root for because either one would likely turn around and try to kill me once they finished.

Horns sounded a fanfare behind us, and we all turned to look out across the blight.

"'All the king's horses' was the truth of it, I'd guess," I said. Seph and Keion looked at me funny, and I briefly told of the connection between the prophecy and the nursery rhyme. Thundering across the blight, riding so powerfully that they swept aside the wolves and the ravens in their way almost as an afterthought, were several hundred black chargers led by the largest of them, a war horse ridden by an elf whose face I recognized. Beside Daddy galloped an elf waving a flag bearing the insignia I'd seen on his wall and his throne: the Elf King of Kiirajanna.

"Oh, that's not *all* the king's horses, nor *all* the king's men," Keion said, crossing his arms and starting to smile. "The king can marshal tens of thousands of riders who will ride to their deaths with him willingly, but that would take days of waiting for them to come in from their homes. What you see now is just the king's horses and men who are close enough to grab and run."

"Still makes a dang fine sight to see," I said.

"That, it does, Alyssa," Prince Charming said, and then he drew his sword with a *shhhhiiinnngggg* sound and spurred his own mount to join in the battle.

The wyvern, seeing the majority of the massive charge wheel in its direction, apparently decided to live to fight another day by flying away. With great pumps of its leathery wings it gained altitude very quickly, soaring off into the still-rising sun.

The riders, all dressed in various shades and materials of green, circled around the librarians and pushed them into a group which they then pressed away from us. There were a few small skirmishes; it thrilled me, for some reason, to watch the prince run one of the librarians through after a dazzling series of parries and thrusts with their swords. I mean, it was real, true, sword battle, and I'd never seen that before. Most of the librarians, though, allowed themselves to be captured peacefully.

"Why aren't they teleporting now?" I asked. It wasn't that I wanted them to get away, but I was curious why they weren't doing it.

"The bowmen are watching for the gathering of energy," Seph explained. "Rangers are more sensitive to it than most, and they can sink an arrow in anybody who starts to try it before the teleporter could get away."

The massive armor-clad war horse carried the king over to us. He leaped off of the horse as it was stopping, landing gracefully on his boots and then sprinting the last couple of steps to me. Suddenly I was enveloped in the mighty arms of the King of all the Elves of Kiirajanna.

Growing up, I'd always fantasized about what it would be like to be swept away in the father's hug I couldn't actually receive, but I'd never imagined it as good as it felt right then.

"Hi, Daddy. I can explain," I said.

"No need, my princess. You are safe," he countered, wrapping me up tightly in his arms. "You are safe," he murmured again. "Why the tears, Alyssa?"

I realized I'd been bawling into his tunic. It took me a second to register why, despite the relief of the rescue, I was feeling awfully sad and sobbing about it. When it did register, though, I sobbed harder.

Finally I got control and looked up at him. My father tenderly wiped the tears off of my cheek and repeated his question. I just pointed back behind to where flames still flickered from the blackened structure.

"Did you see what I did to the library?"

"Nothing more or less than the prophecy set you up for."
And with that, he pulled me to his chest again.

337

DRAIGFUD

literally, stupid dragon; a wyvern.

A Long Ride Home

The ride home went a lot slower than the trip to the library had. Part of that was that the riders who'd come with my father needed to give their horses some rest; they'd ridden them as hard as they could and still expect them to live, he explained. Also, instead of simple meals of sausage and cheese, we ate really well. The king had brought some of his cooking staff along behind, it seemed, and when on the road they didn't count days off.

I told him the story, of course. I told him about how we'd been taken in and fooled. I told him about seeing Stith and his men again, and how I'd smashed Stith's head in with flying books.

Of course, Dad found that part hilarious. He laughed for several minutes, in fact. Every time he'd take a break from laughing he looked back at me, pantomimed books flying and smacking him in the face, and started laughing out loud again.

I told him what I'd heard about the Cult of the Wyrm and the reason behind the previous attacks on me. By the time I got to the end he was ranting furiously at the librarians for resorting to poison in addition to magic, but he stopped when I told him about the pendant.

"Draignerthol? Really? May I see it?" When I pulled it out from beneath my blouse and showed him, he asked, "Where did you get that?"

"Momma gave it to me the night before we left. After Sternyface told me its story, I assumed you'd passed it along to Momma to give to me. At least, that's what the high priestess told me had probably happened."

"No." He shook his head. "Alyssa, that pendant is a legendary and priceless relic of an ancient epoch. No elf, none that I know of anyway, has laid eyes on it for thousands of years."

"Momma did tell me it had been passed down through the family. Like I said, I figured she meant your family."

"No, not mine. She must have meant her family. If so—you know what that very likely means, do you not?"

"I don't dare guess, Dad. So many strange things, so little time to learn about them, it's.... You know?"

"I can imagine, Alyssa. You have had to come to grips with a lot in a very short period of time. Regardless, your having this pendant probably means that your mother—and you, for that matter—are descendants of Rhiannon the White." He looked at me with widened eyes, but continued when I just shook my head in confusion. "You do not understand, do you? Not only are you to be the queen long prophesied, but you also have a pedigree finer than any elf queen's has been for hundreds, if not thousands, of years. Rhiannon the White is our most legendary ruler ever, in the entire history of Kiirajanna. That you are her descendant, my daughter, is—well, it defies words. I am so very—proud, I suppose, but again, words fail me."

"I get the importance of being a descendant of Rhiannon the White, Dad, but how do we know that I am? Mom could'a picked the pendant up at a garage sale."

"It is possible, I guess, but difficult to imagine. That pendant has such a wealth of geas applied to it—magic I can sense now, despite the ages that have passed!—that it is difficult to believe in such a random event. It is tied, if the myth surrounding it is to be believed, to an owner in the genetic line of the throne. I must believe that you, my daughter, are, in fact, a descendant of our most beloved queen of all time."

"Hmm. Could be, I guess. I don't suppose that Momma could actually be Rhiannon?" I asked, wondering about the typical elf lifespan.

"You are kidding, yes? Rhiannon would have to be many thousands of years old. No, it is not possible. Elves used to live hundreds of years, but our lifespan has never been infinite."

"Well, but I saw this picture, though...."

"Go on, Alyssa."

"It was in one of the books in the library. A magical portrait of Queen Rhiannon, it claimed to be. But it was really a spitting image of Momma."

"I have seen the likeness, the subtly elven features, in her face myself, Alyssa. I am fairly confident, given her possession of that relic in addition to the image you saw, that your lineage, on both sides, is royal. But your mother could not possibly be the same person as Rhiannon the White."

"Okay. Well, I don't think anybody has ever followed our family tree back very far."

"I do not think anybody *could* follow your family tree back that far, my dear. That is pre-history, the period on earth before recorded time began that is now only told of in legends. But you say that the pendant kept you from feeling the poison?" I nodded, and he continued, "And that despite you not being an adept at the healing arts. At least, not yet. All that has passed down through the historic writings describe Draignerthol as a powerful magical lens piece, one that serves to gather and amplify the forces wielded by its bearer. It does not—at least, it is said to not be capable of working magic on its own. It is clearly still very powerful, despite the eons that have passed since its creation. As strongly as I stand against its use, I am glad it protected you, though I wonder how much of the healing energy it focused came unbidden from your own subconscious."

"Me, too."

"Naissa is going to want to study it."

"Naissa can kiss my grits, Dad."

"What are your grits, dear?" he asked, looking me over curiously.

"Nothing, really. A breakfast food, made from corn somehow. It's just an old Southern saying. It means that she's not going to get to study it, regardless of how much she wants to."

"I see," he said with a grin.

"Why wasn't Rhiannon called Talaith, too, Dad?"

"I believe she was, Alyssa. She went from Rhiannon to Talaith to Rhiannon the White. Queens are only known as Talaith during their reign. You will also become Talaith upon your ascension to the throne, and then when you step down for the next queen, you will return to being Alyssa."

"Oh. Well, that makes sense. But one more thing, Dad. If Momma has elf blood too, why can't she cross over to Kiirajanna?"

His eyebrows shot up in surprise as he said, "I had not considered that, Alyssa. Tradition required that she stay there, and I here, for the most part, while you grew up on Earth. Once you have gained the crown, though, I suppose we shall have to test the theory." He looked around us at the perfectly manicured forest and nodded. "It would truly bring joy to my heart were your mother to witness for herself the wonders of our realm.”

That evening Keion and Seph called me over to where they sat together, away from the others a bit. I could tell something was wrong by the dark looks on their faces, and the fact that they shared guilty glances between them suggested that it was the same thing with both. In fact, I didn't have much trouble guessing what the topic was about to be.

“Greetings, my friends,” I said, hoping I didn't act over-the-top happy. I'd been dreading this talk all day, but didn't see anything to be gained to starting it off rough.

“Princess,” Keion said, but softened it to “Alyssa” when I flashed a playful hurt look at him. At least, I tried for a playful hurt look; who knows what it actually looked like in the dancing fire's light with my own moods swirling around like a miniature hurricane right behind my forehead.

“We need to talk about—about what you did in the library,” Seph continued, her expression as guilty as I can imagine an elf face ever looking.

“I saved our lives,” I reminded them.

Seph looked pleadingly at Keion in a touch of teamwork that shocked me. He took up her baton and said, “Yes, Alyssa. Yes, you did. But you did so using magic,” he finished, his voice dwindling down to the barest of whispers, barely quivering the last word out.

I shrugged. I'd been thinking about how it would come up for the entire ride that day, and I'd decided it was best to just play it off. Yes, I'd used magic, but I'd saved their, and my own, lives in doing so. “But I saved our lives, is the key part. And I didn't even know I was working magic—oh, come on, quit glancing around like we're kids with our clothes off playing doctor out in the bushes and scared of being caught by the adults. I didn't even know what was going on. They were about to kill you, Seph, and Booboo was hurt too. I reached out and grabbed whatever I could, and since there was nothing in arm's reach unfortunately I happened to grab the blue energy instead. I don't know how I did it, and I probably can't ever do it again. But don't go acting like I just killed Dumbledore."

"Who is this Dumbledore, my daughter?" a voice rumbled from the dark behind me. I didn't jump when his hand clasped my shoulder from behind because I knew he'd come up; I had always been able to sense people entering my space. Now, though, I recognized my ability for what it was.

Magic.

Back on Earth, magic wasn't needed to sense the clumsy footfalls of humans. On Kiirajanna the elves walked with much lighter steps, but my senses were much more acute at the same time.

"Dumbledore is the character of a fantasy book back at home. He's the headmaster of Hogwarts School of Witchcraft and Wizardry."

"And you read about this witchcraft and wizardry?"

"Everybody on the planet has read about this witchcraft and wizardry, Dad. It's one of the top selling book series of all time."

"And this book series makes the use of magic acceptable on Earth?"

Uh, oh. I saw where it was going.

"There is no magic on Earth, Dad. You know that. It's why people dream about being able to use it. Here, where it does exist, it's forbidden to use unless it's hidden, wrapped up inside a ranger's talking to the trees or a hunter's sensing of faraway animals." I glanced over; both Seph and Keion looked as scandalized as I had figured they would. "Oh, come on, you two. They—the powers you have, and what I did by accident back in the library—are the *same* thing."

"Even if they are the same thing as you suggest, Princess,

what we do is not forbidden," Keion pointed out.

"Yes, and what I did is. I get that. And I also know that it saved our lives. Can we at least agree on that?"

"Alyssa—Cousin—we can agree on that. But the use of magic, for the purpose of saving lives or not, has been forbidden, with the harshest of consequences, for many thousands of years."

"Let us not speak of consequences, or of magic at all, until we arrive back at the castle," Dad interrupted Seph. "Once we are there we can take the matter up with the high priestess. It is her judgment to hand down, in any event. Until that time we will focus on celebrating the fact that the three of you journeyed to the library and survived to come back. Am I clear?"

"Yes, Your Majesty," Keion said with a slight bow, and Seph echoed the movement. It shocked me back to being impressed; sometimes I forgot who my father actually was.

"Now, tell me more of this playing doctor, Alyssa," he said, turning his commanding stare back toward me. I gulped in embarrassment that he'd overheard that part of the comment, and then, a little sheepishly, I told him what the phrase meant.

He didn't even bother hiding his chuckles as he went off to his personal tent for the night. As for me, I didn't need any other source of heat thanks to how warm my face got from embarrassment, for having to explain playing doctor to my own father, of all people!

As the ride progressed, Seph and I fell back into our comfortable friendship; it felt by that point like we'd known each other our entire lives. She showed me more of her cool ranger tricks like talking to the animals and trees. She amazed me by singing some gold up out of the ground. Now I could tell that the two manifestations of power were really the same magical force, but I didn't bring it up again. The elves had it ingrained in them from history long past that magic was bad, but ranger and priest tricks were good, and there wasn't anything good I could see to come out of trying to convince Seph otherwise.

Keion went back to being Keion. Prince Charming Keion, that is. He was a favorite of the king's men, and he could boast the loudest and ride the fastest of them all. Sometimes he'd look at me, and his eyes would take on that dark, steamy stare that he'd gotten right after coming out of the poisoning, but it never lasted for more than a moment. He was the prince, and I was the princess, and that, I guess, was that.

Dad and I got the most out of the ride, I think. He told me the old stories that belonged to my faintest of memories, of how we'd moved to Wales when I was a baby, and how I'd grown up speaking both Welsh and English. As he described arriving in a strange land and climbing the stairs of our new home I started seeing the old stones in my mind again. The ancient castle we'd lived in was actually a hold for visiting elves, and we'd moved there because he had needed to maintain contact with Kiira-janna while seeing me raised. It had seemed so huge to me as a toddler, and listening to him describe the seven, eight, and nine hundred square foot rooms and twelve-foot vaulted ceilings made me realize how huge it actually was.

I vaguely remembered dozens of servants, including one young busty girl who held me close for hours every day and smelled like flowers. Not servants, he corrected; they were elves. Yes, they served him as the displaced king of the elves, and they all fell over backward to hold and to touch the future queen of the elves, but none of them was what you would call a servant. Most were scholars, journeying into the world of non-magic to gain ever more knowledge of how the humans lived. There were also special archaeologists and anthropologists, hunters of the past assigned to seek evidences of how human and elf civilization had intertwined over the ages.

Dad told me many cute stories of when I was really, really

young, and he also told me stories about Momma, stories that, if you watched his eyes while he told them, made it clear how much he missed being with her.

She'd had her own horse there, one kept well fed and brushed in what had once been the royal stables of the castle. She and he had spent days flying, hoof beat after hoof beat, across the countryside. It was two young lovers' dreams come true.

"So, with everything so perfect, why did Momma go back to Mississippi?" I asked, and instantly wished I hadn't. Even in the waning light of dusk I saw his face crumple.

"How much did your mother tell you about her parents?" he asked, his voice a soft, throaty whisper that barely made it across the fire to me.

"Nothing, actually. She wouldn't speak of them, other than to tell me how wonderful they were."

"They were that. Your mother's parents—your grandparents—were very well known and respected in central Mississippi. He ran a business—I do not remember which—and she ran several ladies' groups in and around the town your mother grew up in. Unfortunately they were scandalized, as much by their social position as by their own attitudes, when their only daughter brought home a scraggly young man from college. I could not, of course, tell them where I was really from, or what I was destined to be. They would have had me locked up if I had told them half the truth of Kiirajanna. They wanted their only daughter to marry a good man from a good southern family who could support her the way she was brought up to deserve, and who could blame them?

"Your mother and I broke their hearts by running off to Florida to get married. There were a lot of strong words used, most of which your mother absolutely did not mean. But she was young, and so was I, and we neither saw nor cared about the delicacy of your grandparents' position."

"Dad, you can quit apologizing for the situation already."

"I probably can, at that, Alyssa. But your mother cannot. Your grandparents refused to see us off when we left for Wales, and then they swore they would never speak to their only daughter again. Luckily, those ended up being empty, angry words, and it only took about half of a year before the international telephone bills for calls between Wales and Mississippi started. Luckily our holdings have always been fairly immense, but I used to joke that she would drain even that amount dry.

"We proceeded that way, us in our idyllic castle in the country and your grandparents managing their affairs on the other side of the ocean, till just after your third birthday. Then there was a call early one morning from someone else in Mississippi." His voice broke slightly, and I looked over to see a shiny drop on his cheek. A couple of deep breaths later, Dad continued, "There had been an accident. A drunk driver crossed the middle line and drove his large pickup truck right into your grandparents' oncoming car. They were—they were in critical condition, in the hospital, and we needed to get there.

"Of course we left immediately. It only took a few flights and one taxi ride to get to the hospital, but even then we were too late. There was nothing we could do."

His shoulders shook in the firelight as he went silent. I could easily sense how much emotional pain he was in, so I got up and moved next to him, putting my arm around my father to comfort him as I knew he'd done for me.

"Your mother was devastated as much by not having had a chance to say goodbye as by the loss itself," he finally said, his voice soft and far away. "She's such a strong, strong woman, Alyssa. She personally saw to the affairs of the estate, working through her pain with a quiet, lovable dignity. She did make you stop speaking Welsh, though. It reminded her of too much when you did. Then I—my time was up, and I had to return to the throne of the people who needed me. I did not have a choice; no one was available for me to have abdicated to."

"Elf succession seems a fairly fragile thing," I observed.

Dad shrugged and continued, "Once I left, your mother remained barred up in your grandparents' house for a couple more years before she got tired of people looking down at her every time she went out, and then she sold that house and moved up to the town where you lived most of your life. It was really all she could do; all of the people she had known growing up branded her as the silly woman who had run away with the guy who had gotten her pregnant and then left her. And, for what they knew of the story, they were right."

"I—wow," I said, not really sure what I could add that would even make sense, much less help. "Dad, that's a heavy story. And I never knew any of it."

"Like I said, your mother is tough as a unicorn's horn."

"I assume that's pretty tough."

"It is, Alyssa," he said, and he shifted so that he could drape his arm around me. We sat like that, silently holding each other, for what felt like hours.

"When will I become queen and you get to go back to Momma?" I asked as we got up from the campfire to find our beds.

"Soon," he said. "You have come a long way in a short time, Alyssa. I am confident that the people will accept you as queen. Before we test that, though, you still have a little bit of training left to go through."

"Like what?"

"Well, a vision quest, for one."

"A vision quest? Like running off naked into the woods without any food to see what kind of hallucinations I get?"

"Like that, but with less nakedness, and limited running too. It is an important part of an elf's coming of age, and you will need to complete one in order to establish your place among the people."

"Sephaline told me that's when the rangers get their familiars."

"That is correct. It is when those who are destined to be rangers learn their fates. Everyone is expected to come back not only mature, but also with a much better grasp of what their place in society will be."

"Oh. We just kind of did that randomly back on Earth."

"Randomly, and not very well," he agreed.

"Okay, I guess I can do that," I said, ignoring the insult. "What else?"

"That is about it, I think. Once old Sternyface, to use your term, tells us that you are good to go, the queen will meet you and decide whether you are truly ready. Then there will be a coronation ceremony, and you and your newly-selected king will take over the thrones, and finally your old dethroned dad will slink off to Earth to be with the love of his life for good."

"Once you go, I can come visit, right?"

"Sure. The queen gets vacations every other year or so. Or is it every third year at first?"

"You're kidding, I hope."

"About the vacations? Yes. About the chance to visit? No. You will hopefully visit us often, Alyssa. Your mother and I both love you a great deal."

And with that assurance, I went off to sleep.

Letters From Home

My beloved daughter,

Momma's elegant cursive lit up the light pink stationery. It was just a little bit smaller than a normal sheet of notebook paper; Momma had once told me that that was a normal size, back before "I heart U 2" was an everyday cell phone expression. Her handwriting flowed neatly across the page, making perfectly horizontal strips even though the paper had no lines printed on it. At the bottom of the first page the text wrapped around an image of Minnie Mouse. I'd seen the box containing this paper, with matching envelopes, in her room several years before, and I'd asked for a few sheets to draw on, but Momma had shooed me away from it because it was "something special." Back then I hadn't understood, but now that I knew where Momma and my father had met, it made sense why Disney World stationery would be special to her.

Just holding Momma's letter was special to me. It, and a letter from Sarah, were waiting on the desk in my room the night we got back from the library. L.T. somehow knew what they were, the little branches literally quivering as I approached and picked them up. The quiet rustling sound as I walked over to the desk was exciting. I almost cried as I read the addresses on the front. Momma had never written me a letter before. Oh, she'd sometimes put cute notes about how awesome I was into my school lunch, but the few times I was gone for more than a night—summer camp was about it, really—she'd just e-mailed. And why not? E-mail is typed, easier to read, faster and cheaper to get there, and so on.

E-mail is cool.

But it's not hand-written-on-stationery cool.

It was so good to receive your letter, Lyssa.

Okay, I'm happy to say that I started it. All the laying there, looking at Momma's picture, never getting to talk to her, had made me miss her more than I'd ever thought possible. While Dad was making me go from my daily training to my room for dinner and then sleep and then back to training the next morning, I'd used some of my pent-up expressionism by getting a stack of blank paper from the herald and writing a letter to Momma.

It hasn't been the same around here since you left, kiddo. The house is so quiet. I've been tempted to send a note to your father to ask for another one of those monkeys to keep me company. You remember Mwnci, don't you? The monkey he sent that one Christmas?

Of course I remembered Mwnci, though it had been years before I figured out that it was a real memory and not a childhood fantasy. I'd been unwilling to ask Momma about it at first, figuring she would laugh at me for it, but when I finally worked up the steam to tell her, she'd just smiled and confirmed it. Yes, Dad had sent a magical monkey to visit his daughter and to teach her a lesson. The monkey had hidden all my presents, and only brought them out after we'd gone and served the poor and I'd proven that I knew what the spirit of giving and of service really meant. Apparently it was a lesson a future elf queen needed to learn.

And hey, he was a cutie, too. For a monkey, anyway.

Sweetheart, I'm a little worried about some of what you wrote. I know how libraries have always called out to your spirit, and at the same time I know how curious you must be about the prophecies that were written about your birth and ascension. But Kiirajanna is your father's native home, dear. If he tells you that it is too dangerous to travel to the library at this time, then you absolutely must believe him. He loves you every bit as much as I do, and he wouldn't want anything to happen to you any more than I would. At the same time, I know how strong you are, and also how strong-willed you can be. Please, Alyssa, set the trip to see the library off as something that can be done in the future, once you are queen and can bring all your troops with you to pro-tect you.

I stopped to laugh. I had no idea, back when I wrote the first letter, about the whole "all the king's horses and all the king's men" bit, but maybe Momma would have approved if she'd heard that part? Nah, I really doubt it.

The queen's children do sound pretty spoiled, dear. Then again, they've probably lived in that castle their whole lives, waited on by servants. They haven't been through half of what you've accomplished. Don't worry about them, Lyssa. You're worth more than all three of them put together. Besides, some day soon you'll out-

rank all of them, and then you can tell them what you really think! Especially this Prince Charming guy. In the meanwhile, it sounds like he's a great archer, and you probably need to be one, too, so learn what you can from him. Keep your head down, and keep learning your lessons, and some day you can show him just how charming he really is. Not.

After that one night in the library, watching him come back to life right in front of me, feeling his warm, strong heart beating beneath my hand, I wasn't entirely sure just how charming he really was, or not. Momma didn't need to know that, though.

You asked about that pendant—Draignerthol, you call it? It has been in our family for a very long time, and that is about all that I know. My mother passed it down to me when I left home to be with your father and the other elves in Wales. Handing it to you the night before you left felt like the right thing to do, and apparently it was! An ancient and powerful relic, you say? It was always just a dusty old pendant here, though the blue gemstone in the eye was really pretty. I thought several times about having it appraised, but it kept slipping my mind when I'd set out to do it. I hope you learn even more about it, and that you figure out how best to use it for yourself and for your kingdom.

I snorted. Oh, I'd figured out how to use it, all right. Whether that was best for me and for the kingdom was yet to be seen once I got a chance to talk it over with Sternyface.

The rest of the letter, nearly a whole page of it, was pretty much just everyday stuff. Summer school had started, and she was teaching it. The Munfords, our neighbors across the street, had finally replaced their Buick sedan with a Hyundai and were showing it off like it was a Cadillac. The summer camp folks had called to ask if I would be interested in working there this year, and she had to tell them no. That was funny because working at summer camp was where everybody else, other than Momma and Sarah, were being told I was. I mean, we all hated lying to everybody, but nobody wants to be locked up in the loony bin for telling the truth, right?

I'm so happy to read that you found a cousin in Kiirajanna, Lyssa. Your father told me about the small family he came from, but we never had the opportunity to talk much about them. He never brought her up, but your cousin sounds like such a sweet, sweet girl. And a wolverine guardian! That is something. Please, give her a big hug from me for all the protecting and teaching and guiding she's doing. And— what do you do for a wolverine? Can you hug it? Scratch its ears? Feed it treats? Whatever you can do, do something nice for Booboo for me.

Something nice for Booboo. Right. I tried to picture me scratching the little killing machine behind the ears, but could only snort and shake my head.

Love and hugs and kisses always and forever,

Missing you terribly,
Momma
P.S.: My mind is still trying to wrap itself around all that about unicorns and fairies. Tell me more next letter, okay?

I felt a tear run down my face as I flipped back to the first page and read it all through again. It's one thing to look at a photo and think about someone who's dear, but hearing them through their handwritten words on a page speaks directly to the heart. I missed Momma, more than I could even say.

Outstanding to hear from you, Legs! How's "summer camp" going, hey?

The second letter was very different from the first. Far from Momma's neat, consistently-sloped script, Sarah's handwriting looked like it was created by the right hand of a drunken southpaw ape, and that's being a little too mean to the poor ape. She'd written on normal lined spiral notebook paper, and she hadn't bothered trimming the little pieces off from where she'd ripped the pages out. Apparently, to her mind, the blue lines across the page were merely for general guidance, too. Her lines of writing went all over the place: up, down, and sometimes even a little bit horizontal.

It was a mess, but I loved opening and reading it.

I can't begin to tell you how hard this secret is to keep, Legs. "Where's Alyssa this summer?" "She's in elf land petting unicorns!" Oh. My. God. I so want to rub that in peoples' faces. And fairies? And a pet wolverine—is it cute? Can you pet a wolverine? I want to kiss it right on top of its little furry head for watching out for you. Can you do that for me? Just one little smack, right on top of her head, between her ears?

Yeah, that's Sarah for you. She's a sweet, sweet girl, and undeniably the smartest girl in our whole class, but her train of thought jumps its tracks regularly.

You slugged the High Priestess for talking bad about your momma? You rock! It's too bad she had wards or whatever it was protecting her, because she deserved to feel the pain for that. Hope you don't have to work much with her any more! And hey, you have to take that trip to the library. It sounds so cool. Just go, and turn those blue eyes on your dad when you get back. YOLO, right?

Hmm. Somehow I'd forgotten to tell Momma about slugging the high priestess. Well, that's not entirely true; it was less about forgetting and more about not wanting to hear what she might say. Sarah's reaction, though, was priceless.

Sarah had the same take on the royal trio as Momma did, all except Prince Charming. For him, she sent me a *woo hoo* and a lot of little X's and O's and hearts and lips.

I won't bore you with the rest of Sarah's letter, which was just a listing of everybody we knew who'd finished high school with us and where they were at the time. Most of them hadn't left town. Most of them wouldn't leave town, in fact. Honestly, nobody ever leaves that town.

Nobody except me ever leaves that town, I guess I should say.

I folded both letters back up and slipped them into the envelopes they'd been sealed inside. Neither one had a postmark on it, so I assumed Momma had gathered both into some sort of air mail packet to get to Wales quickly.

I was sure glad she did, I thought as my head hit the pillow for the night. My eyes were still leaking little drops of happiness, but I tried to fall asleep anyway.

As much as I was learning to like Kiirajanna, I missed my best friend and my Momma.

UNBENNES

a lady of high rank. The term is not used very often among the egalitarian elves, but it is always used in reference to the High Priestess.

Facing The High Priestess

The first morning after we got back, bright and early, I got to experience the longest half hour I've ever waited for anybody.

First, though, I have to point out the obvious. My bed was very, very nice to sleep in. The King may travel well, with good food and soft pads and all, but that's nothing compared to the joy of slipping into satin sheets on a royal bed.

Aerona glared at me, of course. I mean, she always glares at me, even when she's happy. It's the natural set to her face. But this time she really glared at me, an expression that might've made a stone melt.

"Have a nice time learning the dice, Princess?" she asked, her voice playing at being as sweet as her expression was sour.

"I did," I said, nodding, hoping the situation would go away by itself. "Seph taught me well. It's a fun game. You don't really care, do you?"

She continued glaring silently.

"Look, I know I say I'm sorry too often for the one who will eventually be queen, but I really am sorry to have lied to you.

There just wasn't any other option for us to get going. You would have stopped us, wouldn't you?"

"Yes, Princess, I would have stopped you, or died trying."

"Well, then you see? You're still alive, and I got to go read the prophecy. All's well that ends well, and all that stuff. Right?"

She continued glaring silently, so I gave up and went to croon softly to Little Treebeard. I couldn't imagine a tree being excited to see someone come home, but there she was, trembling leaves and everything. She was a lot more forgiving than Aerona was, too.

A tree. Forgiving. Sometimes I still can't believe this is happening to me. Back in Mississippi, if I'd talked about a tree being forgiving, they'd have locked me right up.

The next morning wasn't quite as much fun. Two burly temple guards knocked on my door very early in the morning. Once I was dressed they followed me like I was a prisoner down to breakfast and then straight to Naissa's office. I sat in the one empty chair that was not behind her desk, and the two guards padded out, closed the door, and then, if the lack of footsteps meant anything, took up guard posts outside.

Well. I really was in trouble.

Truth be told, I'd known it, and I'd dreaded it. It was just that once I'd talked Seph and Keion down off of their high horses, I'd nearly been able to forget this was coming. It really had been a nice ride back with my father. And soon, I supposed, I would get to find out if I had another nice ride back coming—this time a ride back to Earth.

My mind went through at least a hundred different ways I was going to tell Momma about what had happened. "Hi, Momma! Guess what happened to your little princess!" "Well, Momma, you know how you always said to be careful and follow the important rules?" "Momma, I'm home!"

None were any good.

I jumped when the door in the back wall of her office opened. In stepped Sternyface, looking as severe as I've ever seen her. Behind was a face I hadn't dared hope to see, but it filled me with no end of joy.

I might actually get out of this, I realized when I saw my father walk in behind the high priestess.

Granted, he didn't look like he held much hope. He looked like he had just eaten a sour pickle. Worse, he refused to meet my eyes with his, instead staring at Sternyface or at the wall behind me.

"Do you know why we are here, Princess Alyssa?" Naissa said.

What, no 'glad to see you, how was your trip, so happy you got to read a little of the prophecy' warm-up? I wondered. Dad somehow heard my thought, though, because for a moment he flicked his eyes over to mine and held my gaze. Using tiny movements he shook his head. *Don't say it*, I read in his eyes before he stopped looking me in the eye again.

For having been apart for so many years, we really were scarily alike.

With a start, I realized she was still expecting an answer, her face screwing up even tighter into a lemon-sucking expression.

"I am pretty certain I can guess, High Priestess," I said, choosing at the last moment to treat her like the principal. A corner of Dad's lip quirked up, so I must've chosen right.

"Well, then, that is fortunate indeed, for it allows us to not waste any further time. Did you or did you not use magic in the halls of the Library of Alecsanddrha?"

"I did." There wasn't any point even thinking about lying, really, even if that was something I would do in any case.

"Was I not clear in your training that the use of magic is

forbidden and punishable by permanent banishment to the realm of the humans?"

"That it is forbidden, yes, but I do not believe you ever told me of the punishment." It was a small satisfaction to see her blink for a moment of confusion.

She recovered quickly, though. "Be that as it may, you purposely reached out for a forbidden force and used it willfully, is that not correct?"

"I wouldn't say that I reached out for it purposely. It was just there, and I had to grab for something to save the lives of two elves. My two friends."

"That is—very noble. Yet a noble motive does not forgive an evil act, Princess Alyssa," she said. I noticed that, for once, she was not referring to me as a child. Maybe it was time to quit taking lessons from her, and instead to push back a little, I thought.

"I am of the opinion, High Priestess, that it is not evil. I've seen that what you call magic is the same as what the rangers...." I started into a prepared argument, but she cut me off.

"Your opinion on the nature of the various forces involved does not change the situation, Princess Alyssa. You need to be aware that though the two types of power usage may feel much the same, the level of ability is what makes the distinction. Rangers improve the world around them with their powers, and their powers are hardly strong enough to commit mass destruction as in, say, the burning down of a millennia-old icon of the elf race's knowledge and wisdom. You likely believe the same of priests' healing powers, but again, the same rule applies. That is why eons of our people's tradition differentiate the powers and declare what you did, by definition, to be evil. Now, I must ask, would you, knowing the penalty is banishment, knowingly reach out to and use the evil forces of magic if the situation were repeated?"

I'd already thought that question through. "Yes," I said, putting as much certainty as I could into my voice despite the stress of the inquisition. Stress aside, I would have done it again, in a heartbeat. I was sure that the three of us would have died if I hadn't, for one thing. Also, though, I was getting tired of being told something was bad, evil, when I knew in my heart that it wasn't.

"Does your presence, your mission, your future on Kiirajanna mean so little to you, then?"

"No, High Priestess, it does not. I love Kiirajanna, both the land and her people as well as the wonderfully rich history and traditions I've discovered in my short time here so far. Granted, I love Earth as well, and so I have to be honest that the threat of going back to live out my life in the realm of my birth isn't exactly the worst thing you can throw in my face. Even if it were the worst thing, though, the truth is that no, I wouldn't do it differently. Whether you believe it was evil or not, I couldn't stand there and watch my friends, my companions, die and do nothing in the name of tradition. High Priestess, in my judgment, at that moment, the greater evil would have been watching the members of the Cult slit my friends' throats."

"She is ready," my father spoke up for the first time. Sternyface turned a glare his way. "Naissa, she is," he said, returning her glare with his own gaze of iron.

"Am I to leave unpunished in her actions the commission of a crime which has caused others to be banished? How will that be just or equitable? How can either of us go on adjudicating the law when we have looked the other direction on the breaking of one of our most sacred codes?"

"How can you hold it against her that she merely did what she was prophesied to do?"

"Prophecy didn't make her..." she said, but my father cut her off.

"Careful, Naissa. It is your own words from your own tongue that must continue to tell our people about the importance of their adherence to duty, and the prophecies are part of that. You do remember those sermons, yes?"

"Of course I do, Cadfael. Do not mock me, please."

"Cadfael? Your name is Cadfael?" I blurted out. It was the first time I'd heard my father's name. It was fitting, I supposed, since it meant prince of battle.

Both High Priestess and King stopped arguing with each other and turned their gazes toward me. "Alyssa," my father said, "Cadfael is the name adopted by all kings upon our ascent to the throne. Some day you will rule beside King Cadfael, also."

Oh, right—just as Talaith was the name of all elf queens. How could I have forgotten that?

"Perhaps she is not as ready as you suggest," Sternyface said, turning back to glare at my father, who just shrugged.

"She does not know everything, but neither did we at that point, and we were judged ready, were we not? You must remember how much we did not know at first."

"I remember. Though it was a long, long time ago, I do remember." Sternyface turned toward me and searched my face for several long moments, looking for the answer to a question I didn't know. Finally she nodded, once. "Princess," she said, her voice dropping several tones lower and taking on a sound of gravity, "it is my judgment, and apparently your father the king's judgment as well, that your use of magic is in keeping with your duty to the prophecy and should thus go unpunished. You must be advised, though, that we may not be doing you any favors in so ruling. There are some already, and will likely be many to follow, who know of your actions at the library, and of your newfound powers both in transferring sickness to someone and in snatching flames out of the air and throwing them about haphazardly. None will question us openly about our decision, but many will speak behind our backs on the matter. Most will fear you for your power, for it has not been used openly for hundreds of years. Do not be surprised if some capitalize on this general fear to raise the question of your suitability for the office for which you are destined, prophecy or no. In fact, now that the prophecy and the works related to it no longer exist as anything other than charred remnants, and its keepers have been discredited due to their long-standing conspiracy against you and against the crown, it would not surprise me if some began twisting its contents away from what they truly were. I tell you all of this not to make you afraid, but rather to recommend caution and prudence in all of your future words and deeds. We cannot guarantee that the cult that stood against you has been entirely eradicated, but now a second, and potentially more powerful, force may rise against you in the form of the elf people themselves. Do you understand?"

"I do, High Priestess," I said. I thought I did, anyway.

"Well, then, Your Majesty," she said, turning grandly to my father, "it seems we are in agreement that she is ready. It is time, then, to have the ceremony?"

"I believe it is, High Priestess Naissa," he said, equally grandly. "Come, Princess Alyssa," he said, a grin splitting his face as he strode to the door, grabbing my hand on the way. "We have a lot of party to prepare for."

At his walking pace, he was halfway down the hall before I managed to ask, "What party?"

"What party? The party. You are to be acknowledged as the future queen, by the current one. That sounds like plenty of reason for a grand party to me," he said, shooting a grin back at me while continuing his rapid walk.

TYNNU NYTH CACWN AR FY MHEN

literally, to pull a wasp's nest down onto one's head; it's how you feel when you do something that will tick off lots of people at once. Dad says it's a normal feeling for rulers. I was starting to get used to it, myself.

Dad's Side Of The Family

The next day was Sadwrn, so we didn't party much. I spent most of the day with Seph and Dad, of course. Dad took us on another tour of the countryside, one that started pretty much the same as the other trips we'd taken to meet the villagers. He always seemed to genuinely love the interaction with the people, and now that I knew he'd come from being one of them, himself, I understood his connection. Along the way he told me several times that it is a ruler's duty to get to know his or her subjects, to meet them where they are, and that the only way to well and truly lead them was to first well and truly know where they start from.

A wise man, my father is. But that wasn't why he went out to the villages regularly. No, he went out because he loved to do it.

Oh, he always received plenty of love back, and I remember marveling at how much the elves seemed to love him on that first trip. I thought, at first, that he loved going out because of the love showed to him, but somewhere along the way I realized I had it backward. The people, the elf commoners whose daily lives were full of normal, everyday things, loved him because of the sincere appreciation and respect they felt radiating from him on every visit.

I vowed to some day be a ruler like him. As I did it, the high priestess's warning of the fear they would feel when they learned of what I could do came back, but I shoved it down with the assumption that if I just showed enough respect and appreciation for them, they'd get past it.

This trip was different, though, pretty much right from the start. As we left the first village we'd come to, Seph turned to my father with one of her face-splitting grins and asked, "Are we...?"

"Yes."

"Are we what?" I blurted out after several long seconds of silence. I wanted in on the secret, too.

"You will see soon enough, Alyssa," he said. "I promise, you will like it."

We rode along in silence, though I could tell Seph was so excited she was ready to climb out of her seat at any minute. She wouldn't tell me why, though, no matter how many times I gave her the questioning look.

I hate being kept in the dark.

We rode into the next village with the sun at its highest point. Summer had given way to Fall, and I figured based on the direction we'd been going that we were a bit farther north than the castle, and so it seemed normal that the transition from leaf-strewn cart path to perfectly clean clearing made an abrupt sound.

Seph was out of the cart like a rocket. Dad stood by long enough to help me down, a huge grin on his face too, and as soon as my feet were safely grounded he spun and jogged after Seph, who by that point had curled herself around an elf who looked familiar.

He looked very familiar, in fact. He looked just like Dad.

Dad strode up to the guy who was obviously his brother and the pair clasped hands, my uncle's other arm still wrapped around Seph, who judging by the similarities in their faces was obviously his daughter. Every other male elf I'd seen come into contact with my father gave some sort of respectful gesture; some gestures, like eyebrow-wagging, I hadn't recognized as a signal of respect till Keion's class had taught me so. This time, though, neither elf took the time to worry about it. Apparently the bond of brothers between them was strong enough that even royal custom took a back seat.

"Brother," my father said, "I would like to introduce my daughter, your niece, and now, apparently, Sephaline's best friend, Alyssa. Alyssa, this is your uncle, Dafydd."

Seph unwrapped herself so that her father could shake my hand. He looked at me, and then he looked at her, and then he looked back at me, and he said, "My goodness, you two look so much alike. It is so wonderful to meet you finally, Alyssa. Please, can we have some tea in my house?"

I knew enough about elf customs to know that his request for tea in his house wasn't just because he wanted a hot beverage. After all, you generally don't get invited into an elf's home for tea; that's for enjoying outdoors. Wondering what he wanted, I followed him, with Dad and Seph right behind, across the village green and up to a blue-painted round door.

Seph had explained the paint thing. Elves loved, she said, to get out into the woods with nature, and most of their occupations involved something dealing with it. When they were home, though, they liked to differentiate that with bright colors you wouldn't regularly find out in the woods. That was why an elf village looked like a rainbow, with bright blues, bright yellows, bright reds, and so on all intermixed.

Makes sense, right?

I'd never been inside an elf's home before, though. None of them had ever invited me. Now that my uncle had, though, I couldn't wait to experience it, but once I got inside I saw that what I'd thought would be fascinating really wasn't all that different from back on Earth. It was simple, a long, narrow home with three rooms that were separated only by a single architectural log and furniture placement. My uncle obviously didn't do a lot of entertaining, since the first chamber was more of a work area than a living room. It had a couple of chairs and a table, but most of the room was taken up with awls and punches and hammers and other leather-working tools and supplies. We went past these to a dining room table that had been made out of a single wide slab of wood. The five chairs around it were all shaped differently, and each of them was obviously hand-made. A simple pot-belly wood stove sat in one corner with a pot of water perched on it, steam rising from the pot to keep the air inside tropically warm and moist.

The far end of the home held a pantry and food prep area. The sink was topped by what looked like a pump handle; apparently elves didn't sing their water out of the ground like they sang their metals out. Open shelves housed all sorts of foods, from fruits and vegetables to loaves of bread, most likely baked by the village's baker and purchased by trading the leather items I'd seen in the front room.

Industrious was the best word I could find for the house. Simple was another. Unlike the palace, there wasn't any apparent concern given to art of any sort; there were no pictures on the walls, no decorations on the pots or pans or furniture. It was nothing more, or less, than a place to eat, sleep, and work. For all its simplicity, though, it felt incredibly homey.

The austerity made sense, I guess, since most elves prefer to be outdoors in the village green or in the forest for their play or conversation time. Still, it was shocking to see my uncle living in a low hovel while his brother slept every night on one of the best mattresses in the realm, attended by several personal servants and bodyguards.

My uncle caught me looking around. "What do you think of my home, Alyssa?" he asked with a smile.

"It's lovely," I lied. Hey, it was just a little white lie. "It's a little bit different from your brother's digs."

Dad chuckled. "They are not my digs, technically, Alyssa. They belong to the king of the elves. I have had the opportunity to enjoy them for many years, but the time is coming, and fairly quickly, when I will step away from the castle finery for the last time and return to the lifestyle I have envied. A lifestyle suited for a lifetime at your mother's side on Earth, I must add," he said with doe-eyes of longing that seemed sickeningly sweet.

"Indeed. My home is simple, and that is our way. I prefer it that way," my uncle said. Seph nodded from the other side. She'd been silent the whole time, her eyes and her whole essence focused on being with her father again. That much, I understood.

My uncle produced four cups from the pantry and spooned some herbs from a jar on the table into each of them. From the pot on the wood stove he added hot water and then pushed a cup in front of each of us. It smelled lovely, a sort of flowery aroma coming off in the steam. I made a point of inhaling deeply, smiling, and finishing with a slow breath out.

"I have missed your blend of tea, Brother," Dad said as he gently stirred the mixture. "The castle has plenty of tea available, but something—your herbal mixture, perhaps, or just a difference in the surroundings—makes it not quite the same."

Several moments of silence passed as the four of us all enjoyed the beautiful aromas. Spoons clunked lightly against the sides of cups on all sides of the table.

Dad finally broke the silence. "You did not bring us in here to talk about tea, Brother," he said. He'd hit on what was bothering me, too. Elves, I already knew, didn't use their homes as social gathering places. To be invited into a home was either a great honor or something to worry about, the trio of offspring of the queen had taught me.

I was a little worried as a result.

Uncle Dafydd nodded solemnly and stared into his tea for several more long moments before he looked up, first looking his brother in the eyes and then switching his gaze to me. "Dark things are being said, Alyssa. We hear that the grand Library of Alecsanddrha burned to the ground. Worse, we hear that you caused it to happen, with—with magic." He made a strange sign in front of him and then continued, "I pray it is not so, especially of one of my own family." He looked back at his cup, having spoken as much as his burst of confidence had allowed.

Well. They say bad news travels faster than a barefoot rabbit on a hot griddle, but this was a record. I shared a glance with my father, who nodded for me to go ahead and give his brother the story.

I took in a deep breath to begin, but Seph beat me to it. "She did it to save my life, Father."

"Oh? Tell me of this."

I told him the short version of the story, especially the part where Seph was about to get her throat slit and so I reached out for the only weapon I had available: magic! He listened, nodding gravely, looking at my father occasionally with a question in his eyes.

When I finished, he asked, "So, it was an accident? This reaching out and touching the forbidden flames?"

"No, accidental isn't the right word for it. I knew it was there, and I knew what it would do. I was angry, yes, and anger colored my thoughts, but the simple fact is that it wasn't what I would call an accident. I reached out on purpose and grabbed the only weapon I had at my disposal."

"I see," he said, nodding, and then changed direction abruptly. "Brother, you must have had a reason for sending three children into such a perilous situation. One of the children being my daughter, I feel an obligation to ask what your reason was."

My father answered directly. "It was not to be such a perilous situation, for one thing. My rangers had been monitoring the comings and goings of the librarians, but we had no idea they and the Cult of the Wyrm were the same group. The expansion of the blight we assumed was being done to the library rather than by its inhabitants. I thought, wrongly in retrospect, that sending the trio under the cover of secrecy would be best to keep them safe. And another thing, Brother: neither your daughter nor mine is still a child."

Dafydd snorted and said, "Alyssa has not even done her quest yet."

"That will come, and she will be accepted as an adult among elves, but she has grown up a wise and beautiful young woman among her own kind, who do not practice the same coming-of-age traditions as we do. My daughter is, for all practical purposes, already an adult. Your daughter is an adult, and has fulfilled all we have asked of her. Prince Keion, meanwhile, would likely show you a thing or two if he heard you calling him a child."

"Bah. Old age still wins over youth and inexperience."

"I would not be so sure, Dafydd. I saw him fight as the library burned, and his battle skill in the protection of our daughters was legendary to watch. I—well, I think he could take you."

Both Seph and I snickered at his last comment. I glanced at

her, surprised, and her face turned a new shade of red.

Her father noticed, too. "Need I remind you, my beloved daughter, that the prince is spoken for?"

"You need not, Father," she said, glaring at him while her face turned even redder.

My uncle nodded solemnly, a grin just barely peeking through his dour look.

"So, Brother, is the matter of the library put behind us?" Dad asked.

"It has your blessing?"

"Mine, and Sternyface's." Dad looked over at me and winked; I grinned at Dad's use of my nickname for her. His brother gaped momentarily, and then his face, too, broke out into a grin. Seph actually snickered.

"Well, then, I'd say it's time to put it behind us and have a party," my uncle said.

We walked back out through the blue door to a noisy cacophony of fun. While we'd been inside, the village elves had built a roaring bonfire in the middle of the clearing, and several had already taken up position around it with drums, flutes, and stringed instruments. Apparently the stricture against working on Sadwrn didn't include building up a screaming-hot party fire or joining a jam session.

I already knew Dad was a very popular king, evidenced by the reaction wherever we'd gone, but I had no idea how popular he was in his own home village. That carried over to me as his daughter, apparently, as every guy in the village wanted a dance with me that evening, while every brewer and wine maker wanted me to taste the fruits of their efforts, so to speak. In many ways the party was just like the one Dad took me to directly before Seph and I had headed out on our journey: same freestyle joining, same strange haze floating through the air, same wibbly-wobbly dancing. What's-his-name—the elf I'd tagged as Legolas—wasn't there, luckily. I hadn't been offered alcoholic drinks at the other village, but here in Dad's home it was apparently fair game.

Oh, and this time I also had my cousin there, swiveling her hips right beside me. Seph got her share of dancing in, though at times she seemed to be a case of the awkward local girl come home.

I have no idea how late the party lasted. I came to my senses slowly the next morning to the sound and smell of bacon frying. It took me a minute to realize by the blue tint of the doorway that I was asleep on my uncle's bed in his work room. It was another minute before I placed the arm that was draped over me as Seph's. I craned my neck to where I could see into the dining room and saw my dad and his brother working together like they were boys again, Dad mixing what was probably biscuit batter while my uncle dodged hot grease splatters over a frying pan on the wood stove.

They were both giggling, of all things, but quietly. When I moved my head Dad looked in at me and winked. He stopped what he was doing long enough to pour some hot water into a cup, stir, and bring it in to me.

"It is similar to what you know as coffee," he said quietly, handing me the cup.

"Eww. I've always hated coffee," I whispered.

"This will help your head, though," he said.

"My head's fine," I argued. I could tell Seph was coming awake too, so I sat up and, in doing so, realized how much of a lie I'd told Dad. My head wasn't fine at all; it hurt like the dickens whenever it moved, and so I took a sip from the cup he'd handed me. It was good, actually. It was strong, a woody flavor with spices that made it taste like the mulled cider I'd loved as a kid. And it really did calm down the rabid squirrels on crack with nail guns that had jumped to action inside my skull when I'd sat up.

"I can tell," he said with a grin as he went back to cooking.

"You remember what Dad said about there being a special place in the afterlife for men who got young women drunk," my uncle chided my father.

"I don't recall either of us feeding the girls alcohol last night," Dad countered. "Besides, didn't he also say something about what didn't kill us making us stronger when he fed us alcohol to teach us how to hold it?"

"We were boys, though. They're girls."

"That's about the most sexist thing I've ever heard you say, Brother. Surely you did not mean it that way."

I wanted to applaud Dad for making such a good point, but I was scared the sound of my hands making contact would literally make my head explode.

Breakfast was interesting. The biscuits Dad made were lovely, but the bacon grease nearly made me lose the little bit I had on my stomach. Seph's face actually turned a shade of green when she tried to eat it.

The two men seemed to derive an intense amount of humor from the bacon episode. Finally my father took pity on us and suggested, "Sop the bacon grease up with a biscuit and eat the two together. It'll help your stomach process it. And no, you can't not eat it. The food will help your stomach once it settles down."

"Here," Seph's dad said, pushing two shot glasses across the table to us after filling them from the contents of an unmarked bottle. "It'll help."

I sniffed at it and felt my nose hairs almost light on fire. "What—what is it?"

"Don't ask. Just drink it," he said, and my father nodded. "Hold your nose closed when you gulp it down; might make it easier. Here, let's have one too," he said, filling two more little cups and handing one to Dad. Holding the last cup up above his head, he said, "Here's to the hair of the dog!" and gulped it down.

Ah. I'd heard of the 'hair of the dog that bit you' once before, and it had sounded nasty back then. Now, not much sounded nastier than how I really felt, so there wasn't much point fighting. I tossed the contents of the shot glass down my throat and tried to flourish it.

I didn't make it that far.

Oh, Lord. It felt like I'd sucked down an ounce of lava.

Tears came to my eyes as I felt the liquid hit my stomach with a burn. The heat marched right back up my throat, pausing long enough to make my sinuses feel like dumping their entire contents out before it made my ears feel hotter than a skillet left on the sidewalk in mid summer.

I think that my entire body actually quivered.

And then—it was gone. With it went my headache as well as the queasiness. The bacon actually started smelling good again.

I laughed through the tears that still streamed down my face. "What was that?" I asked.

"I told you, the hair of the dog. My own personal concoction I draw through my still back behind the house."

"I believe the word you are familiar with would be moonshine, dear," my father said as he tossed back his own cup. "For some reason unbeknownst to anyone, consuming hard alcohol after a night of overconsumption of alcohol helps take the pain away a little. Sephaline, you should follow Alyssa's lead. It only hurts for a little while."

Seph did as he suggested, and I got to see what my own reaction must have looked like from the outside. Dafydd guffawed once she was breathing again and cuffed her hard on the back of her shoulder.

"I'm proud of you, Missie. Just—don't drink that much again," he said.

"I won't drink that much again. In fact, I'm quite sure I'll never drink anything, ever again," she said, a sentiment I would've echoed had both men not apparently found it extremely funny.

Breakfast successfully downed, we pulled ourselves up into the wagon and started back for home. Seph seemed down, I figured because she'd left her father behind once again. I'm sure I seemed down because, hair of the dog or not, I felt horrible. I'd never noticed the horseless wagons giving a bumpy ride before, but this one was, and every jolt of the wagon made my head feel just a little bit more like exploding.

"So, when we get back," I said when I finally found my voice, "we don't have any lessons planned, right? We can go to sleep?"

"Right on the first," my father said. "You have no lessons for the entire week. Remember, you were already determined to be prepared to meet the queen. Tonight and the rest of this week, then, we celebrate!"

"That means more party, doesn't it?" I asked, not sure whether to be happy or sad.

"Yes, it does. Quite a bit more party, in fact. Everyone from around the realm is coming to meet you, and to feast, and to drink and sing and dance together. It will be the greatest party you have ever seen, Alyssa!"

"Do I have to go?" I knew the answer, but I wanted to make a point.

He sighed. "Yes, dear. You must go, and you must enjoy it. That is tradition, and so that is the rule."

"Oh. Okay. Great. Hey, wake me up when we get to the party part, will you, Dad?"

I fell asleep to the sound of my father chuckling.

CI

literally, a dog. The common elves being pretty free with their affections, this takes a lot to earn, but it's a term applied to a guy who chases after women liberally.

To Party With The Prince

I woke from my hung over stupor just long enough to climb the stairs to the main entrance to the castle, and then the grand staircase up to the second floor. For the first time I felt jealous of Seph, who didn't have to toil her way up the second set of stairs before collapsing in her own room. I sure didn't care what the bed looked like right then; I just wanted one to crash in.

It vaguely occurred to me as I climbed the stairs that the palace staff seemed busier than I'd ever seen them, hanging ribbons and glow-bulbs all around. Splashes of color were everywhere, making a display that any other time would've been pretty, but at the moment just messed with my hung over brain enough that I would've screamed if I hadn't feared the pain it would have caused.

Aerona looked at me when I stumbled in, chuckled quietly, and went back to glaring at the corners of the room as I collapsed, fully dressed, into the bed. Apparently I had "hung over" written on my forehead.

Some time later—I'm not sure how much, but the window

was dark—Seph shook me gently awake.

"What time is it?"

"I have no idea," Seph said. "I woke up a few minutes ago, myself, to the sound of the chief of staff telling me to wake you up for your party."

"Princess, it is approximately half past the hour of eight," Aerona said, her voice cranked up louder than really required to get from where she was to me. I glared at her, and was rewarded with nothing but a slightly upturned corner of her lips before she went back to glaring at the darkness in the corners.

"Thank you, I think," I said as I clambered out of the sheets I'd apparently wrapped myself up in during my tortured sleep and then out of the bed itself. "My head feels better. How's yours?"

"Better," Seph agreed.

"Where's Booboo?"

"I haven't let him into the castle since we got back earlier today. He sensed my foul mood and wanted to take a servant's head off. He hasn't quite gotten over the trip to the library, I think."

"So he won't get to come to the party tonight?"

"He's a wolverine. I think he'll survive being left out. What are you doing?"

"Opening the door? Leaving? Going to a party? Wondering why you're asking that?" I had just been opening the door to walk out.

"Going to a party in the palace dressed like that?" She swept her eyes meaningfully up and down my rumpled pants and tunic a few times.

"Is this one of those fancy ones?" I asked, pronouncing fancy the same way I'd pronounce the word poison. My head felt better, but I still didn't feel like dressing up.

"It's your party, Cousin. If you don't dress up at least a little, everybody will notice."

"It's my party. Why do I care if they notice?"

"Alyssa, people will remember the slight you do them by going down to your first coming-out party dressed like a peasant for the entirety of your reign, however short that may be if you do so. You owe it to your future subjects to dress up and let everyone see how beautiful you are."

"Fine. Is there going to be food there?" I was suddenly very hungry.

"Of course. The kitchens have been going full-tilt all day, it seems. And the faster you put on something you can be seen downstairs in, the sooner you can sample it."

I admit, it was fun getting dressed with Seph there. I remember playing dress-up as a kid, and it was just like that. I held out an outfit, and she gave it thumbs-down. Another outfit, another thumbs-down. Finally, after going through nearly the entire closet that had been started for me when I arrived and had magically grown, an outfit or two showing up in it every week, I pulled out a forest green tunic that came down just past my knees with a matching pair of green pants. She clapped, and I jumped behind the privacy screen to change.

Minutes later I emerged, all clad in green. The tunic was pretty enough, its green linen fabric embroidered in gold thread with tree shapes. The high collars swept down to a clasp, and it opened up again to form a narrow oval shape that Draignerthol shone through. I figured that everyone apparently already knew about my ownership of the ancient relic, after all, so why not display it?

The long sleeves of the top widened as they went, so that if I held my arms out the wrists drooped down by a few feet. Seph nodded appreciatively and sat me down in a chair, and then she went after my hair with a brush. It had grown out from the short spiky mess I'd come to Kiirajanna sporting and was at least long enough to style a little. Using water and the brush she managed to shape it up into a mop of curls that looked nice, at least, to me, and would've done any fashion magazine proud. It was a little quick and rough, but I didn't care—I was ready for food, and I wanted out of the chair and the room.

I launched myself down the hall, but Seph's whisper drew me up short. "Alyssa," she hissed, and I hung back to let her catch up to hear what was so important. "Everybody's downstairs. You need to descend the stairs slowly and regally," she whispered.

I sighed. Dad had picked a bad night to let me get drunk.

As we descended the stairs, it was obvious why she'd said that. There were dozens of elves standing, watching me. Dad was in front, his own black velvet tunic stunning with little sparkling embroidered highlights along its seams. Beside him was Prince Charming, also stunningly decked out in black velvet. Meriel stood by her brother, contempt painted across her face as usual, but Seren rounded out the trio with a broad grin. The sisters were completely decked out, Seren in a bright blue floor-length gown with a swish of sparklies across the neckline and down one side, and Meriel in a futuristic-looking green tunic with metallic gold panels in various geometric shapes. Sternyface stood to Dad's right, wearing her priestess robe as usual. Behind and around were all of the minor nobles involved in running the kingdom and the castle, elves I'd only barely met in passing. Most of their names I'd forgotten, but I hoped Dad would help me out with that.

"My daughter, Prime Princess of Kiirajanna, I and all of your people, your family, your realm, welcome you and salute you. Will you join us for an evening of fun, food, and drink?" Dad said, his voice resonant and ceremonial. He was speaking in the language of the elves, as I'd figured he would, and I was sure I was expected to respond in kind.

I did. Projecting my voice as well as I could, I summoned the ancient language of my father's line and said, "Yes, Father. Friends, thank you for the warm welcome I have received since I arrived in this beautiful realm. I look forward to many more years of peace and joy in service to our home."

Apparently I had chosen my words well; Sternyface actually cracked a smile. Dad lifted my face to his and kissed my cheeks in welcome. Sternyface stepped in behind him and did the same. The rest of the elves, led by the royal trio, greeted me with the strange little hand gesture the trio had taught me. Some bowed, and others curtsied, though Keion and his sisters were careful to greet me very stiffly as equals.

Dad led me into the dining room. Along every table was laid out meats, cheeses, fruit, and breads of all types. Pitchers stood every couple of feet, some full of cool, clear water and others full of either wine or a frothy beer. We sat at spots near the middle of the center table, where everyone could be as close to me as nearly everyone else.

I dug in.

So did Seph. Everyone else followed, too; apparently I had to be the first to eat, and my hunger had helped bring everyone else's wait to a quick end.

Dad chortled after a couple of minutes. "Hungry, dear?" he whispered.

"Very. I didn't realize how hungry last night could make me," I whispered back, though I really didn't need to whisper. The gathering was loud, everybody talking and telling jokes and laughing.

The elves know how to party.

The royal trio had, as position demanded, taken seats directly across the table from me. Seren, it turned out, was the life of the party. She told a couple of very funny stories that came from somewhere in the history books in order to break the ice around us, and when engaged in conversation she proved herself to have a wickedly funny quick wit. Meanwhile the wine softened Meriel's face quite a bit; she actually started smiling at her sister's jokes first and then, gradually, her smile spread to include me.

My own smile spread more and more as I drank more and more wine. It was really good stuff, a nice sweet red. I liked it a lot.

"What was that this afternoon about never drinking again?" my father whispered to me during a lull in the conversation.

"I didn't say it, I just agreed with my cousin. Besides, I didn't mean never as in—well, never. I meant, um, never while I was feeling that bad," I said, making it up as I went. His grin and associated chuckle meant that I succeeded. Sort of.

The only one I couldn't figure out was Keion. He didn't seem to drink a lot, but his friends to the side and behind him kept his glass tipped up full and taunting him to drink more. He was jovial enough, but not joyful like everybody else. He told a couple of hunting jokes, but they fell kind of flat. He smiled a careful smile at everyone else, his lips curled up just enough to look natural, though I could tell from his eyes that it wasn't really a smile.

Then he looked at me, and his smile vanished. His eyes hooded over and took on an intensity that made me feel like a deer being hunted. He stared at me for several long seconds; it got kind of scary. I smiled at him, and he snapped out of the hunter's gaze and looked away, lips forcing themselves up into a smile again.

Most of the night he looked at his friends, at my father, at the ceiling—anywhere but at me. Occasionally his gaze would wander over to my face again, and when I caught him looking I saw the same deep stalking stare I'd seen before. It was always just for a second, and then he'd turn quickly away.

The party moved to the ballroom soon enough. There, the same flutes and drums and other instruments I'd heard in the villages were put together into an actual arrangement. It sounded professional, honestly. I was glad that the trio had taught me some of the less folksy of the elf folk dances, since that was what was being done, and Dad let me know quickly that I was expected to lead the way. It started with a father-daughter couple's dance. Dad was an excellent lead, I found, which was good because they hadn't taught me that one. He said it would be kind of like the waltz, but since I didn't know how to waltz either that didn't do a lot of good. Within a few bars I was gliding along with him, though, in a step-step-glide, step-step-glide pattern.

After the sorta-waltz, there was a line dance. It wasn't like the line dances they did at school, the rhythmic shuffles where everybody stepped and bounced in a synchronous mass. It was actually a line dance, where lines of girls faced off with lines of guys and each beat of the music told us to move closer together or farther apart, depending on where we were in the pattern.

Oh, and meanwhile, servants wandered the hall handing out more glasses of wine.

After a while I noticed how warm it was getting in the room with all the elf bodies moving around, and so I stepped out onto the front porch. It was awfully bright at the doors, and so I moved off toward the darkness, hoping to find a cooler spot where I could breathe by myself for a few minutes.

"We crippled the Cult of the Wyrm, but it is still not safe for you out here in the dark by yourself, Princess," a familiar voice spoke from the shadows. I jumped and turned, the wine making it difficult to do so gracefully.

The prince stepped out of the shadows from behind me, the same hunter's stare he'd been fixing me with all night leading the way.

"I'm not entirely without my own defenses, you know," I said, patting my neck line meaningfully where my pendant was showing through the plunging neckline of the blouse.

"Your defenses are, in fact, impressive, Alyssa," he said, drawing my name out like a song.

I took one step closer to him, moving to where I could see his dark eyes better. They were still intense, but in a beautifully radiant way. His black hair shone in the dim porch light, curls falling down to frame an angular face, his sharp, strong chin casting a shadow across his shoulder. He smelled—strong, masculine. Like warm spices. Was my wine-addled mind playing tricks with me, I wondered?

"Did you come out here to protect me?"

"No."

"Why, then?"

Eyes haunted, he edged even closer to me. Across his face rode some sort of battle of indecision. Bodies nearly touching, he finally sprang. His hand moved so impossibly fast that I didn't have time to reach out for the magical powers I'd only recently come to know.

Before I could jump, or move, or make a noise, he had the back of my head cupped firmly in the palm of his hand, and his other arm pinning me against his muscular body, and then he tilted my head up so that our lips met.

And we kissed.

Getting Over It

"Alyssa!" Seph's voice called down the porch. "Are you okay?"

Keion's lips detached from mine, waking me up from the most amazing dream I'd been having.

Only, it had been real.

While my mind sorted out everything that was running through it at once, Keion shrank back into the shadows. Seph arrived a moment later and reached out to me as my hand somehow made it up to touch my mouth, the lips that had, just moments before, been pressed against the lips of Prince Charming, generating the most incredible energy. I mean, sure, I've kissed boys, but a single kiss had never struck me so deeply.

"Alyssa, are you okay?" my cousin asked again.

"Me? Oh, right. Yeah. I'm—I'm fine," I stammered, my brain still not completely connected to reality.

Had Seph seen it? She'd be indignant if she had; Prince Charming was, after all, "taken." She'd also be pretty jealous, something I really didn't want my cousin to feel toward me.

She must not have, I thought as Seph took my hand and led me back toward the front door to rejoin the dance. She didn't say anything about it, anyway. Until—

"You know, Cousin, the prince is—"

"Taken. Yes, I know. It was—"

"Passion. I know. Us elves, it's part of our heritage. You figured that out already, didn't you? We feel strongly about something, we just—"

"The wine, too. I'm—"

"Right. Must be the wine. You've had a lot of it, and who wouldn't kiss a pretty boy when she's—"

"Drunk. Right. I didn't kiss him, anyway; he kissed me. Hey, is it hot out here?"

"Not particularly," Seph said. "Are you okay?"

"That's the third time you've asked me that."

"It is, at that. And who wouldn't be okay after kissing—"

"I'm heading back in where it's cooler," I said, slipping through the doors into the ballroom, where I could at least pretend to not be able to hear Seph's reminders about my having just kissed the prince. The "taken" prince, at that.

"Alyssa!" my father yelled, striding up to where I stood with a wide grin on his face. "Are you okay?"

"Everybody keeps asking me that, for some reason."

"Well, you disappeared from the party for a while. Keion forsook the dancing to go out and find you, and when he failed to return Sephaline went to make sure both of you were okay."

"I just went out onto the porch to get some kiss—er, air."

"Ah," he said. He looked over my shoulder to where Seph was brooding by the wall. "Ah," he said again. "I presume it was good...air. In any event, as you can see, the party is still going. If you have had enough, of course, you should feel free to excuse yourself at any time."

"I think I will excuse myself now, Dad. I'm still wiped from the gig last night, and the wine has relaxed me to the point of needing to go back to sleep."

"Of course. Good night, my daughter," he said as he planted a gentle kiss in the middle of my forehead. "Sleep well, and pleasant dreams."

As I turned, I could've sworn I heard him chuckle quietly. My face turned bright red, but luckily the ball room by that point was dark enough that nobody could see it.

Dad lied to me about the lessons, but that was okay. The rest of the week featured lots of lessons during the day, good lessons, followed by parties at night. Elves need about as much reason to party as blue jays need to fly—and that's not a lot. Turns out my elevation to crown princess counted, and then some.

The lessons each day were delivered not by the queen's kids, but instead by the queen's senior Lady of the Bedchamber, a position the current queen apparently ripped off from Earth's British monarchy. Regardless of where the title came from, Lady Meredydd, thanks to her extensive travels with the queen, was an invaluable source of knowledge. The queen had given her the mission of educating me every day on the mores, customs, and habits of the group of elves who would most likely arrive at the castle grounds that evening. She proved amazingly accurate, too, teaching me all about the strange eastern elves the day they arrived, and the elves of the great white north just before they showed up. It was a brilliant way of teaching me, too, since I got to go out and practice using what I learned as I learned it.

It was so exciting! All the different groups of elves served the same king and queen, and would therefore eventually be my subjects, but they were all so different. The elves from the north were what I could only imagine the Vikings were like way back when, assuming the Vikings were slender and fairly clear of body hair like the typical elf. But all of the booming voices, all of the great big tents, and all of the massive barrels of lager they brought with them seemed right out of the history books. The eastern elves reminded me of the Durmstrangs from Harry Potter when they paraded in, staves at the ready. The elves from the south lived in a very hot, wet climate, and so they came in wearing not much of anything. It was a magnificent display of elf physique.

The parties grew from night to night. The night after the party I've started calling "the kiss" was the same folks, minus the queen's three kids, as the night before plus the elves who lived nearby in the scattered villages. Seph's dad was there, and he and Seph and Dad and I spent a lot of time dancing around together on the lawn in front of the castle, where they'd moved the party as soon as it was too big for the ballroom. We danced, and we sang, and we completely let our hair down.

I didn't drink much, though. Going from alcohol being a forbidden fruit to it being freely available is only cool for a little while. I was already tired of feeling hung over.

As the parties grew in attendance they grew in amount of ground covered, too. A couple of nights later, when the staff-wielders from the east marched in and set up their barrels of celebratory mead, the party had already tripled in area. By the last day it was way too big to walk around in anything but a matter of hours.

Each evening Dad started the party trip by walking me around to the pavilions where the local leaders had set up in order to introduce me. Each time I tried to do exactly as the Lady of the Bedchamber had taught me.

Padrig, leader of the great white northern clans, she explained, would only choose to respect a leader who was at least as strong as he was. In a queen, what that meant was supreme confidence in the first greeting, as well as unwavering eye contact throughout the introduction. He would try to make me flinch, she said, and I was glad for the warning when the first thing he did was hock a great big mouthful of spit onto the ground by his feet. My father snarled, just as he was supposed to do, and I held him back and excused Padrig's rough gesture, just as I was supposed to do. Padrig smiled at my carefully-chosen and rehearsed words, and apparently at that point I won a supporter for life. He skipped out of his chair and clasped my right hand to his chest in his people's show of eternal bonding.

"Nice job," my father whispered over a flagon of lager later on. Padrig seemed taken by me, he pointed out, so much so that the elf commander gave his son Llew several suggestions, well within my hearing, on how to approach the task of winning my heart and my hand.

That was cute. Llew was ten. Eleven, maybe.

And he looked nothing like Keion, bless his heart. I know, I know, I shouldn't have thought that, but I did. "Taken, taken, taken," I repeated silently to myself several times. Keion was taken.

It didn't work. I kept thinking of the kiss. Taken, yes, but could I just—borrow, maybe? Practice?

The next night, the massive tribes of the eastern seaboard, the ones I've already said came in stomping and bumping staves against the ground, arrived. Their drums sounded all the way across the forest even before we could see them come. Hefin, their leader, saluted me grandly with several amazing twirls of his own staff, a three inch thick and eight foot long hunk of solid oak. Dad introduced me in the long, flowery words that the queen's kids had used the first time, and used the same type of linguistic flourish to announce Hefin's status. My greeting pleased both of them; it was another triumph for Gwenith, the Lady of the Bedchamber, whose name I'd finally been able to coax out.

That night the drums of the northern elves and the drums of the eastern tribes tried to out-drum each other, to the point that Seph told me later that when she left the castle she nearly vibrated down the front steps instead of walking. The rhythms were hypnotic; I didn't need to drink to feel lightheaded.

The elves from the south, when they arrived the next night, were just plain wild. Glynis, their tribal over-queen, wore a cloth bikini that was so skimpy that I wanted to cover Dad's eyes up to protect him for Mom. I couldn't, of course. For one thing, he had to be able to see to make the introductions. For another, Gwenith had warned me that beauty was a trait to be ignored by those tribes.

That night I partied with the southern elves, and it was amazing. Their music was much more of a mix of wind instruments and drums than the other tribes had played, and the dancing circles consisted of more of a pulsing mosh pit than the flailings that I'd participated in near the castle. Not that I've been in many mosh pits, mind you, but I've heard stories.

I danced pretty much all night at that one, standing and pulsing back and forth next to Sephaline, who had also never experienced it.

The lessons the next day were uncomfortable as a result, but they held me, rapt. Gwenith started by telling me stories of the great desert to the west, stories I'd heard a little of from the trio. The difference was that Gwenith had actually been there, a few times. The exotic western elves were masters of water-singing and plant-singing, of course, and their musicality spread into every aspect of their lives. They could make a beautiful multi-harmony melody with just their mouths, and when they started using their hands for clapping and snapping it ended up being a perfectly simple version of a symphony. The desert being the farthest away, the western elves arrived the last night of the party, but their addition to the event seemed perfect.

Walking back toward the castle early in the morning, I heard a catchy drum rhythm from the northern tribe area and decided to take a side trip. Halfway across the camp, I met Keion.

"Hi," I said, not sure whether to be overjoyed or annoyed.

"Hi," he echoed.

"Having a good time?" I asked. Lame, I know, but it was all I could come up with. I was tired, I told myself.

"I am. You?" He seemed as stuck on lame as my own mind was.

"A great time. Have you been to see the southern tribes yet?" I don't know why I asked that. For some reason the idea of Keion ogling the scantily-clad jungle elves irritated me, and I wanted to be irritated right then.

"No. The eastern elves are more my speed. I like training against their staff with my sword."

Oh, right—fighting was what he looked at. Men.

"Say, Alyssa," he said, assuming a pose that made him look an awful lot like the Fonz on the old TV reruns of Happy Days. I could sense how nervous he was, though. He continued, "That, um, remember the other night on the porch?"

"I do," I said. I figured I knew where he was going, but I'd be danged if I was fixing to go out of my way to help him get there.

"Of course. Um, I do too! But it was—well, it was wrong, Alyssa. We can't—um...."

I was beginning to realize that Prince Charming had never actually been with a girl, in any capacity, before. It was entertaining as hell to watch him flounder around like a horse on an ice rink.

It was kinda cute, too, but I stuffed that idea away as

quickly as it came to me. He was, after all, breaking up with me, and we hadn't even really ever been together in the first place.

"Yes?" I asked, curious to see where he would eventually get to.

"Well, the thing is, um, you see, I'm promised. To another girl. I can't, um, well, you're very—I mean, you—we—were awfully drunk that night, right?"

"I was," I said, still leaving him hanging out there. It was mean of me, I know, but he was, after all, breaking up with me.

"Well, good. So that's settled, then."

"What's settled, Keion?" I asked, moving in a little bit closer to him. He'd been dancing again; the musky scent that radiated from his body was intoxicating by itself.

He sighed and finally came to his senses. "Look Alyssa, I like you a lot. I like to think you like me as well. But it can never be, okay? My marriage, once my bride comes of age, will help to cement a diplomatic relationship that your crown will cherish. Your crown, and very possibly my own, as I am highly favored to replace your father. And, as I am certain you already know, the king and the queen cannot be—involved."

"I know that, Keion. You and your sisters have taught me quite well."

"We have, and that is to our credit," he nodded, missing my delicate sarcasm. "I just—well, I did want you to know that you're—well, you're who I'd choose if I got to choose, Alyssa. You're—never mind. I've said enough, more than an honorable man should."

I nodded; he'd come out of it well enough, and he was right. The elf king and the elf queen could never be a couple, and he really was the cream of the crop of the male elves our age. He would then be our king, and I would be our queen, and that, as they say in awfully cliched films, was that. "Thank you, Keion,"

I said. "For—for everything."

He nearly sprinted away, and I also hurried in to go to bed so that I'd be awake for my ceremony as the new crown princess. And, I admit, so that I could quickly turn to dreaming of sharing kisses with Prince Charming.

Because dreams were all that would ever be of those kisses.

FRENHINES

The Queen.

Unbennes is sometimes considered a synonym, but it's not. Not in the slightest, at least in Cysegredig. Unbennes is a queen; Frenhines is THE queen.

The Queen

The next morning dawned way too early.

It was Friday, *Gwener* to the elves. It was a strange name for the last workday of the week, but I supposed Friday would be just as strange to someone who hadn't grown up speaking English.

More than that, it was my coronation day.

No, not the big coronation day. That would come much later, as everybody had seen fit to explain to me every time the subject came up. Today was my first presentation to the queen, my chance to be formally introduced to the crown and its people, my first day as Crown Princess.

So yeah, I was going to get a crown, just not the big one. Apparently the chamberlain had a little tiara thing ready for my head.

It didn't matter. This was a day I'd dreamed of. I mean, what little girl hasn't dreamed of becoming a princess, having a sparkly tiara thrust upon her head by adoring subjects?

Okay, granted, I never dreamed of that. Astronaut, I'd dreamed of, and also President and a few other cool titles, but sparkly-tiara princess wasn't on that list.

The tiara was going to be mine regardless, though. As nervous about it as I'd been at first, I finally settled down into a pleasantly terrified feeling. I just kind of wished that the day I'd dreamed of would've come a little bit later in the day, if you know what I mean.

The queen sent more of her personal circle, including the Royal Chamberlain and the Mistress of Robes, to rouse me out of bed. She probably already knew how much I didn't like getting up, and come to think of it, she probably also knew how much I'd been partying through the week.

Hey, it's my coronation; I'll party if I want to.

The chamberlain carried a breakfast tray of fruits, meats, and some cheese with him. He assured me as he set it on the dresser that it was not in his regular job description to fetch food for anyone. The queen, herself, had asked this favor of him, he explained, because Her Majesty in her wisdom and grace knew how important it would be for a young, thin thing like me to get some food in me before the event. Which was, he reminded me, in the early afternoon, as soon as the queen decided it should be and not one minute later, and by everything that was good in this kingdom and the others, the crown princess had better be ready.

Yeah, yeah.

I thanked him and went over to nibble on the tray's contents while the Mistress of the Robes explained to a couple of her ladies in waiting, who had snuck in behind her, what she wanted of me, my hair, my nails, and everything else once they stuffed me into the dress that one of the ladies carried. The Mistress, it turned out, was wanted in the queen's chambers to help Her Majesty prepare for this momentous occasion.

She left, and the ladies in waiting attacked. There was a bath just across the hall that was primarily used by my father, so they had Aerona stand guard at the door to prevent his accidentally walking in on me—like he wouldn't know what day it was—and the rest of them took to dunking me in the really hot bath water. Every inch of my body was lathered up, and then it was all rinsed and brushed off in the same effort using the most evil bath brush I'd ever seen. Back home, I'm not sure if you'd call it exfoliation or torture.

Once every visible spot on my body was crimson from scrubbing they let me up and out, to be toweled off. Then they wrapped the towel around me securely and marched me back to my bedroom, Aerona in tow with a wicked grin on her face. At least they let me put on my underwear all by myself, but then they started in again, one taking a brush to my hair, another trimming and coloring my fingernails, and the third trimming and coloring my toenails.

As honored as I was at what was literally the royal treatment, I started feeling a little bit abused. Not one of the ladies in waiting was particularly gentle in her job, and there were several times I got a lock of hair and a cuticle yanked at the same time.

But they didn't care.

"What's with the hurry?" I asked the four or fifth, or maybe the eighth, time my scalp was bruised by a rugged yank on a wet tangle.

They ignored me. Oh, right—English. Today in particular, and the entire week at that, I was supposed to be speaking in nothing but my own people's tongue. I repeated in elvish.

"The hurry, Princess?" the toe-yanker said. I noticed, for a brief second, that the pain in one hand's cuticles was slowly going away, and the next second I realized it was because that one had switched sides. "We must have you ready by the high sun," the one at my toes finished. High sun, I'd come to realize, wasn't the same as noon, nor was it necessarily when the sun was directly overhead, of all things. High sun to the elves was when the day's temperature was at its peak, which was generally somewhere around two in the afternoon. It was also when laborers were likely to take a resting nap.

It was also, apparently, when I was to be crowned.

"High sun is still a while away," I said, my grumpiness rising faster'n a cat's with its tail on fire.

"It is, Princess, but we still have a great deal to accomplish to get you ready to meet Her Majesty," the sadist working on my hair crooned into my ear.

Fine.

They buffed and they fluffed for quite a while more, actually. Once my finger- and toenails were perfectly trimmed and polished they got me up and, while hair-mistress kept working, the other two put me into the most god-awful torture device I've ever suffered: a corset. I've seen pictures of servants trying to get corsets tightened around people, the servants standing horizontally to put enough pressure on the tie strings. That was kinda what they did, only worse, bless their bloody little hearts. My body isn't exactly either ample or curvy; I'm mostly a layer of muscle over a ribcage. Tightening a corset over that was excruciating. Apparently, though, they'd fit the dress to the corset instead of to me, and so I had to be made to match the corset in order to wear the dress. That was, anyway, what the hair-mistress kept telling me as I moaned and quietly cursed while the drawstring tightener tried to crush my ribcage into my lungs in order to press my flesh upward to form actual cleavage.

Apparently the act of breathing wasn't all that important for the coronation.

After all that, I have to agree that the dress was stunning. Keep in mind that they don't have power sewing machines in Kiirajanna, which makes the fact that the white dress with silver slashes from waist to floor had over a thousand glistening little pearls sewn on—by hand—all so much more impressive.

And, I admit, it did fit perfectly thanks to the torture fabric from hell. It was both strapless and lacking in arm pieces; the ladies carefully slid lace forearm covers up to my elbows, snugging the fragile fabric ringlet around my middle finger as I'd always imagined in my princess visions.

They sat me back down, then, one of the torture experts changing to a makeup artist while the other brought stuff for the other two. Hair-mistress hadn't stopped brushing my hair even while the corset thing was going on. Now, though, she shifted her work to making curls out of what was long enough.

I didn't hold much hope till one of them brought a mirror around. "Is it to your liking, Princess?" another—the hair-mistress, I think—said. I was impressed; the pale blush color did highlight my cheekbones extremely well.

"It is," I started to say, but just then the door flew open and two people sped in. The Mistress of the Robes apparently had enough free time in whatever torture she was applying to the queen to stop by and see the efforts being done on me. She stood in front of me, looking closely at every detail, and finally she nodded silently. I couldn't help hearing one of my own torturers breathe a breath of relief.

The other was Sternyface. She came around with the pickle-eating face she always wore, but once she looked at me her face broke out into a radiant smile.

"Princess Alyssa, you look absolutely stunning," she said, and I was thrilled by her praise.

"Thank you, High Priestess Naissa," I returned. It wasn't easy to speak in the dress and makeup, but I managed.

She nodded. "Just remember—oh, well, you'll do fine. As uncomfortable as you are in that, you'll need to focus on walking and breathing. This show today is very little about you, or about the queen, and very much about the people who will be watching you. Keep it slow, move deliberately, and you shall do just fine, my dear."

"It is time," the Mistress of the Robes said, startling me. Time? Already? I thought back over what all we'd been doing, and I had to agree that yes, we'd been working on me for a long, long time.

"Her Majesty should already be in her position," the Mistress continued, talking more to Sternyface than to me. "She was leaving when I left to visit Princess Alyssa."

The high priestess nodded and added, "The crowd downstairs is ready, also. Alyssa? Are you prepared to accept the crown?"

Of course I was; I hadn't considered anything else. "Do I have a choice?" I asked, joking.

"Of course you do," Naissa said, looking at me with a surprised look. "You did not know that? It has only been done once in modern history, but—"

"I was joking, High Priestess," I interrupted. I don't think I'd ever interrupted her before, and I'd never done anything even remotely disrespectful after the whole slugging incident, so I expected her to be surprised. She wasn't, though. Instead, she just nodded and turned toward the door.

One of the ladies in waiting slipped my shoes on my feet as I brought them down to stand up. It didn't seem real. As I moved across the room behind Naissa, I caught another glimpse of my reflection in the dresser mirror.

I was—amazed. The princess who looked back at me from the mirror was stunning. My normally spiky, unruly locks that had grown out over the summer had been curled into the cutest little hairdo, one that perfectly accented my face which was highlighted like a pro. The dress looked incredible; the silver slashes shimmered in the sunlight while the pearls glimmered.

Naissa started down the stairs first, and suddenly the castle fell absolutely silent. The loud talking I'd heard from downstairs, typical during a busy dinner, just stopped. I stepped up to the edge of the landing and caught my breath; the floor below was packed. It was a sea of elven splendor.

I started down the stairs, slowly as Naissa had said. It was weird, being the focus of so many pairs of eyes. I looked around, myself, meeting many of the happy stares. Over there, near the door, I spied the elf from the northern tribe—what was his name, again?—who'd taught me how to properly down a horn of liquor. Now there he was, decked out in what must be his finest furs. Across from him stood Legolas, who had instead chosen a long tunic with pants, both of which were cheerfully colored.

I came around through the dining hall and realized how packed the room was. Elves were standing, row after row, on the seats, on the tables, everywhere they could stand. They stood in little obvious pockets of regionalism. Up near where I usually ate were some southern elves, scantily clad as usual, but elegantly so. A few feet farther down the table were some exotic western elves wearing elaborately gemmed veils and silky, billowing tops and pants that reminded me of the outfits I'd seen in Aladdin.

The door of the throne room stood open. Inside, I could see, stood a tightly-packed throng of the most important elves in the land. Padrig, in his northern fur, glared sideways a couple of times at Hefin, whose leather armor was wrapped every bit as grandly and as large as Padrig's fur stood. Both looked to be wrestling for the best spot on the floor, but they were also both smiling at me.

I slowly came around the corner to where I could see Dad. He looked magnificent. His dark curly hair held a bejeweled crown perched perfectly on his head, and his purple furry robe played against the color of his eyes. He was wearing a dress also, sort of. At least, he was wearing a blue tunic that was long enough to satisfy elf propriety for such a formal occasion.

Seph's smile blazed from Dad's right. She shocked me, actually. I'd always thought of Seph as—just Seph. Reliable Ranger Sephaline. But that day, she was radiant. Her long dark hair was curled and cascaded around her face, and she wore a deep green tunic with gold embroidery in the shapes of trees and moons and stars and owls. I couldn't help but grin a great big hello to her.

The trio, of course, stood to the queen's left. They were beautifully decked out, but that was their normal. I tried grinning once at Keion. Unfortunately he obviously had something else on his mind, and so he ignored my grin.

Ah, well. I'd already resigned myself to having to find someone else.

Someone, hopefully, as intoxicating as Prince Charming could be, when he wasn't being an egotistic jerk.

I ripped my gaze away from him. It was easy to keep it away, because it fell on the queen herself.

Other than Momma, I've never seen a more beautiful woman.

The queen's dress matched mine almost identically. She, though, sported both a purple sash embroidered in gold along each edge, and the same purple cape my father wore. Atop her head rested the breathtaking crown of Kiirajanna, a golden masterpiece with emeralds at each point and a strange white stone in the center that practically glowed.

I noticed the queen's smile. She's half human, just like me, but I guess by the time you've been in Kiirajanna for as many years as she had you develop the elf smile. She was wearing it right, to be sure, but I couldn't help but see that it was absolutely genuine. She really was happy to see me, it seemed, a fact that gave me some reason to breathe easier, if I could have breathed at all with the dang corset coiled and roped around my chest.

I was so taken in by her beauty and her smile that I barely even noticed that Naissa was talking. Tuning in, though, I realized that the high priestess was recounting all of the various topics I'd mastered in my stay here. I wondered, mostly jokingly, if she was going to include high priestess slugging in the list. It was impressive, though, to stand there and realize how much I really had learned. It was also good to hear Sternyface talking as though she was proud of me, herself.

The rest of the ceremony went by both way too quickly and agonizingly slowly for someone who couldn't breathe. When Sternyface stopped talking, the queen formally asked me if I were willing to one day step up to assume the responsibilities involved in ruling Kiirajanna. I said yes, of course, and with great honor, hoping all the while that I could get back into clothes I could breathe in before I suffocated. The Chamberlain then put a tiara on my head, and I walked way too slowly back up to my room to the sound of thunderous applause.

No, really. Thunderous. It was *that* loud. That was cool. Cool enough, in fact, that I almost forgot about my need to breathe.

After the ceremony was over I changed back into my normal clothes and asked for, and received, some help taking all the makeup off. Then, tired as heck of all the partying, I kicked everybody out of my room, uninviting even Seph and Booboo for once. I said I was tired, and she bought it, but the fact was that I really wanted some time to myself.

I didn't get much time to myself, though.

Loud rapping at my door interrupted my peace, and I gave Aerona the gesture to get rid of whoever it was. She opened the door a fraction of an inch, shrugged and shot an *I did the best I could* expression my way, and then swung the door inward all the way. "Highness," she intoned, "it is my pleasure to announce Her Majesty, Queen Talaith of Kiirajanna."

The queen bustled through the door, all by herself, completely casual in both dress and attitude. With a single gesture she sent Aerona jumping out of the room, closing the door sharply behind the guard and leaving the two of us alone together for the first time ever. Little Treebeard's branches actually started shaking, and somehow the tree actually leaned over, getting just a little closer to Talaith. I made the mistake of mentally tuning in to my little tree familiar's thoughts, and heard Elvis's All Shook Up once again. Holding back the grin L.T.'s little tree-swoon brought me, I bowed to Her Majesty just as I'd been taught by the three siblings.

In lightly accented English she said, "No, darling, now don't give me any of that cack. This is not a formal visit." She plopped down into a chair and continued, "So, how is our newest crown princess doing now that the pomp and circumstance is done?"

I shrugged. Nobody in any of the classes I'd taken had told me how to respond when the queen asked how I was doing. Did she want honesty? I looked at the smooth, casual serenity of her face and decided that she probably did.

"I'm fine. It's been an emotional roller coaster getting here, but I'm fine now."

"Yes, your path has indeed had its share of ups and downs. Alyssa, I have been watching you through my children's eyes ever since you arrived. I am impressed, I must say. I was fortunate to have elf tutors throughout my childhood who made sure I knew the language as well as much of the culture and the mores of elf society, as did the queen before me and many others before her. You were raised by a commoner in the backwoods of Mississippi—no, there is no insult intended, I assure you, but whether descended from Rhiannon the White or not, your mother has had no noble training at all. Regardless, you managed despite all odds to come here and learn our ways as well as our ancient written language, and you even saved my son's life in so doing." She sighed, and then she continued in a quieter voice, "I have heard that you and he—"

I shook my head and braved an interruption. The last thing I wanted, after a day of being scrubbed, pulled, and corseted almost to death, was a lecture on how her son was *taken*. "We are not, Your Majesty. Is that what this visit is about?"

The ruler sat back in her chair and regarded me with a sideways grin. I realized where her daughters had come by their *regahded* expressions as I watched what had to be several disparate thoughts flit across the queen's face.

"You do realize that he is the leading candidate to replace your father on the king's throne, do you not?"

"I do." I crossed my arms, a gesture I would never, ever have used in front of the queen in public. At that moment I didn't care.

She caught the defiance; her eyebrows shot up. Then they relaxed back down as the queen's face lit up in a sincere grin. "My, you *are* a feisty one. I had heard as much, and to be honest I would have expected no less from the child of Rhys. As greatly as you have vexed the high priestess with it— Sternyface, I believe you have been calling her?—it is my opinion that the trait, moderated with a strong dose of civility and prudence, will serve you well when you replace me."

"Rhys?" I was a little lost, and my expression probably showed it.

Her smile became a look of surprise. "You did not know that your father's real name is not Cadfael?"

"No, I—" I stumbled, trying to work my way through all the nots in her question. "I mean yes, I knew that Cadfael was not

his real name, just as your real name is not Talaith. I just—
well, Rhys is a good, strong name."

"It is, but it was not mine to tell. Oh, dear. I apologize for
assuming that you knew your father's name."

I shrugged. "I just call him Dad. I'm sure he would have
told me his real name, but I never thought to ask. I've had so
many things running through my head since the day I walked
in and found him in our *backwoods* living room."

She was perceptive, I'll give her that. Her smile faltered as
she caught the barb I'd thrown her way over the insult to my
home town. She sighed and said, "I do wish I could start this
conversation over, my dear. I did not infiltrate the king's arm of
the castle in order to insult you or your former home, or to re-
veal your father's real name, or even to discuss your choice of
romantic interest, badly placed as it may be. Rather, I hoped to
simply get to know you more, here in a private and *informal*
setting. We have been kept apart by tradition, which has unfortunately forced me to be the only person in the whole kingdom
who has not yet met my own designated successor."

"About that. Why doesn't the queen get to meet the crown
princess prior to the tiara thing? I mean, most elf traditions
are based on something that makes some sense, more or less,
but I have yet to find a reason for why we haven't been able to
meet till now."

"I do not know, Alyssa. I suspect it has something to do
with a concern that I might unfairly impact your training, either positively or negatively, having already been through it.
Perhaps the desire is to keep the seated queen from jumping to
unwarranted conclusions, as some—other—elves did during
your first days here."

"Okay, I can accept that. So will you be more involved in it
in the future? At a certain point you'd think that the best person to train the future queen is the sitting one."

A knock interrupted us. We sat in silence as a moment dragged out into a few, and then Talaith looked meaningfully at the door and then back at me. Oh, right, I realized—we were in my room, and it was my place to grant permission to enter. "Come!" I called. Lady Meredydd paraded in with a couple of serving ladies bearing a tray that was set down on a small table between Talaith and me. Under Aerona's watchful glare, the queen's lady poured dark, fragrant tea into two dainty white porcelain cups, lifted the top off of the sugar bowl, and then smiled and nodded to both of us before stepping back out.

"I hope you will join me," Her Majesty said with a smile. "Afternoon tea is the one tradition I utterly failed at leaving behind in England."

My eyes conspired with my stomach, which was apparently still irritated at me for not eating all that much from the tray that morning. Hey, it's hard to eat anything while torturers are yanking your cuticles out of your fingers, and it's danged unthinkable to put anything in your mouth while constrained in a corset. The three-tiered stack of goodies looked awfully tasty to my hungry eyes.

"I'd be delighted," I said. "But I have to admit that despite all the protocol training I've received, I know nothing about how to do this."

"Nor would I expect you to, dear. There are a great many rules associated with afternoon tea, some of them more universally accepted than others. Most of the rules, however, will fare perfectly well by remaining back on Earth. You should sweeten your tea before it becomes cold, darling."

I did, adding the sugar first and then the milk as she showed me, and then raised the cup to take a sip out of. I raised my pinky to demonstrate my desire to show good manners, but she shook her head and then demonstrated now not to do that. Fine. No pinky, then. Oh, and then I learned that they weren't cakes; they were scones, she said, and they were best eaten by taking bite-sized pieces broken by hand and spreading butter and jam individually onto them using the butter knife just so. Luckily the finger sandwiches in the second tier and the cakes underneath could be nibbled on just fine without any pinky or breaking by hand nonsense, though they were best approached in the order of scone, then savory, and then sweet. While she explained how things tasted best when eaten certain ways, I looked down at the two forks on my side of the table, wondering why they were there if I couldn't use them.

So much for the rules remaining at home in England. The rules for tea in Mississippi are a whole lot less intense, I think.

Still, it was all tasty, and it really did end up being a lot of fun, just her and I enjoying a tea and chatting. The conversation got lighter as we ate; she told me of her years growing up as the eldest daughter of a well-to-do family. She'd missed her daddy quite a lot when he was away being the elf king, but their position had been a lot different from mine, and her mother's family managed with the story that her father was away helping to right the world for the empire. She managed to see him once a year or so, then, and so no fantasies had been required in her case.

"To answer your earlier question," she said after a brief lull, "no, I will not be much more involved in your training going forward. Some, yes, especially toward the end, but not by any great amount, and not soon in any event. You will be traveling away from Cysegredig quite a lot, in fact."

"Why do I need to leave the castle complex again?"

"This past week you met the four primary clans of your people, but you do not yet really know them, nor do they yet really know you. A ruler must know her subjects well, and so you must travel to each of their home regions."

"Field trips, in other words."

"I suppose so. Extended field trips, at that. You will not be able to return until the clan leadership has blessed your ascension, and that can take what seems to be a very long while."

"Oh. Well, I have to say that doesn't sound like too bad of a time."

Talaith sat back and regarded me once again. "It is tough to say," she said, "whether it will be difficult for you. I was raised in a very proper family, and I had a very difficult time coming to grips with—well, with some of the elf customs in—out there."

I wanted to ask for more, but she'd been clear enough already that she couldn't bias me. Instead, I asked, "And then there's the dream quest I have to go on, too, right?"

She nodded, and I got the impression from the shadowed expression on her face that her own vision quest hadn't gone very well.

"Yes, you do," she murmured, and then changed the subject. "So, tell me more about the grand library, Alyssa. What was this system they had set up to direct the light indoors?"

We chatted for hours, most of it kept light and friendly and completely avoiding any talk of magic. Finally she rose and made a point to look out through the window at the darkened sky. "Well," she said, "I have relished this opportunity to get to know you better, Crown Princess Alyssa, but I am fatigued from the day's proceedings, as I am sure you must be as well. I would hope to enjoy other opportunities similarly, but I doubt that our mutual schedules will permit it often. Should you wish to speak with me in the future, you have but to knock on my door at the opposite end of the hall. I must add that I am pleased with the prospect of you stepping up to the throne when my own time to rule comes to an end. Good night."

She slipped out and Aerona came back in and resumed her

watchful glares. Soon after the queen's departure a couple of ladies whisked the tea setting out, leaving me alone—as alone as I ever was under Aerona's guard—to my thoughts. It had been a busy several months. Naissa's litany during the ceremony had reminded me of how busy it had all been.

And as a result of all of the busyness, I was going to be the Elf Queen.

The Dragon Queen, per the prophecy, I corrected myself as I reached into the bag I'd brought back from the Library of Alecsanddrha. From it I pulled the scroll containing the prophecies and two seminal books on magic. I sat down at my desk and started reading the prophecy scroll.

You didn't think I'd leave them to be burned, now did you?

Kiirajanna Pronunciation and Meaning Guide

The elf tongue aligns very closely with Welsh, but over the years of separation the two drifted apart slightly, so that some differences may be heard. It should be noted, though, that the two languages are still close enough together that young elves traveling to Earth today can readily understand and converse with modern inhabitants of Wales.

The ch sound is aspirated (as in the ch sound in loch).

Afallon: \ a va lyon \ - name of person (antiquity)
Alecsanddrha: \ a lek san dra \ - name of person (antiquity)
Amddiffynnydd: \ am thih feen neeth \ - protector
Awel: \ ah wel \ - brisk breeze
Cadfael: \ cad fiyl \ - prince of battle
Cysegredig: \ kee seh greh deeg \ - sacred place
Darllen: \ dar hlyen \ - to read
Draignerthol: \ dreg nehr thohl \ - mighty dragon
Dwyrain: \ dooee rayin \ - east
Eryr: \ ehr reer \ - eagle
Gogledd: \ goh gleth \ - north
Gorllewyn: \ gor hleh win \ - west
Gwarchodwyr: \ gooar choh dooeer \ - chaperone, babysitter
Gwener: \ gweh nehr \ - Friday
Gwenith: \ gweh nihth \ - blessed (female)
Gwyn: \ gween \ - blessed (male)
Hefin: \ heh vihn \ - summer
Kiirajanna: \ key rah jah nah \ - No known meaning in Elvish
Llew: \ hlyoo \ - lion
Llwdy: \ hloo dee \ - slang: offensive term for humans
Llyfrgell \ hlihfr gehl \ - library
Mwnci: \ moon key \ - monkey
Pen bach: \ pen bach \ - literally, small head. Slang: a grave insult.
Prif: \ preef \ - primary

Rhyddid: \ hree thid \ - liberty
Rhys: \ hrees \ - enthusiastic
Sadwrn: \ sa doorn \ - Saturday
Siawns: \ shawns \ - chance
Talaith: \ ta layith \ - crown, governed region
Twffwllwch: \ too foo hlooch \ - place name
Twp: \ toop \ - stupid, slang: offensive insult
Tylwyth teg: \ teel with teg \ - the faerie folk

About the Author

Dean by day and writer by night, Stephen H. King grew up being asked whether he was "that Stephen King." "Not the author," he'd say until his writing addiction took hold and made that into a lie. Now he writes and reads and blogs as The Other Stephen King--you know, the one who writes fantasy and science fiction. When he's not writing, he enjoys thinking about writing while going on hikes or long road trips. When he's not thinking about writing, it's usually because he's fishing.

Find other Stephen H. King works at:
http://TheOtherStephenKing.com

Read his ongoing thoughts about writing, authorpreneurship, and other key parts of life at his blog:
http://TheOtherStephenKingOnWriting.blogspot.com